ENERVATION

Book Three of the Shadeward Saga

by Drew Wagar

ENERVATION

Book Three of the Shadeward Saga

by Drew Wagar

FIRST EDITION
First published by Fantastic Books Publishing 2019
ISBN (ebook): 978-1-912053-18-6
ISBN (paperback): 978-1-912053-17-9
ISBN (hardcover): 978-1-912053-16-2

Thanks To:

As ever, a huge vote of thanks to my lovely family. This time it's even bigger as they've supported me in a rather drastic change of career – yes the writing is going full-time! I couldn't do this without the support of my wonderful wife, Anita, sons Mark and Joshua and Abbey too. The fact that these books exist and I get time to write them is down to their generosity in allowing me to spend huge amounts of time staring at a blank laptop screen! Anita also gets to read the first 'released' version of the book, so many corrections and adjustments are already done before it is checked further.

To Emma Thompson, Jason Hall and Steph Wyeth – my crack team of proof-readers and commentators. These folks question my spelling, my grammar, my meanings and my intentions during the telling of the story. If it makes it past them you can be very confident that it is cohesive and works. Quite a few changes (in fact an entire new scene) were incorporated as a result of their oversight.

To David Stevenson, who is my 'informal' science advisor on all things Red Dwarf and exoplanet related. He's very generously mentioned my fiction in his proper scientific books.

To my editor Mae, who continues to ask the 'are you sure this is what you mean?' type of questions. The answer isn't always yes.

To Dan at Fantastic Books Publishing who continues to believe in this rather curious cross-genre story which is something of an anathema to more conventional publishers.

And to all of my readers. You folks are ultimately the reason I write these stories. I've always enjoyed writing, but there really isn't a great deal of point in doing so if nobody actually reads what you've written. It's very heartening to know that there is a growing contingent of folks across the world that are waiting for the next 'Drew Wagar' book. I fully intend to keep on writing as a long as I can.

Author's Note

It's fair to say that this third book in the Shadeward Saga has been more than a little delayed. I can only offer my humble apologies for this. I am in control of my schedule, but I'm not in control of the opportunities that occasionally show up and entice me off in new directions. As any creative person knows, doors that pop open in front of you don't always do so at convenient times, nor do they necessarily stay open for long. You have to step through them quickly if you're to take advantage of the opportunity.

My first Shadeward book was set aside for the worlds of Elite, and the second was also pushed back when I had a premonition, ahem, about writing an Elite sequel. Then came another blast from the past with the Lords of Midnight.

Those are completed now and, at last, I can return to Shadeward, to the ruddy starlight of my recalcitrant red dwarf star and the troubled world below it, picking up once again the stories of Kiri, Zoella and Meru. This remains my favourite story of all those I've written. These are my characters, my backstory, my situations. Ultimately I do prefer to be in complete control over everything, it makes the story telling easier.

But writing a book takes time. All of the books I've written have been over 100,000 words, which is a fair bit of text to get down, tweak, edit and sort for publishing. These books are not easy to write and it takes a lot of energy and craft to put them all together.

What I can say is I intend to work on Shadeward as much as I can, I really want to get it finished. Right now I don't think another Elite book is at all likely, but Lords of Midnight very much shows the promise of sequels, so I may need to interweave things. All the dates I have tried to commit to have proved elusive, thus I will simply say – I am writing! – and as fast as I can. There will be a Shadeward 4 to complete this saga before too long.

Beyond that I have big plans. If writing for Elite showed me one thing, it was that folks like my particular brand of political thriller mixed with space opera. Shadeward isn't quite the same, but the universe in which it exists can play host to many different stories.

In the myth and background of Shadeward is some kind of exodus from Earth. There's definitely a prequel there. As you know, Esurio was only one of the worlds to be selected as a colonisation target, so – what happened to the others? We know that technology regressed on Esurio, but what if other settlements had different outcomes; some might be considerably more advanced …

It may not surprise you to find that I've already worked out some of this detail and I'll be doing more work on it in the coming year. My plan is to embrace space opera, themes of exploration and conquest and the detail of what happened before Shadeward. This will, I think, be a set of sixteen books, of which the Shadeward set of four will be a quarter. The entire thing has the rather grand working title of the "Diaspora Saga". All that should keep me going for many years, and give you something to look forward to for a decade to come!

In the meantime though, enjoy this next adventure on Esurio. Thanks to all of you for coming on this journey with me. The reaction to my stories has been heart-warming and inspiring. That people talk about the characters I've created, discussing their motivations and behaviour, loving or hating them (or both!) is a great comfort and reward to me. Writers write because they have to, but every writer wants to know their work is appreciated and enjoyed. Thanks for all the feedback; the emails, the messages, the letters, the reviews, those who have chatted to me at the conventions and the expos. You are what makes it all worthwhile.

Drew Wagar,
April, 2019.

"She remembered who she was
and the game changed."
- Lalah Delia

Lacaille

The most significant terraforming work concerned dealing with the lack of a strong planetary magnetic field. Despite being tidally locked, Esurio was close enough to Lacaille that it experienced sufficient tidal forces to knead its core and keep it molten. Volcanic activity remained present, allowing the raw materials for the atmospheric processors to function. Yet the native magnetic field wasn't strong enough to deflect the extreme forces the planet experienced from its close proximity to Lacaille, the solar wind being hundreds of times stronger than that experienced back on the homeworld. Over millennia, the enhanced atmosphere would be stripped away again by the fierce assault of Lacaille. In order to counter this effect, a magnetic field booster was set to operate, supplementing the planet's own magnetic field, resulting in a potent magnetic flux.

This booster provided a further benefit in the form of widely available power distribution across the planet due to strong interaction with the solar wind. Magnetic induction technology could harness this and provide electrical power at ground level as a result.

With the atmosphere protected and terraforming raising the pressure by a few percentage points, the focus turned to the colonists themselves to close the remainder of the gap. Genetic modification provided adapted eyesight to allow vision into the near infrared and give greater low-light visibility. Increased lung capacity and further adaptions to the low pressure environment resulted in a breed of humans that could have quite happily lived in the highest mountains on the homeworld without much discomfort. Those children became the first to live upon the surface, a generation after the arrival of the colony ship. The lower gravity of the planet provided other benefits, too.

The indigenous life was also carbon-based, with a DNA/RNA complex very similar to that of the colonists, prompting many questions as to the origin of life on Esurio. Evolutionary pressures had produced many unique creatures, though they filled similar niches to those on the homeworld. Few of the animals that came with the colonists adapted well to the new environment and so the colonists turned to domesticating the native species for various uses. The small increase in air pressure had caused a few behavioural issues, but the creatures responded well, with most of them thriving as a result.

With the knowledge that even the most sophisticated equipment would eventually break down and become unmaintainable, it was decided that some of the colonists would be given additional technological capabilities within their biological makeup, aimed at providing the means to administer the fledgling civilisation.

Various criteria determined that female colonists with the appropriate temperament were selected and enhanced, providing them with various abilities. The primary purpose was to allow communication between colonists via the augmented booster, without any other equipment being necessary. The planet's magnetic field was used as a medium for the transmission, with individuals themselves acting as a relay mesh, rendering more traditional radio technologies, which were subject to major interference over long ranges, obsolete. The technology was designed to align itself with reproductive processes, ensuring that subsequent generations would benefit from the enhancement, even if the knowledge of how it worked were to be lost.

The original administrators of the colony worked under strict guidelines to ensure their abilities were governed and used effectively. The settlements prospered for many generations, the necessary knowledge being embedded in song, tradition and writings.

The booster itself was designed to be self-regulating, but it could provide status reports and updates to the administrators in case of any variance outside of its ability to manage. When such events occurred, the administrators would be automatically summoned via their in-built communications mechanism.

It was whilst such an adjustment was taking place that the first flare hit Esurio. It was not anticipated, either by the automated systems that had been set to guard the colony or by the colonists themselves. Lacaille 9352 was not catalogued as a flare star and no flare had ever been observed from the time of its discovery until the present time. Thus the calamity that overtook the colony was as unexpected as it was devastating.

Over nine tenths of the colonists were killed in a devastating holocaust. Most were outside when the flare hit and died as a result of exposure to lethal levels of ultraviolet radiation. Still more were caught by deadly firestorms caused by the pulse of infrared that emanated from Lacaille during the flare.

In the immediate struggle to survive the aftermath, the intentions of the original colonists were lost and the nascent civilisation on Esurio collapsed. Through many generations those who survived began to spread once more across the planet. History became mixed with legend, the origins of the population only dimly remembered. A barely recognisable culture staggered back. It was far different from what had gone before, surrounded by the broken remnants of the past.

What little technology remained was perceived as magic or religious power, its origin misunderstood. Thus wars were fought, empires rose and fell. Thousands of rounds passed. Civilisation emerged from a dark age longer than those known on the forgotten homeworld, but, as always, those who understood even a little of the past grew to be great and powerful.

The powers of the original colonists were still present, yet they had also adapted in the long rounds since they had first been gifted to the people. The booster still operated, unattended, forgotten by all, and yet still its automated systems continued to discharge the task its long vanished makers had designed it to perform. But it wasn't immune to the vagaries of time, it could not operate forever unattended.

If it were to fail …

Prologue

Round 2293, Eighth Pass

The smoke was rising high into the sky, mingling with the thick clouds above. Across the pastoral landscape the scene repeated itself, time and again. Dwellings ablaze; their ramshackle shadewood construction being consumed by flames.

Bodies were being piled in one place amidst the destruction, a heap of twisted and darkened figures, their clothing dirty and soiled, their skin pale and marked with blisters and boils. With a thump of ignition flames began to consume them too.

Black smoke. The burning pyres of the dead.

Plague.

It had swept in without warning, striking down the old and the infirm first, before moving on to the fit and the young. Indiscriminate, it had spread across Scallia, shadeward into Drem and sunward into Drayden, even as far as Taloon. No lands had been untouched by its curse. Untold thousands had died, leaving the land bereft of its people. Some estimates recorded that up to two thirds of the population had succumbed to the blight.

Soldiers stood, surveying their handiwork before stepping back as the flames leapt higher. Behind them stood a group of children, standing meek and scared, clutching to them the few possessions they had. All had lost their families and friends, seeing them fall to the illness throughout the hamlets and villages of Scallia.

The young captain in charge of the detachment looked back at them, counting the few that remained. His face twisted in a grimace.

'Check them,' he said to the two guards beside him. 'You know what to look for.'

Both men moved toward the children, who shrank against the wall of a derelict building. There were eight of them, grubby and thin, the only survivors from this particular village. They were a mix of ages, but none more than seven or eight rounds old.

One by one each child was inspected, the guards looking for the tell-tale marks of pox or rashes. Each was examined, starting with the face and then the arms and legs. The first few offered no resistance, but there was one, a girl with dark hair and bright blue eyes, who objected, snarling and trying to stop the guards touching her. She was subdued and subjected to the check, she seemed healthy enough. The guards moved on.

The last girl was not so fortunate.

A burning red welt was obvious on her upper arm.

The guards looked at each other.

'It's a burn, it's not the plague!' the black-haired girl snapped. 'She caught it on a brand just a few stretches ago …'

One guard pulled the last girl out of the line and took her towards the captain. The other guard remained behind, holding on to the black-haired girl, who was struggling to get free.

'It's not the plague! It's not the plague!' she screeched.

The captain took a look at the girl as she was brought close. She was a tiny thing, perhaps only five rounds or so, with a matt of straw-coloured hair upon her head. She didn't look up, her eyes staring forward past the guard. He'd seen that stare before; it spoke of grief so intense and shocking that there was no way back from it. Doubtless this child had seen her parents die before her eyes, and no help would have come.

Behind them a squeal from the black-haired girl rose above the crackling of the fires. She was struggling to get loose, kicking her legs and flailing her arms as the guard struggled to keep hold of her. A hand was clamped across her mouth.

The captain looked at the guard.

He nodded.

The girl before them saw nothing. It was quick and clean through long practice. The knife was drawn and the stab precise and surgical. The girl gave a short gasp and then collapsed in the dirt.

There was a yell from the guard behind them. The black-haired girl had broken free.

'She bit me!' the guard exclaimed, cursing.

The black-haired girl skidded to a halt in the dust before the captain, looking up at him in fury. The captain almost recoiled; he'd never seen such a fierce expression on a child's face. Utter contempt, utter hatred. The blue eyes were fierce and bright.

She spoke no words, standing before him trembling. For a moment the captain thought she was going to attack him.

'It had to be done,' he said. 'We cannot take the risk.'

Her eyes narrowed, but then she sank to her knees, her hands going out to the body lying on the ground, stroking the hair of her companion, sobbing as she did so.

The captain gestured for the guard to take her away again. She still struggled, but less so this time.

The captain picked up the body of the dead girl and carried it across to the nearest pyre, flinging it upon the flames and then turning back.

'Get these others into the cart,' he instructed.

Beyond the buildings was a wagon, drawn by two hergs. Other children were already sitting in it, huddled together for warmth; the weather had been unusually cool of late. The guards pushed the new children towards it and ushered them aboard. The black-haired girl was last, still glowering at anyone who made eye contact with her.

The guards and the captain climbed aboard, whips were cracked and the hergs snorted, dragging the cart forwards.

They travelled for several stretches to the shaderight, leaving the land of Scallia behind them. The land of Drayden lay ahead, home to the priestesses. The captain smiled, these children would fetch a bit of coin there; the priestesses always had need of drudges. He had few qualms about what he was doing. He was giving these children a chance to stay alive, had they been left back in Scallia they would have surely starved.

He had a total of twenty three now, all clean and free from the plague. That would make a tidy sum.

'I pity the poor soul who gets that last one,' the guard next to him said, nursing his hand. The captain could see blood and a small bite mark.

'Plenty of spirit,' the captain said, with a chuckle. 'She'll need that to survive the rounds ahead. Going to be tough times for a while.'

Daine was close now, the spires of the city visible before them, the great temple of the priestesses rising in the midst of it. The captain repressed a shudder. He had little desire to spend any time close to those strange women. They were otherworldly, possessed of strange powers of the mind and fearsome warriors. It was said they could read your mind and force your thoughts. Wilder stories suggested that their strange rituals involved taking men and cutting out their hearts whilst still alive, then eating them. None had ever seen such things to his knowledge, but he would not have trouble believing it. If they could see into your mind, read your thoughts, maybe they could even turn your body against your will. That sort of power would scare anyone.

They drew close to the gates of the city. The children were all looking around with curiosity, understanding that they were reaching a destination.

They stopped at the threshold, the city guards barring their progress.

'What you have here?'

'Twenty three young recruits for the pleasure of the priestesses,' the captain replied. 'All clean and checked.'

The city guards nodded.

'Twenty three?'

'Aye, twenty three.'

The city guard chuckled.

'What about that one?'

The captain turned to see a small form running down the gravel track away from the city walls.

'Scorch it! Stop her!'

He and his guards had no chance. The girl had too much of a head start and was agile and fleet of foot. She reached the threshold of the shadewood that bordered the road and spun back for a moment to see where her pursuers were.

The captain saw her hair fan out around her and caught her gaze for a brief moment.

'You ...'

Blue eyes and dark black hair.

The girl plunged into the woods.

When the captain and the guards reached the boundary of the woods there was no sign of her.

'She won't last a stretch in the depths of the forest,' one of the guards said. 'Snare or a mulch'll get her in a couple of chimes.'

The captain rubbed his chin.

Somehow I don't think we've seen the last of that one.

But he turned back to the children that remained, ensuring no others escaped. He did not think of the young girl again.

CHAPTER ONE

Viresia, Capital of Scallia

Round 2307, First Pass

Blue eyes, dark black hair.

Kiri was sitting on the wall overlooking the city, her expression pensive. It was an early chime, most folk were still asleep. Lacaille was bright and warm above, comforting and serene once more, so unlike the fury it had unleashed just a few short stretches ago.

Shanza, my beloved dach, slain in that tempest.

An image of the great reptilian beast came to her mind. Her loyal steed, killed by the fire that had risen from Lacaille's wrath and which burned across the lands of Drayden, Scallia and Drem.

We were too slow, we failed in our duty. Shanza saved me, yet paid the price ...

A tear trickled down her cheek at the memory.

Her hair drifted in the breeze that was blowing up from the sun drenched valley below. In the manner of the warriors of Drayden it was long on the right side, but shaved down to the scalp over her left ear.

The damaged city still bore testament to the fierce battle that had raged here only a few passes before. The leaders of Viresia had defied the will of Lacaille, the goddess of the Priestesses of Drayden, and she had swept them aside.

Kiri had faced the King of Scallia himself, besting him in combat before the walls of the city, before a cowardly attack from within the city had almost killed her. That had been the signal for the battle to begin. The priestesses assaulted the city and it had fallen before them.

Her kai, a long metal staff favoured by the priestesses as a weapon, was propped against the wall. It was with this she had despatched the hated prince Torin in the battle. Torin had slain her much-loved mentor, Charis. Kiri had shown no mercy when she caught him, bludgeoning the man to death despite his cries for mercy.

And Drayden had been victorious over Scallia, but the vengeance and the victory had not been without cost.

Tasha …

Kiri had lost a friend that stretch. Tall and athletic, Tasha had been the only one of all the acolytes to show her any companionship in her early time at the temple. She had died at the hands of the Scallians, cut down by bowmen. She had surrendered her own powers to Kiri so she could continue the fight. Kiri had felt her slip away in that moment.

She trembled at the memory. Despite her powers she hadn't been able to stop it.

Rihanna had accompanied her in the attack. That girl had been her nemesis for many rounds. All through her training at the temple Rihanna had taunted her, bullied her. Kiri had given back as good as she had been given. Their antagonism had grown to a dangerous fervour. It had all culminated in a fight where they had nearly killed each other.

But since then, Rihanna and Kiri had been forced to work together. They weren't friends, but no longer the mortal enemies they had been.

Tasha gone, Rihanna no longer an enemy, but who can I really trust? Too many secrets, too many choices ahead …

She got to her feet and walked into the throne room itself. It took her eyes a few moments to adjust from the brightness outside. She stepped forward, her feet echoing on the furler wood flooring.

The house of Tiamoi … this is my secret … this is my house! This could have been my home.

At the far end was a dais, and atop that, a throne. It was here that Nerina had sat giving her proclamations to the conquered people of Scallia, but it would have been King Ioric's throne and King Marek's before him.

Myana would have stood here too, rounds ago. My mother …

It was the murals and tapestries on the walls that drew her attention. Many were pictorial stories of the history of Scallia, some running back into the times of the Voren Empire hundreds of rounds before.

But there was one in particular she was interested in.

On the left side was a mural featuring portraits of the royal Scallian line. She found Ioric, and Torin. Liana was there too, her blonde beauty easy to spot.

What might Liana know about all this? She's my cousin! I must find a way to speak to her …

But alongside was another face.

An image of a woman looked out from the painting, unlike most of the others who looked aside from the painter's perspective. Rich locks of curly dark hair cascaded about a thin, but pretty face with high cheekbones and a determined expression. But it was the eyes that the painter had worked hard to capture.

Blue eyes … blue eyes, dark hair!

She read the inscription below

2258 – 2287. Myana Tiamoi, daughter of Marek Tiamoi, Wife of …

The text had been obscured, erased.

I looked like my mother! So who was my father? Why has his name been struck? If that was the round she died then I must have been born in 2287, that truly makes me twenty rounds old!

There was something strange but reassuring to know when she was born and how old she was. A sense of belonging, having some roots.

Guerrun smuggled me out of Scallia to keep me from the priestesses so it seems, but what happened afterwards?

Her earliest memories were of fire and death. She recalled a pyre and the death of a girl she had once played with, at the hands of soldiers. A word, repeated over and over.

Plague.

She had escaped the soldiers and fled into a forest, coming to the attention of the onlies of Drayden. They had cared for her, and she managed to survive by theft and cunning in their midst until she grew old enough to look after them in turn. Then Choso and his brothers had led her into the midst of the priestesses and Charis' tender care.

But before all that ...

She had a vague recall of an old woman and an old man. She could remember little other than their outlines.

They must have raised me from a babe, but died in the plague.

There were no other answers in the throne room. She heard voices not far away. Priestesses were heading her way. Her heart pounding, she slipped outside and fled.

* * *

Nerina, high priestess of Drayden, looked out from the courtyards of Viresia, gazing sunward down the valley, enjoying the warmth of Lacaille for herself. Far below a river sparkled. Scallia was greener than Drayden by some margin, the climate milder. The shadewood forests here were thicker and more abundant, the landscape better suited for farming and husbandry.

And it is mine now. Scallia and Drem! Soon all the lands that formed the Voren Empire will be mine too. I shall surpass even what Elena achieved and bring unity to this place, under the priestesses, under women, under me!

The power of the priestesses had overwhelmed the might of the Scallian defenders. Their pathetic Lords had bowed the knee to her, after one had been made an example of. Conquering Scallia had taken less than a pass; the kingdom had fallen with the death of both the king and the prince at the hands of the priestesses.

And the queen ...

Nerina turned and walked into the Viresian throne room. Two of the lesser priestesses were already there, having brought the queen up from the rooms in which she had been held. Nerina watched as the Queen was led forward. She walked of her own accord, but when she was released she did nothing, just stood there, unmoving and unaware.

The two priestesses lowered the Queen into a chair. She was dressed in a rich flowing gown of the type favoured by the Scallians, her hair was blonde, her face beautiful.

But her expression was vacant, her eyes blank and staring at something far beyond the walls of the throne room. Nerina watched her for a moment.

Queen Liana of Scallia.

Nerina walked across to her, stepping around her in a circle. Liana did not react. Nerina completed the move, a frown growing on her features.

This is the woman who defied us in the battle, slew many of my sisters, struck Kiri down outside the gates. Her power was greater than ours, yet now …

Nerina probed with an outstretched hand.

Nothing! Even her mind has retreated into the abyss of thought. Is her power gone, or was it taken by another? There are only two who could have done this, and I have tested them both …

Nerina had sent Kiri and Rihanna to pursue the queen when she had been rescued by the youth from Amar. They had followed their orders. Kiri had chased them all the way to Drem and captured her as instructed.

And neither Kiri or Rihanna claim to know anything.

Nerina had issued her instructions for the conduct of Scallia and Drem, sending priestesses to the major towns and cities throughout her new realm. Chief amongst the instructions was the renewed tithe. All the lands would be searched for young women with the gift. If they were found they were to be sent to Daine.

Nerina smiled. More young women meant more power, once she had torn their abilities and absorbed their gift.

Now she had to focus on what came next.

* * *

A bell tolled. Kiri jumped even though she had been waiting for it.

I've been summoned. Rihanna and I both. It's Nerina, she wants to speak to us …

Kiri grabbed her kai, her hand clenched tight around it. She took a deep breath and composed herself. She began walking back to the summit of Viresia.

I must concentrate! My mind must be clear and ready.

Kiri didn't know what Nerina wanted, but she had a pretty shrewd guess. She wasn't looking forward to facing the enigmatic high priestess.

She spied Rihanna waiting outside the throne room. Kiri nodded to her, but neither spoke.

The bell tolled again.

* * *

The doors to the throne room opened. Nerina could see the tall form of Rihanna and the shorter figure of Kiri silhouetted in the entrance.

'Come hither,' Nerina said.

She watched them as they walked, their shoes echoing on the polished wooden floor of the throne room. Much Scallian history was portrayed there, described in carvings and frescoes embedded in the floor. The craftsmanship was impressive, but it held no-one's attention at this moment.

'High priestess,' both of them said, bowing before her.

Nerina said nothing, but walked around them as was her habit.

'We return to Daine,' she said. 'With Drem and Scallia under our control. We have done well.'

'Yes, high priestess.'

'Much of that success can be put at your feet,' Nerina said. 'You fought well against this city, secured it for us. You killed the prince, pursued and captured the queen.'

Nerina gestured to Liana, who had remained unmoved in the chair to the side of the throne room, her expression still blank and unseeing.

'So where ...' Nerina's voice filled with an angry edge and turned to a yell. 'Is the power she wielded against us?'

She saw Kiri and Rihanna both flinch.

'There is nothing but a husk of a woman!' Nerina continued. 'The barest flicker of what she was. This woman ...' She gestured at Liana. 'She struck you down Kiri, do you remember?'

Kiri nodded. 'I remember! I thought I would die ...'

'And she struck Tasha from the sky before you, Rihanna! Do you not recall?'

'I do,' Rihanna said, looking straight ahead. 'She had a power beyond any ...'

'So where is that power? Where is it?'

Nerina spun around, her hand thrust out. Both Kiri and Rihanna gasped in pain and collapsed to their knees.

'One of you knows!'

She heard their screams of torment as she forced her will upon them, but it mattered little to her.

Someone is lying to me, I will find out which one of you it is!

She pushed harder, both Kiri and Rihanna crying out with the force of her assault.

Nerina pushed her way into Kiri's mind. She felt the girl's resistance; that had been expected, she knew her powers to be strong, but they weren't strong enough. Nerina grasped at the memories before her and pulled them close.

Astride her dach, a blast of metallic shock. Tasha tumbling into the courtyard ... arrows and crossbow bolts. Landing beside Tasha. Shock and horror, already dying! There ... the Scallian Queen advancing. Words ...

You can't resist me, little priestess. I am Liana of house Tiamoi, princess of Scallia. I am she who hurt you before. Surrender now and I will spare your life. Or you will suffer pain before I let these men despatch you ...

Yes, she has the power. Trying to attack her, but she is too strong. Astonishment at her strength! Tasha gives her gift ... Liana attacks, trying to steal ... then Torin. Revenge, Hatred! Blood, death and retribution!

The memory ended.

Nerina shifted further on. Kiri cried out as her mind was probed, but it was to no avail.

A cobbled street, poorly lit in the gloom of the far shadeward. Nireus! I have caught them at last. The queen, there she is! And a warrior with a sword … Fool! You can't stand against me. Dead! See, foolish man? Your strength is as nothing, your life is mine. Nerina will want the Queen …

Before her Kiri cried out in relief as Nerina let her go. The memory was clear, Kiri hadn't stolen anything. Nerina turned her focus to Rihanna.

The queen is in our custody. The priestesses assembling on the dock-side. Arrows shoot out at the fugitives. A boy, a girl and a young man running for the ship. Why have the arrows missed? They've jumped in the water, they've made it to the ship, they've escaped! The young man from Amar has escaped!

Nerina released Rihanna. She collapsed alongside Kiri, panting for breath.

'It seems neither of you know what happened to the queen's gift …'

Kiri had managed to get back to her knees.

'High priestess, I caught her, imprisoned her, brought her back as you directed … she is there.' Kiri pointed to Liana.

'And yet her gift is gone,' Nerina replied. 'She is useless to me.'

'We did not take it,' Rihanna said, her voice trembling. 'We wouldn't dare.'

Nerina paced about them both once again.

'Then all is well,' Nerina said, her voice smooth and unruffled again. 'Rise.'

Kiri and Rihanna got to their feet, looking at her.

'Of all the priestesses I depend upon you two the most,' she said. 'Your service has been exemplary. We stand now on the threshold of greatness. We can take all of Esurio and bend it to our will. You will both have an important part to play in that plan. I require your obedience.'

'Yes, high priestess,' both replied, exchanging a look with each other.

'Good. You will accompany me back to Daine with the others. Kiri, you may go. Rihanna, wait for me outside.'

Nerina watched as Kiri and Rihanna exchanged a look before bowing and walking away.

Nerina walked back to the throne atop its dais in the midst of the room and lowered herself into it, placing her arms on the armrests. She closed her eyes.

Merrin!

There was pause, before the answering voice came back across the mental link.

I hear you, high priestess Nerina.

We will be returning to Daine soon, I will leave the lesser priestesses here to keep order. What news from the borders?

All remains secure, nothing has been heard from the shaderight, but we entertain an emissary from Taloon. He seeks an audience with you on behalf of the King of that realm.

Taloon has much within its borders that will serve us well. We must proceed cautiously. Keep him entertained and promise that I will see him as soon as I return, it will be three stretches, no more.

It will be done. Is there something else?

Nerina paused. Merrin lacked imagination, but she had a shrewd ear and eye for detail. That was what made her such a good administrator.

We have captured the Queen of Scallia, she who had the power to resist us ... but her powers are gone.

Gone?

Yes, gone. The queen's mind is addled. Either the powers have been lost, or they have been already taken.

By whom?

There are only two it could be. Kiri, and your daughter, Rihanna.

This time there was a pause from the other end of the link.

Do you suspect their loyalty?

I have tested both and found nothing, but an explanation does not present itself. One, or both, is lying to me. We must watch them both

closely. If necessary we must move that aspect of our plan forward more quickly than anticipated.

We will be prepared here in that case.

Make sure you are discreet!

Always, high priestess!

Nerina dissolved the link and concentrated her mind back on what she had seen. Rihanna had been compliant as expected. Nerina had little suspicion of her, it was Kiri she wondered about.

Perhaps you have learnt how to keep secrets from me, young one. That is both wise and foolish. The question is, if you do have the queen's powers, what do you intend?

Nerina smiled. She had seen the strength of Kiri's gift from their first encounter, after Charis had found her, just a slum-girl living in the gutters of the city. Even then her gift had been extraordinarily strong, and it had grown in the intervening rounds under Nerina's guidance. The girl was still young and raw, but not to be underestimated. Rounds of living on her wits in the slums had moulded a mind that worked on survival at all costs. She was a fearsome fighter and Nerina had opened her mind to all the possible uses of the gift, not just the ones that tradition taught.

I have seeded the ground, the crop is almost grown. Harvest time approaches …

* * *

Kiri and Rihanna left the throne room at a run.

'She doesn't believe us,' Rihanna gasped. 'She forced her way …'

'Shhhh, not here,' Kiri answered. She nodded her head towards the stairs that led away from the elevated mount of the city down to the lower levels. 'This way.'

In silence they made their way down several steps at a time until they were able to access one of the passageways that ran around under the circumference of the walls. Here it was cool and shaded amongst the pillars and arches that supported the walkway above.

Both of them looked around searching for other people, but it was quiet, dank and hidden away. No one else was about.

They looked at each other for long moments.

'I can't stay long,' Rihanna said. 'She'll be wanting to …'

'Won't take long,' Kiri answered.

'She becomes more paranoid with every passing stretch,' Rihanna said, rubbing at her head. 'And we're supposed to be her most favoured? I'd hate to see what she does to those she despises.'

'You're right,' Kiri said, satisfied they couldn't be overheard. The pain from Nerina's forceful interrogation was subsiding. 'But she hasn't found what she's looking for. The queen's power, it's gone.'

'You didn't take it?' Rihanna asked.

Kiri looked away and shook her head. 'No, I didn't take it.'

Rihanna frowned. 'Tasha, maybe?'

Kiri nodded. 'Could be I suppose, though little good it did her. I guess it wasn't you?'

Rihanna gave her a look. 'Nerina would know. None of us can resist her strength, except you maybe.'

Kiri shrugged. 'No, I'm not that strong.' She laughed. 'If I had it, maybe I'd tear Nerina and be high priestess myself!'

Rihanna smiled. 'Reckon you would too.'

Kiri shrugged. 'Well I don't, so that's that. But Nerina is fearful of us, I think she worries we might have plans to do something like that.'

'Testing us, maybe,' Rihanna answered. 'She's suspicious of everyone. And then there are the secrets between her and my mother.'

Kiri's heart leapt. 'I remember, you said before. Something to do with Charis?'

Rihanna nodded, lowering her voice to a whisper. 'Charis always preached a path of peace, not war. It was she who mostly gave council to Launa before she died. I know my mother always voted against her …'

'You think they schemed to get rid of Charis?'

Rihanna shrugged and looked away. 'There was something odd about how you and Charis were sent to Varda the way you were. Almost as if …'

'Someone knew that Torin would attack us,' Kiri finished. 'Someone wanted the war with Scallia.'

'But my mother isn't that clever,' Rihanna said. 'If there was a scheme …'

'Nerina,' Kiri mouthed.

A flash of memory crossed her mind. Charis' words echoing in her head.

Nerina always gets her way.

Kiri's mind raced for a moment. The high priestess was clever enough, but could she have manipulated all of those events to a particular end? Was she responsible for Charis' death at Torin's hand?

'But there's no way to prove that,' Rihanna said. 'It was Torin that burnt the treaty wasn't it?'

Torin said he'd encountered a witch at the Scallian tithe … a witch who had caused him and his men pain …

Kiri nodded. 'We'll be back in Daine soon, there is something we must promise each other.'

Rihanna frowned. 'Promise?'

'Listen,' Kiri leant in close and whispered in her ear. Rihanna's eyes widened as she listened. Kiri stepped back a pace.

'Yes, or no?' Kiri asked after a moment.

'This could be dangerous,' Rihanna said.

'Yes, I know.'

Kiri held out her hand. Rihanna looked at it for a long moment.

'All right, promise,' she said, grasping Kiri's hand in hers. 'You and me.'

'You'd better go back,' Kiri said. 'She's expecting to see you outside.'

Rihanna nodded. 'Be careful.'

'You too.'

* * *

A chime later Kiri walked down through the city streets, noting how the inhabitants moved out of her way as she did so. The Scallians were terrified of the priestesses, having seen what they could do. Kiri had heard that Nerina had killed one of the Lords by crushing his mind as he stood before her.

And she might have done that to me if she had discovered my secrets! I did it once myself … back in Varda …

Kiri had always relied on her physical prowess to deal with her foes. She was strong and quick, now fearsomely skilled with her kai. In her hands it was a brutal weapon, dealing death when she so desired, cracking bone and bruising flesh. Yet, after Charis had died and her rage had consumed her amidst the villagers of Varda, she had struck out, killing with her thoughts. She had been enraged, incensed, out of control.

Her mind was still awhirl. She needed somewhere quiet to sit and think; somewhere where she wouldn't be disturbed.

She walked out of the courtyards of the city, idly wandering down the road beyond until she came to the river that ran out from underneath a mighty series of dams and weirs. It was quite the construction even to her untutored eyes. Fresh water cascaded down from above the city, being funnelled through it to fill reservoirs, pools and fountains within, until it found its way out once more and continued on down the valley to the sunward.

She walked on for a couple of marks, heading down to the river bank, enjoying the warmth of Lacaille and sparkles upon the surface of the water. There, in a copse hidden from view, she sat for a while, still lost in her thoughts, wondering what to do.

Nerina pushes for more power, for more tithes, but in recent times we have been in decline, ever fewer priestesses are found. Our powers stretched thinner and thinner. Nerina is fearful.

She took a deep breath.

From within her robes, Kiri pulled an old and tattered book. It was called the sixth element; one of a series of books that documented the religion of the priestesses. A religion she followed to the letter.

The first five books concerned themselves with the nature of Lacaille, the star above, their goddess. Then it talked of how the religion came to be, emerging from the horror of the past when men had thought they could master the world. How priestesses should use their gifts to heal, to communicate and to administer the people under their care.

But this sixth book was different to the others.

It was concerned with war, the use of the gift to cause pain and inflict harm, how to bend people to your will, how to torture, how to kill. At first such knowledge had been hidden from her, and she now knew why. Her gift was one of the strongest gifts to have manifested in many generations of priestesses.

Since returning to Viresia Kiri had been studying the book, looking for any detail she might have missed, now more focussed on Elena herself and how she had become the first high priestess.

Much of it makes sense now ...

There was one particular passage early on in the sixth book which had caught her eye. Kiri had read it and re-read it. It was brief, but it talked of how Elena began her journey to becoming high priestess. Kiri read it back to herself again, the words echoing in her mind.

'I was smote by pain; fire burned my body and my mind. A refiner's fire it was, cleansing me of foulness and impurity. I cried out, but there was no respite. Lacaille desired a pure vessel into which to pour her will. Then the vision came, my purpose defined. It was vouchsafed by her pureness, Lacaille, and delivered by her servant, the Obelisk; my task was appointed and my road laid before me. I was anointed that stretch, my destiny to be high priestess of Drayden.'

Kiri fingered the pendant that hung from her neck. It was a small metal triangle, elongated to a point. The mark of the priestesses; so she had been told.

To hear direct from Lacaille, what a privilege that must have been! And this Obelisk, what is it? A messenger on behalf of Lacaille?

She sighed and tucked the book inside her robes. She'd found no further answers.

Kiri looked about her. She was alone; no one could be eavesdropping on her thoughts. Lacaille blazed above, warm and unchanging. The heat was soothing and she closed her eyes, enjoying the sensation. She continued running through the events in her mind.

I have kept this secret so far, but what am I to do?

She shivered, despite the warmth about her.

The Scallian girl … I didn't even dare bring her to mind in front of Nerina!

Kiri had thought her no more than a maid of the royal household, but she had been confronted with a power the equal of her own, untempered and untrained, but potent beyond any other she had encountered, save the high priestess herself, Nerina.

Nerina doesn't know about her …

The maid had a name now.

Zoella.

Kiri took a deep breath. The old man, Guerrun, had revealed much.

She's my sister! Separated at birth and never knowing of each other. We are both daughters of Myana Tiamoi, sister of the dead King Ioric. He who I fought … and am responsible for his death. He was my uncle!

She replayed that fight in her mind, its ferocity and conclusion seen in a different light now that she knew who she had been fighting. She swallowed. A sister, an uncle …

I fought against my own people … I am of Scallia, not of Drayden!

Her thoughts whirled in disarray, her stomach clenching. Only she was aware, she'd retained presence of mind to keep her secret from everyone. None in Drayden knew save herself, perhaps not even Zoella, since only Kiri had the mental connection with Guerrun before he died.

I sit here in the city of my ancestors, a place I attacked … Guerrun hid me and Zoella, hoping to keep us safe from the priestesses, knowing our power would be desired by them. Our mother Myana, she was killed by the priestesses! I am of a royal line. This Queen we have captured … Liana is my cousin!

There was no one she could reveal this to, none who she could turn to for advice.

So what do I do? The priestesses raised me out of the slums, they have trained and tended me. Charis taught me their ways and they are right and proper. Lacaille's will must be done, surely? I have believed that, I still believe it! Yet, they killed my mother! If I had grown up here, I would see the priestesses as an evil force, taking our lands, taking our women ... I was hidden away in the hope I would not be found ... I would have fought against them. Now I know, should my loyalty to be Scallia because of birth, or Drayden because of upbringing? What is Lacaille's will for me?

She had no answer to those questions, but as she considered them another thought occurred to her. Kiri felt a warmth rush through her as she considered it. She licked her lips.

Him ... Meru ...

She had saved his life, intervening to make sure he and Zoella could make good their escape, frustrating the priestesses, but keeping it all secret from Nerina.

I want her and I want him. And I shall have them both!

She remembered the last thing she had said to him amidst a heady cocktail of lust, desire, fear and worry. The feelings buzzed within her, submerged for now.

You are mine now, Meru of Amar, mine!

She could sense him, even at great distance, her thoughts and desires imprinted upon his mind. It was disturbing, unsettling. The feelings were strong and powerful, lurking in her mind and interrupting her thoughts when least desired.

My heart burns for a sworn enemy! But an enemy of Drayden, not Scallia – what does that mean for me?

She was startled from her reverie by short sharp squeaks from nearby. She looked up to see a small furry face. It was a marsip, inquisitively sniffing her out and wondering why she was there, its small rodent features twisted in a grimace and its tiny, but folk-like, hands grasping the air before it.

Kiri remembered how she used to hunt them for food; they made for good enough eating if you were starving.

The marsip squeaked again.

'It's all right,' she said, holding out a hand. 'I won't eat you this time.'

The marsip approached, hesitating and running back and forth for a moment, before ducking its head under her hand. She reached down to touch it.

'You're very tame, why ...?'

The marsip snarled and teeth flashed. Kiri yelped in surprise. It had bitten her! She pulled her hand back and the marsip fled.

Blood flowed from her finger. Red. The colour of pain, anger and fear.

Her own lips curled in a snarl and she looked up as the marsip fled, seeking the shelter of the longer greening along the shore.

Without thinking she stretched out her hand. She felt the marsip's presence, felt its tiny mind. Panic, the urge to flee ...

She caught it.

How dare you bite me!

She clenched her thoughts. The familiar metallic sense of power grew within her. A tang she could almost taste.

She heard the marsip shriek for a moment, before it fell and thrashed on the ground. She could feel its terror now, the struggle to survive. She clenched her thoughts again. The marsip shrieked louder, its body contorting and writhing in the dust.

Like this? Yes, like this!

She watched, fascinated, for long moments, enjoying the animal's pain and distress, payment for the blood flowing down her fingers.

The metallic sensation throbbed within her. She closed her hand into a fist with an imperious mental command.

The marsip froze and then lay limp. She could feel it no longer.

She opened her hand, blood was splattered across her palm. She moved to the bank of the river and washed it away. Then she walked across to where the marsip lay, prodding the animal with her foot. It was dead, its body already cooling.

I killed it. So simple! Is that all it takes?

She felt dizzy and lowered herself into the greening until the feeling passed, staring at the corpse of the unfortunate animal. It wouldn't be long before the nargs discovered and made a meal of it.

So easy, just to snuff it out like that ... like a blowing out a candle.

She wrinkled her nose and got back to her feet. She'd been away for chimes now. She needed to get back before she was missed.

Am I strong enough for what lies ahead? The choices ... all are dangerous!

CHAPTER TWO

Straithian Sea, Shaderight of Amar

Round 2307, First Pass

It was no good.

The bile rose in her throat and her stomach heaved. She hung over the side rail of the *Mobilis* and retched again.

Zoella couldn't remember feeling so ill before. She had long since vomited up her last meal and now was reduced to hanging over the edge of the ship clutching her midriff and spitting the foul taste from her mouth. Her insides ached and her head spun.

I hate this ship!

The departure from Nireus had been the anticlimax she had hoped it would be. No sign of pursuit from the priestesses of Drayden. The first stretch had passed without much trouble; the sea had been calm and smooth. The thick grey cloud that had covered the sky had cleared, revealing the strange green hued curtains of light that Turgan had called the 'Alisse', silently drifting above. Minute lights had pricked the darkness beyond.

Just like my dreams of long ago, what are they? Impossible tiny sparkles …

But then the wind had picked up. The sea had transformed from a smooth, almost featureless, flatness to a rolling, tossing sleep-terror. Zoella had been affected straight away, but was alone in her torment. No one else was suffering, not even Ren, who had never been aboard a ship either.

She sank to her knees, still clutching the guardrail in one hand. She had never felt so miserable. The ship pitched forwards and back, undulating under her.

But it wasn't just the sea-sickness.

Loneliness cut through her, colder than the frozen wastes she had hiked through mere stretches before.

Everyone I cared about, killed or taken by the priestesses … and the one I thought might be a friend …

She cast her mind back. King Ioric, he who had rescued her and protected her – slain. Her loyal carn, Raga – slain. Guerrun, her long lost guardian – slain. Her queen, Liana, turned against her and captured. Perhaps she was dead too.

She remembered Liana's ferocity, her attempt to steal Zoella's gift. She'd tied Zoella down, whipped her in a rage. She remembered Turgan's lust, his hand fondling her thighs, reaching up …

More bile. She retched again, dissolving into sobs with the sheer misery of it all.

And Meru … even he's ignoring me!

An image swam into her mind, unwanted and unwelcome, but she was powerless to stop it. Dark hair and sharp blue eyes, a fierce unyielding expression and an unremitting purpose. A black-gloved left hand. Zoella trembled, her entire body shaking with rage.

Kiri!

It was she who had been responsible for all of it. She had killed King Ioric, setting her ghastly flying beast upon him; Zoella could only recall the horror of the snapping bloodstained teeth. Then Raga, who had sought to protect her. Kiri had crushed his skull with her staff and tortured the king's younger brother prince Torin, brutally killing him too. She trembled with the memory.

Murderer! Killer!

Somehow Zoella had fought her off, it seemed she alone had the power to resist the evil priestess. But that had only made Kiri pursue her more. Meru had rescued her and helped her escape, but Kiri had followed.

She caught us …

More killing. Zoella had found the one man who might have told her more about her origins, but Kiri had found him too and murdered him before Zoella's eyes. Whatever secrets he knew, only Kiri knew them now.

Guerrun … But then …

Kiri had done something strange. The priestesses of Drayden had Zoella, Meru and Ren cornered, about to shoot them down whilst they tried to escape on this strange metal ship. The priestesses had an easy shot. Zoella had tried to stop them but knew she couldn't prevent so many.

Yet Kiri stopped them, she let us escape … why would she do that?

It made no sense.

Zoella coughed, spitting more bile out into the rolling ocean beyond the ship.

And since then Meru won't speak to me. Why not? Why's he ignoring me? Did she do something to him? What? Why would she let us go when she chased us for so long?

'You all right?'

Zoella looked up into a round friendly face framed by short blonde hair. It was the ship's engineer, a woman called Mel.

Zoella couldn't manage words. She shook her head.

'Sea-sickness, eh?' Mel said. She took a blanket out from under her arm and folded it around Zoella. 'It's pretty miserable. Not much comfort I know, but it will pass in a stretch or two. You're just going to have to wait it out 'til you adjust.'

Zoella pulled the blanket around her, shivering.

'Thank you,' she managed.

'Your best bet is to stay as close to the middle of the ship as you can, it rolls less. That and sip a bit of water as often as you can.'

Zoella nodded.

She felt Mel crouch down beside her.

'You … ah … alone out here?'

Zoella couldn't help it. Loneliness overwhelmed her, tears streamed out of her eyes and down her cheeks; the pain in her stomach replaced with heaving sobs. She felt Mel put an arm around her and pull her back against the bulkhead of the ship.

'Hey … it's going to be all right. You're safe now, nothing is going to hurt you on board. The crew are a bit offish, but they'll warm up soon enough. Truth is, they're pretty scared themselves … I think your story was a bit more than they were expecting. These powers …'

Zoella tried to stop the shuddering and wiped at her tears. 'Thank you, you're very … kind …'

Mel smiled at her. 'Nothing to it,' she said. 'Anyway, where's Meru? Isn't he …?' Mel stopped, seeing the look that crossed Zoella's face. 'You two had words or something?'

'He won't talk to me,' Zoella said. 'He's ignoring me, ever since … something happened … she did something to him. I don't know what … I might be able to help, but …'

'She? This priestess girl you told us about? She sounds like a right nasty piece of work. Shame we didn't give her a blast from Fitch's rifles when we had the chance!'

Zoella nodded.

'Come on, let's get you below decks and cleaned up. Then we can talk.'

Zoella found herself hauled to her feet; Mel was strong. Zoella was led back inside the ship and ushered into the common room. Mel got her a cup of water and a dampened cloth to clean her face with.

'So what happened back there?' Mel asked as Zoella sipped at the cup.

'The priestess, witch, whatever you want to call her,' Zoella said. 'She killed so many of my people. Meru rescued me in his flying machine, but still she chased us. Through the mountains, forests and the frozen wastes, right into Drem.'

'But why?' Mel asked. 'What for?'

Zoella huddled closer into the blanket. 'For this power, this gift,' she answered. 'The priestesses can take powers from others, steal them, add them to their own. It makes them more powerful. I was able to resist …'

'So this … what was her name?'

'Kiri.' Zoella spat the name.

'She's after you? Trying to take your power?'

Zoella nodded.

'But ...'

Zoella looked up. 'She let us go. When you found us at the quayside, she deliberately stopped the other priestesses. Kiri let us go ...'

Mel frowned. 'And you think that has something to do with Meru?'

Zoella sighed. 'She did something to him. I'm sure of it. Why chase us all that way and then let us go? Makes no sense.'

'You're worried we can't trust him?'

'I don't know,' Zoella said. 'Kiri caught him once before. She tortured him I think, trying to find out where I was. I don't know what he went through, but she has some hold over him ...'

'I'd better let Coran know ...'

'I don't want to cause trouble!' Zoella looked alarmed.

Mel touched Zoella on the arm. 'Hey. I can see you care about him. He's lucky to have a friend like you. We're worried about him too. Come on, cheer up. We're getting further and further away from that witch all the time. There's no way she can cross the ocean. Try to put her out of your thoughts.'

Zoella pursed her lips, stifling a yawn. She shivered.

I wish I could! Kiri will find a way ...

'You're still exhausted. You need rest,' Mel said. 'Bet you haven't slept at all. You've been putting salve on your back too, I hope?'

'I ...'

'Thought so, come on.'

Zoella allowed herself to be led down to the sleeping berths. Mel was right, it felt good to be looked after. Mel helped her into a bunk, checked the welts on her back where she had been whipped by Liana, and then rubbed salve into them and gave her a small measure of Coran's Ochren.

'Medicinal,' she said, with a wink.

The liquor was strong and made Zoella's head swim, but in a more pleasant way than the slow rocking of the ship. Zoella found herself dozing off.

Dreams flickered at the edge of her mind.

* * *

Coran and Fitch were in the deckhouse of the *Mobilis* when Mel joined them. Both were looking out at the forward deck as the ship pitched back and forth.

'I hope this sea doesn't get any rougher,' Coran muttered. 'Not happy being out here on a single engine.'

'Two stretches out of Nireus,' Fitch replied. 'Got a long ways to go yet. Think the ship'll hold together?'

'She'll hold,' Mel said, walking up behind him. 'I'm more worried about our passengers.'

'The witch girl?' Fitch said.

'Don't call her that,' Mel replied.

'Why not?' Fitch returned. 'She's got magic powers. She's a witch.'

'The poor girl has a name; she's called Zoella. Seems to me she's as much a victim of what's going on as anyone else. Her story is miserable. All death, murder and angst over these strange powers.'

'Shouldn't have taken her aboard,' Fitch said. 'No good'll come of it.'

'We couldn't just leave her behind,' Mel retorted. 'Anyway, sounds like we have her to thank that Meru is still alive.'

'Shouldn't have let Meru go either,' Fitch added.

'Are you going to constantly hark back over old ground?' Coran snapped. 'What's done is done.'

'I warned right from the start we was playing with stuff we didn't understand,' Fitch said, facing both of them. 'So we've learnt that these confounded witches are real. Fantastic. We've learned that they still have a death wish on all the people of Amar ... wonderful! But those same scorchin' witches now know about us. And since one of them chased Meru across the whole forsaken continent we just put to our tiller you can bet your last coin they are going to come for Amar – and just to compound it all we've got one of them on board!'

'She's not one of them!' Mel snapped.

'And there's no way they can know where Amar is,' Coran said.

'Really?' Fitch said. 'You saw what that witch girl ...'

'Zoella!' Mel interrupted.

'... what she can do. She can put a thought in your head, sure as shades is shades she can see what's in your head too – your thoughts, your feelings and anything you know. She can kill you just by thinking it – she admitted it! Don't suppose we can keep any secrets from her or her kind. How do we really know she isn't one of them? She'd be a perfect spy, playing on our sympathy. She might already be doing stuff inside our heads and we'd never even know.'

Coran looked at Mel and she returned the look.

'See?' Fitch said. 'You're thinking it too.'

'Meru has vouched for her,' Coran said.

'And Meru's in his right mind is he?' Fitch said. 'He's been through the wringer that boy and no mistake. What if this witch girl ...' He glared at Mel before she could say anything. 'What if she, or any of the others he's met, has done something to his head?'

'It's not her,' Mel said. 'She's worried that the priestess girl might have done something to him, says he's acting odd ever since we left Nireus ...'

'Then either way we have a problem,' Fitch replied. 'We can't trust him, he's being manipulated. I say we're leading the enemy straight into our home camp. We should pitch this girl overboard, and her little friend, right this spell, just to be safe. Might be safest to dump Meru too.'

'No one is being pitched overboard,' Coran rumbled. 'Least of all Meru ...'

'Mark my words then,' Fitch said, pushing past both of them and striding to the door at the back of the bridge. He pushed it open and stepped outside, pausing for a moment. 'You'll regret that you didn't. You made a mistake when you went looking for the witches and you made a mistake not keeping hold of Meru back when we found that cursed speaking contraption. Third time is the charm, so they say. You're leading an army of witches right into our home port. Don't say I didn't warn you.'

He slammed the door and was gone.

Coran sighed. 'I thought we'd have a happy ship once we were homeward bound.'

'Fitch is overreacting …' Mel began.

'Is he?' Coran asked. 'We don't know what happened back there. These witches are real, Mel. Far more powerful than we feared and in enough numbers to destroy a city with ease. You heard Meru tell us what they did to Viresia – they wiped it out in minutes. What do you think they'll do if they find Amar?'

'Amar has some weapons. Catapults, the coastal defences, archers …'

'You think they'll hold against an aerial attack where the invaders can kill you by thinking it?' Coran glared at Mel, who didn't answer. 'Fitch is right, we've been stupid. We've alerted them to our presence and reminded them of some ancient vow – they're pledged to exterminate us. All those old legends warning of witches with magic powers – remember how we laughed? Turns out it's all true! Worse than true. They're going to come for Amar. Maybe Fitch is right about our passengers too …'

'You can't!'

Coran clenched the helm hard in his hands, his knuckles showing white through his skin.

'Not without proof, no,' he said. 'If she's telling the truth she might be handy to have on our side – maybe even the only effective weapon we'd have … what do you think?'

Mel considered it for a moment. 'She's just a girl. She's hurt, scared and lonely,' she answered. 'I believe her. I don't see her in the same light as these priestesses. They did try to kill her, we all saw that. I think she's been running from them all her life.'

'Maybe.'

'Zoella isn't one of them, I'm sure. Like you say, she might be the only defence we have.'

'I'll trust your judgement,' Coran said with a smile. 'What about Meru? And no, I won't pitch him overboard either.'

Mel frowned. 'He's not right. Zoella says he was caught by this priestess girl, the one who was chasing them … the one called Kiri. Zoella thinks he was tortured, or something. Lacaille knows what she might have done to him.'

'You think he might be a liability?'

'I think we need to know what happened back there. He's ignoring Zoella it seems, won't talk to her. She's pretty upset about it.'

Coran nodded.

'And I need to check on the one remaining engine,' Mel said, with a grin. 'I've done my bit with the girl. Now we need to sort Meru. Over to you captain.'

Coran grimaced. 'I knew you were going to say that.'

* * *

Meru and Ren were sitting over the bow of the *Mobilis,* watching the sea roll under the ship, parting into foaming torrents as the ship continued on its course. Ren shrieked with delight every time the spray splashed across him. Both seemed oblivious of the rough sea, though the weather was clearing with every mark they progressed. Snatches of clear blue were shining between rents in the clouds above.

'Can't see it no more,' Ren said, pointing up into the sky.

They'd been talking about the strange light in the sky they'd seen after leaving Nireus.

Meru nodded. 'No, the sky is too bright now.' The light they had seen was no longer visible and the fainter lights that had accompanied it were also gone, lost in the brightening sky between the clouds. Even the green curtains of light were harder to see now as Lacaille's influence grew once more.

'Skyship,' Ren said. 'How'd it get up there?'

Meru thought about it. Two stretches before they'd seen a light, rising in a swift arc across the sky. He'd first thought it might be a flying machine like the one he'd appropriated from Caesar's hangar, but it was too high, beyond the mountains and beyond the clouds, never more than a point of light. It had crossed silently above them and then dropped towards the far horizon, its speed constant and smooth.

Less than a chime later it had appeared again, now at a different angle in the sky, but behaving in the same way. They'd had ample chance for all the crew to look at it through Coran's scope, which, if you could hold it steady enough, had shown the light to be an elongated shape with three distinct sections; a blunt 'nose', a bulging mid-section and a tapered stern. More than that they couldn't make out.

But to make out even the smallest shape at the distance it must be huge … huge beyond imagining.

During his adventures in Scallia Meru had found an ancient research station, with long abandoned machinery pointing at the sky. He'd learned the devices were called radio telescopes and they seemed to have once sent messages up into the sky to where the skyship flew.

Ships in orbits, high above the sky.

After watching the skyship a second time, Meru had gone below decks and tried to work it out. He made some calculations on a piece of paper, rewriting them and scribbling again, the answers made no sense.

It's above the clouds, beyond the mountains, beyond even the horizon! So far that we can't hear it. Horizon is about twenty five marks away give or take … how high is the sky? Let's say it's fifty marks. The 'scope makes things about twenty times bigger than they really are …

He'd written the numbers down, and used the figurings of distance that he'd learnt as an apprentice timekeeper on Amar. He knew the maths worked for things on the ground, but the answers for the skyship were unbelievable.

But that means it's something like five marks long! And if it is truly that big, it's moving at a speed of hundreds of marks every minute. That can't be right …

Meru had tried, but he couldn't see the error in his maths. Either the object was much closer and they should be able to hear it, or it was far away … and stupendously huge and fast. Neither made any sense. How could a flying machine be the size of a city and travel at such a speed?

Ren was still waiting for an answer.

Meru sighed. 'I have no idea,' he said. 'Another mystery for us to solve.'

'Magic!' Ren said.

Meru nodded and laughed. 'Maybe it is, it doesn't make much sense!'

Meru knew where to find the answers though. Back in Scallia, in a cavern hidden away not far from the deserted city of Dynesia, they had found a machine.

Caesar. Even now, I'm not quite sure what it is ... not a person, but a ... thing!

An intelligence of some kind; a machine, a mechanism. It called itself 'Caesar', and by its own definition that was shorthand for Computational Atmospheric and Environmental Service facility. Much of what it spoke about was confusing and peculiar, but Meru had recognised enough to understand that it was a device that their ancestors had used, perhaps even made, long ago to help them.

The crew of the *Mobilis* had discovered it. It was Caesar that had warned them about the flares and given Meru access to the flying machine. Later he'd discovered the abandoned radio telescope facility somewhere across Scallia, in which he'd found more machines, broken down, but leaving tantalising hints as to what their ancestors had been capable of.

And this light in the sky, it's a vessel in orbit, somehow going around and around this world of ours, this planet ... Esurio. Caesar would know ... if only I could ask him ... it ... him!

He stared back out to sea. For now, Scallia was behind and Amar ahead. Amar was home, but he had no great desire to return there. Meru shivered.

What are they all going to say when they find out the truth?

There wasn't anything he could do about it now. It was just the way things had happened. None of this had been expected. To start with it had been an adventure, a way to escape the problems at home and then a quest across strange lands. He'd not meant to deceive anyone, not really. He was caught in it now.

And then there was her.

Blue eyes, dark black hair.

Every time he slept, even if he closed his eyes for a brief moment, there she was. The witch-girl, the young priestess of Drayden. He'd watched as she'd led the attack on Viresia, intimidated by her prowess as a warrior. She could wield her metal staff with a devastating ferocity. He'd watched her great reptilian beast kill the King and saw how she and her fellow priestesses had attacked and subdued Viresia killing many within, Zoella's loyal carn amongst them. Later she'd caught him with the intention of forcing the location of Amar from his mind. She'd forced her way inside his thoughts.

But something happened ...

Then the flares struck, forcing them to flee. She'd been injured, he had a chance to kill her, but they'd cooperated in order to survive. Some sort of understanding had grown between them despite her vowed intent to murder everyone who shared his ancestry.

And then ...

She'd caught him once again, fleeing amidst the ruin of the attack on Nireus. She could have killed him. Instead ...

The same feelings washed over him again. He couldn't stop them. Burning desire, her scent in his nostrils, her mouth pressed hard against his, her fingers clawing into his back. The last words she had spoken, still echoing in his mind.

You are mine now, Meru of Amar, mine ...

He shivered again, his body responding despite his wishes. She'd done something to him and he knew there was no way it could be undone, because he wanted it more than anything else he'd ever known.

Her name was on his lips, her face in his thoughts. Her body, somehow always bereft of her clothes, the subject of lurid dreams that taunted and tempted him every sleeping.

'Kiri.'

Another secret I'm keeping ...

The *Mobilis* pounded on through the waves. Amar was getting ever closer.

* * *

Coran watched them for a moment. The pair were laughing and joking together. From the story that had been told Coran understood Ren to have been a native of Drem, orphaned by the flares and found along the way by Meru and Zoella as they had ventured into the Shadeward.

Another passenger ... another complication. At least he doesn't have magic powers!

The joking seemed to stop. Meru was looking out to sea, pensive all of a sudden.

'Hey,' he called, raising his voice so they could see him.

Both turned around to look. Ren was on his feet and bowing his head.

'He's only the captain,' Meru said, giving him a jab. 'Not the king ...'

Coran smiled. 'Yeah, belay all that stuff. You guys all right out here?'

'Ship running well,' Ren said. 'So fast!'

His young eyes were bright with enthusiasm. He seemed to have adapted well to the ship, despite never having been aboard one before.

Kids take it all in their stride though ... always have done.

'Good. Need you to run along inside Ren. I need to have a chat with Meru.'

Ren nodded and scampered off towards the mid-section.

Coran sat himself down on one of the raised deck hatches, bracing himself against the motion of the *Mobilis*. He fixed Meru with a look.

'So,' he said.

Meru didn't answer, but looked away out to sea.

'You need to level with us,' Coran said. 'What really happened back there?'

'Did Zoella send you?' Meru replied.

'Zoella?' Coran frowned. 'No. It's Mel who's worried about you. Truth is, we're all worried. This girl, Zoella, has the same power as these witches. We need to know what happened and what we're up against. You sure that this girl we've got on board is safe?'

Meru turned, an alarmed look on his face. 'Zoella isn't a priestess,' he said. 'She's from Scallia, not from Drayden. Her people were attacked and killed!'

'Yet she has the same power,' Coran said. 'How do we know she's telling the truth? How do you know she hasn't twisted your mind and she's a spy? Fitch wants her overboard right this spell and I can see ...'

'Fitch knows nothing,' Meru said. 'Zoella is no spy. Her people were attacked just like ours were. These priestesses steal power from other women ... Zoella just happens to have it. She's innocent ... she ... it's not her who ...'

Meru stopped.

'This Kiri girl?' Coran prompted.

Meru looked away.

'Come on boy, tell me. What's with her?'

Coran saw Meru look out to sea again before turning around. Coran saw him swallow.

'I rescued Zoella and her queen, Liana, when they were attacked by the priestesses,' Meru said. 'I didn't know what to do, but Zoella had been kind to me. She would have been killed if I hadn't, I couldn't just leave her. The three of us escaped in the flying machine ...'

'All very noble,' Coran said. 'I'd have probably done the same.'

'There was this one priestess. Young, powerful. She tried to stop us. She chased us. They had those flying reptiles. Dachs they're called. She came after us, chased us into the mountains. The flying machine was damaged, we crashed. Zoella got out with Liana. I didn't. The priestesses caught me.'

Meru stopped.

'It's all right,' Coran said. 'Keep going.'

'She ... she ...' Meru's lips were tight, Coran saw him shudder.

'This Kiri girl. What did she do to you?' Coran whispered.

Meru looked down. 'She got ... into my mind. She could read my thoughts. She made me think of Zoella so she could find her. She found out about the *Mobilis*, about Amar ...' Meru's voice cracked. 'I tried, but I couldn't stop her, she hurt me, she ...'

Coran placed his hand on Meru's shoulder. He could feel the young man shuddering.

'Hey. It's all right. No one could have done any better. Doesn't seem like it's possible to defend yourself from this mind reading stuff. You did the best you could ...'

Meru's shudders slowed. 'Zoella wants to help,' he said. 'I know she does. I just don't want anyone inside my head again ... not like that ...'

Coran considered it all for a moment. 'Do you know why she let you go?' he asked.

He felt Meru tense. Meru shook his head. 'She chased us all that way. She came alone. She wants Zoella's power for herself. The other priestesses were there. Maybe thought she had another plan and it didn't work out ...'

Not convinced, Meru ...

'Then we're doing the best thing,' Coran said, keeping his voice even. 'Staying as far away from her as we can. Every spell we head sunright we're putting more distance between us and her.'

Meru nodded. 'The priestesses don't know how to cross the sea. They don't have anything like the *Mobilis* ...'

'That's just as well,' Coran said, thinking it through. 'How would I know his girl, what does she look like?'

Meru sighed. 'You can tell her apart easily enough; she wears a black glove on her left hand.'

'A black glove?'

Meru nodded, but said no more.

'Come on. You've had a tough time. But ignoring folks isn't the answer. You'd better square off with your friend too. She's as miserable as you are.'

Meru nodded.

'We're heading to Amar,' Coran continued. 'Like you say, the priestesses can't reach us there, least not for passes or rounds. Plenty of time to figure out what to do.'

Coran pulled Meru to his feet.

'But if you get any suspicion that you're being contacted or ...'

Meru shook his head. 'I don't think they can do things like that at distance. They have to be close by, their powers aren't that strong.'

'Nevertheless,' Coran said. 'You get a suspicion of anything like that, you tell us. Yes?'

'Aye, captain,' Meru said.

'Good lad.'

* * *

A burning landscape, swept with golden sands under a crisp azure sky. Lacaille was centred straight above, as if looking down upon the ground. All about was a wall of impenetrable stormy clouds, swirling around and around, dozens of marks high. Yet here in the centre, all was calm.

The eye! The Obelisk!

Her gaze drifted away from the clouds and the light of Lacaille, now focussing on something else. She could see a vast construction, towering up from the landscape below, reaching far into the heavens, as high as the clouds themselves, perhaps even above them. It took the form of a vast tower, wide at the base and then tapering as it rose. Sunlight flashed from its sides.

Metal!

She had seen it before, in dreams and imaginings and in symbols. An isosceles triangle, but huge, towering into the heavens. Wasn't it the mark of the priestesses? She had been given a pendant with this symbol. What did it mean?

Waves of power were pulsing from it. She could feel it pounding outwards, washing over her, invigorating her. She felt the gift rise in her with each pulse, strengthening and building, growing to crescendo ...

The source! The Source of Lacaille!

But the pulses faltered. Her own power failed and lapsed. She saw strange green glows flicker in the heavens, before they too evaporated into nothingness.

Then came the heat, a gasping shortness of breath. She could see animals howling in fear and pain as something struck them down, something invisible. She felt her own skin crackle and burn, something snatching the breath from her lungs. Pain and darkness ...

Zoella jolted awake, almost banging her head on the bulkhead above her. Her breath coming in gasps and wheezes, her heart pounding in her chest. She felt a hand grasp hers.

'Hey, you all right?'

She blinked. Meru's face swam into focus. His hand felt hot in hers.

'I ... yes,' she managed. 'A dream.'

Meru handed her a cup of water and she took a sip.

'Your dreams normally mean something,' Meru began.

Zoella looked at him, but didn't respond.

'Look,' he said. 'I didn't mean to abandon you ... I'm sorry. This must be really horrible for you after everything that's happened.'

Zoella pursed her lips. He seemed contrite.

'I only offered to help,' she said.

'I know,' Meru said. 'I just ... she invaded my mind ...'

'Kiri,' Zoella said, her voice cold.

Meru nodded.

'She got inside my mind, saw things, got into my thoughts. I couldn't stop her ...'

Zoella swung her feet down from the bunk. 'The gift is not supposed to be used like that. I truthfully don't know what it is supposed to be for, but I'm sure of that at least. It's meant to be used for the benefit of all, not twisted into a weapon as the priestesses do.'

Meru nodded. 'I just don't want to feel anything like that again, it ... it was horrible.'

Zoella nodded. 'I understand, I didn't mean to make it worse.'

She held out her hand. Meru smiled at her and took her hand in his. She held it tight and didn't let go, turning to face him and looking him in the eye.

'So why did she let us go?' Zoella demanded.

She felt his hand twitch in her grasp. He shook his head and pulled his hand away.

'Maybe she had a plan to capture us herself,' Meru said. 'But it didn't work out. I don't know. What do you think?'

Zoella kept her gaze on him, pursing her lips.

'I have no idea,' she said, her tone hard. 'I can't think of a single reason why she would let us go after chasing us all that way. It doesn't make any sense to me at all.'

Meru looked away. 'No, it doesn't. But she did. She must have had her reasons.'

Zoella nodded, but didn't say anything further. Meru wouldn't make eye contact.

'We're going to have a bit of a council of war,' he said, after a pause. 'A plan of action. The rest of the crew would like you to be there.'

'I will be. Give me a spell.'

Meru nodded and left. Zoella took a deep breath.

You are still lying to me Meru. You might have convinced the others, but you're lying! I can feel it. You and … ugh! Kiri! Something has happened and I will find out what it is.

She gathered her thoughts for a moment before climbing down from the bunk. She walked towards the door …

Pain flashed at her temple, a headache that pulsed across her forehead. She yelped and staggered, grasping at the door handle to steady herself. The pain grew worse, like a drill burrowing into her skull. She cried out and sank to the floor, pushing her palms at her head, trying to ease the pain.

Then the agony came. She screamed.

* * *

Meru had just reached the deck when he realised something wasn't right. Coran, Fitch and Mel were all on the deck behind him, looking over the stern of the ship. Meru could see the engine covers on the rear deck were open. Daf and Creg were standing nearby, hands on hips.

And the single remaining engine wasn't turning.

Oh no, don't say we've broken down out here. We're hundreds of marks out to sea!

'What's happened?' he called. 'Engine broke?'

They looked around at his voice. Mel shook her head. 'The engine's fine … well, it's not broken at any rate, it's …'

'The 'tricity,' Coran said. 'It's gone.'

'Gone?' Meru echoed.

Coran pointed up.

The *Mobilis'* curious sails were fully deployed as they had been for the last stretch. Where they would normally be crackling with the discharge of the 'tricity, with faint sparks of blue flashing about them, now they were still and silent. The ship was rolling in the waves, adrift. None of its lights were operating.

'Breakers? Coils?' Meru asked.

'All checked, there's nothing wrong,' Mel replied.

Coran straightened.

'That also means the bilge pumps aren't running,' he said. 'Daf, Creg, you'd better get below and start cranking.'

The two big men nodded and jumped down into the interior of the *Mobilis.*

'But …' Meru looked around the ship. The wake of the *Mobilis* was fading into the swell of the sea. The ship was dead in the water.

'… how can the 'tricity be gone?'

It was then they heard the scream from below decks. Meru ducked back down, scrambling through the hatch into the crew compartment. He found Zoella curled up on the floor in her berth, screaming and pummelling her forehead with her hands.

'Zoella!'

He tried to pull her hands away, but her strength was beyond him. She flailed, pushing him back against the door, all the time screaming in agony. Coran and Mel appeared at the hatch.

'What's happening?' Coran demanded.

'I don't know, she's just ...'

Zoella gave another ear-splitting scream, her fingers tearing at the skin on her scalp and drawing blood.

'Help me!' Meru said, grabbing one of her arms and yanking her up. Coran grabbed the other and between them they tried to wrestle her under control. Her strength was wild and fierce.

'Mel, help us, can't hold her!'

The lights in the berth flickered and came back on. At that same moment Zoella went limp in Coran and Meru's arms, her body slack. The ship vibrated. The engine had come back to life.

Mel pulled up Zoella's chin and looked at her.

'She's in a dead faint. Out cold.'

'Help me get her back into a bunk,' Coran instructed.

Together they wrestled Zoella's unconscious body into the lower of the two bunks in the berth. She looked pale, her breathing ragged, her face marked with the scratches she had inflicted upon herself.

'Check the ship,' Coran said to Mel. 'Meru you stay with her.'

Mel ducked outside, but wasn't gone long. They heard the engine slow and come to a halt. Meru had just managed to clean the blood from Zoella's face when Mel came back.

'Everything is back on,' Mel reported. 'Same as ever, 'tricity is flowing as you'd expect. I've throttled back for the time being, 'til we can figure this out.'

'So what happened?' Coran demanded.

Mel shook her head. 'I don't know. It just stopped. One moment everything was spinning normal, next it wasn't there. There was nothing, no 'tricity, nothing. But it's not something we did, the *Mobilis* is fine.'

'But that can't be,' Coran said. 'It's always been there, always! It can't just not be there suddenly, can it?'

'Seems so,' Mel said, with a shrug. 'But it's never happened before.'

Coran looked at Meru. 'She's got something to do with it,' he said, gesturing to the unconscious Zoella. 'She must have. Can't be a coincidence she gets the screams when the 'tricity fails and then goes out like a light when it comes back on.'

Meru looked back, worry etched on his features. 'She doesn't know anything about 'tricity, her people don't even know it exists ...'

'Then how do you explain ...?'

'Obelisk!'

All three jumped and spun round as Zoella sat up behind them, screeching out the single word. She was staring at them, her face pale and drawn, shocked as if she'd seen some horrific vision.

'Zoella?' Meru whispered.

'It needs me,' she said, looking at the three of them, her expression confused and fearful. 'It's calling me. I must go to it, before it's too late. Before everything is killed.'

'Go to ... what?' Meru asked.

Then she fainted again. Meru caught her and lowered her back down.

Coran let out a sigh of frustration. 'Just what in Lacaille's name is going on? Shades. Meru, when she wakes up ... find out!'

CHAPTER THREE

Daine, Capital of Drayden

Round 2307, Second pass

Kiri stood on the balcony outside her room, enjoying the warmth of Lacaille as it shone down from above. Its face was unmarked by the dark blotches that had tainted it in the previous pass, but she sensed pause since the devastation of the flare was a respite.

We have brought peace to these lands. Would Charis be proud of what we've achieved? This was not the way she foresaw. Had the leaders of Scallia not schemed against us, we might have avoided all the bloodshed too. But they are gone now and Drayden itself, Scallia, even Drem to the Shadeward … All lies under our control. But we haven't completed the task appointed. Thus the flares will return …

The priestesses had returned to Daine, the capital of Drayden. Her room felt strange to her. Yes, it was still the same familiar place, nothing had changed, but it no longer felt like the safe place of refuge it had once been.

It hasn't changed … I have.

Kiri could see the red sand-stone pyramid of the temple across the piazza. Above it a few riders on dachs came and went, delivering messages throughout the realm. Within, Nerina would be preparing to reveal whatever plans she had concocted.

But Nerina is right. I did take Liana's gift … I never intended to, it was an accident! But now I have it, I cannot reveal that. Nerina suspects, but she cannot prove it. So what will she do? My ancestry remains a secret too, but for how long? A tiny slip and all will be revealed. If Nerina discovers I'm an heir of Scallia …

Kiri wasn't sure what the outcome of that revelation would be, but she doubted it would go well for her.

It would give her a reason to take my gift, my loyalty questioned. Nerina always gets her way ...

Kiri shivered.

My secrets must remain so for now.

Kiri thought about Liana too.

She's my cousin, what might she know about my family? Did she know about Zoella and Myana? Zoella was a maid in Viresia, so perhaps not ... too many things I don't know!

And then there was Rihanna's story. She and her friends had been pressured into attacking Kiri, before the flares, before the war on Scallia. Her mother, Merrin, had put her at risk. Kiri, defending herself, had almost killed Rihanna. Charis had intervened on her behalf to stop Merrin's demand for an execution.

Charis got me out of there, at risk to herself. They put me on probation and sent me into that conflict in Scallia. Did Nerina know what was going to happen there? Did they know Torin was going to turn on us? If so, why would they do such a thing?

Kiri frowned.

Nerina always gets her way ...

So what was it that Nerina wanted? Kiri thought about it for a moment.

She was furious when she found Liana's power missing. Angry like I've never seen her before. She wanted her gift, she was desperate for it. Why?

Kiri's mind kept racing.

She wanted to do something with that extra power. And I must be the next most powerful priestess after her. Perhaps she was hoping to take my gift for herself? The priestesses can't pool their gifts, so she would have to be very much stronger than me to do it. Now her plans are thwarted!

Kiri swallowed. Everything Nerina had done had a single aim. More power for her. The tithe from Scallia, tearing power from the young women, taking on Scallia, searching for Liana. All save the last had resulted in more gifts being taken.

She sees herself not just as high priestess, but empress! Empress of old Voren. She wants to do what Elena did … more! She wants to have everything subject to her. With Liana's power she would have been unstoppable, but she doesn't have it, so she still needs the rest of us … for now. If she finds a way to increase her strength enough though … It's Amar, she wants Amar. More women … more power!

Kiri's thoughts turned in another direction.

If I were the stronger … I must be close to her equal, thus she fears me. And Nerina doesn't know about Zoella! Her gift … if I had that there'd be no way Nerina could take me. I am of a royal line. The ancient kings and queens of Voren are my ancestors through Scallian birth. I could be …

She gasped at her own audacity, but the thoughts wouldn't go away, they swirled, growing in strength and ambition.

Then an image of Zoella filled her mind. A softer, kinder face than hers, framed in brown hair. Sisters they might be, but they looked little alike. Kiri knew nothing of Zoella's background other than that she had ended up as a maid in the palace in Viresia. Had Ioric known who she was? Had anyone? Did she?

And she is an heir too. I have a sister, estranged yes, but a sister … If I am to confront Nerina I must have her gift. Whilst she was just a maid that was easy to consider … but can I really tear my sister? But without her power …

Thinking of Zoella brought other things to mind.

She licked her lips.

And I can sense him too, I can find him. When I have the means …

The plans that had half formed in her head were brushed aside. His face filled her mind. She knew what was coming, it had been plaguing her ever since that encounter in the boat-room in Nireus.

No, not again!

But, in truth, she wanted it. The feeling kept coming back, each time more powerful than before. It didn't matter what her conscious mind tried to focus on, it was overwhelmed in a rush of desire.

I want him.

The urge was primal, instinctual, overpowering. When she had broken into his mind to interrogate him she had done something else. She had forged some kind of connection and ever since then …

Meru …

She let the feelings wash over her until they subsided once more. They were getting stronger each time they returned. Her room felt claustrophobic, her clothes damp and clingy. She opened the door and stepped into the corridor beyond, wanting some fresh air. Her heart was pounding so hard in her chest she was surprised she couldn't hear it echoing off the walls.

She walked down past the doors of the other priestesses with whom she shared the accommodation. Rihanna's room was not far away, but few of the priestesses were in residence now, most were employed with tasks around the temple. It was quiet.

She walked on, forcing herself to breathe, feeling her heart slow from its fierce beat. She leant against the corridor wall to compose herself.

There was a sound from ahead of her. Some sort of cry or moan. Frowning, she moved forward. It was coming from the rooms before her. There was a heat in her mind, a strange warmth that compelled her forwards. Her skin itched, craving something she couldn't define.

The cry had come from Rihanna's room. Kiri knocked. There was no response. She pushed open the door and walked in.

'Rihanna, are you …?'

Kiri stifled a gasp, her eyes widening in shock.

Rihanna was naked, astride an equally naked young man. She had him pinned to the bed, her hands on his shoulders, her thighs bearing down on him, her back arched and head flung back. Both were oblivious, lost in their combined ecstasy.

Kiri stared, unable to avert her eyes. A redness flooded her vision, lust coursing through her own body, lighting her from within. Unbidden, her own hands swept across her body, touching her breasts and sliding down her midriff. Her eyes closed as her mind wandered. The fire was stronger, almost burning her. She moaned.

'What are you doing?'

Kiri blinked, Rihanna was turned towards her, looking at her, her expression a mixture of annoyance and surprise. Beyond her the young man was propped up on one arm, looking back with curiosity.

'I ... sorry ... I don't ...'

'Spying on me?'

'No! I didn't ...'

'You can have him after I finish if you want.'

'What?' Kiri's voice filled with genuine alarm. 'No!'

'Always the prude,' Rihanna said. 'You never change, do you?'

She got up from the bed and walked towards Kiri, hips swinging, shaking her bright red hair, at ease with her nakedness.

'I'm sorry, I'll go, I don't know why ...' Kiri stuttered, retreating.

Rihanna turned and smiled at her as she came close, pushing the door closed, preventing her escape. Kiri backed up against the wall.

'I know what ails you,' Rihanna said, her voice dropping low. 'I know what you've done. That boy isn't it? The one from Amar you talked about. You can't run away from it.'

Kiri avoided her gaze, looking down at the floor. 'I'm fine, it's just ...'

'It's burning you up,' Rihanna said. 'Every time you think of him, it's lighting you up like a fire inside ...'

Kiri looked up, her breath coming in short, sharp gasps.

'I can't stop it, I can't control it ...' Kiri said, feeling her hands shake. 'It's like I'm going mad ...' Tears sprang into her eyes. 'What's happening to me?'

'Hey ... don't fret. They should have taught you these things,' Rihanna said, her voice now soft. 'I guess there was never time, you joined the priestesses so late, never grew up with all this ...'

Kiri bowed her head, 'I don't want it, but then I do ...'

'Don't be scared,' Rihanna said, her voice dropping to a whisper. 'You know the priestesses have different callings. Many are warriors, like you and I. Others are healers ...'

Kiri remembered her old mentor, Charis. Charis had taken her in when all others despised her. She was just a dirty girl from the slums after all. The 'guttersnipe' they called her. Charis had seen her potential and trained her as a healer.

'I know all this,' Kiri said, brushing aside the sad thoughts of Charis.

Rihanna smiled. 'So. The others, they're birthers.'

Kiri looked up and wrinkled her nose at this, causing Rihanna to laugh.

'Still the same old Kiri,' she said. 'It is an honourable part of our society! Without the birthers how would we keep the population? They get to choose from the pick of the men within the realm, selecting the strongest and most virile to take to their beds.'

Rihanna looked around at the young man behind her. Kiri saw her run her tongue over her teeth as she looked back

'But to make babies …' Kiri said, her face still twisted in distaste.

'Yes. They bear babies. We need girls for the priestesshood. A few baby boys are tolerated, but men are never in short supply.'

'But what does this have to do with what's happening to me?'

Rihanna smiled at her. 'Where the warriors use their gift in conflict and the healers used theirs to treat wounds, the birthers use the gift to make an indelible bond with the men they choose, leading to loyalty and fidelity from the men and a greater chance of healthy offspring …'

'Are you saying …?'

'You've bound yourself to that boy of yours,' Rihanna said. 'Accidently, I guess. But he will consume your thoughts and you will consume his.' She shrugged. 'You've made that bond, it's done.'

Kiri knew Rihanna was telling the truth. She couldn't deny it.

I did this to myself. I didn't listen, now I'm stuck with …

'How do I break it?' Kiri whispered.

'Break it?' Rihanna shook her head. 'I don't think you can. You must feel how strong it is …'

Kiri didn't answer. She didn't have to. Rihanna was right, she could feel it. It had been there for a pass or more, ever since she had forced her way into his mind.

And I don't want to break it. I just want him. I want him here and I want him now!

She groaned, turning and thumping her fists against the wall, her eyes bright with lust. The moment passed, she caught her breath and turned back.

'You mustn't tell anyone.'

'I'll keep your secret,' Rihanna said, with a girlish giggle. 'But you're going to have to square with it sometime. It will not leave you, nor will it leave him. And it will only get worse the longer you deny yourself ...'

'Deny myself?'

Rihanna laughed. 'You've never been with a man, have you?'

Kiri didn't answer that question either. A tremor of panic passed through her. A man had come for her once, when she was younger, just an 'only' in the slums. He hadn't known she had a knife. There had been blood and screams. That one would never bother a woman again ...

Rihanna stepped close. 'You feel it, don't you? Burning in your thighs, quickening your breath, hotness, you want it ...'

Rihanna ran her finger tips down the side of Kiri's cheek, across her neck, still further down between her breasts ...

'Stop it!'

Kiri felt her face flush. Memories flooded back, how she had caught up with Meru in the boathouse in Nireus. How they had embraced, kissed ... had there had been time she would have taken him there and then. She had almost lost control of herself.

'I can see you do,' Rihanna said. 'It's in your mind, isn't it ... those thoughts ... they scare you ...'

'No, don't!'

Rihanna took her hand, whispering in her ear.

'It's all right,' she said. 'You don't need to fear it. I can help you.'

'But I don't even know what ... ' Kiri stared at her. 'What do you mean, help me?'

Rihanna smiled, looking back to the young man, still prone upon her bed and then back to Kiri. 'For once, this is something I know more about than you. You need some lessons.'

'I can't … I don't think …'

'Like anything else,' Rihanna said with a wink. 'This is an art, the more you practice, the better you get. Come …'

Kiri felt Rihanna squeezing her hand, pulling her further into the room.

She was about to protest again, but Rihanna silenced her by placing her finger against Kiri's lips.

'Trust me,' she said, her voice little more than a whisper. 'You'll enjoy it. And when you find that boy of yours once more … you'll be ready.'

Kiri was horrified and curious all at once. In her indecision, Rihanna turned and led her towards the bed.

* * *

'They're all talking about her,' Merrin said. 'In fact, they talk of little else since her return from Drem.'

Nerina did not react, but her voice was tight. Both priestesses stood atop the temple, looking out across the city. Lacaille blazed in the sky above.

'Our erstwhile slum girl grows in stature each stretch so it seems,' Nerina said. 'It was Kiri, not Nerina, who slew the King of Scallia. Some say she vanquished Drem too.'

'She'll always be a guttersnipe.'

Nerina shook her head. 'Where she came from is of less interest now than where she is going. Let us assume she has taken the Queen's power, perhaps even unknowingly. What does she intend to do with it?'

'She's just a child. We should tear her now, quietly, silently. Like the others over the rounds.'

Nerina looked across at Merrin. 'You are a talented administrator, but leave the strategy to me. Kiri hasn't turned against me, not yet.'

'Maybe she plots even now.'

'Maybe she does,' Nerina replied. 'And if she grows the love of the people and garners a following then she becomes a threat. Until then she is mine to use to as I see fit.'

'So what will you do?'

Nerina smiled. 'For the time being, the stronger she becomes, the more useful she becomes. I can gain no further increase from tearing the feeble abilities of tithed girls from the provinces. They are too weak. I want power concentrated first, then I will take it.'

'Kiri already is powerful …'

'I have a task in mind for her, it will test her loyalty. I want her as powerful as she can possibly be before I tear her. But it is time to think of contingencies. We must find a way to test her limits, determine whether she truly has the Queen's power or not.'

'And if she does?'

'That depends on whether she has lied to me or not,' Nerina said. 'If she does plot against me then we will have to arrange her downfall carefully. She is a heroine this stretch; that must be undone for the next if we are to tear her. Until then she remains a valuable member of our society.'

'I still think we should tear her now and be done with it.'

'We can afford to wait a little,' Nerina said. 'The next move is hers.'

* * *

A faint smile crossed Kiri's face. Rihanna had been right, such things were pleasurable. She had no idea what she had been missing out on. The lessons had been … different, but she had learnt quickly. With her rank as a priestess, the men of the temple were hers to choose from. She had experimented for herself, her confidence growing. Her lust had been sated for a while, but the desire remained. It smouldered, biding its time, but at least now she had some control of it.

Her thoughts turned to Rihanna and the easy familiarity she possessed with the men of Drayden. The thoughts broiled away somewhere deep within her, biding their time.

She was right, I am going to have to deal with that. Yet as Empress, everything would be subject to my will, my bidding ...

For now though she wanted to focus on her immediate plans. A knock came from the door behind her.

'Come in,' she called. The door opened.

It was Pootle, her manservant, laden down with pressed clothes and fresh bedding. He was a short rotund fellow with a crumpled, but friendly expression. The hair atop his round face was cut down short, with the exception of a braid on the right side, hanging at shoulder length.

'I'm here to change your room, mistress, if that be pleasing to you.'

She nodded, gesturing for him to come into her chambers.

'It is good to see you once again, mistress,' Pootle said. 'You've been on such a journey. Quite the talk of the temple you are again.'

She smiled at him; she had missed her manservant's bumbling and talkative manner.

'And what are they saying about me now?' she asked.

'I wouldn't presume to know everything of course,' Pootle replied.

'Of course,' Kiri said. 'But you'll tell me what you do know, won't you Pootle?'

Pootle began pulling the old sheets away from her bed. 'Talk is that you're becoming the most powerful priestess in the ranks,' Pootle said. 'That perhaps you're in-line to become high priestess after Nerina. Some still sneer about ...'

'About where I came from,' Kiri said, her eyes narrowing. 'The guttersnipe? No prizes for guessing who that was.'

'Horrid lies,' Pootle said.

Kiri shrugged. 'No, it's true enough. But I've come a long way since then.'

'You have indeed, mistress,' Pootle affirmed. 'Many admire you. There are many stories of Scallia and Drem circulating amongst the servants. They all talk of you.'

Kiri considered that as Pootle placed new linen on her bed.

'I hear people talking about you as young and fresh,' Pootle said. 'Not weighed down by tradition and old thinking. Somebody who decides what to do and gets things done. If it's not too presumptuous, I'd say you'd caused quite a stir.'

Kiri licked her lips.

'You are presumptuous,' she said. 'But I like that about you. Dress me.'

Pootle finished with the bed and moved across to her, removing her clothes and replacing them with new in a business like way. Kiri had long since got used to being undressed and dressed by him. It had seemed so odd when she had first joined the temple priestesses. Yet everyone had their role, and this was his. Pootle had always been good at his job and he had a knack of keeping his ears open too.

'I daresay Priestess Nerina isn't best pleased though,' he said from behind her, tightening the draws on her tunic.

'Why?'

'She's always been the young one,' Pootle said. 'Now, here's you, equally gifted, even younger.'

'Is that what people say?'

'They think it,' Pootle said. 'They like your story, you weren't born to this life. You've earned it through hard work and application. That gets you a respect none of the other priestesses can attain.'

Kiri sat down as Pootle turned his attention to her hair, brushing and braiding it before fitting the slim tiara that marked out the priestesses. He dabbed a little sweet-smelling perfume on either side of her neck before standing back.

'There,' he said.

'Thank you, Pootle'

'If there's nothing else, mistress?' he asked.

'No, that's fine.'

'I'll attend to the laundry then.'

Kiri watched as he gathered up the old bed linen and retired from the room, closing the door behind him.

She turned her thoughts back to Nerina.

So the people also see that Nerina thinks only of herself. But for the sake of Drayden and all the other lands we must complete the task appointed, or doom will take us all. The wrath of Lacaille will return. Amar must be our next priority.

Kiri licked her lips. Zoella's gift. Meru. It all could be achieved.

And yet, Lacaille's will be done. What does our goddess want? How would she determine our ways? Elena told us to complete the task appointed, surely that is what we must do? The conquest of Amar, is that not her will?

A bell tolled, ringing out from the temple. It rang continually; a warning. A summons for the priestesses.

Kiri frowned. She had only heard those tolls on rare occasions, when some imminent danger threatened the city. She walked out to her balcony to see what was happening. Nothing seemed amiss, but the ringing faded and then stopped.

What was that for ...?

Pain flashed across her temple and she staggered back from the balcony, pressing her hand against her forehead in surprise and dismay. A headache was pulsing there, sharp and intense. It intensified, causing her to cry out in pain and alarm, staggering back to fall upon her bed. She heard screams from the nearby rooms.

Not just me ...

The pain ratcheted up, excruciating, burning into her skull. Amidst the torment a strange image formed in her mind. A bizarre tower, stretching far into the sky, burnished metal gleaming in the light of Lacaille, a wall of furious cloud ...

What is this?

A sense of dread descended on her, a desperate urge to reach the place to avert some unknown calamity.

Words formed in her mind, shocking as their meaning inflamed her mind.

The Obelisk Commands! The Obelisk Requires! Obedience and urgency!

Terrified, Kiri fell to her knees, her hands clasped before her. She cried out again as pain suffused her body but even as she set her mind against it, she welcomed it. A brief snatch of thought was all she was able to muster.

Like Elena in the sixth element! Purification!

Changes must be made! Lacaille must be sated, all must be set right or death and destruction will blossom, fires will come more devastating than any you have known.

Kiri fought the trembles that racked her body. The voice of the Obelisk was speaking to her, directing her, anointing her …

What must I do, Obelisk, great servant of Lacaille?

Come to me, faithful one, servant of Lacaille. You are chosen! Come to me! This you must do! Carry out the task appointed! Changes must be made!

Kiri gasped.

Chosen? Chosen! Changes must be made?

Then another image replaced the first. Concerned faces, she saw a woman with closely cropped blonde hair, a stern man with a full beard and a young man she recognised …

Meru!

The pain relented a touch. She made out a strange grey room, festooned with pipes with a simple sleeping bunk above her. Off to one side was a small circular window through which she could see …

The sea!

Voices, heard or imagined, buzzed in her ears.

What's happening? I don't know, she's just … Help me! Mel, help us, can't hold her!

And then, as quickly as it had arrived, the vision and the pain were gone. All Kiri could hear were faint moans from somewhere nearby.

She continued to kneel there, her hands clenched, her body in shock and her mind dazzled, her breath coming in short sharp gasps. Sweat cooled and the shivers brought her back to herself. She could scarcely credit what had happened.

The Obelisk spoke to me! To me! It commanded me in the name of Lacaille herself. I am chosen, anointed! And then I saw … through her eyes …

It was clear what she had to do.

The task appointed!

* * *

Nerina stood at the very summit of the temple, looking sunright across the city of Daine. Before her the grounds of the temple were spread out below, beyond them were the houses of the rich and well to do of the city, beyond that a wall, fixed with watchtowers at intervals around its perimeter. Daine had always been a major city, even in the time of the Voren Empire; it was fortified with defence in mind.

Outside the wall lay the slums. Nerina had never visited them and she never intended to, they were none of her concern.

Below people were running to and fro in alarm. She could see some priestesses being carried in stretchers, others staggering towards the infirmary, supported by their manservants.

Strange visions. Almost as if there was some meaning behind all the ancient words.

As ever, Merrin stood alongside her.

'Our priestesses?' Nerina asked.

'A count is being made. So far, none are hurt. Shaken, disturbed, but there seem to be no lasting effects,' Merrin replied. 'But as to what it was …'

Nerina nodded. 'Have we learnt any more?'

'Only that the priestesses alone were affected,' Merrin replied. 'Those with the greater gift more so. Those who lack the gift noticed nothing and, of course, none of the men.'

'It feels like a weapon has been turned against us,' Nerina murmured. 'But by whom?'

'Who could attack us thus?' Merrin asked. 'It cannot be the doing of our own people.'

'No, but we can use it to our advantage.' Nerina smiled. 'It would seem that Lacaille has issued another incentive to action.'

'Many saw an image,' Merrin added. 'A tower …'

Nerina held up the pendant she wore around her neck, fingering it. All the priestesses wore a similar emblem; a stylised isosceles triangle.

'And a sense of warning,' Nerina said. 'That some doom would soon transpire. Yes, I felt it too. I will search the libraries. We must know the nature of this vision. There are equally pressing matters though, our borders … If word gets out that the priestesses can be weakened in this manner …'

'The shaderight borders are secure,' Merrin replied. 'We have had reports this stretch that those of Keriak have backed away. They do not have dachs and the way is rocky and barren. They have seen what became of Viresia and dare not challenge us.'

Nerina nodded.

'This is good,' she said. 'We have conquered Scallia and Drem. Keriak we can deal with in time, but make sure there is a show of strength aplenty. For now my thoughts are with Taloon.'

Merrin nodded. 'Their emissary is with us and anticipating an audience with you.'

'A man?' Nerina asked.

Merrin nodded.

'Then he should be easy to manipulate,' Nerina said.

'He is old,' Merrin said. 'And wily, I would say.'

'Taloon has always provided the tithe as directed, what brings him to us now?'

'It seems the King wants to re-iterate the alliance of Taloon and Drayden.'

Nerina chuckled. 'As well they might. They have seen what we do to those that defy us. All fear us now. An advantage we will make much use of.'

'We could simply take them anyway, we have the strength now …'

Nerina shook her head. 'There is no need, when they already prostrate themselves before us. We can ask what we may and … I will be asking much.'

* * *

Kiri made her way down through the accommodation buildings and across the piazza towards the temple, her steps uncertain, her thoughts in disarray. Here she had once been tested with all the other acolytes – the choosing – how long ago it seemed! The temple rose above her; she never failed to be impressed by its sheer size and remarkable design. It rose hundreds of hands into the air, a vast redstone pyramid.

Around her, other priestesses were talking and arguing. Some still looked distraught after the strange visions. Many had seen things, Kiri overheard talk of towers and storms. Others had only received the blinding pain; some had fainted and were still overcome.

But no one has talked of the Obelisk … was that message only meant for me?

Within the temple pyramid, visitors might have expected it to be dark, but the interior was lit by hundreds of mirrors which were set to reflect Lacaille's light within the corridors and rooms. Before her she could see the great hall where she had been chosen as an acolyte, but she turned aside, walking down the now familiar corridors to another doorway, flanked by two guards of the temple. The meeting hall of the priestesses was much smaller, but no less imposing.

Once she had been here to be subject to the judgement of priestesses, for an alleged crime. Just a girl from the slums, a guttersnipe they had called her. She had been summoned and judged. It was here that Nerina had spared her life, called her to be an acolyte. She had learned the way of the priestesses over many rounds. This stretch she was one of them, standing proud, with a string of achievements behind her. None dared defy Kiri any longer.

The headache had gone, but she could still recall the vision of the tower and the group of people clustered around her. It had not seemed like a dream. She had been there. But that wasn't possible, so …

I was seeing through her eyes. Zoella's eyes! She experienced the same thing as we did.

The priestesses had talked of little else for the last chime. All had felt some measure of pain, most had seen the image of the tower, but despite listening for a while, it seemed that none had seen or heard anything else like she had.

The Obelisk! As in the sixth element, it called to me! Me alone? It said I was chosen!

The guards stepped aside and the doors opened. Kiri stepped through, seeing many of the other priestesses already assembled. Ahead, Nerina sat in her customary place in the centre chair, draped in her black garments as ever she was, her face pale and enigmatic, her black hair with a single silver streak, finished with an ornate tiara.

Benches were set to either side, lit by upturned metal oil burners, fashioned to resemble the shades from the forests. They were lit, flames leaping from them, to warm and light the interior further. A thin film of sweet-smelling smoke laced the air.

Kiri looked down at the marbled floor passing beneath her feet, with its interlocking red and sand coloured tiles. Rihanna was already sitting on the benches, waiting. Their eyes met. Kiri ventured a small smile. They hadn't spoken since …

Since I caught her love-making and she taught me!

She took her place, sitting next to Rihanna, watching as all the other priestesses filed in.

Kiri turned to Rihanna.

'I … meant to … thank you for …'

Rihanna smiled by return. 'I hear you've been studying hard.'

Kiri blushed and looked away.

Rihanna laughed. 'You are such a strange one. The fearless warrior, slayer of kings! Yet shy when it comes to men and–'

'Shhh!'

She looked across to where Merrin was sitting opposite, her face twisted in an unpleasant sneer as she looked at Kiri. Kiri threw her a fake smile in return. Kiri sensed something new, there seemed to be some sense of smug satisfaction about her.

'I see your mother is happy to see me once more.'

Rihanna smiled. 'At least she noticed you. She hasn't said a word to me yet, despite not having seen me for almost a pass.'

Kiri had often envied many of the women in the priestesshood, with their families and relations, but right now, being an orphan seemed to have its advantages. Only herself to worry about, no need to deal with annoying relatives …

But I wasn't an orphan, as I've learned …

She clenched down on those thoughts, now was not the time. She didn't know who might be listening … or trying to listen.

'What do you think that pain was caused by …?' Rihanna began.

'Rihanna,' Kiri interrupted. 'I need to announce something to the priestesses, the pain … something happened to me, something … remember what we promised each other back in Viresia?'

Rihanna nodded. 'Yes, but …'

'We must play our parts, keep this secret … I need you to do as we discussed … there's no time to–'

Kiri was cut off. Rihanna nodded in acknowledgement. Nerina got to her feet, her movements elegant and measured. She stepped forward, her shoes clicking on the tiles.

'Priestesses,' she said. 'We have won a mighty victory. Viresia sought to defy us and paid the price of their folly. Drem capitulated in fear and Keriak have bowed their heads in obedience. We return with a string of captives and renewed commitments to the tithe. Our strength is restored. The legacy of our inaction under Launa and her ilk is banished to history. None dare challenge us. We are strong once more!'

The priestesses cheered. Kiri exchanged a look with Rihanna before joining them.

'Yet, we still have much to do,' Nerina said, as the cheers subsided. 'Just this stretch Lacaille has reminded us that the task appointed is overdue. She is displeased. Pain she has sent, to remind us of our duty …'

Kiri found herself on her feet. Nerina stopped speaking, turning her gaze upon her. Kiri could sense the eyes of all the priestesses turning to her. Silence fell in the hall. Words came to her, almost wrenched from her despite herself.

'I ... I was given a message,' she managed to say, her voice stuttering. 'From Lacaille!'

Maybe this isn't such a good idea ...

She saw Nerina's eyes narrow. A gasp went up from all about her. No one spoke. Kiri shifted her weight from one foot to the other. She looked around, seeing Merrin glaring at her, and then turning towards Nerina. Both exchanged a knowing glance. Nerina looked back at her, her expression impassive.

'A message?' Nerina said.

Kiri nodded.

Nerina gestured expansively. 'Then I am sure we would all like to hear it.'

Kiri swallowed.

'When the pain we all endured struck me, I was forced upon my knees,' Kiri said. 'I cried out for it to stop, but it would not relent. Then I saw a vision, a great tower wreathed in cloud ...'

'Many of us saw such things,' Nerina said.

'But then words ... words came to me.'

'Words?' Nerina's voice was flat. 'Explain.'

Kiri nodded, her confidence regained. 'A voice called out the Obelisk commands. The Obelisk requires. Obedience and urgency. Changes must be made. Lacaille must be sated, all must be set right or death and destruction will blossom, fires will come more devastating than any you have known.'

A muted mumble of conversation drifted around the hall of the priestesses. Kiri heard brief snatches of conversation

'... the forbidden book?'

'Elena's commandment from the Obelisk?'

'It can't be ...'

Kiri looked around her and back to Nerina. Nerina's expression was unreadable and Kiri could sense nothing from her.

'I was scared,' Kiri said. 'Terrified. I did the only thing I could do.'

'And what was that?' Nerina asked, a trace of impatience filtering into her words.

'I asked,' Kiri replied. 'What must I do, Obelisk, great servant of Lacaille?'

The conversation around her dropped away, first to a whisper and then into silence. Kiri saw Nerina tilt her head up, her gaze still fixed on Kiri.

'And was there an answer?' Nerina asked, her voice quiet but still carrying throughout the hall.

Kiri nodded.

'Come to me, faithful one, servant of Lacaille,' she said, her voice cracking. 'You are chosen. Come to me. This you must do. Carry out the task appointed. Changes must be made.'

There was uproar as she spoke the words.

'Blasphemy!' someone called. Kiri wasn't sure, but it might have been Merrin. Kiri stepped back a pace. Snatches of conversation drifted around her.

'... claiming the Obelisk out of the forbidden book spoke to her, the audacity!'

'... it could be her! She has the strength and the gift in great measure ...'

'... setting herself up to be Elena incarnate? How dare she ...'

'... she has risen far from the lowest ranks, why not ...'

'... guttersnipe has gone too far ...'

'Enough!' Nerina's voice silenced conversation in a moment. All heads turned to her.

'It is clear this message is of great import,' she said. 'We all understand the ramifications of it. If Lacaille commands and speaks to us through the Obelisk as was done long ago in our books of lore, we would be fools to ignore it.'

Nerina looked at Kiri.

'We must seek the meaning behind these words,' Nerina said. 'It seems that task falls to you, Kiri. It seems there is much still to be done. Come with me, now.'

Nerina beckoned to her. Kiri stood still, noticing that Merrin was walking towards them and stood alongside Nerina.

'The rest of you wait here,' Nerina called. 'We will return shortly.'

She looked at Kiri, her eyes narrowing. 'Follow me.'

Kiri followed Nerina and Merrin out of the hall. The door closed behind them. Nerina gestured to a side room a few paces along.

'Wait for us,' Nerina directed. 'We will call for you.'

Kiri opened her mouth, but no words came. Her choices were stark; submit or confront. After a moment's hesitation she capitulated and opened the door to the room, venturing inside. The door was pulled closed behind her.

She heard rapid footsteps outside and then there was silence.

CHAPTER FOUR

Straithian Sea, Shaderight of Amar

Round 2307, Second pass

The sea-sickness had passed, but Zoella still looked pale and ill. Fitch had given her blankets and a warm drink. Mel had throttled the engine back up to a cruising speed, but there seemed to be no repeat of the strange sudden loss of 'tricity, at least for now. Coran, Mel, Fitch and Meru sat clustered around her. They were all in the *Mobilis'* common room. Ren was cuddled up with her, clutching her close.

'You had a dream?' Meru asked. 'You've had dreams before and you said they came true, what was this one about?'

Zoella looked around at the expectant faces all about her.

'I saw some kind of tower,' she said. 'It was huge. Taller than anything I've ever seen. There were clouds and storms all about, swirling around. All seemed well; there was a sense of peace and tranquillity despite the weather. But then ...'

'What did this tower look like?' Coran asked

Zoella held up the pendant she wore. The silver chain was tarnished with age, but the pendant itself was bright and shiny, as if it were new. 'It was metal, it looked just like this.'

She turned it over in her fingers. Guerrun had given it to her. The others leaned forward to get a better look.

'This is the mark of the witches ...' Fitch said, before Mel gave him a look. 'All right! The priestesses! But we saw these in Dynesia, in that courtyard with all the slaughtered people ...'

'They use it now,' Meru said. 'But Guerrun said it was older than them ... what did he say? The mark of the gifted ... he called it the tower too.'

'And this is the tower you dreamed of?' Coran asked. 'The same?'

Zoella nodded. 'But it was enormous, metal, a huge thing reaching into the sky … Lacaille was clear in the sky above, not just in the sky, but right above. It called me. I've got to go there. If I don't everything will be killed.'

'Go there?' Mel echoed.

'We don't even know where it is,' Meru said.

Zoella shook her head. 'I just know I've got to go there.'

Coran frowned. 'You said Lacaille was above you in your dream?'

Zoella nodded.

'As in straight up?'

Zoella nodded. 'Yes, but …'

'Wait a moment,' Coran ducked out of the common room and could be heard next door in his own room, rummaging around for something. He returned a moment later with a carefully rolled parchment.

Space was made and it was unfurled on the table.

'The map of Esurio?' Meru asked.

'You remember how you figured out how to navigate?' Coran asked.

Meru nodded. 'The angle of the pass and the height of Lacaille in the sky gives you … the height of Lacaille. Oh … I see what you mean!'

Coran nodded and looked at Zoella. 'You're sure Lacaille was straight up? I mean, absolutely above?'

Zoella nodded. 'Yes. It seemed so strange, but yes, that's where it was. Why is that important?'

Coran traced his finger down the map. Zoella could see Drem, Scallia and Drayden marked on a large continent. To the right she could see the island of Amar, their current destination. But Coran wasn't pointing to any of them.

His finger had stopped at a dotted line at the base of the map. It was unmarked. The area below the line had been torn off, lost long ago.

'The far sunward,' Meru whispered.

'What does it mean?' Mel asked. 'You've lost me.'

'The further sunward you go, the higher Lacaille rises in the sky.

Remember in Drem? That's the far shadeward, Lacaille drops to the horizon. In the opposite direction …'

'You think this tower is in the far sunward?' Mel asked.

'Has to be if Zoella is right about where Lacaille is in her dream,' Coran said. 'Look, these lines on the map are converging. You can work it out …'

Meru counted up the divisions on the map.

'You're right,' he said. 'Lacaille would be overhead in the sky at the point these lines converge … but the map stops way before that, there's nothing here.'

'And that's a long way,' Mel said. 'Easily as far as the journey from Amar to the continent, maybe even more.'

Coran nodded and turned back to Zoella.

'And after you finished screaming …'

Zoella swallowed and nodded.

'I heard it somehow. It was calling me. Asking me to come to it. In my dream something went wrong, there was heat, and that ghastly blue light that came from Lacaille. Animals and people died horribly…'

'And at that moment …' Mel began.

'The 'tricity cut out and left us stranded,' Fitch finished.

Coran sat back.

'Mel, you remember during the flare when we saw that green light in the sky, those strange patterns?'

'They were coming from Lacaille, from the sunward. They were linked with the 'tricity,' Mel said. 'When they were glowing so bright there was too much, the engines overloaded.'

'It's all connected somehow,' Coran said. 'This dream, the tower, the lights, the 'tricity, these powers … everything, it's all connected. Got to be.'

'All of us have been warned of these flares,' Meru said. 'Zoella in her dreams, us by Caesar in that hangar …'

Zoella was looking distant again.

'The tower,' she said, fingering the pendant. 'The eye, the Obelisk, that's what it's called …'

Meru turned to look at her, 'What did you say?'

'In my dream, that's what it was called. The eye, the Obelisk ...'

'Obelisk!' Meru said, looking around at the rest of the crew. 'I've been an idiot! Don't you remember?'

'No,' everyone else replied after a moment.

'Sandra Morino,' Meru said, 'and Caesar too, they said something about an Obelisk.' He paused, his eyes darting from one side to another as he tried to recall. 'Her voice, her warning – you must remember. We heard it on the radio.'

Fitch nodded. 'You're right boy. She said something about losing contact with the Obelisk, that she didn't know if it was still working ...'

'And Caesar had that report,' Mel said. 'On the glass panel. Obelisk status ... it had failed, it wasn't responding!'

'The tower is the Obelisk,' Meru said. 'It's the same thing, it has to be. It must provide the 'tricity somehow, and ...'

'It's breaking down,' Zoella finished for him. 'I know it is. And if it fails, it won't just be your 'tricity we lose.'

She got to her feet. Ren pulled at her, worried.

'Everything is going to die.'

They all looked at her. Zoella was trembling from head to foot. Mel reached out a hand to steady her.

'So,' Fitch interjected after a moment. 'What are we going to do?'

Zoella turned to him. 'I've got to go to it, it needs me.'

'It's clear this is some kind of warning,' Mel agreed.

Fitch frowned. Coran was shaking his head.

'We've got to get to Amar,' Coran said. 'We haven't delivered our warning to them yet.'

'They'll have already been hit by one flare,' Mel said. 'Damage is already done ...'

'Not just the flares,' Coran said. 'The danger from the witch-priestesses. Amar is going to have to prepare.'

'This is more important,' Zoella protested. 'If the tower fails, the flares and the priestesses will be the least of our problems. The blue light, it burns skin, it hurts ... it kills!'

'You've just had a bad dream, lass,' Fitch said. 'Can't be chasing off into the sunward on a hunch ...'

'Zoella's dreams come true,' Meru interrupted, seeing frustration growing on Zoella's face. 'We can't ignore it. I've already seen that blue light, it blisters your skin right off!'

'It hurt me,' Ren said, summoning the courage to say something. 'Burns and scalds!'

'I've got to go!' Zoella added, stroking the small boy's hair.

'Hold your hergs,' Fitch said. 'How do you get to this tower, eh? Where is it precisely? How far away? The map is incomplete, torn and missing, it's all uncharted. Could be anything towards the sunward. Why, Meru was shipwrecked in a storm that came up from that direction. Is it sea, or land? Who knows what hazards there are. What kind of traipse is it? You don't know!'

'We'll find a way,' Meru snapped.

'All right, say you do make it there,' Fitch continued, glaring at Meru. 'What are you going to do when you arrive? Both of you are experts in this strange device that makes 'tricity and magic powers are you? You know how to fix it, I suppose?' Fitch looked at Zoella and Meru, neither responded. 'Thought of that? No, didn't think so. Snuttin' kids!'

'Caesar,' Meru said, after a moment. 'Caesar knows. We should go back to Dynesia. He had better maps than we did! We could find out more about it ...'

Coran shook his head. 'Meru, that's a long journey in the wrong direction. We have a half crippled ship in the midst of the ocean. 'Tricity might fail again at any moment. Sensible thing is to do as Fitch suggests and get to Amar, make repairs, give our warning. Then we can consider another voyage.'

'But ...' Meru began.

'We don't have time,' Zoella said. 'I know we don't have time!'

'We have a duty,' Coran continued. 'We've got to bring a warning about the flares and the priestesses back to Amar.'

Meru was about to protest, but Mel raised her hand.

'Captain's made his choice. Course is set.'

Meru sighed. Zoella looked like she was about to protest again, but took her cue from his resigned face.

Coran looked at Zoella and Meru. 'Listen. I hear what you're saying and I don't doubt it. Right now the risk is too great with too many unknowns. Safety of the ship has to come first. We'll get back to Amar, give our warning, make repairs. Then I promise we'll deal with this tower and Obelisk business.'

Meru looked at Zoella. She rubbed at her forehead and shook her head but said nothing else.

'Right then. Let's get to it,' Coran snapped. 'Meru, pass is almost due, figure out our position and we'll set a course. Mel, best speed to Amar.'

Zoella still looked unhappy, but Meru gave a reluctant nod.

'Aye captain.'

* * *

Meru busied himself with the timers aboard the ship and squinted through the double axis sextant set before the bridge of the *Mobilis*. Zoella watched him set up the equipment. Towards the rear of the ship she could hear the thrum of the ship's single working engine increasing. Mel had been repairing it for a spell or two. It seemed she had finished.

'What did you mean back there?' Zoella asked. 'Caesar, knows? Who's Caesar? Radio? Sandra … these names and words are strange.'

Meru explained about their voyage across the sea and the receipt of the radio message that had led them into Caesar's hangar. Zoella listened in amazement.

'You remember I told you we'd found a voice?' Meru said. 'That was Caesar. I guess he's some kind of machine left behind by our ancestors hundreds, thousands of rounds ago. You could talk to him, ask him questions, but he wouldn't always answer them. He could show pictures of far off places, describe things … and he mentioned the Obelisk.'

'What did he say about it?'

'Not much, he just said it had failed, that it wasn't responding,' Meru replied. 'Other stuff that didn't make sense …' He thought about it for a moment, trying to recall the words. 'Something about winds, a warning to check the Obelisk … most of what he said we didn't really understand, but it didn't sound good.'

'Then we must go there,' Zoella said. 'We need to find out. If we don't …'

Meru nodded. 'Yeah, but if the 'tricity fails while we're at sea and doesn't come back on … starving to death out here won't be nice. This ship can't move without it.'

Zoella shivered, unable to stave off the feeling of fear that surrounded her. She could see the Alisse, the strange green hanging curtains of light in the sky, streaming away from Lacaille.

Time is short, I'm sure of it.

Meru turned back to the sextant, looking through the aligned glasses.

'Still no sign no sign of Mayura,' he murmured.

'Mayura?'

'Start of the pass,' Meru answered, adjusting the instrument again.

'All this left by our ancestors,' Zoella said, her voice low. 'Thousands of rounds ago, what does it mean? If it was all so important, why haven't they left us records, or guides? We shouldn't be guessing our next step.'

Meru drew back.

'When I was flying to Viresia I stopped at this strange place en route,' he said. 'It was old, abandoned, all broken down, but it was full of the same sort of things as Caesar's cavern. Something to do with sending messages into the sky. I think our ancestors had all sorts of things they could do that we don't know about, I think they set lots of things up, but it's all so old now, most of it is broken, lost or just forgotten about. No one understands how it all works any more. Remember we talked about how many rounds there were?'

Zoella nodded. 'It's two thousand three hundred and six rounds … but since what?'

'Since we started counting time,' Meru replied. 'I think our ancestors had all these amazing abilities, but something went wrong. Now, after all that time, most of it is gone, broken and forgotten. We don't know how it works. Even this ship, we only just about understand it and we certainly couldn't build another one. It does seem that the 'tricity, your gift, all these machines … they're connected. What we do know is that people have been fighting each other for as long as anyone can remember. We found the remains of people killed long ago in Dynesia. Your city was destroyed, all that knowledge lost, if you imagine that through all of history …'

'All that time,' Zoella said. 'And our history is lost, so much we don't know, so much we need to know …'

Meru squinted through the sextant.

'Ah … there it is,' he said.

'Can I see?' Zoella asked.

'Sure,' Meru said. He guided her to the instrument. 'Look through here, you can see that Mayura has just touched the edge of Lacaille.'

'That marks the start of the pass?' Zoella asked. She could see a faint indentation against the limb of Lacaille, growing into a curve as Mayura began its transit.

Meru nodded. 'Now I have to measure the angle that Mayura passes. That, along with the height of Lacaille in the sky gives us a position we can check on the map.'

Meru worked for a few moments before he had the numbers he needed.

'There,' he said. 'Let's see where we are. Come on.'

He vaulted up into the bridge, where Coran and Mel were waiting. Zoella followed behind him. Meru crouched over the map and ran his fingers down it.

'Here,' he said. 'We're about one third of the way to Amar from Nireus by this reckoning. There's your course.' He showed the plot to Coran.

Coran nodded. 'Lacaille to the sunward, two points to starboard. Not far off. Mel, how is the engine?'

'So far so good,' she replied. 'I've checked best I can, everything looks to be neat and tidy thus far.'

'Best speed then,' Coran said.

'I think we can cruise at three quarters full,' Mel said. 'For now at least.'

'Good work,' Coran said. 'Keep the ship moving. Let's get home.'

For many stretches the *Mobilis* cruised across the undulating seas of Esurio. Fortunately for Zoella, the weather stayed fine for the most part. She had remained untroubled by any further dreams, the 'tricity seemed to be flowing, even Lacaille was calm. Their progress across the sea was swift and uneventful. The crew busied themselves with bits of maintenance work that Mel ordained were necessary. Zoella spent time with Ren, cleaning and tidying the ship from stem to stern.

'Never seen the ship so clean,' Coran commented to both of them, looking around at the scrubbed interior walls, floors and portholes. Zoella smiled and Ren gave a jaunty salute.

'Ingratiating themselves is more the way of things,' Fitch grumbled.

'Just because you don't like hard work,' Coran said. He gave Zoella a wink and ruffled Ren's hair. 'Good show.'

The ship continued on its way.

'If our measurements and course are good,' Meru said at the first chime on the following stretch, 'we should sight Amar ... in the next stretch or so.'

He was on the early watch, with the rest of the crew still asleep. Zoella, standing next to him, caught a hesitation in his voice. He was hopeless at hiding his feelings.

'Don't you want to go home?' she asked.

He looked at her before dropping his gaze. 'Not really.'

'Why not?'

Meru didn't answer.

More secrets? Why can't he just tell me? This isn't about trust, this is about hiding things he doesn't want to reveal ...

Zoella changed tack, anxious to avoid another uncomfortable impasse in their conversations. 'What is Amar like?'

'It's an island,' he replied. 'A big one, but still an island. Much of it is rocky and uninhabitable. Most folk live on the sunward and shaderight sides. Freezing cold streams and rivers flow down from the mountains to the sea. The main city is on the coast on the shaderight side, Amaris. A port; with fishing and trade. It's where … where I came from.'

'Do you have friends there?' Zoella asked. 'Family?'

Meru got to his feet. 'Got to check the course,' he said, turning away.

Zoella sighed and placed her head in her hands. The sense of loneliness returned.

Fleeing Nireus was supposed to solve problems, not make more …

She was interrupted by another set of footsteps. Zoella looked around to see Mel walking towards her.

'Anything to report?' Mel asked.

'No,' Meru replied. He stomped past. Zoella saw Mel watch him for a moment before turning to Zoella.

'That boy still in a mood?' she asked.

Zoella nodded. 'I seem to keep saying the wrong thing.'

'He's in a huff and no mistake,' Mel replied. 'Gave him a piece of my mind and it doesn't seem to have made much difference. What was it this time?'

'I only asked about this place we're going to. Amar. I thought he'd be pleased we're almost there, but no …'

Mel nodded. She took a look at the ship's controls and then settled herself down beside Zoella.

'Did Meru tell you about how we first met?'

Zoella shook her head.

'We found him adrift, clinging to a piece of wreckage from a ship,' Mel said. 'Fitch wanted nothing to do with him as you might expect, but Coran quickly figured out he had the smarts. Turned out his ship had been sunk in a storm and that he was a timekeeper, which came in pretty handy for us. Said he had no family that would miss him, so we never took him back to Amar.'

'Really?' Zoella asked. 'He's an orphan?'

Mel grinned. 'There's the rub. With no family there's no way he could be even an apprentice timekeeper. That's a rank in Amar and you have to pay for it, you don't just decide to be one. He's got to have had someone back there looking out for him. Coran and I have a bet on what the truth is. We reckon he's run away from something, bad blood, argument, something like that. I don't think he ever expected to be away for so long. If he does have folk back home they'll have long since given him up for dead. Maybe that's what he's worried about.'

'So he's lying about that too,' Zoella replied.

'He's keeping secrets,' Mel said. 'That's for sure, but there ain't no one aboard this ship who isn't. Don't be too hard on him.'

Zoella pursed her lips.

Mel smiled at her. 'To be fair, we've all got mixed feelings about going home. I'm not sure we'll get much of a welcome in Amar either.'

'Why not?'

'We've broken the law you see.'

'How?'

'The senate and the councils of Amar decreed that no one should travel out of sight of land rounds ago. The history of our island has been hidden from most folk. Scared of it. They don't know of the exile, Nireus, or any of the lands you came from. Everything is just myth and legend. They want it to stay that way. We're coming back with a story of what's actually there. I don't think they'll be all that delighted about that.'

'Then why return?'

'Got to be done,' Mel said. 'We've got to warn our folk, haven't we? Coran is firm on that score, whatever the consequences. I think he's right.'

Zoella looked out of the windows of the wheelhouse. The sea was as unending as ever, but the ship was still moving fast. Amar couldn't be that far away now.

'What might they do?' she asked.

'No idea. Still, we'll find out soon enough. What about you?'

'Me?'

'I figure you must be pretty scared about all this,' Mel said. 'You've got these powers too, only reasonable that you should be worried about what reception you might get. For most folk on Amar these powers are nothing but half-remembered stories of witches and evil from long ago. Safest not to mention them I think.'

Zoella nodded.

'I wish I never had them,' she said. 'If I could give them up I would. They've caused nothing but grief and hardship.'

'You've got to have them for a reason,' Mel countered. 'That old man of yours kept you safe, made snuttin' sure you survived. Your dreams, this Obelisk thing. Once we figure it all out I'm sure they'll be important.'

Zoella nodded.

'And we won't let anything happen to you,' Mel continued. 'Let Fitch grumble. He always grumbles; he'll come around eventually. He just doesn't like change.'

'Your captain …'

'Coran always has to have an eye out for trouble,' Mel said. 'But he's said you're staying and that's final. He'll keep you safe and that young lad safe, have no doubt of that.'

Zoella smiled when she thought of Ren.

'That little one thinks a lot of you,' Mel said.

'He lost everything,' Zoella said. 'Doesn't talk about it, but his home was scorched when the flares hit.'

'And you've looked after him since,' Mel said. 'You've got a heart for it. I can see that. But sometimes you need looking after yourself.'

Zoella looked around. 'Thank you for everything you've done for me.'

Mel put an arm around Zoella's shoulder. It felt warm and comforting. Tears sprang into her eyes and she found herself sobbing.

* * *

Daf and Creg were stationed at the forepeak of the *Mobilis* when Amar came in sight. First a series of mountains rose from the sea, wreathed in misty cloud. Before long, the wider island could be seen growing before them. It looked lush and green, much as they remembered it. Lacaille blazed in the sky above and the sea was flat and calm.

Cheers greeted the news and everyone rushed up on deck to get a view, glad of the change and looking forward to setting foot on dry land once more.

'Your course was pretty much perfect,' Coran said, grinning at Meru. 'Down to the spell, nice work.'

Meru nodded, but didn't respond. Coran rolled his eyes at Mel, who shrugged. Meru took over at the helm.

'Let's hoist our flags,' Coran instructed, climbing down from the wheelhouse. 'Amaran colours. Haven't flown them in a while!'

Daf and Greg busied themselves at the masts and the maroon flags embossed with a white fellin were soon fluttering in the breeze above.

Ren was watching the approaching land with fascination.

'Amar?' he asked.

Zoella nodded beside him. 'Yes, far across the sea we've come.'

Mel had grabbed the 'scope from the bridge and was looking through it at the coastline.

'I can see the harbour well enough,' she said. 'Looks like all the ships are home and moored, there's no smokes. Fisher-folk should be out to sea at this time of the stretch.'

Coran gestured for the 'scope and looked for himself.

'No ships out at all,' he agreed. 'Nothing. Seems strange.' He adjusted the course of the *Mobilis*. 'We'll come wide through the harbour entrance and see where we can moor up. Doubtless they've seen us by now, they'll be wondering who in the world we are …'

The *Mobilis* continued to cruise forward, closing to around a mark from the coast.

'I can see folks on the harbour wall,' Mel said, having retrieved the 'scope. 'Definitely seen us, quite a commotion it seems.'

'None of them have seen a 'tricity powered ship before.' Coran watched the lower levels of the coastal city grow clearer. 'Going to give them something to think about that's for sure …'

Fitch was watching the coastline too, squinting and leaning on the handrail. He jolted upright and spun around, his expression full of alarm.

'Get down!'

A shrieking noise followed his sharp yell and then a huge plume of water rose from the sea perhaps a hundred hands off the portside bow. Spray lashed across the deck and a wave caused the ship to rock.

Zoella had no idea what had just happened. Ren squealed and ran into her arms.

'They're attacking us!' Mel exclaimed. 'Can't they see our colours?'

'Turn us to starboard!' Coran yelled. Meru was already swinging the wheel. The *Mobilis* came about, turning away from the harbour.

Another whistling shriek. The crew could see a lump of rock arcing through the air towards them. The thump of impact was closer now, water erupted close by, showering the crew. Zoella could see the water running off the deck and splashing back down into the sea.

They could see a pair of contraptions at the end of the pier, large wooden constructs festooned with twisted ropes. As they watched, part of one was being winched backwards by a team of men and hergs clustered around it.

'Catapults!' Fitch called out. 'They're flinging rocks! If one of those hits us ...'

With a faint cry, just audible over the distance, the weapon was triggered again. The crew watched in horror as a large rock was flung towards their ship, whistling and tumbling through the air.

'It's going to hit!' Fitch yelled.

The *Mobilis* rang like a gong. Tremors ran through the deck, throwing everyone to the floor. Ren squealed again as he and Zoella lost their footing.

Before them, just short of the bow, part of the forward hull on the port side had been buckled by the impact.

'They'll rip us to shreds,' Coran muttered. 'Daf! Creg! Raise a white flag!'

Amidst the commotion, the two burly men made their way towards the foremast and were soon busy yanking on the ropes which raised the flags.

'Amar has never attacked a vessel before,' Mel said.

'Times have clearly changed,' Coran muttered. 'Meru! Bring the ship around again, keep our stern towards the harbour, it'll make us a harder target.'

The *Mobilis* turned again.

Daf and Creg yelled. Coran could see the flags were up.

'Come on,' he muttered. 'Stop the attack. Let's be friends.'

The whole crew held their breath looking at the pier, trying to see if the catapults were being reloaded.

Ren was still whimpering in Zoella's arms. She did her best to comfort him, keeping her hands over his ears and murmuring reassurance to him. Moments passed and the whistling sounds of incoming rocks did not return. She looked up.

The crew looked around at each other.

'Look!' Fitch said, pointing to the harbour.

Two flags had been raised over the entrance, Amaran colours.

Coran gave a low whistle.

'Looks like they're going to let us in,' he said. 'Meru, bring us about, quarter speed into the harbour. Nice and slow.'

'Aye, captain.'

The engine of the *Mobilis* throbbed again and the ship turned back towards the coastline.

'Could just be making sure they have a perfect shot,' Fitch muttered. 'At close range one of those rocks will go through us like a scalpel through parchment.'

'Where else are we going to go?' Coran asked. 'Ship's damaged.'

Fitch shrugged.

'Don't make any sudden moves,' Coran instructed.' Everyone stay on deck where you can be seen.'

The *Mobilis* cruised forward, the steep harbour walls growing before them. Along the top they could see people milling around stony emplacements spaced evenly along the walls. They could make out the large catapults stationed at each position.

'None of this was here before,' Meru said. 'Where has it all come from?'

'Looks like they were expecting trouble. These catapults ...' Coran began.

'More dangerous than our rockets at this range,' Fitch said. 'Amar has had 'em for many rounds, but they've never been brought out like this before. A normal ship could be smashed to smithereens if it was hit.'

'So we saw,' Mel said, eyeing the dent in the *Mobilis*.

The *Mobilis* cruised into the lee water within the harbour walls. They could see all the fishing vessels were moored up, not a single ship was at sea.

Coran jumped up into the bridge and looked around the harbour.

'There,' he said, pointing. 'That quay, we'll tie up there.'

Meru brought the ship around and reduced power to the engines. Already they could see a crowd of people was building at the base of the quay they were heading for. As they came closer it was obvious many were soldiers armed with swords and bows.

'Doesn't look too friendly, does it?' Mel said, under her breath.

'Let's hope they don't lynch us the moment we step off,' Fitch said, tucking a knife into his belt.

'No weapons,' Coran said. 'These are our folk. There's to be no violence from us.'

'Captain ...'

'No weapons.'

Fitch sighed, pulled the knife out and put it away in one of the bridge lockers.

'If I die, I'm blaming you,' he muttered.

'Noted.'

Daf and Creg were now standing fore and aft, ready to jump ashore and secure the ship. Meru brought the *Mobilis* alongside and reduced the power, letting the ship drift the rest of the way. With the faintest of jolts, the ship came to rest and was made fast with ropes.

The soldiers surged on to the decking, the crew of the *Mobilis* backed up against the bridge bulkhead.

'You the captain?' the lead soldier demanded.

'Aye,' Coran replied, squaring up to him. 'Captain Coran of the *Mobilis*.'

'You're coming with us,' the soldier replied. 'All of you.'

'Are we now?' Coran replied. 'Under whose authority?'

'The council and senate have decreed all vessels entering port are subject to inspection and seizure ...'

'Seizure?' Mel said.

'Crews to be interred for processing ...'

'Now just wait a spell,' Coran began, but he was pulled aside by the soldiers. Behind him the others were wrestled into a line.

'You boy!' the soldier called. 'Your name?'

Coran saw that the soldier had turned his attention to Meru. He stood just before Zoella with his head hung down, she was looking around her with eyes wide with fear. Meru muttered something under his breath.

'Speak up!'

'Meru,' Meru managed to say.

There was muttering between the soldiers.

'Meru? Meru Farstone?'

Meru looked up, sighed and nodded.

The soldier gestured to his companions and Meru was pulled out of the line.

'What are you doing?' Coran demanded.

'Abducting the son of a senator,' the soldier said. 'That ties up with piracy too. Not going to go well for any of you.'

'We're no pirates!' Coran stammered. 'Senator? Meru ... what?'

'Told you he wasn't on the level,' Fitch said from somewhere behind.

'Meru?' Mel demanded as Meru was led away. 'Meru! What's all this about? Meru!'

But he was gone, hustled away into the crowd.

'Lock 'em up!' the soldier called.

The rest of the crew of the *Mobilis*, along with Zoella and Ren, were marched away.

CHAPTER FIVE

Daine, Capital of Drayden

Round 2307, Second pass

'How dare she!' Nerina's face was flushed, her pale cheeks aflame. She and Merrin had walked further down into the temple, reaching the far end of the corridor. Both looked around to ensure that they couldn't be overheard.

'The impudence,' Merrin agreed. 'It was blasphemy, claiming to be the servant of the Obelisk. Lies! She should be punished for such heresy, cast out of the priestesshood. I told you she would make a move against you, and here it is.'

Nerina shook her head.

'She has committed no sin as measured by the elements,' Nerina replied. 'She is a true believer, I am sure she believes the Obelisk spoke to her. We cannot cast her out. See how many who trust her, believe in her? She has risen from the slums to the ranks of the priestesses, she has defeated the King of Scallia in battle.' Nerina paced back and forth. 'She is powerful … and she knows it. Now we can be sure she has taken the Queen's power. She seeks to challenge me for the role of high priestess!'

'We have to get rid of her, overpower her …' Merrin countered. 'It must be done now, both us together … we can do it.'

Nerina shook her head

'No, not yet. I want her … both of them fattened before the slaughter. They are still useful right now.'

'This is too risky.'

'We can't assail Kiri now. You heard what she claimed, to be the "chosen one" of the elements! How can we smite Lacaille's messenger?

All heard what she said. This is a clever move, elevating her position in the ranks, but claiming it is Lacaille herself who puts her there. We must not underestimate her.'

'She can't be that strong.'

The blazing light that illuminated the interior of the temple, steered by mirrors all around, faded around them. Cloud must be blocking the light of Lacaille. Nerina lowered her voice in the gloom.

'We do not know her true strength,' Nerina replied. 'Probably she does not either. No, we must be more subtle than that.'

Nerina's fists were clenched, she looked about her for a moment.

'Perhaps,' she whispered. 'Perhaps we can solve two problems in one … Amar! Yes, that could be the answer.'

'Amar?' Merrin asked.

Nerina turned to look at her. 'Yes. Amar, a land untouched by us in generations. What gifts might languish there, undiscovered and untapped?'

'There are easier lands to grasp …'

'There are,' she said, 'But Elena's imperative still holds and we can use recent events to fan the flames here. Those of Taloon can prove their loyalty to us by dealing with that problem. Taloon has what we need to cross the ocean. They are seafarers, they have a mighty fleet of vessels. Our price for peace with Taloon? They conduct war upon that foe on our behalf, led by our most zealous priestess …'

Merrin smiled. 'With those ships we might win a mighty victory over evil and fulfil ancient vows.'

'And if our chosen one really is the anointed of Lacaille, how can she fail?' Nerina replied, with a faint laugh. 'Our holy war, our task appointed. She has been told to carry it out. Elena understood well how to motivate the priestesses, this will keep them fighting. I will make an impassioned call to arms to rid this world from the curse of those exiles, endorsing Kiri's vision.'

'And if she fails or is killed in the attempt …'

'She was misguided or deluded,' Nerina finished. 'We can claim to have tested her and found her wanting.'

'What of the flares?' Merrin asked.

'What of them?'

'They will continue to inflict suffering upon all peoples. Nothing we can do will change that. You know as well as I do that there is no link between them and a holy war we declared in the past. If they don't stop when we destroy Amar the faith in our religion will fade … our authority will go with it!'

'The flares last for a few rounds only,' Nerina replied. 'Elena knew this and used it to unite the priestesses, to accomplish her objectives in a certain time. We have the same opportunity. It matters not whether it is true, what matters is that the priestesses believe it. With Kiri's vision they all believe it anew. By the time we subdue Taloon and Amar the worst will have passed, the flares will stop … seem to stop … because we have done what Elena and our goddess Lacaille commanded us to do. We will have Esurio under our dominion and will be seen by all to have delivered it from destruction.'

'Then, our plan is …'

'We must secure Taloon. Kiri will go as our emissary. She has the support of the priestesses, to her the religion is all-consuming. We need that single-mindedness. She has the admiration and love of many for what she went through. She found the location of Amar. Now she claims to be the chosen one of Lacaille. We will send her away for another victory! When she is out of sight, she is out of the minds of most who remain here.'

'And in the meantime?'

'We consolidate our gains here. We must choose our moment to deal with her carefully, she must be disgraced and weakened first … and how that must be done is our next move.'

The clouds had moved. Light blazed around them once more, filling the temple with Lacaille's warm orange glow.

'If you cast her out amongst the carns, don't be surprised if she returns at the head of the pack,' Merrin replied.

'Very poetic,' Nerina said. 'I know what I'm dealing with. For now we can use her to subdue Amar and Taloon at no danger to ourselves. If she dies in that attempt … so be it.'

'If she succeeds she will be more popular than ever, and perhaps even more powerful.'

'We will be ready for that. And if she does not swear her loyalty to me then, she will be torn.'

'It may not be enough.'

'Then we must ensure that there is another ready to challenge her,' Nerina replied. 'I have always indicated that your daughter is my natural successor, that's what they have all believed until now, perhaps we should remind Rihanna of that … and that Kiri might threaten that assumption.'

Merrin nodded. 'Rihanna and Kiri have struck up a friendship …'

'It can be used,' Nerina said. 'Rihanna is ambitious and strong, but she does not have Kiri's cunning. Both can be nurtured.'

Merrin didn't reply for a moment. Nerina's eyes narrowed.

'Do you not support my intentions?' Nerina asked. 'Your daughter belongs to me, remember? As all your other offspring.'

'Yes, high priestess,' Merrin mumbled.

Nerina stepped closer, her voice dropping to a whisper. 'Or I can take your own gift now and put your daughter in your place this very spell. Have I not given you everything you ever wanted? Or have you decided to serve another?'

Merrin looked up. 'No, I serve you. I always have. I always will. It will be done.'

'All Esurio will be ours, Merrin,' Nerina said. 'Sacrifices have been made for the greater good. It is for us to subdue this world, order it appropriately. You have served me so well for so long, your children given as offerings to that end. We are close now. Do not falter and you will have everything you want. It seems likely Kiri will be the one that survives. If so, once I tear her, I will give her to you. Think of that sweet satisfaction.'

There was a flicker of desire in Merrin's eyes.

'Yes, Merrin,' Nerina said. 'Every last piece of Charis' work undone, her name scrubbed from the annals. Once torn you can throw Kiri back into the slums, or keep her as a drudge in your household as the fancy takes you. Imagine that! Kiri serving at your pleasure, Charis' apprentice! Whip her, abuse her, do what you would with her. Throw her back to Handela and have her tortured … I don't care.'

'You promise to give her to me?'

'Once Amar and Taloon are dealt with and I have the gifts I need, she will be yours. Come, we must return. Go to the priestesses. I will see to Kiri.'

* * *

Kiri paced in the anteroom like a cornered fellin. Dozens of thoughts ran through her head.

I should have stayed quiet. Now Nerina will truly consider me a threat. What was I thinking, announcing things like that?

It had felt so right though, an imperative was upon her. She had to speak out. It was Lacaille's will; nothing could thwart that, could it?

Some of the priestesses believe me, some don't, but would there be enough support for me to challenge Nerina, here and now? What about Merrin and the others? Are they plotting now to tear me, murder me? I don't even have my kai …

Sweat chilled her and she shivered.

The door creaked and opened. Kiri spun around, her hands outstretched, ready for whatever was coming.

It was Nerina.

'Be at peace, young one,' she said, a smile on her face.

Kiri lowered her hands.

'Quite the revelation,' Nerina continued, stepping into the room and closing the door. 'It must have been alarming for you. You spoke with great conviction.'

'I only told what I heard,' Kiri managed to say. 'I didn't understand it all.'

'The Obelisk speaks to few,' Nerina said, assuming her usual habit of walking around the person she was talking to. Kiri remained unmoved as the high priestess completed her steps. 'And none for some generations of the priestesses. You still surprise us little Kiri. Your coming to us was no accident if Lacaille herself seeks to choose you.'

'You're not … not angry?' Kiri asked.

Nerina looked baffled. 'Angry? Why would I be angry? That one of ours is honoured by a revelation from Lacaille, has been found worthy to stand in her presence and receive direction? I am proud, Kiri. Proud of us, proud of you. It underlines that we are taking the right and just approach. Many things have brought you to this point, the mentoring of dear Charis, your dedication and your service in Viresia. Lacaille has seen and noted your conduct.'

Kiri blinked in surprise.

'It seems clear that a great destiny awaits you,' Nerina said.

'I didn't ask for Lacaille to speak to me, I truly didn't,' Kiri said. 'I didn't mean to …'

'Peace, young one,' Nerina said, her voice soft. 'Do not fear. We will support you in this. The task appointed. It remains incomplete, yes? Elena's great directive? Amar itself?'

Kiri nodded. Nerina continued.

'Amar lies across the sea far to the sunright, it seems we must subdue it, we cannot ignore this renewed directive. The Obelisk demands your attendance too, you must do as it says unquestioningly.'

'But I do not know how to find the Obelisk …' Kiri began. 'Or even where to start looking.'

'The servant of Lacaille will not leave you without further instructions,' Nerina replied. 'Thus you must listen, and follow the path before you – to Amar it would seem. None since Elena have had such clear instruction, thus I believe both tasks fall to you. The will of Lacaille in the subjugation of Amar followed by the Obelisk's request. The question is do you have the courage to do so, will you undertake this?'

Kiri stood straighter, her mind made up. 'I will see it done!'

Nerina smiled.

'And you will succeed,' Nerina said. 'You were born for this Kiri, raised out of the slums for a purpose. Come, we must return to the priestesses. I believe the solution to at least part of your quest already presents itself …'

'I don't understand.'

'Lacaille has already provided. Follow me and see.'

* * *

Merrin returned to the main hall of the priestesses ahead of Nerina and Kiri. Within, the priestesses were still muttering between themselves at Kiri's words, discussing what they might mean for Drayden.

Rihanna was standing on her own, awaiting Kiri's return. Merrin walked up to her.

'Daughter.'

Rihanna looked up. 'Mother.'

'Quite the performance from your friend, wouldn't you say?' Merrin asked.

'Kiri has always been … different,' Rihanna replied.

Merrin smiled. 'Different, yes that's one way to describe her I suppose. A shame that she's supplanted you in Nerina's affections.'

Rihanna frowned. 'Nerina respects us both.'

Merrin laughed. 'Really Rihanna, you can be so naïve. Kiri is playing you for a fool. This was no great revelation from upon high. It's all part of her scheming, to differentiate herself. She has studied all the works of Elena and understood them well. How can we possibly ignore one chosen by Lacaille?'

'If Kiri says she's received a word from Lacaille, then I believe her,' Rihanna countered.

Merrin scoffed. 'Then Kiri already has what she wants.'

'And what is that?'

Merrin turned and looked back over her shoulder. 'You out of the way, so she can realise her ambition. She wants to be high priestess after Nerina. Perhaps she even wants to depose Nerina.'

Rihanna shook her head. 'Kiri doesn't want that. I would know. She would have told me.'

'Like she told you in advance about her revelation?' Merrin asked, seeing the look upon Rihanna's face. 'Oh, she didn't tell you, then? Interesting friendship you have.'

Rihanna paused before replying. Merrin turned back.

'Kiri would have shared it with me,' Rihanna said, her voice uncertain. 'There just wasn't time.'

'The same way she hasn't told you how she stole the Queen of Scallia's powers?' Merrin asked.

Rihanna looked at her mother in shock. 'She hasn't done such a thing. She told me she hadn't.'

'How do you explain how powerful she has become?' Merrin smirked. 'Even Nerina is concerned now. She's lying to you Rihanna. Using you.'

Rihanna shook her head.

'Listen,' Merrin said, whispering in her ear. 'Nerina admires strength. Kiri is strong and growing stronger. Nerina gives out the choice assignments so that those with the gifts have opportunities to learn and grow. Remember how quickly Kiri was pushed to become a priestess? Remember Varda?'

'Varda?' Rihanna said, looking around.

'Shhhh,' Merrin said. 'Not so loud.'

'What about Varda?' Rihanna hissed.

'Kiri was sent there, don't you recall?' Merrin said. 'Accompanying Charis.'

'It was an attempt at reconciliation with Scallia. Charis went to make peace ...'

Merrin smirked. 'Charis may have thought so, but Nerina knew better. War was already inevitable. Charis refused to see it. Nerina knew what would happen.'

'And she still let them go?'

'Charis was a fool,' Merrin said. 'Nerina wanted a war, to put men back in their place. It's our right to take back the lands, subdue them and rule them. The path of peace we pursued for rounds made us weak and craven. It was a test for Kiri; could she fight, could she overcome? She did. That is why Nerina has favoured her until now.'

Rihanna looked away.

'And now Kiri has her own ambition,' Merrin said. 'She cares for no one but herself.'

'She's my friend. I trust her.'

'Touching that you still believe that,' Merrin replied, offhand. 'She is clever and manipulative, I'll give her that. You watch. Nerina will appoint her some special task this stretch and exclude you. Perhaps that will persuade you where you now lie in Nerina's affections …'

* * *

Kiri followed Nerina back into the hall. Nerina clapped her hands for attention.

'It seems that priestess Kiri has indeed received word from Lacaille herself,' she said, her quiet voice carrying throughout the hall. 'We will all support Kiri in her fulfilling what has been asked of her.'

There were a few mutters amongst the priestesses, but there were nods of assent from all around. Kiri looked around at the assembled faces, noting all the gazes that were upon her.

'For now though,' Nerina continued. 'We must return to our immediate business. Be seated Kiri.'

Kiri nodded and sat down in her previous position. She turned to Rihanna.

'I …'

Rihanna's look was cold and hard. Kiri saw Merrin smirking from behind her.

Nerina was still speaking. 'Now, we must celebrate what we have achieved! The subjugation of Viresia in the land of Scallia. Thus, I have gifts for you all!'

Kiri blinked in surprise.

Gifts?

Nerina clapped her hands twice. The doors to the hall swung open once more.

The temple guards stood either side of the entrance. Between them, roped together in a line and bound at the wrists, were girls dressed in tattered smocks. Kiri's eyes widened.

From Scallia ... girls taken from Viresia ... oh no!

The girls were forced into the hall, huddled together in the centre, looking about as the priestesses surrounding them looked down. Aside from Nerina and Merrin there were twelve priestesses ... and twelve captives.

Merrin had stood up and was standing beside Nerina as she gestured to the guards. One by one the ropes were removed from the girls. They huddled closer, trembling, clutching at each other in fear.

Nerina raised her arms.

'Drayden is in the ascendancy,' she called. 'We will realise the ambition of Elena in our lifetimes. We will see the task appointed complete. We will subdue all lands to our will. This is the will of Lacaille!'

'The will of Lacaille!' the priestesses echoed.

Nerina's lowered her gaze and looked from left to right, a smile growing on her face.

'Feast, my priestesses!'

The priestesses rose from their benches. Arms were outstretched, hands clutching and grasping in the air. As Kiri watched three of the girls slumped to their knees with a shriek, their faces going blank as the priestesses stole into their minds. Those not caught cried out in terror, trying to run towards the doors, but it was to no avail. Swift mental ties caught them, subduing them and they fell to their knees before the priestesses that had caught them.

Next to her, Kiri saw Rihanna stretch out her hand and another girl fell, whimpering before her. About her the moans and cries of satisfaction rose from the priestesses as the power of the stolen gifts surged through them. Kiri knew well that feeling, the fierce glow and warmth of it bursting through her body, akin to the physical joys so she'd heard tell, but even stronger, more desirable …

But this is wrong!

Then there was only one girl left.

If I don't take her they'll ask why, they'll know! But I can't … these woman are of Scallia … my people … my home …

In split second Kiri reached out her hand. She sought the girl's mind. She felt the girl pull back, shrieking in fear.

Do not fear! I will not harm you, but you must do exactly as I say or you will suffer the same fate as these others …

The girl's eyes widened in shock, staring into Kiri's, suspicion and confusion mixing on her expression.

Fall on your knees! Now! Do it!

The girl dropped before her, staring up, quivering with fright.

Let your face go vacant, open your mouth as if your mind has gone …

Kiri continued to stretch out her arm towards the girl, her fingers miming the actions of the other priestesses. She lowered herself down on her knees, moaning, imagining the wonderful flow of power that would have come to her. It was tempting, the feeling was so pleasurable, so addictive … she almost changed her mind there and then. She fought the instinct to seize the girl's gift, it was there, glowing before her, tantalising, within reach, all she had to do was reach out …

Now, slump to the floor, keep your eyes open but do not move. Lie still! They will carry you away, do not resist, say nothing, do nothing! I will come to you later and help you escape …

Kiri could hear the faint echo in her mind. The girl's gift was not strong, but she had enough wits about her to ask the question.

Who are you?

I am Kiri. I will see you safely back to Scallia …

My name is Gemma …

There was still fear, but there was gratitude too. The girl slumped to the floor, lifeless like all the others about her.

Kiri heard the sound of heavy breathing in her ear.

'So good!'

It was a young priestess sitting on her other side. Kiri turned to look at her. Her face was flushed, her lips parted in a lustful smile. Kiri managed to nod. She tried to repress her distaste and revulsion.

'Nothing like it, is there?' the girl continued. 'Sweet joy to take these Scallian wastrels ...'

Kiri didn't answer.

As Kiri had expected, Nerina soon summoned more guards. Each girl was carried out, like a sack thrown over the shoulders. Kiri watched as Gemma was picked up. She remained as limp as the others. Then they were all gone and the doors were closed once more.

I will have to find her later ...

'Now,' Nerina said. Kiri saw Nerina cast a glance in her direction. 'To business. We have a guest.'

The priestesses looked at her expectantly.

'You know of our conquest of Scallia and Drem and you know of the task appointed to us by our first high priestess, Elena,' Nerina said, striding down through the centre of the hall, before whirling around at the far end. 'Lacaille warns us that we must not delay. Kiri has received a directive from the Obelisk itself. What must be done?'

The priestesses looked at each other, muttering.

One volunteered. 'The exiles ... they must be destroyed. But they were supposed to be in Nireus ...'

Nerina pointed at her. 'Correct, but we conquered Nireus and the exiles were not there. Lacaille was appeased, but not sated. The flares warned of in the elements will continue to return. If we are not swift, so will the pain! But we found one ... we found an exile ...'

The priestesses except for Kiri and Rihanna gasped.

'Didn't we, Kiri?' Nerina asked, her gaze falling upon her.

Kiri tried not to flinch, she nodded.

'Tell us of him,' Nerina instructed.

Kiri swallowed. Meru's image formed in her mind, but she was too anxious for any other feelings to well up.

'He … he came from over the seas,' Kiri managed to say. 'From a distant land called Amar. It was there his ancestors had fled from Elena's wrath long ago …'

'Elena Drayden was victorious over Kashif Amar, the leader of exiles,' Nerina said. 'She overpowered him and his evil people, but they fled and we never knew where they had gone until now. They have named their land after their leader as we have done. They exist, they continue their evil … why they even had a flying machine straight out of the legends!'

More gasps.

'It was …' Kiri began.

'I saw it too,' Rihanna interrupted, her voice hard. Kiri looked around at her to be greeted with an unfriendly stare. 'A metal beast that flew through the air …'

'But this exile escaped,' Nerina continued. 'Across the sea in a ship, fleeing back to Amar. We could not pursue … not until now.'

Rihanna glared and then looked down her nose at Kiri before turning away.

Nerina walked back along the hall and seated herself in the centre chair, facing the doors.

'To complete the task appointed, we must venture across the sea. This is a further test of our resolve, priestesses of Drayden. The lands hereabout are under our dominion, or fearful of our wrath, all respect the tithe once more. But to reach this Amar … we need ships.'

'And Drayden is landlocked,' Merrin said, speaking for the first time.

'Precisely,' Nerina said. 'We have no ships, no sailors, but we have an ally that does. An ally that knows of our increasing strength and thus wishes to serve …'

She clapped her hands twice again, the doors to the hall swung back a second time.

A man stood there, dressed in a strange and outlandish fashion. Most surprising was a huge hat like a flat saucer, perched on his head with an enormous wide rim. His clothes were loose fitting, swaths of fine linen swirling about him as he walked forward. His skin was dark, the whites of his eyes contrasting with the flesh of his face.

Like Tasha ... did she come from Taloon then? She was my friend, but I never asked ...

His pace was quick. He looked neither to the right nor left, but strode straight up to Nerina and then bowed low before her. He was a big man, over twelve hands tall.

'Well met, emissary of Taloon,' Nerina said, her posture languid and relaxed. 'I, Nerina, high priestess of Daine in the land of Drayden, welcome you.'

'It is an honour much anticipated, high priestess,' the man replied, with a deep baritone voice. 'I am Vandare, from the court of King Karquesh of Taloon.'

'We are pleased to receive you, Vandare of Taloon,' Nerina replied, still formal. 'How fares Taloon? Is all at peace within your kingdom?'

'It is,' Vandare replied. 'And we are grateful to the priestesses of Drayden for their role in keeping the security of our borders.'

'As well you should be,' Nerina said. 'A duty we take seriously indeed. The world remains a dangerous place. Taloon has proved itself a trusted ally in the past, we hope that remains the case.'

Vandare paused for a moment before responding. 'Where Drayden goes, Taloon will follow, high priestess. Never doubt our commitment, or our tithe, to you.'

Nerina got to her feet.

'Your words are salve to my soul, Vandare,' she said. 'We have much need of allies now.'

'Taloon stands ready to serve, of course.'

'Rise,' Nerina said, taking Vandare's hand. He stood up. The contrast between the pair could not have been more striking. Nerina barely came up to Vandare's shoulder. He was an older man, so it seemed to Kiri, his dark face lined with age under the strange hat.

'High priestess,' he acknowledged.

'The flares,' Nerina said, dropping her voice. 'Have they caused harm?'

Vandare nodded, 'Fires swept much of our land and many have died. Stone buildings and caves provide the greatest safety. But the flares themselves? We are at a loss ...'

'Lacaille herself,' Nerina said. 'She has told us what must be done. This is her wrath, purging the unrighteous from amongst all the peoples. Her punishment has descended upon us all because we have not heeded her words.'

'Lacaille?' Vandare echoed.

'The goddess,' Nerina replied, stretching her arms wide. 'She who directs us all.'

'Ahhh,' Vandare replied. 'Of course. What does she command?'

He doesn't believe, but he is cautious ... and wise.

'Our ancient texts describe the flares,' Nerina said. 'They are a punishment for us being remiss in eradicating evil from our lands. Long ago, we were set a task to destroy that evil, but we failed. That responsibility still lies heavy upon us. We call it the task appointed, we must complete it.'

Kiri swallowed, the remorse in Nerina's voice was compelling.

That task has been a cornerstone of my life for so long now, the hated exiles ... but now? Meru is an exile and he was not as Elena said he was ... he said the people of Amar were peaceable. Can they truly be cursed by Lacaille? And yet, Lacaille has spoken to me, told me to carry out the task ...

'What are you obliged to do?' Vandare asked.

'There is a race, a race of evil,' Nerina said. 'Once they rended the soil of our world, tainted the air and defiled everything about them. Their abode was in the far shadeward, a city called Nireus. Long ago we sought to destroy them and we almost did, but many of them fled before us. Fled across the sea. They became known as the exiles. We knew not where they had gone.'

'And now you do?' Vandare queried.

Nerina nodded. 'Across the sea, a land called Amar.'

Vandare paused once more. 'We have heard rumours of it. An island far beyond the horizon to the sunright …'

Nerina straightened. 'They must be destroyed.'

Vandare frowned.

'Taloon has a fleet of ships,' Nerina said. 'Warships. We require them.'

Kiri watched as Vandare assimilated that bit of information.

'It would be a dangerous voyage, to make war upon an unknown foe at such distance …'

'We have a duty,' Nerina said. 'My people would accompany yours in this quest. We would seek an end to these flares. Our combined might against the evil …'

'My King would have to make such a decision,' Vandare said. 'I am merely an emissary. I will take your request to him immediately.'

Nerina smiled.

'I will send my own honoured emissary with you,' she said gesturing towards Kiri. 'Priestess Kiri will go on behalf of Drayden, our sole representative. She has been anointed by Lacaille's servant.'

Kiri heard Rihanna stifle a gasp next to her and exchange a look with Merrin. Kiri could sense an intolerable smugness emanating from the older woman.

But Kiri's thoughts were driven elsewhere. The exiles, the wrath of Lacaille and Elena's directive buzzed in her mind, but they were thoughts too large for her to deal with at that moment. Two things flickered to the forefront of her mind.

If I go to Amar … Meru and Zoella. I can have them both!

'Kiri will accompany you back to Taloon,' Nerina said. 'She will ensure that my … request … is presented to your King on my behalf with all the necessary detail.'

Vandare looked at Kiri for a moment before bowing to her. 'Such assistance would be most welcome.'

He didn't sound at all enthused by the prospect.

'Your King's response will set the tone for the ongoing relationship between Drayden and Taloon,' Nerina said. 'Long may it continue.'

Vandare bowed before Nerina again.

'We are your humble servants, high priestess Nerina,' he said.

Nerina sat down, crossing her legs as she did so.

'I hope so, Vandare of Taloon. I hope so. Now, you must rest before your voyage back to Taloon. We will speed your way.'

It was clear he was dismissed. Vandare bowed once more and then stood, turned about and strode away, the doors opening for him and then closing again behind him.

There was silence in the hall for a long moment before Nerina turned her attention to Kiri.

'You will escort him back to Taloon,' she instructed. 'You will fly by dach, taking my order to their king. The attack on Amar must commence as soon as they are able.'

Kiri nodded. 'Yes high priestess. But if the king refuses?'

Nerina's eyes narrowed. 'Then Taloon will no longer have need of a king. They have few with the gift in that land. Subduing them should present little problem. If you have need, we are but a dach's flight away. Once the fleet is ready to depart I will send others to accompany you.'

Kiri hid her excitement and anticipation.

If I am careful I can achieve it all. Amar lies before me. The peace that Charis hoped for might come to pass for all lands, not just ours.

Nerina rose to her feet again and clapped her hands one more time. 'Dismissed!'

The priestesses began to file out. Next to her, Rihanna got to her feet and stepped away. Kiri could see Merrin was watching them both.

'Rihanna, wait ...'

Rihanna glared at her. 'No, why should I?'

'What's the matter?'

Rihanna's lip curled into a sneer. 'Always you have to be the chosen one, don't you? Always special, always favoured. Seeing visions of Elena's Obelisk ...'

'But I did, I'm only telling what I saw!'

Rihanna scoffed, shaking her head. 'And you didn't even tell me? I thought we were supposed to be friends now?'

'There wasn't time. There were only moments before …'

Rihanna shook her head. 'You lied to me, Kiri. You're unbelievable. Using everyone for your own advancement. You can't treat people like that, but it's the way of the gutter I guess.'

'Rihanna!'

'I know what you're trying to do. You think you can be high priestess. Ha! You're not that special, one of these stretches you're going to learn that.'

Rihanna left, leaving Kiri standing amidst the few remaining priestesses. She let tears pool in the corners of her eyes, gritting her teeth. Merrin sniffed with satisfaction and turned to leave. Kiri was left on her own in the hall.

She wiped away the tears and then laughed.

I hope our little show was good enough! Rihanna is a better actress than me. Merrin seems convinced we are at odds once more. Let's hope that message gets to Nerina.

Kiri's thoughts drifted back to the words her old mentor had spoken to her long ago. She felt tears well up as she saw Charis' tender face, heard her soft voice once more.

You have a remarkable gift. You are precious child, not just to me, but to all Drayden. You should have always been here in the Temple. We saved you, it is true. But my fondest hope is, in time, it will be you who saves us.

She gritted her teeth with determination.

'I will, Charis. I will!'

CHAPTER SIX

Amaris, Capital of Amar

Round 2307, Second pass

Coran and the rest of the crew had been marched within the walls of Amaris and upwards into the city. They were led into the city jail and from there escorted to a large cell.

'I demand to speak to someone in authority,' Coran said, eyeing the entrance to the prison.

'You'll get your chance,' the soldier replied. 'In, now.'

'I'm a citizen of Amar,' Coran replied. 'You can't do this.'

'You're a pirate,' the soldier replied. 'And you're under arrest.'

Coran was shoved forward. Daf and Creg looked ready to start a fight, but Coran shook his head. He raised his hands in submission.

'All right!'

Coran walked into the cell and the others followed in.

The soldiers bolted and locked a heavy furler wood door behind them and they heard the sound of feet marching away.

Coran looked around the cell, there was nothing within save for a small window at the far side.

'Lovely accommodation,' Fitch said. 'So glad we came back here to warn the good folk of Amar. Really pleased with the reception, the banquet in our honour … very nice.'

Coran cast a look at him, but didn't deign to reply.

'And pirates?' Mel asked. 'Why would they say that?'

Coran shook his head. 'Something's happened. They must have been hit by the flares, lost some ships. I don't know. Must be something else going on.'

'What's going on,' Fitch began, 'is that little snut timekeeper of yours didn't tell us ...'

'Meru didn't know what was going to happen,' Mel replied.

'Didn't tell us his daddy was a senator of the snuttin' city though, did he?' Fitch retorted. 'Failed to mention that, didn't he? Must have slipped his mind! I told you he was lying.'

'Yeah,' Coran muttered. 'He could have told us that.'

'So he lied to all of you,' Zoella said, crouching down against the wall of the cell and wrapping her arms about her knees. 'He lied to me. Is there anyone he's not lied to?'

'We always knew he was running from something,' Mel said. 'When we found him adrift in the sea ...'

'Told you we should have chucked him back in,' Fitch said.

'He's paid his way since then,' Coran said. 'As well you know.' Coran looked at Zoella. 'And he rescued you too, remember?'

'I do,' Zoella replied, glaring back at him. 'But that doesn't excuse this, does it? You sure he was even telling the truth about being shipwrecked?'

'He was way out in the Straithian Sea,' Mel said. 'Adrift, like I said. We found him clinging to the wreckage of his ship, sunk in a storm and about to be eaten by a squidder.'

'Squidder?' Ren asked.

'Something big that lives in the sea,' Mel replied, waving her arms around. 'Lots of tentacles.'

'Could have been lies,' Zoella said.

'You don't deliberately swim out into the sea and put your life at risk,' Coran said. 'He was shipwrecked. I knew the captain of his ship and the storms that come up from the sunward are real enough.'

'When we got him aboard he claimed he didn't have any parents,' Mel said. 'But he'd never talk about it.'

'Orphans don't get to be timekeepers,' Coran said. 'It's a privileged rank, but it's below the station of a senatorial family.'

Coran looked around at the rest of the crew, his gaze ending at Zoella.

'Either way, he's got some explaining to do.'

Zoella's lips were pursed. 'Yes, he has.'

* * *

Meru had been led up into the higher circles of the city. The city of Amaris was built into the cliffs on one side and extended out to sea on a natural promontory to the other, rising a thousand hands to the cliff tops and then extending further on top of them. The roads from inland led to the top of the cliffs with most of the city save the senate buildings set out below in tiers like an ornate cake constructed of smooth redstone.

Meru knew it formed a natural arc around what was locally called Saddle cove; the promontory reaching out like a welcoming arm into the sea.

Standing at the edge of a large piazza and looking over a low wall he could see the harbour far below. The *Mobilis* was easy to spot, its shiny hull distinct from the small wooden vessels all around it.

Upon reaching the piazza he'd been instructed to wait. Two guards stood alongside him. They didn't restrain him, but it was clear he wasn't going anywhere. Another guard had walked into the buildings on the other side of the piazza. Meru recognised them.

The Senate. Where my parents worked.

Figures emerged from the building. Meru didn't need to see their faces to recognise them. He'd know them anywhere.

They were walking towards him, a woman and a man, also escorted by guards. The woman broke into a run on seeing him.

'Meru! By the shades, it is you. You're alive. Alive!'

Meru found himself pulled into a crushing hug. His breath was knocked out from him.

'Mother ...'

She drew back and slapped him across the face.

'How dare you put your father and I through that? We'd given you up for dead. Lost at sea, drowned. Thought we'd never see you again. No message, nothing. You thoughtless, hurtful child!'

Meru tried to interject, but his mother was in full flow.

'Shipping away on a common fishing trawler without saying goodbye. Then the ship is overdue and it doesn't come back. What were you thinking? You've been lost for almost a round and a half.'

'I ran away mother.' Meru managed to shout.

'Why, in Lacaille's name, why?' she protested. Meru looked up at them; Henoch and Hannah Farstone, his father and mother.

'Henoch,' his mother said, exasperated. 'Say something.'

'Your conduct was reprehensible,' Henoch said. 'Inexcusable. The anguish you put your mother through …'

'You haven't changed then,' Meru interrupted.

'How dare you,' Henoch snapped.

'Please,' Hannah said, pulling at her husband's arm. He pulled away.

'No Hannah, the boy needs to be brought to heel.'

'No I won't!' Meru shouted. 'I've been out there.' He gestured to the wide open ocean behind him. 'I've seen things, done things. The senate needs to hear what I've got to say …'

'The senate will do as it sees fit,' Henoch replied. 'According to rule and custom as is right and proper. Those who abducted you will be dealt with as the pirates they are.'

'They're not pirates. They didn't abduct me, they rescued me.'

'… will be dealt with in the proper manner after due process and sentenced according to their crimes.'

Meru pushed forward. 'No father. You've got to shut up and listen for once! There is danger out beyond the sea. We went there, discovered what it was. All Amar needs to hear this. The myths and legends are true and we need to prepare.'

'Nonsense.'

'It's not nonsense, it's true. And if you don't start paying attention then lots of folk are going to die.'

'I've been to see your companions,' Henoch replied. 'Two known criminals, a captain with no licence and his woman, a decidedly untrustworthy looking fellow and two urchin refugees from Lacaille knows where. Hardly reliable witnesses.'

'She's from a distant continent,' Meru said. 'Her …'

'Just because some vagabond girl claims to be from over the seas means nothing …'

'She's no vagabond, her name is Zoella,' Meru retorted. 'She saved my life more than once. She's the bravest, truest and the kindest person you could ever wish to meet.'

Henoch glared. 'You will be dealt with too. They've clearly brainwashed you. It will go all the worse for them. They will be summoned to the senate shortly and we will find out what they are really about. You will stay with your mother until summoned.'

* * *

The crew of the *Mobilis,* along with Zoella and Ren, were led from the cells. They were escorted upwards into a council chamber, a vaulted room in the midst of the senate buildings, with a lofty domed roof. The light of Lacaille streamed in far above, providing a warm airy feeling to the interior.

That feeling did not extend to those in the room. Before the crew sat the senate of Amar, a group of five elderly men seated atop ornately carved chairs. They, in turn, were placed upon a raised dais, allowing the senators to glare down upon their subjects. There was a sixth chair, alongside, unoccupied.

Four guards flanked the crew for a moment before they were dismissed. They filed out and the doors were locked behind them.

'Who speaks for you?' the first senator asked.

Coran stepped forward. 'I do.'

'And you are?'

'Captain Coran of the *Mobilis.*'

'The metal vessel?'

Coran nodded.

A door opened and another man stepped through, carrying a stack of papers under his arm. He walked with alacrity, pacing on to the dais with a nod to the other senators before he sat down.

'Henoch,' the first senator said. 'Good that you could join us.'

'Apologies for my tardiness,' Henoch said. 'A matter of discipline. My son was abducted by these … pirates. I was gratified to find him intact, though whether his mind can be repaired remains to be seen.'

Coran looked around at Mel and the rest of the crew. All of them were looking at him.

'Told you he was a lying toe-rag!' Fitch whispered.

'I am Senator Janaid,' the first senator said, turning back to Coran. 'Your accent betrays you as from these shores, and we saw your vessel fly Amaran flags. Yet, this ship is not known to us. From whence do you come?'

'I am from Amar,' Coran answered. 'As are most of us …'

'Most of us?' Henoch interrupted. 'There are no other lands.'

'There are,' Coran replied. 'We have been there.'

Henoch almost rose out of his chair, but Janaid held up his hands.

'Explain who you are,' Janaid said. 'And what you are doing here.'

Coran took a deep breath.

'I am from Amar,' he began. 'Six rounds ago I was first mate aboard a trawler. We were caught in storms and driven beyond the horizon, out of sight of the smokes of Amar. My crew and I fetched up on an island. There we met Mel …' Coran indicated Mel, standing next to him. 'She had likewise been marooned there, shipwrecked before, unable to return home.'

The senators listened, but none spoke. Coran continued.

'Our ship was damaged, but we attempted repairs,' Coran said. 'But Mel had found something else. On those islands was a cavern, hollowed out of the rock. Within was a landing stage, and moored there … the vessel that now rests in the harbour.'

'The metal vessel?' Janaid asked.

Coran nodded. 'We call it the *Mobilis*. It was dilapidated, broken down, covered in debris and dirt. But it had been deliberately preserved. Someone had gone to great lengths to store it safely.'

'Store it?' Janaid asked.

'It was ancient,' Coran said. 'How old we can't tell. Certainly many hundreds of rounds. We didn't know what to make of it at first. There seemed to be no sails, no means to row or steer. But Mel had been there for rounds. She had worked out its secret.'

The senators looked at Mel.

'Well?'

'Coran is right,' Mel said. 'It is very old. It is completely made of metal throughout, immensely strong. It has sails of a sort, but they do not catch the wind. It catches something unseen …'

'A power we call 'tricity,' Coran explained. 'Within the vessel were instructions and guides, written in our language. Many were ruined with age, but enough remained for us to make repairs to it.'

'Preposterous!' Henoch exclaimed. 'Ships sail by the wind, everyone knows that. Senators, these are pirates. Abducting our people for their own purposes, twisting their minds with idle nonsense and preying on our ships. Whether Lacaille has grown in brightness in recent passes is moot. Our vessels have oft failed to return because someone has been pillaging them. Mystery solved! The perpetrators stand before us.'

'That ship lies within our harbour,' one of the other senators interjected. 'Willingly venturing within. Why come in at all if they are pirates? We all saw it. It clearly had a motive power beyond our understanding. A search of the vessel has revealed no evidence of plunder aboard, Henoch. Please, continue.'

Coran bowed his head. ''Tricity seems to be a force that emanates from Lacaille. It is our belief that our ancestors harnessed this energy for all manner of purposes, including that which drives the *Mobilis*.'

'So you have found an extraordinary vessel,' Janaid said. 'Why did you not return it to Amar immediately?'

'We found other things aboard the ship,' Coran said. 'Amongst them, a map.'

'A map? Of what?'

'Of our world,' Coran replied. 'Our ancestors called it "Esurio".'

The senators mumbled amongst themselves. The word was familiar, but it was seldom used, referring to something vast and incomprehensible.

'Describe this map,' Janaid asked.

'It shows Amar,' Coran said, 'and some way to the shaderight, the islands where we were shipwrecked, the Scattered Isles they are called. Beyond that ...'

'There is no beyond,' Henoch snapped. 'How long are we going to entertain this nonsense?'

'Honourable Henoch,' Janaid said. 'We are here to establish what has transpired. Let us hear the explanation before we cast judgement.'

Janaid indicated for Coran to continue.

'The map shows a great continent far to the shaderight,' Coran said. 'It is marked "Voren". Books that accompanied the map told stories of our ancestors living in the shadeward of this land, a place called Nireus.'

The senators' faces had gone pale.

'The stories also told of how an army of witches from the sunward realms, a land called Drayden, had assailed them, causing them to flee.' Coran said. 'They were exiled from Nireus, forced to flee before these witches, finally coming to Amar itself.'

The senators were muttering amongst themselves.

'As we feared ...'

'If this knowledge were to leak out ...'

'Must be suppressed! But it may already be too late ...'

Janaid stood up and the senators fell into silence.

He took a moment to compose himself.

'This knowledge is known only to the Senate,' he said, placing a hand against his forehead and rubbing it. 'You speak of events that have been consigned to history and locked away for the benefit of all.'

'You actually knew?' Coran said, his voice rising. 'I suspected the knowledge existed ... but you knew and suppressed it?'

'It is forbidden to speak of it,' Henoch said. 'The horrors of the past are best left buried.'

Janaid nodded. 'It is not taught, as well you know. Our past is ignominy, best left there … and yet … What did you do next?'

Coran stood tall. 'I took it upon myself to determine the truth of these legends.'

That was met with gasps from the Senators.

'You travelled across the sea to Voren?' Janaid managed to say.

Coran nodded. 'We did, we discovered much, and returned to warn the people of Amar based on what we found. There is great danger coming. Lacaille will flare, bringing fire and devastation …'

'You should not have returned,' Henoch said. 'To disturb long rounds of peace with this. Our people must be protected …'

'Protected, yes,' Mel interrupted. 'By knowing the truth. The flares are real and the witches are real, they remain and they still consider us their enemy. They seek us and they wish us harm. We can hide no longer!'

The senators were on their feet, gesticulating at each other. Janaid tried for long moments to restore order.

'Colleagues. Colleagues! Enough of this unseemly row.'

'And this ridiculous tale?' Henoch shouted. 'A map I will give you, and there is no doubt this vessel of yours has some remarkable capabilities. But witches? Magical powers? We are losing ships to piracy, nothing more. But this, this is all patent nonsense. Stories with which to scare us, to save their pitiful hides. I ask you. What is more likely? Flares and Witches, or common piracy? I say lock them up and throw away the key – sink that vessel and have done with it.'

The senators remained arguing. Despite the hubbub, Zoella stepped forward. She closed her eyes and raised a hand.

'Zoella, no,' Coran exclaimed.

Silence!

The crew of the *Mobilis* winced as the mental imperative jolted their minds, but they at least had some prior experience of Zoella's power. Three of the senators fell to their knees, one toppling over in shock.

Janaid and Henoch stared at each other before their attention turned to the girl before them. They had not noticed her before, now every gaze was upon her.

Her deep brown eyes stared back at them, her features resolute, demanding attention. Her arm was held out before her, her palm towards them. All heard the words that resonated from her mind.

Listen, and listen well. I am not of Amar, I am of a land far from here. These people mean you no harm and neither do I. But across the seas are those that do. They swore an oath to destroy your ancestors, and they are coming. Heed my words.

'What is this witchcraft …?' Henoch managed to whisper.

Zoella turned to regard him and he flinched back.

I am no witch. Those you call witches are the Priestesses of Drayden, your sworn enemy, they that persecuted your ancestors and forced you to flee here. They have pursued me. This power I use, this gift? This is their strength and something they seek to take from wherever they might find it.

'But this was so long ago,' Janaid said, his voice hushed. 'Generations have passed since we fled. It's ancient history. Surely they can bear us no grudge after all that time?'

They consider your destruction to have been ordained. Even now they seek a way across the sea. They destroyed my home city when we would not bow the knee to them.

'Then you have led this ancient foe back to our very doorstep!' Henoch raged.

Coran stepped up alongside Zoella.

'We came back to warn Amar of the flares and this imminent attack.' Coran raised his voice. 'You've already seen one such flare and the strange green lights in the sky?'

'Yes,' Henoch replied. 'The lights grew in the sky and caused much consternation …'

'They're called the Alisse,' Mel added. 'They too are a warning.'

'Some ships at sea were lost,' Janaid whispered. 'There were stories, but we assumed it was piracy. None have ventured out since, it's a crisis but not a …'

'Worse will come,' Coran said. 'All must be sheltered from them.'

'These flares will strike Amar?' another senator asked.

'Yes,' Coran answered. 'When dark spots cover Lacaille and the Alisse is seen, the flares are due once more. We have learnt much about both them and our ancient foe, but we must alert our people to our history, no more can we keep it quiet. History is coming back to haunt us!'

The senators looked dumbstruck. Zoella pushed the point home.

The priestesses believe that Lacaille is a goddess and that she herself has commanded your destruction. They believe the flares have come as a result of them not destroying you. That is why they will come.

'What must we do?' Janaid asked, his face ashen.

'We must prepare first against the flares, and then for an invasion,' Coran said. 'And tell the truth to everyone.'

Henoch was shaking his head.

'This knowledge is too dangerous to reveal,' he said. 'The people will panic, and deaths will result. Far better we supress this knowledge.' He cast a dark eye towards the crew of the *Mobilis*.

'The fishermen talk of nothing else,' Janaid said. 'They are scared and will not sail out any longer. Fish stocks will be depleted in mere stretches.'

'They're cowards,' Henoch replied. 'A few lost ships and they refuse to sail? Lacaille is calm, who is to say it won't remain so? As for these witches …' He glared at Zoella. 'One example is not evidence of an army preparing to attack. The sea lies between us and any force – how could they come in strength enough to lay siege to us? Amar has defences enough.'

Zoella concentrated once more, this time projecting the images she recalled of the attack on Viresia. The senators reeled back as their minds were filled with the sights of fire, soldiers dying and the huge reptilian dachs swooping about the beleaguered city.

All this will come to pass here if you don't make preparations.

There was a long silence before the senators began to confer in whispered conversations. Janaid turned back to them.

'You will be held under house arrest,' he said, 'until such time as we decide what to do with you.'

'You must act now,' Coran yelled. 'The flares …'

But guards had been summoned and the crew were marched out.

* * *

Meru sat, arms folded, looking out at Lacaille from the inside of his parents' residence in the city of Amar. Two guards were discreetly located outside to prevent him from leaving.

His mother, Hannah, sat opposite him, a drink of chai held in her hands.

'It is good to have you back,' she said.

Meru swallowed.

'We came back to warn everyone,' Meru said. 'But instead they've locked my friends up.'

'Meru, look at it from the senate's perspective,' Hannah said. 'You disappeared. We all thought you were dead. Then you arrive in a strange ship with a wild tale, consorting with criminals …'

'They're not criminals.'

'They've broken the law at the very least,' Hannah said. 'Two of those men are known thugs, convicted of brawling in the taverns …'

'You don't know them,' Meru said, turning to glare at her. 'Yes, they're rough, but they're good men.'

'And this captain,' Hannah continued. 'By his own admission he's sailed out to sea. You know that's a violation of rules. It's forbidden.'

'The rule is stupid,' Meru countered. 'The senate are deliberately hiding the truth from everyone. It's all been covered up because they're scared of dealing with it.'

'But the story is so fanciful … magic in faraway lands, surely it's all …'

'It's true, mother,' Meru said. 'All of it is true. Zoella and Ren are from those places. I've been there, seen the flares, seen the witches. They're real!'

Hannah stopped and took a sip of her chai. Meru huffed and looked away. She continued to look at him.

'I can see you believe it.'

Meru turned. 'But you think they've brainwashed me? Like father does? Why would they? Why would they come back here if not to warn Amar? Why come back at all and risk all this? It's because they're telling the truth.'

Hannah thought about it for a moment and then nodded.

'I will do what I can,' she said.

* * *

The crew of the *Mobilis* had been given quarters in the city. They were rather more civilised than the cells they had been held in, but they were not free to leave. Guards stood at the entrance to the residence they had been escorted to. Within, each had their own room, with servants on hand to provide for their needs.

Senator Janaid had advised them that the senate was discussing their revelations and would report back before the stretch was out. In the meantime it seemed all they could do was wait.

'Got to hand it to you young lady,' Fitch said, grinning at Zoella. 'You've got spirit. They might have killed you on the spot for showing what you did.' His grin faded. 'Let's hope it hasn't condemned us all to death for witchcraft.'

Zoella glared at Fitch. 'They were wasting time and they weren't listening.'

Coran smiled at her. 'You can be very convincing.'

'And a little bit scary too,' Mel added. 'Remind me not to get on your bad side.'

'More powerful than witches she is,' Ren said, grabbing hold of her hand. Zoella pulled him into a hug.

'I'm not sure of that,' Zoella said. 'But if my powers can be used to help, then they should be used.'

A heavy sounding bell tolled. All of them looked up as the front doors to the building were unlocked and swung open. Two guards stood there, flanking a third figure, who stood, shoulders slumped, between them.

They recognised him.

'Meru!' Mel called.

He walked in and the guards closed and locked the doors behind them. Meru looked up and managed to gaze at most of them before dropping his gaze. He couldn't hold Zoella's fierce glance.

'I guess … I owe you all an apology,' he said.

No one moved for a long moment.

'And a flamin' good one too,' Fitch snapped. 'Didn't tell us you were the son of a snuttin' senator, did you? Did it slip your mind? Did you think maybe they'd forget or something? You've put us through the fire because of your lies. They thought we'd abducted you! We could have been killed …'

'I'm sorry,' Meru flinched as Fitch berated him.

'Sorry ain't good enough, boy,' Fitch snapped, stalking towards him. 'I've a mind to take it out of your hide.'

'Fitch. Enough.'

Coran's voice was soft but arresting. Fitch backed away, grumbling under his breath. Coran turned his attention back to Meru.

'But you'd better explain yourself.'

Meru sighed and backed up against the wall, looking down at his feet.

'I … you've met my father I think. Senator Henoch. Henoch Farstone.'

'Charming fellow,' Coran said. 'Very welcoming.'

'He's always wanted me to follow in his footsteps,' Meru said. 'Be a senator like him. I was schooled for it, endless lessons in administration, figurings and numbers, stretch after stretch. I hated it, but I had to do it. Tests and checks, every stretch was study all stretch long. But I wanted to see what was beyond our city, beyond our land, wanted to do something that mattered. My father, he wouldn't allow it …'

'You ran away,' Coran said.

'I tried many times, but I was always caught and brought back,' Meru said. 'I got whipped and punished for it, but it didn't stop me. Then I came up with a plan. I learnt the arts of timekeeping from the guild, easy for me to gain access as a senator's son. One of the apprentices was booked for passage on a ship, but he was ill. I agreed to take his place. I took his place on the Bethany …'

'And got shipwrecked.'

'On my first voyage,' Meru said. 'Pretty unlucky. Then you found me and …' He looked up. 'It was adventure! It was everything I wanted. I should have told you, but I didn't think it would matter. I never knew what we'd find, all the things that would happen. When we were coming back, I wanted to say something, I just didn't know how. I should have told you. I'm sorry.'

Fitch snorted. 'We all knew you were lying anyway.'

Meru looked at Coran and Mel, who were both nodding.

'Your story didn't really add up,' Mel said. 'Probably would have done the same thing myself by the sound of it … your father …'

'Is a complete snut,' Coran finished with a smile.

'Whereas you're only mostly a snut,' Mel said. 'Come on.'

She held out her arms. Meru swallowed and walked across, allowing himself to be hugged.

'Lies never help much, Meru,' she said. 'Next time, come clean with us, yes? Crew's got to trust each other.'

To her surprise she found he was crying, sobbing in her embrace.

'I let you down,' he managed. 'All of you.'

'Scorchin' hell,' Fitch muttered. 'I think I preferred him when he was furlin' about …'

Mel glared at him, but Meru wiped at his eyes and stood up.

Coran held out his hand. 'Mel's right, no secrets in this crew. Understood?'

Meru took it. 'No secrets.'

Meru looked across at Zoella, who had remained silent throughout. Both Coran and Mel spotted the look.

'Time to get some food ready,' Mel said. Coran got up beside her.

Fitch frowned. 'We only just ate.'

Mel gestured to the doorway, by angling her head and giving Fitch a glare. Fitch rolled his eyes and stomped out, still muttering.

'Come on Ren, Daf, Creg,' Coran called. 'You can help too.'

Meru watched them go, dropping his gaze to the floor. The door closed, leaving him alone with Zoella.

There was a long moment of silence.

'At least you admit you lied to them,' Zoella said, breaking the silence, her voice sharp. 'Anything else you care to admit? Something about Kiri, perhaps?'

Meru took a deep breath and paced in a circle for a moment.

'I saw what she did,' he whispered. 'I saw how she killed. How she chased us, tried to capture us. All of it. I know what she's like ...'

'And?' Zoella voice remained sharp, edged by a tremble.

'When she caught me,' Meru managed. 'After the flying machine crashed, she had me tied up. She broke into my mind, read my thoughts ...'

'You've already told me this,' Zoella said. 'I offered to help, you turned me down.'

Meru winced. 'I know. But that's not all, there was something else. Something happened. I thought she was going to kill me. She had several chances to do so, but she didn't ... she couldn't. I ... Then I saved her life in the flare, she would have died ...'

Zoella's lip curled in distaste. 'You should have let her die. She's a beast, a murderer. She killed Ioric, Torin, Raga my carn. She killed Turgan and Guerrun. Who knows who else she has killed before and since?'

'It's not like that,' Meru argued back.

'How so?' Zoella demanded. 'They're dead, she's not. I can't believe you didn't take that chance ...'

'I couldn't kill her,' Meru said, his voice soft. Zoella stared at him, incredulous.

'Why not?' she cried.

'She was helpless,' Meru whispered. 'Injured after the flare. We'd fallen out of the sky when her dach was slain. We had to work together to survive. If I'd left her there she would have died.'

'You should have left her.' Zoella's voice was cold. 'I would have.'

'I almost did, she even wanted me to kill her.' Meru argued back. Zoella gasped in disbelief. 'We fought. I had my knife at her throat. But I'd learnt something about her power. When she entered my mind I could hear her thoughts, she could hear mine. There was fear and anger, but there was something else … gratitude, acceptance, the beginning of trust … I couldn't kill her, not in cold blood. I grabbed her hand … and I asked for a truce.'

Zoella stared at him.

'A truce? With that murderer?' she said, her voice cold. 'After what she did? Why Meru? Why?'

'I needed her to survive too. I was alone …'

'After how she killed? How could you even consider it …?'

'Zoella …'

'You should have slit her throat when you had a chance. Maybe Turgan and Guerrun would still be alive. Ever think of it like that?'

'It was Kiri who let us go,' Meru whispered. 'At the harbour in Nireus. She promised not to kill me … she let us both go. She stopped the priestesses. It was her.'

Zoella's jaw was clenched, her lips pursed.

'She only let us go so she could follow us to Amar,' Zoella said. 'So she can find us, so she can sense where we are. She is evil, Meru! She's tricked you, don't you see? She wanted the location of Amar and now she has it. She can probably sense where one or both of us is. She wants my power and she's committed to destroying all of this.' Zoella gestured around her.

'No …' Meru shook his head. 'I don't believe that.'

'How can you say that?' Zoella stared at him, incredulous. 'You've seen what she's done …'

'I sensed her thoughts,' Meru said. 'Heard them as clear as I'm speaking to you now. She couldn't lie to me, I couldn't lie to her. This is the truth, I know it is. She's not who you think she is. Yes she's killed, but she's never done it without reason. There is more to her …' Meru looked away for a moment.

Zoella's eyes widened in shock.

'Shades. You have … feelings for her? Oh … Meru …'

Zoella felt sick, the betrayal burning up inside her. Meru reached out towards her, but she recoiled, stumbling away. 'Get away from me.'

'She's been brought up to believe we're the enemy, taught how to fight and kill …'

Zoella backed away from him.

'She has killed everyone and everything I ever cared for,' Zoella said, her voice icy. 'If you harbour any sentiment for that beast of a woman, you are no friend of mine.'

'Zoella, don't …'

Zoella spoke over him, her voice shaking with the effort of forming words.

'Know this. If I get a chance, if the opportunity comes my way, be it dagger, sword, rope, bare hands or the power of my mind …' She shook her head. 'I will not hesitate.' Her expression was taut and brutal. Her hands were clenched in front of her. 'I will kill her.'

They stared at each other for a long moment.

'Zoella …'

Anger and upset overwhelmed her. She lashed out, slapping him hard across the cheek, sending him reeling back. She screamed out at him.

'No, get out of my sight. I never want to see you again!'

Zoella pushed past him and ran from the hall.

* * *

Zoella sought the emptiness of the room she'd been given. Her face was twisted in despair, her breath coming in great heaving gasps. She ran within, pulling the door closed behind her and backing up against it, sinking down until she was crouched up on the floor, her arms wrapped around her legs, curled up.

Then the tears came, hot and scalding, dripping down her cheeks. Sobs shook her and she wept, head resting on her knees.

How could you, Meru? How could you?

It stung. Her insides clenched and hurt. She could barely breathe now, her sobs making her gasp.

I saved you from Liana, I saved you from the ice and this is how you repay me?

His image came into her mind. How she'd met him in Viresia when he'd turned up out of nowhere, wandering into the city and escorted by the guards. Then later when he tried to defend her against Torin and then how he'd rescued her and Liana in his flying machine.

And then she got hold of him!

Zoella remembered the blast of emotion she had sensed in the frozen wastes of Drem. Kiri had been searching for them, pursuing them. Zoella had felt Kiri's rage, her aggression, but there had been something else too, a burning sense of …

Jealousy! She was jealous …

Zoella remembered how she had touched Meru's mind when she found him with Ren. He'd been in some kind of fever: insensible, delirious, writhing, his mind in terror.

I thought she'd tortured him, but what did she really do? Why be so jealous just because I had touched his mind?

As she thought about it there was flash of pain across her forehead.

He's mine, how dare you!

Zoella yelped in surprise, her vision tunnelling in around her. A vision flashed before her eyes. Astride a dach, mountains below, clouds whistling past, the air rushing past. A black-gloved hand clenching reins …

Zoella gasped in horror.

Kiri!

Zoella felt shock and surprise come back to her through the strange link, but it was severed before she was able to react to it. The mundane walls of her room came back into focus around her.

She was trembling with fright before anger lit within her and she projected her thoughts outwards, wrestling the connection back.

The images of the mountains and the clouds came back to her. Recognition flickered in her mind. Kiri's voice echoed in her head.

You!

Yes, me. Murderer.

How did you …?

What did you do to him? What did you do to Meru?

A flash of feelings crackled over the link. First there was amusement, then worry and concern over secrets revealed, before a hot sense of desire burned through. That was extinguished by a blast of jealousy.

He's mine. Mine! Leave him alone.

The ferocity of it startled Zoella, but she faced it down.

What did you do to him? Answer me.

Then Zoella could sense intense concentration, a feeling of the communication between them being honed and directed. She realised what Kiri was trying to do.

Trying to locate me!

No!

Zoella severed the link, berating herself for what she had done.

There was a soft knock at the door.

'Go away!'

'Zoella,' the soft voice came back from the other side. 'It's me, it's Mel. Let me in.'

Zoella didn't respond, but she didn't object when the door opened and Mel let herself in.

'What's happened?' Mel said, coming across and kneeling beside her. 'Zoella, what's wrong?'

Zoella sobbed again.

'Hey,' Mel said, pulling her into an embrace. 'Was it Meru? Honestly that boy. What's he done now?'

Zoella wasn't able to answer.

'Still arguing?' Mel asked.

Zoella nodded.

'Was he lying again?' Mel asked.

Zoella shivered and shook her head.

'No … worse. He was … he was telling the truth,' Zoella stuttered between the sobs. 'And there's something … something else I need …'

'Hey, hey,' Mel chastised her. 'One thing at a time. Come on …'

Shouts came to their ears and there was a sharp knocking on the door to her room.

'Zoella? Mel! You in there?'

It was Coran's voice.

'We're here,' Mel said, raising her voice. 'Coran, this is not a good time …'

The door opened and Coran burst in, he looked flustered. 'Where have you two been … oh … I'm sorry, but we need you both.'

'Why?' Mel demanded.

'Come quickly!'

'What is it?'

'Trouble,' Coran replied and left.

Zoella saw Mel look at her, she wiped at her blotchy eyes.

'I'll be all right,' Zoella said. 'We'd better go.'

Mel nodded and helped her to her feet.

* * *

Mel and Zoella ran down through the house and out through the front door. The rest of the crew of the *Mobilis* were stood in the courtyard of their residence, looking up. In the streets beyond, the residents of Amaris were milling around in the streets, pointing upwards. Some were yelling, others crying.

'What is …?' Zoella asked, still wiping her eyes with the back of her hand. Her vision was blurry.

Ren ran across to her, dragging her forward before pointed up. 'Look! See!'

Zoella looked up. Lacaille was a great golden orb in a clear sky as ever, but her heart lurched at what she saw. Dark stains were splattered across the familiar disk.

The darkness again!

'Oh no,' she said. Her heart thumped in her chest. 'Flares are coming.'

Even as she watched the blotches were changing shape, growing and writhing before her eyes.

She saw the senators from the stretch before had gathered at the entrance to their residence. Coran was already talking to them, with Meru alongside him. As she came closer she heard Coran talking to Janaid.

'What must be done?' Janaid said. His face was pale.

'You must heed the warnings,' Zoella said. Coran, Janaid and Meru turned to look at her. 'You must get people under cover and secure as much stuff as you can.'

'The whole city? That's impossible ...'

'Zoella is right,' Coran said. 'She was caught in one of these flares on the mainland. Tell us.'

Zoella looked Janaid in the eye. 'There is a blast of fierce heat which can set fires burning all over the place. Anything that can burn will burn. Then there is a blue light which stings the skin without heat. It gives you a painful rash if you are caught in it. I saw my land ablaze, thousands were killed because they were caught in the open.'

'You mean, the whole island could be hit?' Janaid asked.

Zoella nodded.

'I saw it too,' Meru said. Zoella noticed he stood away from her, not making eye contact. 'She's right, fire consumes anything in the open.'

Janaid now looked shocked. 'How long do we have?'

Zoella looked up at Lacaille. The writhing darkness was growing on its face.

'Chimes,' she said. 'A stretch if we're fortunate.'

Janaid blinked.

'You must act now!' Coran said. 'The citizens, ships in the harbour, stockpile water and food in safe places ...'

Janaid nodded. 'Yes, yes ... will you help me? Such a crisis ...'

'Of course!' Coran said. 'Set us free and we'll help, that's why we're here. It's why we came back.'

Janaid looked at them. 'Then you're freed. I'll clear the legalities with the senate later. We must save the city!'

CHAPTER SEVEN

Daine, Capital of Drayden

Round 2307, Third pass

Kiri had woken long before the first chimes of the stretch. She took her kai with her, the thick metal weapon reassuring in her grip, and made her way down to the dormitories beyond the temple. Already she had gathered together a small pack of clothes, food and water, intent on keeping her promise. Nerina would be expecting her after breakfast, she would have to hurry.

The dormitories were quiet as she suspected, but two guards were on duty. Both women looked up as she approached.

'Priestess Kiri.'

She nodded in acknowledgement.

'I have need of a servant this morning to assist me with errands,' Kiri replied primly. 'One of those Scallian captives will do.'

'I will retrieve one for you, priestess.' one guard said.

'I will choose myself,' Kiri replied. 'My needs are specific.'

The guards exchanged a knowing look. Whilst Rihanna had an appetite for men, Kiri knew many of the other priestesses preferred the company of women. The docile and compliant behaviour of mindless young women who'd had their gifts torn away appealed to many of the priestesses. Kiri couldn't help but repress a shudder.

The guards didn't stop her though, seeing nothing untoward in her request. Kiri made her way within, stretching out her senses in an attempt to find the Scallian girl she had spared the previous stretch.

Gemma? Gemma!

It didn't take long. The girl's fear was palpable. Kiri could sense the despair and the homesickness and then the faint pang of surprise and hope that radiated out from somewhere nearby at her insistent call.

Kiri found the room and opened the door. The room inside was bare other than two simple wooden beds. Upon one Gemma was sitting upright, her thin face pale, her dark eyes wide. She was dressed in the same simple linen frock as before.

'Quickly now,' Kiri whispered. 'Walk before me. Do not make eye contact, do not speak. Just plod along as if that is all you can do.'

Kiri could see the girl was trembling, but she got to her feet and did as she was told.

To the left …

They made their way back along the corridor and the exit where the guards remained standing.

Say nothing!

'This one will do,' Kiri announced. 'I will be keeping her for some time. Drudgery and cleaning for the most part.'

'The others are being sold at the fifth chime,' the guard replied. 'Auctioned off to the wealthy houses.'

'The spoils of war,' Kiri said, fixing a false grin on her face.

Condemned to a life of slavery for the rest of their rounds, without the will to resist. Is this truly Lacaille's will? For certain the priestesses should rule, but should our rule not benefit everyone rather than just taking for our own needs and wants?

Kiri placed a hand on Gemma's shoulder and marched her forwards. Once they were out of sight of the guards Kiri turned aside.

'I'm taking you to the eyrie,' Kiri said. 'We will take a dach and I will fly you to the border of Scallia. There are clothes, food and drink in this pack. From there you must take your own chances. Reach Viresia if you can. Do you understand?'

Gemma nodded. Kiri could feel the sense of hope and astonishment from her.

'You spoke true …'

Kiri nodded. 'I keep my word.'

'But why?' Gemma whispered. 'Why are you doing this?'

Kiri pondered that for a moment. It was a good question. What would Nerina do if she discovered all this? There was no time to debate it. She felt sure it was the right thing to do. She couldn't save all of them, but she could save this one.

'I can tell no one,' Kiri said, with a smile. 'One stretch I will return and you will know why. Remember my name. Kiri.'

Gemma's face betrayed her puzzlement.

'Come!' Kiri said. 'We must be quick.'

The eyrie was a large timber-framed building set away from the temple of the priestesses on the opposite edge of the plaza. Kiri led Gemma around the edge of the open spaces, moving between the buildings in order to reach it without being seen.

The entrance was an unassuming furler wood door, but as they entered Kiri heard Gemma's gasp of surprise at the scale of the interior. She looked around her once again, remembering how she had first gazed upon it herself.

In form it was akin to a vast herg stable, with the floor covered in dried reeds from the river, which were replaced on a regular schedule. Rather than pens for hergs though, the building vaulted upwards with perches arranged in a spiralling circular fashion around a large open central space. Upon the perches sat the dachs.

Kiri felt Gemma's terror at the sight of the big winged creatures.

They were imposing creatures. In the wild they would hunt hergs, their talons able to rend and grasp them, sweeping them into the air before the unfortunate prey would be ripped to shreds by the fierce jaws. Teeth there were aplenty and many an adversary had found their death in such a way.

Like King Ioric of Scallia … my uncle, killed by my own lost dach … Shanza.

Kiri hadn't known. How could she?

Most of the dachs were dozing. Like all the creatures on Esurio, none of them slept in the way that people did, something Kiri had always wondered about. One spread its dark green leathery wings as it caught sight of them. Kiri gave a short whistle and it left its perch and dropped down to the ground before them, the reeds rustling around them as it landed. Gemma retreated, cowering behind Kiri as the great beast undulated its neck and brought its head close to sniff at them.

'Don't be afraid,' Kiri said, reaching out to touch the dach's head.

How I miss Shanza, but she gave her life to save me in the flares ...

Kiri pulled Gemma around throwing some dach-leather riding gear at her.

'Get changed, quickly.'

Gemma did as she was told. The dach lowered its neck and Kiri hoisted Gemma up.

'Sit back at the neck joint saddle,' she called before jumping up herself, seating herself behind Gemma. The girl leant back against her. Kiri recalled the last time she had sat like this.

With Meru before me ...

The familiar sense of lust grew in her once more and she had to shove it aside.

Fly!

The dach swept its wings in the crucial first down stroke and leapt into the air. Gemma couldn't repress a screech of horror as the dach surged upwards. Kiri felt the girl tense in front of her.

The building fell away around them, the dach making for the central opening far above. In moments they were through and out into the warm air. It was a cloudless sky, Lacaille a blazing arc of fire to the sunward.

The dach circled twice, gaining altitude all the while, before turning and heading into the shadeward.

* * *

Two figures stepped from the shadowed overhangs of the eyrie, moving into the light as the sound of the dach's wings faded into the distance. The first was dressed all in black, her skin pale, almost wraith-like, her hair dominated by a silver streak all tied up in an intricate tiara. The second was taller and rather more plump, dressed in a dark maroon gown. Her hair was a bright auburn red, her face drawn into a frown.

'So,' Nerina said, looking upwards. 'It seems you were right, Rihanna. Kiri has her own schemes and ploys.'

'I'm sorry to bring you ...'

'Shhh,' Nerina said. 'It was right of you to tell me. It is better that I know. I'm only sorry that she's done this to you.'

'I thought we were friends now,' Rihanna said. 'But all this time ...'

'Kiri thinks only of herself,' Nerina replied. 'A lifetime of living in the gutters has shaped her mind thus. Don't be hard on yourself. This is not the first time a hand of friendship has been extended, only for her to cast it aside.'

'Where has she gone?' Rihanna asked. 'That was the Scallian girl you gave her to tear, why should she ...?'

'She is concealing things from you, from us,' Nerina said, her voice catching. 'From me.'

Rihanna looked at Nerina in surprise. 'High priestess?'

Nerina looked away, holding an arm up. 'I'm ... I'm sorry. It's just ... I've tried so hard with that girl. After Charis died I took her in, tried to guide her and ...' She shook her head.

Rihanna scowled. 'And this is how she repays you ... repays all of us, with lies, concealments and falsehoods!'

'I've given her so much, perhaps I indulged her too far,' Nerina said. 'It's my fault she's become so wayward.'

'No!' Rihanna cried. 'Kiri's always been selfish, thinking only of herself. She uses people to get her own way. It's her fault, not yours.'

'I took over as her mentor,' Nerina said. 'The responsibility lies with me.'

Rihanna shook her head. 'You can't blame yourself. Kiri keeps secrets, I know one of them. She swore me not to tell ...'

'And so you shouldn't,' Nerina said.

'I must. It's important that you hear it,' Rihanna said. 'I know why she is so keen to get to Amar, and what her claim about the Obelisk is all about. I should have told you, but Kiri made me swear ...'

'Amar?' Nerina asked.

'The boy we found at Viresia, the one with the flying machine,' Rihanna said. 'Kiri interrogated him, forced her way into his mind. But she was careless, she ...'

'Forged a birther's bond with him,' Nerina said, nodding. 'I had my suspicions. That would explain much. She's driven by her longing for him?'

'It's burning her up,' Rihanna said. 'She can't control it. She'll do anything to get her way.'

Nerina thought for a long moment.

'Will you do something for me, Rihanna?' Nerina asked. 'Of all the priestesses I have you're the only one I can trust with something this important.'

'I will do your bidding, high priestess!' Rihanna said. 'Of course!'

Nerina looked upwards at the blue sky visible in the opening above.

'Follow Kiri,' Nerina said. 'Find out what she is doing with this Scallian girl. Be stealthy, do not be seen. Kiri must not suspect.'

Rihanna nodded. She raised an arm and gave a mental order. A dach flew to her, landing before her and bowing its neck low. Rihanna ran her hand across its head, her eyes narrowing with intent before she vaulted aboard the winged beast.

'Go now, report back when you can,' Nerina instructed. The dach launched itself upwards. Nerina watched until it was lost from sight.

The sad and heartbroken expression on her face dissolved, replaced by a wry grin.

'Too easy,' she muttered to herself. 'It seems you are the only one who is a challenge, Kiri. You alone who have been able to keep secrets from me.' The grin faded into a frown. 'But I will know what they are, young one, I will know.'

* * *

The mountains on the borders of Scallia were rising up around her. The air was chill at this altitude, laced with thin clouds. Kiri could see the edge of the shadeward forests that she knew ran almost to the city of Viresia. She had flown these skies many times now.

At a mental instruction the dach began to descend, performing lazy banks and turns to reduce its height. Kiri spied a clearing and the dach made for it, rearing up as it landed, clawed feet outstretched. Dust billowed around them.

Kiri jumped down and gestured for Gemma to do the same.

'I've come as far as I dare. You must make your own way now.'

Gemma nodded, shedding the heavy riding gear. Kiri handed her a sack of provisions.

'Be quick, it is only a few stretches march to Viresia from here,' Kiri said. 'Hide in the forests and don't let yourself be seen in the open until you are close.'

'Thank you,' Gemma replied. 'For everything.'

'Just stay alive,' Kiri said. 'That is the only thanks I need. Beware the priestesses. Don't use your gift if you can. It will only bring attention to you.'

'But what of you?' the woman asked.

'Do not fear for me,' Kiri replied.

Gemma hoisted the sack. 'Why?' she asked. 'Why did you save me?'

Kiri licked her lips.

'For Scallia.'

Gemma frowned.

'There's no time to explain,' Kiri said, gesturing for her to go. 'I am of Scallia myself. Quickly! We may have been followed, run and hide.'

'Thank you then, Kiri of Scallia! I won't forget this.'

Kiri watched as Gemma plunged into the shadewood. The shades were thick and dense here, but with Lacaille's light behind her she'd be able to follow her own shadow in the right direction.

Kiri of Scallia! I have done what I can. Now I must return before I am missed.

She mounted her dach and with an imperious instruction the mighty beast took back to the sky.

* * *

Another dach descended through the mountains, gliding down from where it had been perched moments before. It landed in the same clearing that Kiri had just departed, folding its wings and bowing its neck to allow its rider to dismount.

Rihanna leapt down, grabbing her kai from the harness and looking around the clearing.

She had found a rocky ledge, not far away, from where she had been able to see what Kiri was doing. She saw her land and leave the Scallian girl behind before flying away once more.

She closed her eyes and concentrated for a moment, seeking communication. The answer was swift.

You have news?

Nerina's mental voice was unmistakeable. Rihanna responded.

Kiri dropped the Scallian girl just over the border and then left. She's flying sunwards now, I assume she's heading back to you.

You have not been seen?

No, I stayed far off until Kiri departed.

The girl?

Ahead in the forest somewhere.

Find her. We must understand why Kiri would go to such lengths to rescue her.

What should I do after I find out?

There was a flicker of mirth across the connection.

The girl has a small gift. Take it, enjoy it as your reward for your service. Then kill her, there must be no witnesses.

I understand.

I will wait to hear from you.

* * *

Kiri turned her dach about until they were heading sunwards once more, the dach's wings flapping as the beast strove to gain altitude over the mountains. Before her Lacaille's massive orb dominated the sky, serene and …

She gasped.

A black stain … another sign!

It was creeping around the edge of the great sphere of light, a cankerous mass of writhing darkness. Kiri had seen it before and knew it for what it was.

Lacaille grows angry once more, we have not completed the task appointed. I must go to Taloon, and hence to Amar. Time is running out!

At her mental command the dach pushed harder, straining at the air, its lithe body undulating as all of its muscles joined in the task of flying as fast as it could.

It was then that something tingled on the edge of her mind. It felt as if one of the priestesses were trying to probe her thoughts. She looked around, but she and the dach were alone in the sky.

How can that be?

The feeling would not go away. It was as if she was being watched. It was edged with the familiar metallic sense of power that accompanied the gift. Kiri kept looking about her, expecting something, but not sure what it was.

Then a face came to her. She recognised it straight away.

Zoella!

Her image formed in Kiri's mind. Her soft expression, brown eyes and wavy hair. Strange feelings coursed through her; worry, concern, upset and hurt. The feelings were strong, impossible to ignore.

Why? Why is she …?

Another face, another she recognised.

Meru!

Kiri's feelings surged in response, unbidden. There was nothing she could do about them.

She's been with him! What's she doing? Concern for him? No ...

Kiri caught sight of a room, dim and shuttered, a table, a bed ...

Fury consumed her, her anger spiralling out of control.

He's mine, how dare you!

Then it was dashed away, the vision fading in moments. Kiri clutched at the reins to steady herself, clenching her thighs against the dach below.

Before she had a chance to recover, the vision came back, pounding at her, the metallic sensation in her mouth and nostrils, pungent and overpowering. She reeled from the intensity of it, almost losing her grip on the reins. Her own fury was met with anger from the other end of the connection. Zoella's face appeared once more, her gaze determined, her lips pursed. This was no longer the gentle maid of the Scallian household she'd encountered before.

How did she do this? To communicate with me from wherever she is ... to be able to find me ... I can't do that! Her powers ...

You!

Kiri could not help her feelings of astonishment from leaking across the connection. Zoella would know that too. It was impossible to keep secrets across the mental link.

Yes, me. Murderer.

The anger and ferocity was not what she had expected. Brief flashes of images flickered between them. The death of King Ioric, the battle with Torin ... the old carn that had leapt upon her. The anger and bitterness were sharp.

I was only defending myself! And Torin deserved what he got after what he did to Charis and I!

She fought to transmit her own images. Images of Torin lying about the treaty. Images of the death of Charis, images of her own pain and the crossbow bolt that had impaled her hand.

Her thoughts turned to the question dominating her thoughts.

How did you ...?

But her own questioning was swept aside. Kiri winced under the mental barrage as Zoella's rage echoed in her head, demanding answers.

What did you do to him? What did you do to Meru?

Kiri almost laughed.

As if I would tell you …

Then she realised that even thinking of the denial was foolish. Perhaps she'd already revealed too much. The thought of Meru lit up a different part of her mind and she struggled to damp it down. Too late, the desire and lust blossomed once more. Kiri couldn't help it.

She's been near him, close to him, talking to him, lying to him about me!

Now jealousy blistered into her mind.

He's mine. Mine! Leave him alone.

Kiri felt the link flicker for a moment under the tumult of feelings from both sides, but Zoella didn't relent.

What did you do to him? Answer me.

Kiri's mind was working a few steps ahead.

If this link is so strong, maybe I can use it to my advantage!

She concentrated, trying to determine the source of the connection. She could sense the power. Her head turned left toward the sunright. The distance came to her, and she looked. It was far beyond the horizon, but she knew.

No!

Zoella must have realised what she was doing. The link crackled and fell apart. Kiri was left alone on the back of her dach once more, flying through the azure skies of Esurio.

Kiri was gasping for breath, but elation surged through her. Maybe Zoella hadn't found her answers, but she had.

Amar. I know where it is!

* * *

Rihanna stretched out her thoughts. The faint sense of the girl was ahead in the shades, less than a mark ahead. She was gaining on her. Rihanna slipped between the shade trunks, running on the soft muddy ground. The terrain was dropping towards a river, she could hear the noise of the water ahead.

There!

The Scallian girl was walking down the bank, looking for a way across. The river was fast flowing and deep enough that wading would be dangerous. Rihanna, concealed behind a shade, watched her for a few moments. It would be easy enough, there was no way the girl could escape.

Rihanna stepped out, twirling her kai.

The girl took a moment to notice her. Rihanna felt the fear, heard the sharp screech of dismay and saw the terrified expression on the girl's face.

To her credit, the girl fled without a pause. She dropped the pack she carried and ran away as fast as she could. Rihanna smiled and stretched out her hand.

In her mind she could feel the girl's muscles straining, her heart pounding, the feel of her feet on the banks, the breath in her lungs. It wouldn't take much.

Rihanna clenched a fist.

The girl cried out in pain as cramp stole up her thigh. She stumbled and fell, rolling into the tall rushes at the water's edge. By the time she'd recovered Rihanna had closed the gap, standing over her with her kai ready.

The girl scrambled away, but then the kai was at her throat.

'Don't move,' Rihanna said. 'I'll make this painless.'

'Please, don't hurt me!' the girl whimpered. 'Please …'

Rihanna rolled her eyes and then stretched out her hand, palm outwards, seeking the girl's mind.

The girl's howl of fear faltered on her lips as Rihanna suppressed it.

Who are you?

Gemma … my name is Gemma … please!

Why did Kiri rescue you?

I don't … I don't know …

Rihanna's grip on her mind clamped tighter.

Why did Kiri rescue you?

Gemma's thoughts were a whirl, confused and hard to read. It seemed she didn't really understand either. Rihanna pulled at her memories, forcing her to play back events in her mind. Gemma winced as she recalled what had happened.

Rihanna could see Kiri's familiar face in Gemma's memory and pursued it. Kiri was talking …

'Be quick, it is only a few stretches march to Viresia from here,' Kiri said. 'Hide in the forests and don't let yourself be seen in the open until you are close.'

'Thank you,' Gemma replied. 'For everything.'

'Just stay alive,' Kiri said. 'That is the only thanks I need. Beware the priestesses, don't use your gift if you can. It will only bring attention to you.'

'But what of you?' Gemma asked.

'Do not fear for me,' Kiri replied.

Then Gemma asked the question Rihanna was looking for. She clenched Gemma's thoughts even tighter, mindless of the screams from her as her memories were wrenched open.

'Why?' Gemma asked. 'Why did you save me?'

Rihanna saw Kiri lick her lips.

'For Scallia. There's no time to explain,' Kiri said, gestured. 'I am of Scallia myself.'

The memories came to an end. Rihanna released her mental grip.

Kiri is a Scallian? How can that be? She's from the slums of Drayden. How could she possibly be from Scallia? She fought the Scallians! She really is keeping secrets from us all, the lying bitch!

Rihanna straightened, trying to assimilate the information.

She looked back down. Gemma was lying in the reeds, gasping for breath and clutching at her head, moaning and whimpering.

No need to prolong this any further.

The girl still had some presence of mind. As Rihanna released her thoughts, Gemma staggered to her knees, crawled, staggered up and ran. Before Rihanna could stop her the girl had thrown herself into the raging torrent of the river. Rihanna tried to grasp hold of her mind, but the girl was sucked under the rapids and disappeared. Rihanna ran down the river bank trying to locate her, but there was no sign.

Drowned most like.

She cursed, pacing back and forth for a moment. She threw out her senses, but there was no sign of the Scallian girl. Rihanna walked back towards the forest edge where she had encountered her. The pack she had dropped lay in the reeds. Rihanna looked through it; it contained clothes, food and water.

As good as dead out here without this.

Satisfied, she concentrated, casting her thoughts outwards once again. The answer was swift.

You found the girl?

I did.

And?

Kiri rescued her because she was Scallian.

But, why? Of course the girl was Scallian ... we all know that ...

Not the girl ... Kiri herself!

There was a long pause in the mental connection between herself and Nerina.

Kiri is Scallian? How can this be? Charis found her in the slums here in Drayden!

I don't know ...

There was another pause.

You've done well, Rihanna. Return home now. I must consider carefully what to do next.

The mental connection dropped. Rihanna smiled to herself.

Yes, you must. And so must I.

* * *

Kiri had returned to the eyrie, seeing to the dach and discarding her riding gear. It was the first chime, with luck no one would have noticed her absence. She went to her room and changed into her travelling gear and then walked to the temple.

The guards allowed her within. It was still early and thus quiet.

She walked down the familiar corridors, enjoying the bright light of Lacaille that was spread about the interior by the intricately positioned mirrors. She passed the doorway which led into the room in which she had once rested, just after she had nearly been stoned to death.

She paused, thinking for a moment. Then she pushed open the door and went inside, closing it behind her.

The room was as she remembered it, the bed with its tapestry-like decorations of Lacaille, the desk with the mirror in which she'd first seen her true reflection, even the brush she remembered was still there.

Without knowing why she sat down and looked at herself once again.

The face that looked back was different now. Before, she had been gaunt and thin, her body only a hair's-width from starvation. Many rounds of good food and exercise had nourished her. She looked healthy now, her face fuller, with her bones less prominent. Her hair was now cut in the manner of the priestesses, the right side grown long and the left side shaved down to the scalp. The triangular pendant hung from her neck, glittering in the faint light from the window.

I was just an only then, now I'm a priestess. I swore an oath to Drayden … I swore to defend it, swore to fight for it and, if necessary, die for it. I have done for Scallia what I can … for now, my loyalty lies here. It is what Charis would have wanted.

The memory of her old mentor almost brought tears into her eyes. But that was another vow she had made. She remembered the words.

No longer the healer. No longer! I say goodbye now, Charis. I loved you, but love has no place in these times. I will shed no more tears for you until this task is finished.

She took a deep breath.

Amar, and then this Obelisk …

'I am chosen,' she murmured to herself. 'I am special. I will see this task done.'

There was a twinge in her mind, a faint metallic taste on her lips.

Rihanna!

Kiri?

Yes, I'm here.

It has gone as we planned. Our little act seems to have worked!

They believe our friendship broken and that we hate each other again?

Yes. My mother behaved exactly as you said she would. Nerina took me aside immediately, as you suggested I revealed the secret about your boy from Amar …

Kiri smiled.

Well done! Nerina will trust you again now. I will be sent to Taloon this stretch I'm sure, but we can stay in touch. We must find out what Nerina and your mother are trying to do …

There was a pause before Rihanna answered. Kiri sent a question.

Was there something else?

No, sorry, just thinking! Be careful.

I will.

The mental connection faded. Kiri took a deep breath before getting to her feet and walking out, closing the door behind her.

She strode down the corridor, her kai in her hand, clicking on the marble flooring in time with her steps.

* * *

Nerina waited in the meeting hall of the priestesses. Kiri was due any moment as she had requested the previous stretch.

And you have been busy already, haven't you, young one?

Nerina paced about the hall with measured steps. Rihanna's information had been interesting enough, but not everything had been revealed, just tantalising clues as to what was motivating Kiri.

So you're from Scallia, you admitted that. How did you find that out? Who told you of this?

Nerina turned the thoughts over in her head. Kiri had been secretive ever since the attack on Viresia, and more so since the encounters in Nireus.

What did you find out? And what do you plan?

Perhaps Merrin was right, perhaps she should take Kiri's gift, right here and now. Rihanna's revelation of how Kiri had defied her instructions was sufficient justification in terms of the law.

But Kiri's revelation about being chosen by the Obelisk prevented that. There was too much support for her amongst the priestesses. Whatever Nerina did, she had to retain her own standing. Kiri was in a unique position. She had no family, no friends that could be leveraged to force her hand.

That leverage lies elsewhere. And I can encourage it ...

Nerina smiled, a plan forming in her head.

The door swung open. Kiri stood in the entrance, her kai clutched in her right hand. Nerina could see she still wore the black glove on her left.

'We have no need of sparing practice this stretch,' Nerina said. 'You will not need your kai.'

Kiri nodded and placed the weapon aside before walking into the hall across the coloured tiles underfoot. Her stance was proud and erect, confident and assured.

She knelt before Nerina.

'High priestess.'

'Rise, young one,' Nerina said. 'We have much to discuss.'

Nerina saw a muscle twitch in Kiri's face, but she said nothing.

'You must depart for Taloon immediately,' Nerina said. 'Your task is to gain their agreement to ally with us in an attack on Amar. Accompany this Vandare back to his home and make the demand of the King himself.'

'I understand, high priestess,' Kiri replied. 'If they refuse?'

'Then you must return here,' Nerina said. 'And we will take what we need from them.'

'We could do that now,' Kiri said. 'And save ourselves the trouble.'

Nerina nodded. 'We could, but fighting to sunright whilst our shaderight borders are yet to be secured does not seem advisable. Let us try diplomacy first. Charis taught you much about that, and what to be on the lookout for.'

Kiri looked away for a moment, before nodding.

'I will make sure they join us,' Kiri said.

'Excellent,' Nerina replied. 'And then we can proceed to Amar itself. Time is pressing once more. Lacaille grows impatient.'

'I have seen the dark spots growing once more. The flares will come soon.'

'You must make haste indeed,' Nerina said. 'But it seems to me you have more than one reason to finish the task appointed.'

Kiri frowned and Nerina watched, amused, as the colour drained out of her face.

'I …'

Nerina laughed. 'Don't tell me I can't sense a birther's bond when it is under my nose, young one.'

Kiri swallowed.

'It … it was an accident,' Kiri said. 'I didn't mean to …'

'What is done is done,' Nerina replied. 'I know how hot it burns within.'

'I would undo it if I could,' Kiri said, her voice unconvincing.

'No. Use it,' Nerina said. 'Let that fire within you motivate you to take Amar. He will be your reward if you succeed. When you are victorious, you can bring him home as a spoil of war. I'm sure you'll find a use for him then.'

Kiri nodded. Nerina saw her take a deep breath and the colour returned to her cheeks, there was no mistaking the feeling of lust that emanated from the girl. Rihanna had been right.

'And then,' Nerina said. 'The quest for the Obelisk itself.'

'I have heard nothing else since,' Kiri said. 'I have no direction.'

'I suspect we must complete the task appointed first,' Nerina said.

'Perhaps Lacaille herself is testing you, seeing if you are worthy to undertake that greater task.'

'I will devote myself to this.'

Nerina paused for a moment, taking her customary walk around. Kiri waited as Nerina completed her footsteps.

Now we will see.

'Perhaps we may need other compensations for the King of Taloon,' Nerina said. 'We might offer gifts to make him think more highly of us.'

Kiri looked up. 'What do you mean?'

'Vandare tells me he has an eye for women of class and distinction,' Nerina said. 'He has many wives. You would do well to make yourself aware of all their customs. Vandare seems quite knowledgeable, for a man. It appears that in Taloon the women are sickeningly subservient.'

'None here would endure such an insult,' Kiri said. 'None amongst the priestesses!'

'Indeed not,' Nerina said. 'Perish the thought. But we have one amongst us we could send, surplus to requirements now ...'

Kiri's eye's widened. 'You don't mean ...?'

'Another spoil of war,' Nerina said. 'Liana, the Scallian Queen. She retains enough wit to be bedded by this King, and her beauty is without question, no?'

'I suppose ...'

'And without her gift she is useless to us,' Nerina said. 'And Scallians are ours to do with as we wish, aren't they?'

'Yes, high priestess.'

'Then take her, offer her to the King of Taloon if he will have her. She can serve us best by cementing an alliance with Taloon.'

Nerina saw Kiri swallow, but she made no further objection.

'So,' Nerina finished. 'Will you go, make an ally of those of Taloon and dispatch Amar as Lacaille directs?'

Kiri gave the traditional response.

'I will see it done.'

'Good, I know you will,' Nerina said. 'With the alliance with Taloon secured we can venture across the sea and put an end to these flares forever. You will stand mighty in the ranks of the priestesses with such a success.'

'I wish only to serve you,' Kiri replied.

Is that true, young one? We shall see!

CHAPTER EIGHT

Amaris, Capital of Amar

Round 2307, Third pass

The lethargic administration still took precious chimes to stir, and Coran had to lose his temper more than once to get them moving. Runners were dispatched with messages, riders on hergs were sent out towards the other townships and villages around the island. The warning was stark and the instructions terse; secure water and food, take shelter in stone buildings or caves and carry with you whatever essentials you could save, avoid the 'blue light' of Lacaille and wait until the firestorm passes before venturing out.

The crew of the *Mobilis* were much in demand explaining their warning again and again to the various authorities within the city, overseeing the preparations, giving advice, whilst all the while watching the darkness grow upon the face of Lacaille.

'Get the streets swept clean, anything that can burn must be cleared or moved underground wherever possible,' Coran instructed. 'Zoella, Mel, Ren, you help me organise emergency housing for the citizens in the shadeward side of the city, we can use the city itself as a shield against the heat.'

Mel nodded. Zoella pulled Ren alongside her.

'You can help me,' she said.

'Meru, Fitch, Daf and Creg, get yourself down to the harbour,' Coran said, gesturing towards the docks. 'Strip all the ships of their sails, splash their decks with water and fill their bilges as high as you can without sinking them. Let's hope we can keep them cool enough to stop them catching fire.'

The crew dispersed. Meru paused for a moment.

'Zoella …'

Zoella looked at him, pursed her lips and shook her head. She turned away.

'Come on boy.' Fitch yelled. 'Work to be done.'

Meru sighed and left.

'I know he's hurt you,' Mel said to Zoella. 'But don't leave it too long to fix things up.'

'I don't want anything to do with him,' Zoella replied, her voice hard. She snatched up some packing crates and started hefting them. 'Ren, give me a hand with this.'

'Zoella …'

'No,' Zoella snapped, glaring at Mel. 'He's made his decision, and I don't want to talk about it. We've got work to do.'

She gestured upwards. Above them, growing like a canker across the face of Lacaille, the dark spots grew, their ominous presence expanding each and every spell of the chime.

Coran set them to work, each organising an aspect of sorting out the chaos around them. Hundreds of folks were being crammed into the administrative buildings and more were flooding in from the surrounding countryside. They worked, chime after chime and still more came.

'So many people,' Mel said, 'And little enough space for them all.'

Zoella nodded, looking at the crowds of people still thronging the streets below. They were carrying packages, baskets of food, barrels of water. All the provisions were being carried inside.

She could see Coran talking with the senators, issuing instructions. She recognised Henoch, Meru's father. She could see the family likeness, though Henoch was grey haired and perhaps a little taller.

'You're Zoella, aren't you? The girl from across the sea?'

Zoella looked around at the voice that had come from behind her. She caught sight of a woman, dark haired, through it was also streaked with grey. Her eyes were brown, almost familiar.

'Sorry to interrupt,' the woman said, already looking apologetic.

'Yes, I'm Zoella,' Zoella replied.

'My name is Hannah,' the woman said. 'I'm … I'm Meru's mother.'

'Oh …'

'I wanted to ask you something,' Hannah began.

'We're quite busy,' Zoella said, looking at the provisions being stacked and moved around her.

'It won't take long,' Hannah said.

'I can do work,' Ren said, grabbing a box. 'You go.'

Zoella sighed. 'Just for a spell then,' she replied.

Zoella followed Hannah outside and away from the crowds that were pushing through the streets.

'You're his friend,' Hannah said, as they reached one of the piazzas that served as crossroads through the city. In the centre there was a fountain, surrounded by benches and trees.

'No, not really,' Zoella said.

Hannah frowned, gesturing to one of the benches. They sat down.

'I thought …?'

'We're not exactly on speaking terms right now,' Zoella said. 'Not after …'

'He lied to you too didn't he?' Hannah said. 'I'm sorry, I guess we're somewhat responsible for that.'

'His lies are his own,' Zoella said. 'He needs to take responsibility for them.'

'We forced him out you see,' Hannah said. 'My husband wanted him to join the senate as a scribe, but there was too much wanderlust in the boy. I knew, but I didn't do anything. I should have. They were always arguing. I didn't know what to do. Then Meru ran away. I thought he'd died, that we'd never see him again …'

'He was heartless to do that to you.'

'Perhaps, but we weren't looking out for him either. Trying to force him into something he didn't want to do. It was the biggest mistake. I'm just glad he's back now.'

Hannah paused, looking up at the mottled disk of Lacaille before turning back to Zoella.

'I saw him with you and the others,' Hannah continued. 'He looked happy, as if he was doing what he was supposed to do. I'm sorry, I assumed you were friends, he spoke so highly of you …'

'We were,' Zoella looked away, tears springing into her eyes. She blinked, wiping them away. 'Why, what did he say?'

'That you had saved his life, that you were the kindest and bravest woman he'd ever met.'

Zoella looked around in surprise.

'He said that?'

Hannah nodded. 'I wanted to meet you, I thought that you two were… well, I'm sorry to have wasted your time.'

Hannah got up to leave.

'Wait,' Zoella said, holding out a hand and grabbing the other woman's arm. 'What were you going to ask me?'

Hannah settled back down on the bench.

'I only wanted to know if he was content in whatever he was doing. He was so miserable here, so down. With you, all of you, he seemed alive again, I haven't seen him like that for rounds. I wanted to hear what he was like.'

'He is happy,' Zoella said after a moment's thought. 'He loves the adventure. I am grateful to him. He is brave and so very inquisitive. He rescued me too, without him I would have been captured by the priestesses, but …'

Zoella's voice tailed off.

'You said he lied to you,' Hannah prompted.

'After he rescued me he was captured by one of the priestesses,' Zoella said. 'That same girl killed my king, my prince and my loyal carn in front of my eyes.'

'She sounds terrifying.'

Zoella looked at Hannah. 'She is. Vicious and evil.'

'What happened? What does she have to do with Meru?'

'I don't know,' Zoella said. 'But something happened between them. Something ...'

Zoella felt the nausea rise in her again. Hannah could see the distasteful look on her face.

'This girl and Meru ...?'

Zoella nodded.

Hannah thought about it for a moment.

'Misplaced affections are the hardest to steer,' she said, after a moment. 'He's lucky that he still has a friend like you that cares about him.'

Zoella couldn't answer.

'A mother would always say this I suppose,' Hannah said. 'But I know he doesn't mean to lie and deceive, he has a good heart under it all.'

Zoella got to her feet. 'Maybe he has and maybe he hasn't,' she said. 'But he's done something I can't forgive, not now, not ever. I'm sorry, he and I ... we aren't friends, not any more.'

Fresh tears were brimming at her eyes but she brushed them aside.

'Zoella ...' Hannah reached towards her.

Zoella got to her feet, avoiding the older woman's reach.

'There's work to be done, time is running out.'

She walked away.

* * *

Ren waved at her as she returned, and she stepped into line behind all the others who were helping load provisions inside the buildings.

'All right?' Ren asked.

'I'll be fine,' she answered.

'Keep at it,' Coran called from nearby. 'We'll be ready in a stretch at this rate.'

'We can cram it all in,' Zoella answered. 'We just need ...'

High above, the light of Lacaille began to flicker.

Zoella looked up in horror. She heard the people about her moan and start pointing upwards. The fear around her was palpable.

Too soon! Lacaille hasn't gone black yet, this isn't how it happened before – we should still have plenty of time.

Yet, even as she watched a tinge of blue was souring the light above her.

'We're out of time,' Zoella wailed, looking out from the doorway of the administrative buildings. 'It's upon us. Everyone inside now!'

Beyond the city streets in the distant sunward they could see the horizon was darkening. A mist was growing there too, a wall of cloud that was rising from the Straithian Sea far away. It was billowing, forming faster and faster, like a thundercloud, but at ground level, sweeping in across the sea.

Heat!

'Ring the bells,' Coran yelled. Janaid called out the directions and the bells began to ring outwards from the city centre, more and more joining in a sonorous toll, alerting all to seek shelter.

Below, across the city, they could see crowds of people trying to make their way inside buildings, the cries of tumult reached their ears. Panic and terror, the screams of the frightened; both adult and child.

Zoella gasped in horror.

Too soon, it's not supposed to happen so fast. We're not going to save everyone … those down in the harbour!

Her heart lurched. There was a crush of people at the gates of the city, the way back from the harbour was blocked by a milling throng.

'Coran!' she called. 'Meru and the others … they're still down there!'

* * *

Meru heard the bells as he was standing on one of the quays, helping to wrestle a sail down from one of the fishing vessels moored there. He looked back at the city and then up at Lacaille. A flickering blueness was writhing around the edge of the huge disk of light in the sky. Already they could see the Alisse cascading in the sky.

'Oh no.'

Daf, Creg and Fitch were with him, as were the crew of the hapless fishing vessel.

'We've got to go,' he yelled. 'The firestorm is coming now. It's early.'

Already folks were deserting the quay and running back towards the city. The bells grew louder as more and more of them took up the warning.

The light was fading and the sky taking on a blueish tinge.

'Everyone run,' Meru yelled. 'Seek cover.'

Daf, Creg and Fitch leapt from the sailing ship, helping the crew off and then they all raced up the quay, their feet pounding on the wooden planks until they reached the stonework of the harbour. Dozens of people were all around them, pushing and jostling to get back into the city.

Meru skidded to a halt and looked behind them.

The dark stains on Lacaille now covered perhaps two thirds of its surface, their edges tinged with red fire, strange curling arcs could be seen jutting out, reaching into the sky, their extremities blue and otherworldly.

'We ain't getting in this way,' Fitch said.

Meru looked back at the city.

'No way we'll ever get inside in time,' Meru agreed, looking at the crowd of people before him. A strange hissing sound reached his ears and he spun about looking for the source of it.

The sky on the sunward horizon was now a dark arc, foreboding and grim, creeping higher in the sky. Before it a mist, or something like it, was rolling in across the sea. It would reach the land in moments.

'What in Lacaille is that?' Meru whispered.

'Nothing good,' Fitch said. 'We've got to get under cover, otherwise we're gonna get cooked outside.'

The crowd of people were going nowhere.

'This way,' Meru called, signalling to Daf, Creg and Fitch.

He ran back down towards the quays.

'Where in blazes?' Fitch asked.

'To the *Mobilis*,' Meru answered. 'We'll have to take shelter there. It's metal ...'

They ran as fast they could down to the quay where the *Mobilis* was moored. Daf and Creg jumped aboard, wrestling with the forward deck hatch, spinning the locking wheel housing open. The hatch swung back with a thump. Meru pushed Fitch before him and he dropped inside.

'Get to the starboard cabins,' he yelled. 'Shaderight side of the ship.'

Others from amongst the fishermen they had helped followed them, seeing that the crowd of people trying to get out of the harbour was in vain. Meru beckoned them over and one by one they began clambering inside the *Mobilis*.

'Get in too.' He motioned to Daf and Creg. 'Nothing more you can do out here.'

More and more people were jumping on to the ship. Below, through the hatch, Meru could see Daf, Creg and Fitch manhandling people out of the way of the ladder that led down from the hatch.

'Keep moving. Fast as you can!'

The light was fading, a deep gloom settling across the city. The sky was going dark, fading from a bright azure to a deep violet, tinged with blue and green strings of light. It was still awe-inspiring to Meru as he gazed up at the spectacle. For those around him and further on up into the city it was terrifying. He could hear screams of fear. People were panicking.

There was a crush of people around him now, forcing their way forward, trying to get aboard the *Mobilis*.

How many can we get aboard? Not enough ...

The buildings on the far point of the island were covered in the mist. Then screams reached his ears. He watched as the mist rolled towards the crowds. As it hit them there were more screams and people flailed around before being hidden from view.

'It's not mist ...' he muttered. 'It's steam.'

It was rolling up the quayside now. More people screamed as it touched them, some throwing themselves into the water as it approached. There was a crush around the hatch.

Meru was almost pushed aside, but a big hand grasped him and pulled him back.

Daf!

The big man tossed Meru down through the hatch. Meru hit the interior deck with a thump that knocked the wind out of him. Above, Daf retreated in, trying to close the hatch behind him. Dozens of hands were grasped around the edges trying to pull it back open. Screams filled the air about them.

Meru saw a whiteness grow above the hatch. The light faded. Screams of fear turned to yells of pain and agony. The hands around the hatch vanished. A blast of steam forced its way inside. Daf yelled and yanked at the hatch, it closed with a resounding clang. He spun the locking mechanism before falling from the ladder and landing with a thump on the deck plating below, yelling in pain.

He held up his hands in shock and surprise. They were red, raw and blistered.

'Let me fix that,' Fitch said. 'We need water, cold water.'

A loud hissing sound echoed around the ship. They heard the metal of the ship creak and groan, vibrations tinkling and popping up and down the hull.

'It's outside,' Meru whispered. 'If it gets in we'll boil alive.'

One of the glass portholes on the port side cracked.

* * *

Zoella couldn't just see and hear the panic, she could feel it too. It was a stampede, a rout. There were still hundreds trying to get into the city from the harbour and the streets were full of running people.

No ...

Above, Lacaille was fading fast, the great black blotches beginning to coalesce, the cracks between them churning with an angry fire. Already she could feel the heat, she knew what was coming next.

All these people ...

The strange mist had reached the edge of the harbour. Zoella jolted from the sudden feelings she sensed.

Pain!

She tried to see what was happening. Those at the back of the crush of people were fleeing in random directions. Zoella saw the mist overtake some of them and saw them reeling, flailing about for a brief moment before falling to the ground.

Burning … the others, the others are down there! Meru.

She watched as the mist enveloped the harbour, sweeping in across the ships and obscuring them. Screams erupted from the city below as first the harbour area and then the walls were obscured.

But they were mercifully short.

'Zoella move!'

Coran grabbed her, pulling her back from the doorway of the building and wrestling her inside. She pulled Ren along with her. People pushed and shoved around her as they continued to cram inside the building. She heard Coran yell instructions to close the doors as she fell to the floor.

She could sense the fear and pain all about her, a counterpoint to the agony in her heart. Doors closed with thumps nearby, the interior lit only by candles.

People were shouting and jostling, calling out the names of family and friends, trying to find each other in the dim lighting.

'Meru? Where is Meru?'

Zoella saw Hannah being pushed back through the crowd, losing her footing. Zoella forced her way over, grabbing at the woman's arm and pulling her up. Hannah struggled against her.

'It's me, I'm here.'

Hannah recognised her.

'Zoella. Where is he? Where is Meru?'

'He was down in the harbour,' Zoella cried. 'The flare came too soon …'

'We've got to find him.' Hannah began moving towards the doors, Zoella trying to hold her back.

'You can't go out there,' Coran yelled, somehow managing to stand before them. 'The flare will kill anyone outside.'

As if to underline his words, screams rent the air from outside the door, flames flickered and the scent of smoke was upon the air.

'No please, I must, he's out there …' Hannah dissolved into sobs. Zoella pulled her close.

Meru.

Guilt hit her like a hammer blow. The last words she had spoken to Meru echoed in her mind.

I never want to see you again!

Tears sprang into her eyes. Their friendship broken, all left unresolved, anger in their parting words. She'd never get a chance to put it right now. Mel had been right.

She clutched Ren and Hannah close, all three weeping in their close embrace.

* * *

The screams were loud in the confined space of the *Mobilis*. Meru winced and jolted as another man yelled close by. He'd stumbled against the outer bulkhead of the ship.

'Get away from the hull,' Meru shouted over the din.

'Snuts, it's red hot,' Fitch said from alongside. 'Got to stay to the middle of the ship.'

Another porthole cracked.

Fitch looked at Meru. 'Don't know how long we can take this, if one of those portholes goes …'

Meru nodded. 'We've got to get everyone further into the ship, down in the forward hold will be safest, then lock all the doors between us and the deck.'

'Aye,' Fitch agreed. 'Daf, Creg, get the hold open. We'll get these people moving.'

The two big men pulled up the hatchway near the bow that led down into the hold of the ship. A ladder led down from the hatch into the darkness below.

'I'll bring a light,' Fitch shouted to Meru.

Meru watched as Fitch grabbed one of the glowing orbs from a rack on the bulkhead and clambered down into the hold with it.

'Should be enough room,' he yelled back up. Fitch secured the light to one of the cross beams and braced the bottom of the ladder. 'Send people down.'

Meru signalled for the people around him to move forward. One after another they clambered down the ladder into the gloom below.

'Hurry!' Meru said, dragging each one forward. Some were hesitant about descending into the darkness.

There was still nothing to see beyond the portholes, just a swirling gloom outside. To his right another porthole cracked with a sharp tinkling sound. Meru could see the cracks growing in it. The heat was stifling, he felt sweat running down his face, back and chest.

At last the crowd of folks above had worked their way down. Daf and Creg motioned for Meru to descend. He swung himself on to the ladder.

As he did so a ghastly hissing noise sounded above him and the room above the hold filled with vapour. He heard a yell, he couldn't tell if it was Daf or Creg.

He slid down the ladder using only his hands.

'Daf, Creg!'

Both men were through the hatch above, steam was billowing around the hatch way as they wrestled it closed. A roar of anger and pain echoed throughout the hold as they struggled against the intense heat.

Then, with an echoing clang, the hatch locked into place.

The steam stopped and the only sound that could be heard was the gasping breaths of those around him.

'I think we got everyone,' Meru said, wiping the sweat from his eyes. 'Wow, it's so hot down here.'

'Safe for now,' Fitch said. 'How long will this flare last?'

'It was over in a spell or two last time,' Meru said. 'I don't think the heat will last that long.'

'Going to be touch and go then,' Fitch whispered.

'Why?' Meru asked. 'We can just wait it out.'

Fitch shook his head. 'This hold is watertight, reckon it's airtight too.'

Meru looked about him in the gloom. The lamps cast a faint illumination about him. All he could see were scared faces receding into the darkness. He looked back at Fitch.

'You mean …'

Fitch nodded. 'If it doesn't pass before we run out of air, we're all going to suffocate down here.'

* * *

Zoella, Hannah and Ren were still huddled close within the ground floor of the administrative building. The air was filled with smoke, people were coughing and spluttering all around them. The urge to get outside was almost overpowering. Coran had to knock down two folks who'd tried to get to the doors.

They could hear fires raging outside and see the flicker of the flames around the door jambs.

If those fires catch, we may be roasted alive inside here anyway.

Ren was whimpering in her arms. She pulled his head towards her and planted a kiss on top of it.

'It will be all right, you'll see,' she said. 'The flare won't last long, I promise.'

This is how he lost his family in the previous flare … poor child!

Ren coughed, the fumes about them were becoming intolerable. Zoella could feel the acrid smoke burning into her lungs.

We can't last much longer like this …

She could see some people around her had already succumbed, fainting and collapsing on the floor.

'Can't … breathe …' Ren's voice was a whisper. He choked, struggling in her grasp.

'Just a little longer,' she managed to croak.

* * *

Conditions aboard the *Mobilis* were no better.

Meru gasped, struggling to breathe, the heat was suffocating. Sweat dripped from him. He watched as the droplets hit the floor of the hold and then evaporated. The air was thick and humid, stinking from the odours of so many in close confinement.

One by one folks were fainting, collapsing where they stood, no one was able to help, none had the energy or strength.

'Air's going bad,' Fitch managed. 'Less than a spell I reckon.'

'We've got to open the hatch,' Meru whispered back.

'And let that steam in?' Fitch replied.

'Maybe it's gone.'

'Maybe it hasn't,' Fitch said. 'Climb the ladder and feel the hatch then, see if it's cooled.'

Meru nodded. He looked up at the ladder, it should be an easy climb, but with a woozy head …

Nothing for it but to try.

He grasped the rungs and pulled himself up. His limbs felt weak and shivery, he had to concentrate on putting one foot and then one hand up a rung at a time and then heaving himself upwards. His body felt lethargic and heavy.

It seemed to take him an age to reach the heavy hatchway above him. It was even hotter up here, the air seemed so thick and humid it was almost like water. He swayed on the ladder for a moment, almost overcome.

'Well?' Fitch called up.

Meru reached out his hand to grasp the wheel that would unlock the hatch. He reached out to grasp it …

He yelled, and almost fell off, struggling for a grip on the ladder, his feet slipping.

'It's still burning hot!' he said in dismay.

* * *

Zoella's eyes were closed, the fumes were intolerable now, every breath was an effort, each gasp a painful wheeze of poison.

Maybe this is how it ends. The flares are going to kill us all ... What of the Obelisk? We're too late, this is it ... suffocating the darkness ...

Redness flooded her eyes even behind her eyelids. A blast of cool air washed over her.

She opened her eyes. For a moment she could see nothing but a bright flow as water streamed from them. She blinked, trying to focus.

She could see a figure in the doorway, the door opening, wider and wider. There was brightness beyond, not the ruddy glow of flames, but the orange of Lacaille's natural light.

It's over!

'Ren ... Hannah ... Look.'

In her embrace the others stirred, coughing and spluttering but then looking towards the light.

Coran and Mel were standing in the doorway, pushing open the doors. The air was fresh, invigorating, cooler. Zoella struggled up and pulled the others to their feet with her. Coran was gesturing to her and she staggered forward.

For long moments she stood there gasping, staring out of the doorway.

'Oh no ...'

Fires were still burning around down the street before them. Bodies were strewn about, some of them on fire too, smoke billowing from them and casting a pall over the city. Above, the darkness across the face of Lacaille was retreating, the light about them growing brighter by the moment.

Zoella raised her gaze past the carnage. Through the drifting smoke she could see people emerging from the buildings, staggering out into the streets as they realised the worst had passed.

Beyond the streets Zoella could see the harbour. Several of the boats were aflame, settling into the water. She could see bodies strewn all over the quays. Her heart leapt in her throat.

The *Mobilis* was still there though, its bow swung out into the bay, but still tethered at the stern. She could see no sign of anyone alive.

'Coran … our friends …' she cried.

Coran looked at where she was pointing, taking in the view in a single glance.

'Get the fires out,' Coran yelled to Mel. 'Before they do any more damage. Folks will be hurt, find them, get them out in the open.'

'I want to help find our friends,' Mel protested.

'Need you here,' Coran replied. 'Ren, you stay here with Mel.'

'I want to …' Ren protested.

'Stay there, Ren,' Zoella said. 'Coran's right.'

'I'm coming too.'

Zoella turned to see Hannah behind her, wearing a determined expression. Zoella saw Coran about to protest.

'He's my son,' Hannah insisted.

'Meru's mother,' Zoella added by way of explanation.

'All right then, let's go.' He grasped hold of Mel's arm. 'We'll find them. We'll … do what we can.'

Mel swallowed and nodded without saying a word, but pulled him into a hug.

'Be careful.'

They released each other. Zoella felt another pang of guilt as she watched them.

I shouldn't have said what I said …

Coran pulled Zoella behind him.

'Quick now. Let's hope they found some way to stay out of danger.'

Coran led the way down to the harbour and the three of them picked their way through the scorched bodies of the dead. As they approach the walls of the city, the crush of bodies grew worse. Some had panicked and been crushed as the crowd had tried to escape.

They had to scramble up staircases and lower themselves over the wall, the main gate was blocked with bodies. Zoella could see that the bodies were no longer burnt now, but the upturned faces were blistered.

As if they'd been boiled alive ...

She couldn't help herself, she was looking for a familiar face, horrified and saddened as she looked, but grateful when she didn't recognise any of them.

They reached the quayside.

'Meru!'

'Fitch!'

'Daf, Creg!'

There was no answer, but no sign of their friends either. The *Mobilis* was close by now, drifting in the harbour. Zoella could see that the rope securing the bow had caught fire and burnt away, with the ship secured only at the stern. The outside deck was strewn with more bodies and more were floating face down in the water.

Coran ran to the stern mooring and hauled on the rope, calling for Zoella and Hannah to help him. The *Mobilis* slowly drifted back in. He jumped aboard.

Zoella helped Hannah on to the stern. The hull was steaming; she could feel the heat through the soles of her shoes. There were bodies everywhere, all dead, all blistered from the heat that had swept through.

'Might be worse up ahead,' Coran whispered. 'You ready?'

Zoella nodded, looking around her in despair. Hannah seemed unmoved, her face set.

'None of these are our friends,' Coran said, looking about him. 'Don't give up hope just yet.'

They walked up the deck of the ship, past the metal hatches that secured the engine bays. The ship seemed to have fared well, its metal structure unaffected by the heat. They reached the deck house. Zoella could see the glass windows had been shattered. Coran vaulted up and rummaged around.

'Nothing up here, damage is all fixable. Where did they go?'

Zoella pointed to the bow.

'Look!'

Coran climbed down and looked to where Zoella was pointing. Bodies were crammed around a hatch on the forward deck, just above the entrance to the galley.

'Looks like someone got inside in time,' he said, looking at Zoella. She nodded and they ran forward.

Coran didn't hesitate in pulling the bodies away from the hatch. Zoella watched, sickened, as they slipped into the sea and bobbed away, but there was nothing she could do for them now.

Coran gripped on the hatch wheel and turned it, spinning it up and then heaving on it. The hatchway opened. They both peered within.

The interior was dark and gloomy, the normal illumination was either switched off or broken. They could see no one inside.

Coran jumped down and helped Hannah clamber down the ladder from the deck, Zoella slid down a moment later. They walked forward and aft, looking in the galley, the crew quarters and the common areas. The ship was deserted.

'There's no one here,' Zoella said, her face a mask of despair and her voice cracking into a sob. 'They must have been caught in the crush, they're all dead somewhere in the harbour ...'

But Coran was shaking his head.

'The hatch was sealed from the inside,' Coran said. 'It must have been, nobody would have had time to close it from outside. I just don't understand where ... The hold!'

'What?' Zoella and Hannah said in unison.

'To the bow.'

Coran leapt past her and ran to the forward compartment of the *Mobilis*. Zoella had never been here before. She ran up behind him, seeing him wrestle with another hatch set in the floor. Around her she could see all the portholes were cracked.

'Crew entrance to the hold,' Coran said, turning the wheel. 'Never normally use it, as we unload from the stern …'

Coran yanked up the hatch and pushed it aside, peering down into the darkness.

'Meru? Fitch? You down there? Daf, Creg?'

There was no answer from the darkness below. Coran swung himself on to the ladder and slid down, Zoella followed his movements, leaving Hannah above. Within a moment both stood on the planks that covered the keel of the ship.

Bodies!

All around them were prone forms. The air was hot, humid and stale, rank and foul smelling.

Coran picked up something from the floor. Zoella recognised it.

'Fitch's hat!'

Fitch was lying just beyond, Coran shifted over, pulling Fitch's body towards him.

'Fitch, Fitch!'

The man groaned and his eyes flickered open, taking in the sight of Coran looking at him.

'Ah, you've found my hat, wondered where I'd dropped it.'

'Where's Meru, where's …?'

'He's here,' Zoella screeched, scrambling over two other bodies in her haste. Both grunted and began to move.

Meru was lying face up, his hands at his throat, Zoella could see burns and scald on his fingers.

'Meru? Meru!'

She pulled at him, managing to yank his body up and cradling him in her arms. 'Wake up. Please, wake up.'

She smoothed his dirty hair out of his face. His skin felt cold and clammy.

'Meru? Don't be dead, don't be … Coran.'

Coran came up behind her. Zoella looked up.

'I think … I think he's gone …' she said, between sobs.

'No … no I'm not.'

She felt him convulse in her arms and then his eyes opened. Meru looked confused for a moment, before his gaze fastened on Zoella.

'Zoe–' he reached out towards her.

She pulled him into an embrace, scrunching her eyes shut as she hugged him close.

I'm sorry!

Around her, more and more people were moving. It seemed a good number had been saved. She opened her eyes to see Daf and Creg before her, helping Fitch to his feet alongside Coran.

She craned her neck around and looked up to the hatchway, calling to Hannah.

'He's alive. He's going to be all right.'

* * *

The spots on Lacaille's surface were receding once more, life began to return to normal in Amaris. Many had lost their lives, some still caught in the open when the flare burst upon the island, others broiled alive in the hissing steam that had rolled across the harbour. Some had been trampled underfoot in the panic-stricken rush to get indoors in the last few moments.

It took several stretches of hard work to bury the bodies of the dead. The death toll just in the city was in the hundreds, and it became clear that hundreds more had been killed further inland.

The city itself had fared better, its stone work unaffected by the heat. Here and there fires had broken out. All the crops still left in the fields had been destroyed.

'We survived,' Janaid observed, looking out across the city.

'Most of us,' Coran replied, with a heavy sigh.

'Without your warning the death toll would have been far worse,'

Janaid said. 'We have enough provisions to survive until we can tend to the fields. We, the senate and the people of Amar, owe you and your crew a huge debt of thanks.'

'We're not out of the shades yet,' Fitch said from alongside them. 'Worse is coming.'

'Worse?' Janaid gulped.

'He means the priestesses of Drayden,' Coran said. 'Trouble you haven't seen yet.'

* * *

With the immediate priorities of the injured, damage and fire dealt with, the senate organised a council of war. The crew of the *Mobilis* were now listened to, the senators hanging on every word.

'They will come in ships,' Fitch said, addressing the senators. 'It's the only way to cross the sea between their lands and ours. Thus the attack will first come from the sea.'

'And in what type of vessels?' Henoch demanded.

'We saw only vessels of traditional build whilst we were on the continent,' Fitch answered. 'Timber built, much like our own ships here, though designed for warfare.'

'Then your vessel will have the mastery of the seas,' Henoch said.

'The *Mobilis* is only one vessel,' Coran answered. 'There are no others, least none that we know of. We have arms that might prevail against a handful, but the *Mobilis* cannot resist a fleet.'

'Our catapults then,' Henoch said. 'A wooden vessel will not survive a blow from a rock!'

'True enough,' Fitch said. 'But the priestesses will know that. Meru, describe what you saw at Viresia.'

Meru stepped up. 'The priestesses have trained flying creatures, their wingspans as wide as our ships are long. The creatures are called dachs. I saw Viresia, a proud and well defended city in Scallia, subdued in minutes by an aerial attack. The priestesses flew in, dropping burning brands of some substance that spread fire wherever it landed. Viresia had archers and other defences, they were defeated swiftly.'

'Then what can we do?' Janaid asked. 'We have no way to defend against a foe from the air. Our fate seems sealed.'

'We have two chances,' Coran said. 'Fitch has mastered the art of some of our ancestor's weapons, devices that fly through the air and explode, causing great harm to anything nearby. Others can shoot at great range. We have tried this on the priestesses once before and found them effective enough to deter them. But, again, there aren't enough to fend off an invasion.'

'Your second chance?' Henoch asked.

'During our travels in Scallia,' Coran said. 'We encountered an … an intelligence. Once again it was built by our ancestors long ago to serve their purposes. Alongside it were other machines, some of which could fly.'

'I learnt to fly one,' Meru interjected. 'It was easily the equal of the priestesses' dachs.'

'But if these devices you speak of are in Scallia …' Janaid began.

'Yes,' Coran said. 'We need to go and get them.'

'How long will that take?' Henoch asked.

'It took us five stretches from the Scattered Isles,' Meru said. 'Perhaps one more than that to get there from here, and the same to return.'

'Say twelve stretches,' Janaid mused. 'And how soon before these priestesses reach us?'

'It's a thousand marks,' Meru said. 'Even if they set out now it would take them four times as long even with a favourable wind.'

'Our own vessels can travel perhaps fifty marks a stretch,' Henoch said. 'Perhaps more. Say twenty stretches from the point at which they set out.'

'Of course,' Coran said. 'There's no way to know when that will be.'

'Yes, there is.'

Everyone in the hall turned to look. Zoella had been silent up to this point, but now she had something to say.

'I can hear one of them,' Zoella said. 'Sometimes I can see what she sees. I will know when they leave. I have seen nothing yet. We have time.'

'Time enough to get to Scallia and return with reinforcements,' Coran said. 'But we must depart as soon as possible.'

'Agreed,' Janaid said, nodding. 'We will see to it that your ship is given all the provisions it needs. Prepare as fast as you can and sail upon the earliest stretch!'

* * *

The senate was as good as their word. The *Mobilis* was repaired, provisioned and readied for another voyage. The crew worked for two stretches to ensure everything was ready. The first chime of the following stretch they were prepped, ready to sail once more.

Hannah saw Meru standing on the far side of the Amaris piazza, looking out from the high vantage point across the bay of Amar.

Above, the warm smooth orb of Lacaille dominated a quarter of the clear blue sky, unmarred by even the faintest whiff of cloud. The rest of the sky was flecked with the swirling green patterns of the Aura, twisting and coiling above them, a delicate and beautiful river of light flowing from Lacaille over their heads and then fading away towards the shadeward.

She strolled across the piazza, avoiding the train of wagons and visitors still jamming the boulevards in and out of the city. Meru turned and smiled at her.

Once clear of the immediate hustle they were able to enjoy the wide expanse of the wall that served as the upper boundary of the city of Amaris. Hannah looked over the edge before stepping back with an expression of distaste.

'I will never get used to that view.'

'It's a long way down,' Meru replied.

She remembered when Meru was much younger, how he'd always tease her by running close to the edge.

The cove far below provided a smooth area of calm water, deep blue in the middle, rising a shade to aquamarine by the time it reached the coast. Beyond that lay the Straithian Sea and, so the stories said, other lands.

Stories that my son has confirmed!

Hannah could see the strange ship that Meru had returned upon. It was three times as long as any other ship in the harbour, and glinted in the light of Lacaille, its metal nature obvious even from here.

'So you're going with them again.'

It wasn't a question.

Meru looked at his mother.

'I have to,' he replied. 'They need me. I navigate the ship. Without me …'

Hannah smiled.

'I wasn't going to stop you. I just wanted to wish you a safe voyage, or whatever it is the sailors say.'

'Calm seas is the usual farewell.'

'Calm seas then.'

Meru smiled. 'Thanks Mother. I'm sorry about …'

'It's done and past now,' Hannah said. 'You've found your calling, you're doing what you should be doing. These people, they seem good folk …'

'They are,' Meru said.

Hannah nodded.

'And the girl you're travelling with, Zoella. She thinks a lot of you. She seems like a good friend.'

Meru looked away and didn't answer.

'Your dealings with this other girl … this priestess …'

Meru turned, with an angry look upon his face.

'Her name is Kiri,' he snapped. 'And she's not evil like everyone says she is!'

Hannah held up her hands. 'I don't mean to pry.'

'Then don't.'

Meru stepped away and then turned back.

'I'm sorry, it's just that everyone is judging me, telling me what I should think, no one listens …'

Hannah thought that for a moment.

'So what is she like, this Kiri?'

Meru sighed.

'She's … she's strong, tough. A warrior of her people. She fears no one. She has such skill with weapons. So determined, so … alive.'

'Pretty too I guess?' Hannah asked, with a wry grin.

Meru's expression grew distant.

'She has these eyes, these … deep blue eyes. Her hair is dark and she's …'

Hannah watched her son's expression. She didn't need to ask any more.

'Just … be careful,' she whispered. 'Will you do that for me? I only want the best for you. Zoella does too. Our worries only come from concern for you.'

'I will, Mother.'

Footsteps thumped alongside them. They turned to see Henoch striding up to them.

'Wife,' he said and then looked at Meru. 'Son.'

Hannah bowed as was custom. Meru nodded in acknowledgement and looked into his father's eyes, a frown creasing his forehead.

'You'll be travelling once again I assume,' Henoch said.

'I will,' Meru replied.

'I suppose that nothing I say will have any bearing on your decision to leave?' Henoch asked.

'I won't stay here, if that's what you mean,' Meru answered. 'We have to go.'

Henoch nodded, and looked out across the bay.

'These … friends of yours,' Henoch said, rubbing his chin. 'Pirates and vagabonds.'

'They're not …' Meru began, stepping forward, incensed.

'I was wrong,' Henoch said.

Meru gasped and stopped. Even Hannah looked surprised.

'Yes,' Henoch continued. 'I was wrong. About a great many things. These people … your friends are good people. They saved this city and many lives. My counsel was poor and my judgement awry.'

'Father …'

'Hannah tells me I contributed to you running away,' Henoch said, still looking out across the bay. 'Quite what is so bad about a life of honourable service in the senate I fail to understand, but it has been my life and it was wrong of me to try to impose it upon you.'

Meru swallowed.

'Then …?'

'Go,' Henoch said, turning to look at Meru. 'Go on this …' He waved his hands, 'quest, adventure, whatever you call it. Go with my blessing. It seems Amar needs adventurers more than it needs senators at this time.'

Hannah stifled a sob and then pulled them both in a close embrace. After a moment, father and son put an arm around each other.

'I will do this,' Meru said. 'And I will come back! I will come back, and willingly.'

Hannah kissed his forehead and Henoch hugged him close.

'May Lacaille favour you.'

* * *

Zoella was sitting at the end of the quay gazing out to sea when Meru sat down next to her. She looked across at him with a smile.

'Just said goodbye to my parents,' he said. 'Got permission to go this time.'

'I'm glad you were able to speak to them again,' she replied, with a light laugh. 'Your mother loves you very much. Your father too, in his way.'

Meru nodded.

'That's a precious thing,' Zoella added. 'I never knew my parents, not even their names.'

Meru swallowed, paused and then summoned up the courage to speak.

'I'm glad to be able to talk to you again,' he said. 'I didn't mean to push you away the way I did.'

'I shouldn't have said what I said,' she answered, looking back out to sea. 'Sorry for hitting you too.'

'I probably deserved it,' he said. There was a pause, and then, 'Can we be friends again?'

Zoella took in a deep shuddering breath. 'Do you still …? Is what you said about …?'

'Kiri?' Meru asked. 'Let's not talk about …'

Zoella turned and glared at him.

'We have to,' she said. 'Otherwise you and I … Well, there won't be a you and I, will there? I want to be your friend, but we have to trust each other.'

Meru rubbed his forehead. 'I won't lie to you again Zoella. I won't. I know what I felt from her; she isn't all evil, not just a killer like you think she is …'

Zoella pursed her lips, trying to stop her body from trembling.

'I know what I saw …'

'And I know what I felt.'

Zoella took a deep breath.

'All right,' she managed to say. 'For the sake of our friendship … I'll accept what you say. She has some feelings in her anyway … I know she wants you. That's very clear.'

Meru looked at her. 'How do you …?'

'I sensed her,' Zoella said. 'Just before the flare, she was trying to find out where we were. I'm sure she knows where Amar is now. I think that's what she was after all along, either from you, or from me. The priestesses will come.'

'They were coming anyway,' Meru said. 'Kiri or no Kiri. It was just a matter of time once they discovered I came from Amar, way back in Viresia.'

'Perhaps,' Zoella said.

'She had doubts,' Meru said. 'She thought all Amarans were evil, me included. When I saved her life she was shocked to discover I wasn't. It changed her, Zoella. It really did.'

'If you say so.'

'Maybe ... maybe I'll be able to convince her to stop the attack, or at least negotiate terms between Drayden and Amar ...'

Their conversation lapsed into silence broken only by the water lapping at their feet.

'What you said before,' Meru said. 'If you meet her ...'

Zoella chewed at a fingernail. 'For your sake I won't try to kill her,' she said after a moment. 'But if she attacks me I will defend myself.'

'I can't ask for more than that,' Meru answered, his voice a whisper.

'And know this,' Zoella said. 'If you're wrong ... If she kills again and you choose to seek her out, if you go to her despite all that ... I won't stop you.'

'If she kills again, you'll be proved right,' he said. 'And if that turns out to be the truth, there's no way I would go with her. Why would I?'

She looked at him. 'If you do, our friendship will end upon that stretch, never to be reconciled. Do you understand?'

She saw him swallow, saw his gaze study her face.

Yes. I really mean it, Meru.

* * *

As the ship rounded the harbour and turned out to sea, Coran pushed the throttles up and the *Mobilis* surged forward, her mighty engines churning a frothing wake at her keel.

Coran grinned, happy that he was master of his vessel once again, with nothing but the horizon ahead.

Crew all aboard. Mel, Fitch, Daf and Creg, Meru, even Zoella and little Ren. Things always seem more straightforward when away from land!

He knew it was an illusion, trouble lay ahead and time was short. Defending Amar was one thing, but there were still Zoella's troubled dreams of the Obelisk to consider too. They would have to see if they could wrestle any other information from Caesar.

Fitch vaulted up into the bridge beside him.

'All stowed and ready for sea,' he said. 'Mel reports all's well with her damnable engines.'

'She said that?'

'No,' Fitch replied. 'What she actually said isn't repeatable for the most part, but the general gist was about cobbling things together in a rush.'

'Best we can hope for,' Coran replied with a chuckle.

Fitch rubbed his chin. 'Didn't want to mention this when you were convincing the senate and all,' he said. 'But there's a big flaw in this plan.'

Coran turned to look at him. 'Oh yes? What's that then?'

Fitch was looking ahead as spray splashed up from the *Mobilis*' rapid progress.

'You've assumed that infernal contraption on the mainland is going to give you what you want.'

'Caesar?' Coran replied. 'Why wouldn't it … he … it?'

'Call me sceptical,' Fitch said. 'But it's got a mind of its own. You want to use its flying machines, and anything else useful that might be lying about, to fight a war against these witches. What if it don't like that idea? What if it says no?'

'Then we take them anyway,' Coran said. 'What is it going to do? It's a talking table.'

Fitch looked at him. 'Don't underestimate it, is my advice,' he said. 'All this while and we're still dabbling with things we scarce understand.'

Fitch left the bridge, leaving Coran musing over his words.

The *Mobilis* surged onwards, ploughing its way across the Straithian Sea towards Scallia.

CHAPTER NINE

Airea, Capital of Taloon

Round 2307, Fourth pass

Kiri circled her dach above the high parapets of Airea. It was an impressive city. Nestled in a natural sandy bay and flanked by the sea on one side and the harsh desert on the other, it was positioned in a narrow belt of green. From the air the reason was obvious, the city was built on a river delta that now flowed within its streets.

Kiri took in the sight and signalled for the three dachs to close up their formation. Together they began to descend.

The city had a central thoroughfare that ran almost its entire length, splitting it in two. It was flat and paved, crossed here and there by lofty bridges. Unlike the redstone of Drayden, here the building material was a startling white, forcing Kiri to squint into the brightness as they approached. The end of the thoroughfare ran straight for perhaps a mark, ending in a vast palace constructed out of the same material. Its spires were the grandest in the city. The entire city was ringed by a defensive wall, it appeared as a majestic circle of white from the air.

From above, Kiri could see that the spires were wrought out of coloured glass that flashed and sparkled in the light of Lacaille. The craftsmanship was obvious. Even beyond the palace there were minarets and towers as far as she could see, there was no evidence of the slums that disfigured the outskirts of Daine.

A rich city indeed.

Between the buildings she could spy the water courses, see people both walking on the streets and moving about in boats. In some places large lakes had been created, perhaps for the wealthiest residents to gaze out upon. There were well tended gardens and flowers everywhere. She could make out markets and stalls, there was a large oval area too, an amphitheatre with a sandy floor. The city was a riot of colour.

But no fields, no crops. Where does the food come from? And where are the workers?

To the sunright at the opposite end of the thoroughfare lay the harbour. At a glance Kiri could see dozens upon dozens of vessels moored, with many out at sea about their business. Some of the ships were of decent size, with multiple masts and expansive decks. People were milling about below her as she descended. She signalled again, ensuring the dachs stayed together. Some began to point upwards as the priestesses from Drayden were spotted.

From her perspective she could see all of them were dark-skinned. A pang of sorrow clutched at her.

Like Tasha. Was Taloon her home before she came to Daine? Was she tithed from here? I'll never know. I should have asked …

Kiri made for the wide expanse before the palace itself. It seemed the obvious place to be received by the King of Taloon, and Vandare had said he resided in the palace.

Clouds of fine sand were swept into the air as the three dachs landed in unison, their wings back-flapping as they came to rest. A crowd of people, having seen their flight descend and wondering from where they had come, was growing about them, yet keeping a respectful distance. Kiri looked at them. She had never seen so many people with dark-skins and short cut dark hair. It reminded her how far from home she was.

Her dach bowed its head and Kiri slid down, walking forward towards the palace a few paces.

Vandare and Liana came up behind her, each flanked by the junior priestesses who had flown them.

The gates to the palace remained closed. Kiri could see a few guards in evidence on its lower levels, but there seemed no other movement. She looked around at Vandare.

'Must we announce our presence?' she asked.

Vandare bowed low.

'The King will be aware,' he replied.

Before Kiri could answer, a horn blared out from the palace, followed by a second and a third, each playing a different note. A short theme of music played and the gates to the palace swung open.

As they did so Kiri could hear drum beats sounding before her. In the dark corridor beneath the palace, something was moving. Kiri squinted to see better, but the brightness outside was still dazzling.

Something big …

She blinked in surprise as a creature emerged into the light of Lacaille.

It was huge. Her first thought was that it had to be three, perhaps four, times the height of even the biggest hergs of Drayden. The creature was moving ponderously, on four legs that were each the size of a mature shade. Its head was vast too, but in proportion to the body, a wide flat expanse of greenish flesh. As Kiri watched the head came up, revealing a neck that stretched almost the height of the creature again. Kiri could only estimate how tall it was, but it had to be stretched up somewhere near fifteen hands into the sky. Kiri could see a long muscular tail drooping behind it, counterbalancing the huge body. The creature's fans ran all the way up its neck, flushed red as they cooled the blood of the enormous beast.

As it stretched up, the creature emitted a deafening sonorous trumpeting sound that set the dachs squawking in fright and made Kiri flinch and back up a pace. She'd never heard anything so loud in her life. The creature stamped a foot on the ground and the tremors ran through her body.

Beside her Vandare was chuckling. She spared him a pointed look before regaining her posture and stepping forward, legs astride and her kai held forward in her right hand.

The creature was flanked by soldiers on hergs and Kiri could make out more of the vast animals following in a line behind. The lead one had a contraption on its back. Kiri realised it was a throne, covered with an ornately decorated fabric tent. She could just make out a man within.

The King?

Her thoughts were answered a moment later as Vandare bowed the knee. Remembering the etiquette she had been instructed in she copied his movements, as did Liana and the priestesses behind her.

The drums grew loud and the creature approached. It stopped only a few paces away. Kiri looked up into a vast fleshy face. Before her, huge nostrils flared, sucking and blowing on the air as if investigating her scent. She could make out the creature's three enormous eyes, they were as big as her fist. The dachs cowered before it, bowing their own heads low and emitting keening noises from their jaws.

As the great beast came to a halt the drums stopped. The trumpets sounded again, playing a bright marching tune for a brief moment. A rope ladder was thrown down from the throne high above and a man began his descent. The soldiers alongside dismounted from their hergs and stood to attention.

The man descended. He was big too, a bulky muscular physique was swathed in brightly coloured, almost garish, cloth. He had an ornate hat upon his head. His skin was a deep brown, much like Vandare's and the other inhabitants of Taloon.

He dropped the final distance to the floor with an energy that belied his size. He was about the same height as her, but twice as wide and she guessed perhaps three times the weight. Behind him, another man followed, taller, but thinner and muscular.

As she had been directed she bowed her head as they approached.

'Rise, rise.' The King's voice was rich and melodious, cultured and bold. 'Vandare, you will introduce me forthwith.'

Kiri, Vandare, Liana and the two priestesses got to their feet.

'Sire,' Vandare said, with a further short bow. 'May I present Kiri, priestess of Drayden and emissary of Nerina high priestess of those same lands. '

'Ah …'

Kiri looked into wideset deep brown eyes. She felt an intense sense of scrutiny and saw his gaze move up and down her body, appraising her.

'King Karquesh of Taloon,' he said, holding out his hand. The word Taloon was said with great emphasis on the second syllable. His hand was big and fleshy, festooned with rings bearing large gemstones.

As she had been instructed, Kiri took the hand and planted a kiss upon it.

'As enchanting as you have been described,' Karquesh said. 'No wonder you are held in such esteem. Though I had expected you to be taller somehow.'

Kiri blinked in surprise, unsure what he meant.

'I have been keen to meet you in the flesh, so to speak,' Karquesh continued. 'The victor of Varda, the black-gloved vanquisher of Viresia. Rider of dachs and slayer of Kings! Your reputation precedes you.'

Kiri was still nonplussed. Karquesh grinned.

'Word of your exploits has travelled far, Kiri of Drayden. We take great interest in the affairs of our neighbours. I look forward to knowing you better. It is not so often we entertain mighty warriors of your ilk in our humble land.'

Kiri wasn't sure whether she imagined it, but she got the impression that the King's companion coughed and went to stifle it.

'It is an honour to stand in your presence, your majesty,' Kiri managed. 'On behalf of my high priestess I bring you greetings from Drayden.'

'Of course, of course.' Karquesh beamed. He turned aside. 'My cousin, Taryen, advisor to my court and Prince of Taloon.'

He gestured to the man behind him, who stepped forward. Kiri looked up at him. He was more than two hands taller than she was, muscular and even darker skinned. He was looking at her with a cold expression and she sensed a wave of animosity from him.

So, we're not welcome here by all.

Her thoughts focused back on Karquesh as he spoke.

'I hope we will see some evidence of your prowess before your visit is over.'

Kiri didn't know how to answer that either, she only sensed subtle amusement from Karquesh. She turned to her companions.

'May I introduce Liana, once queen of Scallia, now subject to Drayden.'

Karquesh turned his attention to Liana. Kiri looked herself. Liana was a little taller, her bright blonde hair shining in the light of Lacaille, her riding gear unable to hide the obvious curves of her body. Kiri sensed the arousal and appreciations of Liana's form as Karquesh swept his gaze across her.

Which is all to the good. A bargaining chip I can use.

Karquesh held out his hand in the same manner.

'My Lady ...'

Liana took the hand and kissed it in the same manner, but she said nothing.

'Adrella and Tali, my assistants,' Kiri said.

Karquesh bowed to the other two priestesses. They curtseyed in return. Kiri saw him turn his attention to the dachs behind, appraising them.

'Remarkable beasts,' he said. 'We have none here in Taloon.'

'The heat,' Kiri said. 'They prefer cooler climes.'

'You train them, and they fight for you?' Karquesh asked.

Kiri nodded. 'Yes.'

'And how many such beasts do you have in Drayden?'

Kiri caught herself before answering.

He probes ... as well he might.

'A good number,' Kiri replied, remembering Charis' words from long ago.

Karquesh chucked.

'And what do you think of our phaunts, priestess Kiri?' he asked, gesturing back to the procession behind. 'Magnificent beasts, are they not?'

'They are truly a sight to behold,' Kiri said, still gazing at the huge creature in awe of its size.

'Have you nothing like them in Drayden, then?'

Kiri shook her head. 'No, they are unknown to us.'

'Good, good,' Karquesh replied. He turned about. 'But, where are my manners? You must be tired after your long flight. Vandare, my good man. Accommodation is prepared, the very finest. See to it that our guests are rested. At the eighth chime we shall have a banquet in their honour.'

Kiri saw Taryen's gaze had remained unmoved. He continued to look at her as their entourage walked away.

* * *

'They come to demand our subservience.'

Karquesh kept smiling until the door to the palace closed behind him and the servants had departed. Then his expression fell.

'Indeed,' Karquesh replied, looking back at his cousin, Taryen. Vandare stood behind them. 'And we would be wise to consider it.'

'Bow the knee to these women?'

'These are no ordinary women,' Karquesh replied. 'Priestess Kiri's reputation is no idle boast. Survivors from Viresia reached us here in Taloon. These priestesses overpowered that city, armed with bowmen and all manner of traditional defences, within minutes. Kiri herself slayed the King it is said.'

'Exaggeration,' Taryen spluttered. 'Incompetence and laziness on the part of the defenders of that city. This Kiri, she's barely a woman, let alone a warrior.'

'All the more reason we should understand her better,' Karquesh replied. 'What say you, Vandare? You have seen more of them than we.'

'I saw no demonstration of their skill in battle during my short stay,' Vandare replied. 'But they are certainly feared by all around them. It is said they wield a power of the mind with which they can control others. I travelled here alongside them. They are proud and haughty, and they seem sure of their abilities ...'

'Magic spells and sorcery?' Taryen said, with a laugh. 'Child's tales.'

'We should find a way to gauge their strength,' Karquesh said. 'You know what they want from us?'

Vandare nodded.

'Our fleet,' he replied. 'They intend to wage a war on a foe across the sea. Being landlocked, Drayden has no sailing vessels.'

Karquesh nodded.

'I thought as much,' he said. 'They need what we have. It will be interesting to see what they intend to offer us by way of return.'

'We should refuse,' Taryen said.

'That will mean war with Drayden,' Vandare said. 'The priestesses are not famed for their patience. Scallia was confident they could resist, Drem put up no defence at all ...'

'Taloon is strong.' Taryen said.

'But we have no need of another war,' Karquesh replied. 'Kerun might be quiescent for now, but we have enough troubles of our own with the unrest here ... and no word of that must reach our visitors.'

'The catacombs?' Vandare asked.

'There was another riot whilst you were away on your errand,' Karquesh said. 'Put down once again, but those responsible for inciting it still elude us.'

'And our food?'

'We have recovered much, but some was smuggled away, there has been sabotage to many of the mechanisms. The slaves have been put to work repairing it, but ... there will be shortages before long if these attacks continue.'

'They are organised,' Vandare replied. 'This seems to be no random act of insurrection, it is planned and executed.'

'Double the guards down there,' Karquesh said, nodding. 'We must find the perpetrators, they must be caught. Take care of it personally, Vandare.'

'Yes, sire.'

'And as for these priestesses – we keep the peace with Drayden, is that understood? We will hear what they have to say.'

'But women, dictating our ways?' Taryen growled. 'We should take these emissaries now, show them a woman's true place and send them back whipped, bound and shaven as a message.'

Karquesh looked at him.

'Then perhaps it is good fortune for all that I am King and you are the Prince.'

'An accident of birth, nothing more,' Taryen growled. 'With your leave, cousin?'

Karquesh gestured and Taryen stalked away.

'His insolence has not abated I see,' Vandare said, speaking in lowered tones.

'No indeed.'

'He means to take the throne.'

Karquesh chuckled. 'Of course. He believes it should have been his from the start.'

'He will kill you for it. Many of our seafarers would agree with him. A tougher line, both inside our realm and outside it. Some say we should have razed the cities of Kerun, and not drawn up a treaty with them. Many believe these rebels amongst the slaves should be executed without mercy.'

Karquesh didn't answer for a long moment.

'Kerun, no. An enemy subdued looks inwards and doesn't foster guerrillas. We will treat with Kerun, not drive them to extinction. These rebels though, yes. Death ... once they are found, if they can be found.'

'And the priestesses?'

'Perhaps the visit of this legendary priestess Kiri might be put to use in other ways.'

'How do you mean?'

'I am still pondering it,' Karquesh replied. 'Make sure their needs are met, the best of our hospitality must be on display. Prior to the banquet we will have a parade. I would like Taryen and Kiri to meet properly.'

'That will be an interesting encounter.'

Karquesh smiled and nodded. 'Yes indeed.'

* * *

King Karquesh had not been lying when he had described the accommodation as the very finest. Kiri had been given a vast apartment in the highest spire of what she learnt was called the Queen's Tower. It seemed odd, as Taloon had no queen.

The apartment had a sunken bath, gilded decorations of all sorts, lush and vibrant tapestries adorning the wall, with thick carpets underneath. Everything smelt of exotic perfumes, large plants decorated every corner and servants were on hand with giant handheld fans to waft cooling breezes across her.

She'd had scant chance to enjoy it though. Dozens of ladies-in-waiting swarmed around her, apparently to ensure she was ready for the banquet. She had been bathed, scrubbed, her hair untangled, washed, washed again and then brushed, dried and then adjusted for what seemed like a whole stretch. One had tried to remove her black glove, but she had slapped at the woman's wrist in anger. The glove remained firmly in place on her left hand.

Without Pootle she would have preferred to dress herself, but women of rank in Taloon didn't undertake such chores. Kiri was not used to wearing a dress. The last time she had worn one Charis had dressed her prior to her trial at the hands of the priestesses in Daine.

How long ago that seems now ...

Kiri sighed. Charis was gone and she was in charge of her own destiny now. The King was insisting on his banquet in her honour and etiquette demanded she follow the local customs.

But that hadn't been all. Next came another flock of women bearing a succession of powders and colours. Her skin was dabbed and dusted, her eyebrows trimmed with tiny scissors and her hair twisted into an ornate swirl atop her head before falling back down around her shoulders. Every spell she was instructed to hold still for more colour to be applied. They even coloured her lips. It seemed both the city and the people within shared a love of bright and radiant hues.

I'm going to look like a painted doll once they finish.

It was relaxing though. She had never been pampered like this before. Even bumbling Pootle hadn't taken anywhere near this long in preparing her for an important meeting. The banquet seemed to be the social event that the entire royal household was circulating about and no negotiation would happen until that ritual had been conducted. She would have to wait. Taloon put great stock in its socialising.

The material was floaty, awkward and revealing, so unlike the practical flight gear she wore when riding the dachs, or the close-fitting leather armour she had worn when fighting. That was comfortable and familiar, not like this flimsy attire. She felt exposed and vulnerable, though the dress was light and airy, which was a comfort in the oppressive heat.

Yet, if you have to wait, you may as well try to enjoy it.

The dress she had been given to wear was a bright cyan, chosen, so the women had said, to compliment her eyes. It came with matching shoes that had curious extensions to the heels, increasing her height as she stood up. She felt as if she was tottering forward and took a moment to regain her balance. The women about her tittered in surprise, but fell silent when she glared at them.

They walked her over to a large oval mirror that was positioned in the far corner of the room, adjacent to the windows. Light was streaming in. Her new shoes clicked on the flooring as she walked across.

I must look ridiculous, I hope they've done this to Liana and my companions otherwise I'm going to ...

She stopped.

The woman in the mirror was unknown to her. She was thin and tall, her skin a glowing tan in the light from the window, the familiar scars obscured and hidden by the dabs of powder. Her body was trim and curved, the dress revealing enough of her form to appreciate a generous measure of feminine grace. The shoes stretched out her toned legs, accentuating them. Dark hair was perched atop her head, accompanied by falling ringlets about a narrow face, with more cascading around bare shoulders. Blue eyes stood out, matching the hue of the dress.

They were right about the dress. The colours too.

The woman stared back at her. A woman of substance and allure, mature and sophisticated, aware of the presence she generated and the effect she had on those around her. Kiri stared and looked at her reflection for long moments, admiring herself.

I look like a Queen!

Memory flickered in her mind.

None know this ... but I am a Queen, I am royalty! Of the house of Tiamoi of Scallia.

Visions flashed before her eyes, the hardship of the forest and the slums where she spent her childhood, the fights and the constant struggle for survival. Then the battles to prove herself in the Temple; becoming a priestess, mastering the arts of war and conflict.

But this ...

Softer, subtler. Here was a woman who could turn the mind and body, not pummel it into submission. Here was a woman who didn't need the hard blow of a kai to make her point, nor even the gift to subdue or coerce her opponents. Here was a woman who deserved praise and adulation, who expected it and embraced it. This was no slum girl, no warrior, no mere priestess. This woman was all of those and more. A woman to be feared, to be loved, admired and revered.

She's me ...

Kiri caught her breath.

And I'm truly as much a Queen as Karquesh is a King. It's my birthright! Elena strove to be high priestess. Nerina likewise with Drayden. But me ... I could take it all. Drayden, Scallia, Taloon, Amar too! I could reunite the lands. Not just Queen ... I could be the most powerful ruler these lands have ever seen. Empress of Voren ... Empress Kiri!

Her mind spun with the possibilities. The woman who gazed back at her was calm and controlled, yet her eyes burnt with a fierce determination. Kiri smiled. The woman before her did likewise. She was beautiful and intimidating.

I like this vision of me!

Schemes and plans already half-formed in her mind, solidified in her consciousness. She could see with clarity the steps unfolding before her.

I am Elena's heir in purpose. I have the royal blood of Scallia flowing in my veins. The Obelisk itself anointed me, I have the gift, I have the skill, I have the line. I have done things that no others have done. I have the right! It is prophecy, it will come true. I will be Empress Kiri!

She staggered back, blinking at her audacity.

* * *

Karquesh appraised the young priestess as she walked into the palace grounds once more. She was slight, with a gait that was short of elegant; she was not used to the footwear she had been provided with. No longer wearing the tough leather riding gear she had arrived in, she was wearing a bright cyan gown, a colour often favoured in Taloon. She had been dressed well and her skin and face were cleansed from the dirt of travel.

She was too thin for his tastes, her frame not quite petite, but neither voluptuous in the manner he preferred, but there was something about the way she stood that spoke of authority and grace. She saw him and he beckoned to her, still watching as she walked towards him.

Her legs were hidden by the gown, but her arms were bare, Karquesh could see the firm muscle tone there, so unlike the women of Taloon. Her trademark black glove was still in place on her left hand.

This girl, this woman ... attacked and defeated the capital of Scallia. And the glove, what is that story? Some deformity of the hand perhaps? I should like to see her abilities ... and as for the powers of her mind ...

Kiri bowed as she approached. Karquesh gestured for her to rise.

'You are rested from your long voyage?' he enquired.

Kiri nodded. 'Your hospitality is quite wonderful,' she replied.

'Your accommodation is satisfactory?'

'More than satisfactory,' Kiri replied.

Karquesh nodded. 'Excellent. The banquet is at the last chime, but for this stretch I am at your disposal. I thought you might enjoy a tour of the city.'

'That would be most kind of you.'

'Come then,' Karquesh said. 'I have made preparations.'

He clapped his hands and one of the enormous phaunts emerged from between arched columns that lined the edge of the palace grounds. The beast was led to them by a pair of handlers and stopped nearby, trumpeting softly. As usual, it was equipped with a set of canopied seats secured to its back by a complex harness, the howdah. He saw her once again take in the beast's enormous size. It was far larger than the strange flying creatures the priestesses employed.

But their beasts are equally fearsome in their own right. To be attacked from the air …

Moments later they were seated side by side in the howdah, protected from the bright light of Lacaille by the fabric above.

Guided by Karquesh, the phaunt proceeded through the city. Karquesh pointed out the spires and the landmarks. Kiri showed polite interest, but it was clear that the markets and the theatres interested her little. She showed more interest in the architecture and the construction.

Studying it to see how she might attack it from the air, perhaps?

'The city of Airea is ancient,' Karquesh said as they continued to move through it aback the phaunt. 'We have records going back a thousand rounds or more. Airea has been here all that time. Much of its construction is a mystery to us, we can no longer build such marvels ourselves, but we maintain what is here as best we can. The stone of the city is immensely hard and does not crumble over time like the rocks we mine from the hills. How this is done is a mystery, but we are grateful for it.'

'Your city is beautiful,' Kiri said. 'A wonder. It is grander than Daine I think.'

'I have heard tell of your city too,' Karquesh said. 'It is said there is a golden temple in its midst that reaches to the sky.'

'Not quite that high,' Kiri replied. 'But the temple is a wonder too, it is made of redstone, a pyramid that stands in the centre of Daine and looks over all about it. The insides are lit by a multitude of polished mirrors.

'I should like to see that one stretch,' Karquesh said,

They stopped for refreshment after a couple of chimes, enjoying fresh fruit juices that had been prepared by some of the market traders who ran around them bowing, fawning and attending to their every need, anxious to please.

The girl seemed to enjoy the fruit. She drank a cupful and then asked for more.

'This tastes wonderful,' she said. 'Fresh and sharp, from what fruit is it made?'

'We call it the Seetruss,' Karquesh said. 'Do you not have it in Drayden?'

Kiri shook her head. 'No, it is unknown to us.'

The phaunt reached the city walls. They disembarked and walked up the wide flight of stairs to the top, gazing out over the harbour below. Hundreds of ships were visible in the bright blue sparkling waters. The harbour was built upon the terminus of the river delta, with two arms that stretched out far into water. Within those protective stone arms, dozens of large wooden quays had been built, around which uncounted ships were clustered. Most were merchant vessels of various types, some carrying cargo, others fish and other food products. The harbour was bustling with activity. They could hear distant shouts and conversations as ships were directed in and out, moored, loaded, unloaded and set on their way again.

To the far side of the harbour lay the military vessels. The biggest had many masts, their sails furled and stored for the time being, but their purpose obvious even from a brief inspection. Shields were stored along the flanks, with the prows shaped into aggressive looking points below the bowsprits. Others were smaller, with curved rams visible just below the waterline. Dozens of oars could be seen jutted out from the sides.

Karquesh saw Kiri scrutinise them the moment they came in sight.

A warrior, after all.

He pointed them out to her.

'There are three main types,' he said, gesturing to them. 'We call them the Aries, the Lacus and the Telum. Of the three the Lacus is the dull one, it is nothing more than a means to transport soldiers and their arms.'

'And how many women do they hold?' Kiri asked.

'Women?' Karquesh laughed and then stopped at the look on Kiri's face. 'Why none … ah … my apologies, priestess Kiri. The women of Taloon do not go to war.'

'None of them?' Kiri asked. 'Why not?'

Karquesh shook his head. 'Such things are …' He turned back to the subject of the ships. 'They carry up to forty soldiers apiece and can cover fifty marks a stretch. Some are built just for … people, others for cargo and provisions.'

'Can the phaunts be carried?' Kiri asked.

'Of course,' Karquesh replied. 'In the bigger ships. They are trained for it and they are a major asset in warfare.'

'I thought they might be,' Kiri said. 'Then you could carry our dachs too.'

'I dare say we could,' Karquesh agreed. 'If you could persuade them to reside aboard the ships.'

'Our dachs are quite disciplined,' Kiri said. 'They obey their priestesses. The other ships?'

'The Telum are vessels equipped with weapons,' Karquesh said, gesturing to a smaller series of vessels. 'Upon their bows are powerful crossbows, and they carry heavy weights and various means of setting other ships alight. They serve a single purpose, to sink opposing vessels.'

'And the Aries?'

Karquesh nodded, the girl was paying the utmost attention now. He could almost sense her filing the information away inside her mind.

'Ah, yes,' he said. 'Of all the ships, these are my favourite. They are small, but sleek and fast, rowed by the strongest. You see the bow, how it curves down to the water instead of up from it?'

Kiri nodded.

'The ram,' Karquesh said. 'Below the water is a vast metal spike. These ships are driven hard into other vessels, breaking their hulls and sending them to the bottom of the sea. Our neighbours to the sunwards have reason to fear the Aries ships.'

'Neighbours?' Kiri asked.

'The land of Kerun,' Karquesh said. 'It is why we have an army and a fleet. We are oft at war with them, but we won a decisive victory against them not long ago and they have not bothered us for rounds. They are a tough and cruel people, they live mostly amongst dunes of sand, but they raid our cities along the coast with cunning ships and vicious crews. I once saw one of their vessels cut in twain by one of ours. It sank in moments, taking all its crew with it. Such is the nature of war.'

They turned from the harbour and walked along the wall. It arced around the entire city, perhaps two marks in diameter, encircling everything within. After a while she stopped.

'There is one thing I do not understand,' she said. 'Where are the farmers? Where are the crops? The fields?'

Karquesh smiled and pointed out beyond the walls.

'Away from the city walls and the river there is desert stretching far to the shaderight and the shadeward. Nothing grows out there. Kerun to the sunward is arid too.'

'But the fruits … they were fresh. They could not have been transported far, if at all.'

'Another wonder of the ancients,' Karquesh admitted. 'Would you like to see the ancient secret of Taloon, priestess Kiri?'

She nodded. 'It has already been a stretch of wonders,' she said. 'But I would see more.'

'Very well.'

Karquesh led her down from the walls and they returned to the phaunt, mounting it once again. It took them back to the centre of the city where they disembarked once more. Yet, instead of climbing up through the city heights, Karquesh led her down stairs to levels below the ground. They passed a series of guards, who stood back away from the king.

To begin with the passageways were cut from stone. They were narrow and rough, but before long they widened out into great vaulted spaces. There were huge ranks of fresh plump vegetables and fruits being tended and boxed.

'This way,' Karquesh gestured.

In the centre of the space was a large metal circle set in the floor, perhaps forty hands in diameter. In the very centre was a lever. Karquesh waited until Kiri was alongside and then pulled it.

With a faint vibration, the disk descended through the floor. Karquesh chuckled at the alarmed look on Kiri's face, but also noted how she recovered her balance and composure.

They continued to drop down until the rock ended, the disk now suspended in the air in a vast space. Blazing light surrounded them in all directions as they caught sight of a vast underground space that stretched out in all directions.

Karquesh smiled in satisfaction. Kiri's mouth had dropped open in absolute astonishment. He heard her gasp and stagger as she took in the view.

'Shades ...' she whispered.

'One of the great secrets of Taloon,' Karquesh announced. 'Come, I will show you.'

CHAPTER TEN

Shadeward of Dynesia, Scallia

Round 2307, Fourth pass

'There it is,' Coran said, looking out through the bridge windows of the *Mobilis* and pointing ahead. 'Dead slow.'

'Dead slow, aye,' Mel replied, pulling the throttles back to just short of their idle setting. The faint churn of the engines dropped to a muted thrum.

The river had narrowed and the rocky cliffs had split in two before them. The *Mobilis* couldn't travel much further upstream.

It didn't need to. The dark opening of a cave could be seen on the port bank. The entrance was smooth and regular, cut into the rock by some unknown means. Odd fixtures jutted from the walls, rusty with long rounds of disuse. Everything was hung with vegetation.

Coran swung the helm over and the *Mobilis* turned inwards.

'Daf, Creg, be ready fore and aft.'

The cave loomed over the ship as they entered, the warmth of Lacaille replaced by a welcome dampness in the air and the sound of dripping water. The crew squinted in the darkness, waiting for their eyes to adjust.

The cave widened out inside and they could see the quay, set at right angles to the entrance.

'All looks undisturbed,' Mel said.

'Just as well,' Coran said. 'The thought of those priestesses getting hold of this.'

Mel swallowed. 'I hadn't even thought of that.'

Coran looked at her. 'They're fearsome enough with their flying dachs and magic powers, let alone if they were able to use this stuff. We need to ensure we're the only ones who can use it, take what we can back to Amar.'

Mel's observation was proved to be correct. The quayside was as dirty as before, but they could only make out the footsteps they had left the last time they had visited. Daf and Creg made the ship fast against the moorings and Mel cut the engines.

'All secure.'

'Let's go pay Caesar a visit.'

* * *

Coran led the way, with Mel, Fitch, Meru, Zoella and Ren following behind. Daf and Creg stayed behind to mind the ship. Fitch switched on and then handed out the lightglasses. They entered the narrow corridor that led away from the quay into the rocky heart of the cliffs.

'Watch your step,' Coran called. 'The floor's uneven and there are a few surprises along the way.'

'Surprises?' Zoella queried.

Meru pointed at a small alcove on the right side of the passage. Zoella peered and gasped.

A skeleton lay on the floor, the bones bright in the light. It was lying on its back, its arms held up with hands clamped around its head.

'Look familiar?' Meru asked.

'The priestesses,' Zoella said in a whisper. 'Here? When?'

'Long time ago,' Fitch said. 'Long before us and our woes that's for sure. There's more up ahead. Watch out for 'em.'

They came across a second skeleton a little further up, this one was propped against the wall, but in a similar position. Zoella looked into the empty eye sockets, wondering what sights they must have seen.

And who killed them? And why?

The tunnel opened out into a cave, their footsteps echoing around the small interior. Opposite the entrance they had come through was a large metal door, with a wheel, a lever and a small panel of buttons set in it.

'Just like last time,' Coran whispered. 'Least it seems that no one has been here. That's good news.'

Meru gestured to the door. Zoella looked.

There were more skeletons, all clustered below the door. This time their bones were blackened and burnt, dismembered and scattered.

'What happened?' Zoella whispered.

'I guess it must have been the flares, they struck before and these people were caught in a firestorm down here and …'

Meru's voice trailed off. Zoella trembled at the thought of being trapped underground as the flames consumed her.

Coran peered at the door.

'Let's hope this still works,' he said and then raised his voice. 'Unlock!'

They all looked up as there was brief hiss of noise. Then a voice echoed around them.

'Entry to this facility is restricted to authorised personnel only. Please enter your access code. Frequency forty eight point seven megahertz.'

'What was that?' Zoella asked.

'One of the voices I was telling you about,' Meru said. 'It's sort of a machine I guess. This one seems to only have one job, guard the entrance!'

'You remember the code?' Fitch asked.

'I sure do,' Coran replied, pressing the numbers into the small panel set in the door. 'One, two, three, five, eight, one, three …'

On the final number a heavy clunk echoed out of the door. Coran pulled the lever down and swung the wheel. As he did so more thumps echoed around the cave. Air hissed out for a moment and then the door folded in on itself.

A corridor led inwards. Zoella watched as overhead lights flickered on.

This magical 'tricity …

Coran led the way further in. They climbed on to a walkway suspended above the rocky floor which led to another door like the one they had just come through, but without the numbered buttons. Coran swung the wheel and pulled the lever down. The door folded back in the same manner.

Beyond was darkness, but to Zoella's surprise, Coran marched forward with his lightglass aloft.

'Try not to hold your breath,' Meru said. 'This next bit is a bit unnerving …'

Zoella and Ren looked at each other and then followed.

She could tell she was in some vast empty space by the way the sound from their movements faded away, but the darkness was impenetrable, their light glasses showed nothing other than the smooth floor they were standing on.

'Any moment now,' Coran said, standing still at the front of the group.

Zoella heard a hum from somewhere far above. It was deep and throbbing, the movement of some kind of powerful machine …

Light burst around them, the hum faded away in the intolerable glare. Ren squealed beside her and she felt him grab hold of her leg and pull himself close.

She blinked as her eyes adjusted.

Before them was a grand cavern, a huge empty space at least five hundred hands high, shaped like the inside a vast inverted bowl. Above, massive blazing orbs were casting a bright glow all about them, suspended in an enormous chandelier hanging from the roof. More lights were festooned around the cavern in concentric rings. The floor was also lit by lights embedded in the ground, illuminating bays and walkways.

Zoella looked around in astonishment. All about them were machines of different types and sizes, all arranged in their bays and organised side by side. She recognised one of the machines as being identical to the one Meru had used to rescue herself and Liana from Viresia.

'Welcome to Caesar's cavern,' Meru whispered, his voice hushed.

Zoella continued to peer about her. The machines were arranged around the circular edge of the cavern, except for in one area where a vast pair of doors could be made out. In the centre a series of glass partitions rose in multiple levels. Zoella followed as the crew moved across to it.

Within was a large central table, with a glossy black finish, around it were chairs made of some strange coloured material she didn't recognise.

'Let's hope he remembers us,' Coran said.

'Where is this Caesar you were speaking about?' Zoella asked.

Coran tapped a finger on the table top. 'Here ...'

A musical tone sounded and a picture of a hand appeared before him. Zoella gasped in surprise.

'Identify for palm print identification please.'

The voice had come from with the table. It was male, with a soft yet peculiar timbre.

Zoella watched as Coran placed his hand on the image, matching his fingers and thumbs to it. The image glowed for a brief moment around Coran's hand.

'Identification confirmed. Welcome, Coran, captain of the *Mobilis*.'

'Hello Caesar,' Coran replied. 'Do you remember us from last time?'

'Details of our last encounter have been stored in memory as a permanent record, along with those of your companions Mel, Fitch and Meru. Sensors detect two additional individuals whose identity is unknown. Please state your names, ranks and designations, if available.'

'I don't like the way he can tell who's about,' Fitch grumbled.

'Their names are Zoella and Ren,' Mel said, ignoring him.

'Welcome Zoella and Ren,' Caesar said. 'Please speak for identification purposes.'

Ren pushed forward. 'I'm Ren. What do you want me to say?'

'That single sentence is sufficient. Your voice pattern indicates you are a child, is this correct?'

'It is,' Mel said with a grin and then looked over at Zoella.

'I am Zoella,' she said. 'I don't have a rank or a des ... desig ...'

'Rank and designations are optional parameters,' Caesar replied. 'Identities have been recorded and stored. You have been granted read-only access to monitoring systems alongside your companions. Would you like a status report?'

Zoella looked at the rest of them.

'I don't understand what it's saying.'

Fitch laughed. 'Join the troop, sister.'

Coran smiled at her. 'Neither do we most of the time. Caesar, a status report would be welcome, thank you.'

A spinning circle appeared on the table, turning from red to green.

'Many sensors feeds remain unavailable. Uplinks remain unresponsive. Diagnosis has been unable to determine the precise cause.'

Text began to appear on the table. Zoella stared in surprise.

'How does …?'

Facility status summary: Poor.

Power: Poor. 23% of Magnetic Induction Panels remain operative.

Comms links: Failed. Not responding, no data.

Satellite links: Poor. One Lagrange point facility remains operating.

Obelisk status: Failed. Not responding, no data.

Internal integrity: Good. Minor atmospheric leakage detected.

Hangar assets: One class six personnel shuttle lost. Telemetry at point of loss indicated catastrophic airframe damage. All other vehicles serviced according to schedule.

Terraforming Status summary: Warning!

Atmospheric Pressure: Good. 950 millibars.

O_2 *Mix: Good. 22%.*

Pollution: Excellent. No harmful oxides or excess carbon detected.

Humidity: Good. Average 55%.

Magnetic field strength: Critical! 14 Microtesla and falling. Atmospheric loss due to solar wind erosion in progress, check Obelisk status.

Zoella's eyes widened as she read the display. Meru nodded.

'The Obelisk!' he whispered. Caesar continued.

Astrometric Condition Status summary: Critical!
Orbital eccentricity: Good. No anomalies.
Semi-major axis: Good. No anomalies.
Solar output: Critical! 790 W/m^2*. Fluctuating due to ongoing flare activity.*
Ultraviolet flux: Critical! Fluctuating on high frequency band between 110 and 315 nm.
Flare activity: Critical! Solar cycle now at maximum. Flares are likely at any time with radiation peaking in infrared, ultraviolet, microwave and x-ray frequencies.

Status report ends.

'Flares likely at any time,' Fitch grumbled. 'He's got that right.'

Zoella pushed past him.

'The Obelisk,' she said. 'What is it? Where is it?'

The display of text faded out and was replaced by a vast map which was overlaid with markers pointing to specific places. She recognised some of them. Viresia was marked, as was Nireus. She could also see Daine.

Caesar spoke once more.

'The Obelisk is a magnetic field booster positioned at co-ordinates zero zero, the substellar pole of Esurio. Its purpose is to supplement Esurio's latent magnetic field and prevent atmospheric erosion by Lacaille's solar wind. It has a secondary function of providing electrical power distribution across Esurio. It has a tertiary function as a communications relay for administrative purposes.'

The map moved. Viresia, Daine and Nireus moved upwards and another large continent was revealed below. A flashing cross hair appeared in the midst of a bright coloured area of the map.

'The Obelisk is located here,' Caesar said. 'Obelisk status is marked as failed. There has been no data connection with those systems for three hundred rounds, seventeen stretches and four chimes.'

'Far to the sunward,' Meru said. 'A really long way sunward.'

'Way off the map,' Coran agreed. 'The substellar pole, what does that mean?'

'The substellar pole is the location upon the surface of Esurio whereby Lacaille is positioned directly overhead from the perspective of the observer,' Caesar replied.

Zoella's eyes widened. 'That's what I saw!' she exclaimed. 'Lacaille, overhead and a great wall of cloud.'

'Please specify your observations,' Caesar requested.

Zoella looked around at the rest of them. Coran shrugged and indicated she should continue.

'I had a dream,' Zoella said. 'I saw a tower, made of metal, reaching high into the sky. Around it was a huge wall of cloud ...'

The map on the table disappeared and was replaced with a moving image. Zoella gasped as she saw in exquisite detail the images she had seen in her vision. The others gathered around to look. The table was displaying a view of a vast metal edifice, reaching high into the sky. A vast swirl of cloud rose behind it, moving as they watched.

'That's it ...' she whispered. 'Just like in my dream.'

'This is the last library stored visual record from the Obelisk site observation cameras taken before the communications failed,' Caesar said. 'The cloud is the internal structure of the substellar vortex.'

'Vortex?' Meru echoed.

'Satellite imagery will aid understanding,' Caesar said. The image on the table changed, the map being overlaid with streams of white and grey. 'This is a live feed of cloud cover on Esurio. The vortex is a permanent storm condition that persists around the substellar pole of Esurio.'

Over the familiar continent of Voren they could all see wispy traceries of cloud, sweeping in bands across the land. The further sunward they looked the more twisted and complex the cloud became, sweeping inwards into a gigantic angry looking spiral. The spiral was centred on the position of the Obelisk. They could just make out a small clear area right at the heart.

'It looks like an eye,' Zoella said.

As she said the words the image enlarged, centring on that location in a series of snap movements. They could see a circular area free from cloud and a metal structure at the very centre.

'This is the maximum resolution available,' Caesar reported.

'What you saw is real then,' Coran said.

'Never doubt Zoella's dreams,' Meru added. 'They come true, every time.'

'Query,' Caesar said. 'Zoella, how often to you receive such dreams or visions?'

Zoella shrugged. 'I don't know, maybe twice a round or so. Why?'

'Have these visions contained warnings?' Caesar continued.

Zoella was conscious of everyone looking at her.

'Yes. In the last one I felt compelled to go to the Obelisk,' Zoella answered. 'And that bad things would happen if I didn't ...'

'Why are you asking?' Meru demanded of Caesar.

There was an uncharacteristic pause before Caesar answered.

'This unit is programmed to assimilate any additional sources of data in case of the failure of primary data feeds.'

Zoella looked at Meru and then whispered. 'What does it mean?'

'No idea,' he said.

'All very interesting,' Fitch interrupted. 'But not why we're here. You going to ask it about your plan?'

Coran nodded. 'Caesar, we need your help.'

'Please specify request.'

'We need to borrow your machines.'

'Please specify which machines and for what purpose.'

Coran shrugged.

'What machines are available?'

On the table, text appeared once more. A list as Coran had requested.

Facility asset summary:
3x Class 6 Personnel shuttles.
4x Class 7 Surface reconnaissance vehicles.
2x Class 7 Mining vehicles
2x Class 3 Personnel transports
1x Class 3 Medical transport
1x Class 2 Equipment transport

'We need all of them,' Coran said.

'Please specify purpose,' Caesar replied.

Coran sighed, looking around at the rest of the crew.

'You'll have to tell him what's happening,' Mel said.

'Caesar,' Coran said. 'We need help in defending our island against an invading force.'

'Specify the nature of the invading force,' Caesar replied.

'A bunch of psychotic women with magic powers are hell bent on murdering us,' Fitch said.

'Please elucidate the scenario,' Caesar said. 'Magic does not exist, it is a pre-technological explanation for sleight of hand tricks or complex phenomena ...'

'Fitch,' Coran snapped. 'You're not helping ...'

'The people of Drayden wish to destroy us,' Mel said. 'They intend to attack our island of Amar.'

In a moment the map was back with two locations highlighted. The crew could see the markers over the island of Amar and the city of Daine.

'What is the motivation for the attack?' Caesar asked.

'The priestesses of Drayden believe that Lacaille is a goddess,' Meru said. 'And that Lacaille has ordered them to destroy us. They believe that will prevent the flares.'

'That is an incorrect premise,' Caesar replied. 'Lacaille is an M2V class red dwarf, not a deity. Sacrifice of life will have no effect on future flare events. They should be advised of their flawed reasoning.'

Fitch laughed. 'Yeah, why didn't we think of that?'

'We can't reason with them, Caesar,' Meru insisted. 'We've tried. I will try again, but we need to be able to defend ourselves regardless.'

'You intend to use the hangar assets to defend the island of Amar from attack by the people of Drayden?'

Meru looked at Coran who nodded.

'Yes,' Meru said. 'The priestesses have trained dachs, flying creatures, to help them. We've got to be able to counter that.'

'This unit is an automated diagnostic, forensic, reference simulation and decision making aid, providing terraforming support to the colonists of Esurio. It is not a tactical or strategic military decision making aid. Conflict between Esurio colonists is strictly prohibited by original statute and is not permissible.'

'Caesar, these priestesses don't care about your statutes,' Meru said.

'This unit is not programmed for offensive or defensive duties. The hangar assets will be ineffective in warfare as they do not carry any weaponry.'

'You won't help us?' Mel asked. 'But we will be wiped out. Surely that isn't permissible either?'

'Conflict should be averted by mediation,' Caesar replied.

'We have tried that,' Coran said. 'They are intent on destroying us.'

'This unit cannot permit a violation of statute,' Caesar replied. 'Hangar assets cannot be used for military purposes without override from an administrator.'

'We're scorched then,' Fitch said. 'Told you it would be a waste of time coming here.'

'Administrator?' Coran snapped. 'Caesar, the people you served have been dead for hundreds of rounds, there are none of these administrators left. You have to help us! Let us use the machines to defend our home!'

'This is an incorrect assertion,' Caesar answered, his voice as flat and toneless as ever.

Mel frowned, trying to follow the conversation. 'Which bit?'

'Coran stated that there are no administrators left,' Caesar replied. 'This is an incorrect assertion.'

The crew looked at each other in surprise.

'I don't understand,' Coran said.

'There are administrators,' Caesar replied. 'You have one in your company.'

The crew looked around at each other.

'Who?'

Caesar's answer was immediate. 'The individual designated as Zoella is an administrator.'

The crew looked around at Zoella. She looked bewildered.

'I'm not an … whatever it was!'

'Incorrect,' Caesar replied. 'Your bio scan indicates you have the signature nano-infusion which is the mark of an administrator.'

'Nano-infusion? What is nano-infusion?' Meru asked.

'Not now, Meru,' Coran interrupted. 'Caesar, can Zoella command you to allow us to use the machines in this hangar?'

There was another pause.

'That is affirmative,' Caesar replied.

Coran looked at Zoella and gestured to her.

'I'm not …'

'Zoella, we need this, you know we do,' Mel pleaded. 'If we're to have a chance of stopping the priestesses. We've come all this way …'

Zoella swallowed and nodded.

'How do I … ?'

'You must request hangar asset override against current policy,' Caesar replied.

Zoella looked at Coran, Mel and Meru. Ren gave her an encouraging push from behind.

'Go on, do it!'

Zoella stood before the table.

'I request hangar asset … override …' she stuttered, trying to remember the words. 'Against current policy.'

'Identify for palm print identification, please.'

The table was dark now, other than the glowing outline of a hand print. Zoella placed her hand on it and it grew brighter.

'Identity verified. Nano-infusion levels confirmed. Administrative access granted and override confirmed. Zoella, you are now a level two administrator. Hangar assets are at your disposal.'

'Now what?' Zoella asked.

'I can fly one of the machines,' Meru said. 'But the others ...'

'All hangar assets have autonomous piloting and navigation capability,' Caesar replied. They can be given rendezvous coordinates or follow a designated target. For travel overseas the ground units can be carried aboard the personnel transports. Would you like all hangar assets prepped for immediate roll out?'

Zoella nodded. 'Yes. Prepare the ... the hangar assets.'

'Instructions confirmed,' Caesar said. 'All hangar assets will be prepared immediately.'

Coran grinned at her. 'Well done! Now, let's get moving. We need to get all of this stuff back to Amar. There's work to do.'

The crew were ready to move when Caesar spoke again.

'Query,' he said. 'Administrator Zoella, are you able to contact the Obelisk?'

Zoella shook her head. 'I don't understand. Contact it? How?'

'All administrators have access to multiple facilities via mesh communication and remote telemetry. Are you able to contact the Obelisk?'

Fitch laughed again.

'I don't know what you're talking about,' Zoella said. 'I dreamt about it, saw it, is that what you mean?'

'Did the Obelisk provide any instructions?' Caesar demanded.

'Tell him what you saw in your dream,' Meru said. 'It's got to be important. Tell him!'

'Please provide all pertinent details,' Caesar said.

'It was asking me to come to it,' Zoella explained. 'In my dream something was going wrong, there was heat, a fierce blue light that came from Lacaille. Animals and people died from burns and ran screaming as they were consumed ... it was horrible ...'

'What does it mean, Caesar?' Coran asked.

Again there was a pause.

'Your testimony matches current data,' Caesar replied. 'The Obelisk is a magnetic field booster positioned at co-ordinates zero zero, the substellar pole of Esurio. Its purpose is to supplement Esurio's latent magnetic field and prevent atmospheric erosion by Lacaille's solar wind. There is no direct data feed from the Obelisk. Your testimony confirms observations of reducing magnetic field strength and associated fluctuations.'

Zoella and Meru looked at each other and then spoke at once.

'We still don't understand, Caesar. Simple words, please.'

'The Obelisk is malfunctioning,' Caesar replied. 'Failure of primary capability appears to be accelerating. The initial impact will be intermittent loss of electro-magnetic induction power distribution. Upon Obelisk failure, power distribution will halt and atmospheric erosion will reach critical values. Flare generated ultraviolet, x-ray and microwave radiation exposure will rapidly increase to fatal levels as ozone layer depletion rises exponentially.'

Meru was listening intently.

'I'm still not clear,' Mel whispered. 'But that sounds very bad.'

'If I'm right,' Meru said, his face going white as he thought it through. 'First we're going to lose all the 'tricity ...'

'Like when the *Mobilis* was adrift?' Coran asked.

Meru nodded. 'But for good.'

'And what else?' Mel demanded.

Meru swallowed.

'And the next flare that goes off is going to kill everyone.'

Silence greeted his comment, interrupted only after a moment by Caesar's toneless voice.

'Imprecise,' it said. 'But essentially correct. Precise arrival time of flare intensity of fatal levels is unknown.'

'How long do we have?' Zoella asked.

'Available data is insufficient to make a precise determination,' Caesar replied. 'However the Obelisk was designed to be self-regulating and only to contact the Administrators in the case of irresolvable systemic failure.'

'It was calling to me,' Zoella replied. 'It needs me to go to it. It's urgent, I know it is.'

'This unit concurs with your conclusion,' Caesar replied. 'Obelisk failure is likely within a short interval of passes. Its repair must be prioritised or all human life on Esurio will be in peril.'

'We've got to go to the Obelisk,' Meru said.

'Now wait just a snuttin' minute,' Fitch interrupted. 'We've got to get back to Amar. Remember that plan? Saving ourselves from the crazy magic women with the death wish? What about that?'

'If we don't fix the Obelisk we'll all be dead,' Meru shot back.

'He's right. We've got to go,' Zoella added. 'I know we have ...'

'And you know how to fix it do you?' Fitch argued. 'We've already had this conversation. You don't know nothing! No offence to your new found administrator powers young lady, but a couple of dreams isn't exactly going to qualify you to fix some ancient machine from thousands of rounds ago is it?'

Zoella swallowed. Fitch shook his head.

'I thought as much. And how are you going to get there? Look at that map, there's a massive storm between here and there. Even if you did know what you were doing, I don't see how you can get there.'

'Environmental conditions at the substellar pole are dangerous,' Caesar said. 'Penetrating the substellar cyclone will be fraught with difficulty due to wind intensity, static discharge and high levels of precipitation. The personnel shuttles have insufficient maximum altitude to avoid the cyclone but are certified for storm conditions and should be able to make the transit. However, caution is advised.'

'So, we can fly there,' Meru said. 'See? It is possible.'

'It's madness, that's what it is,' Fitch replied.

'Caesar,' Coran said. 'Is there another way to fix to the Obelisk?'

'Without precise data on the current issues with the Obelisk facility it is impossible to make a determination,' Caesar replied. 'Fault simulation indicates the most likely problem scenario is a failure of sensor inputs and auxiliary systems. This will require on site repairs.'

'Which you won't be able to do,' Fitch argued. 'Because we don't know how the damn thing works.'

'The Obelisk has a similar audio prompted interactive facility as I do,' Caesar replied. 'If members of this group are able to arrive at the Obelisk facility, it should be able to guide you through the necessary diagnostic and repair procedures.'

'There you go,' Meru said, glaring at Fitch. 'It can tell us how to fix it.'

Fitch straightened and folded his arms, looking over to Coran.

'It's your call then, Captain,' Fitch said. 'Another crazy quest, or doing something practical to save Amar.'

Coran sighed.

'We could try both,' Mel said. 'Split up …'

'Yeah, like that's worked really well in the past,' Fitch said.

'Enough, Fitch,' Coran said. 'Mel's right. We've got to defend Amar, but this Obelisk thing … If what I'm hearing is true then if we don't fix that then there won't be an Amar to save. The question is who …'

'I have to go to the Obelisk,' Zoella said. 'I'm the administrator. It needs me.'

'And I can fly her there,' Meru said. 'I know these machines better than anyone.'

'We need her in Amar,' Fitch countered. 'She's got the same power as the witches. She's got to fight with us!'

'That's a good point,' Mel admitted.

'Then we have to fly to the Obelisk, fix it and get back to Amar as soon as we can,' Meru said, looking at Zoella. She nodded.

'We've got to get to it,' Zoella said. 'If it fails we all die, your people and the priestesses … everyone!'

'What about getting the other machines to Amar?' Coran asked.

'Caesar said they can fly themselves, or they can follow the *Mobilis*,' Meru said.

'This statement is correct,' Caesar added.

'We can't let you two go off alone,' Mel said.

'What choice is there?' Meru asked. 'Coran is needed to organise Amar since the senate is so useless. Fitch knows all about the weapons we have and how to make them better and you need to keep the *Mobilis* running. You need Daf and Creg to man the ship. There's no other choice, Zoella and I have to go. We've done it before, we can do it again.'

'Meru, you know what happened last time,' Mel said.

'But we know so much more now,' Meru said. 'More about the world, more about flying, more about the people … and I'll have Zoella to keep me safe.'

She looked at him and smiled. 'I'll try.'

Coran looked around at the crew.

'I don't like it,' he said. 'But I don't see an alternative. Zoella and Meru will go to the Obelisk and try to fix it before returning to Amar. The rest of us are heading back to Amar right now before those priestesses find a way to invade. Let's not waste any more time. Jump to it.'

* * *

Zoella and Meru were sitting at Caesar's table. There was little more they could do whilst the machines in the hangar were prepared. The crew of the *Mobilis* watched as a series of small vehicles had emerged from recessed compartments in the hangar walls to check and adjust the machines. Caesar had indicated it would take two or three chimes for everything to be ready.

Zoella was looking at the various maps and readouts he was able to provide for them. The huge spiral of cloud over the Obelisk's position was hard to grasp in her mind. It was as big, if not bigger, than an entire continent; a storm that had raged forever.

'Cyclonic forces are significant,' Caesar said in summary.

'Bad weather then,' Zoella said.

'Imprecise, but essentially correct,' Caesar replied.

'Very bad,' Meru said. 'Hundreds of marks of thunderstorms and high winds.'

'And … what did you mean by should be able to make the transit?' Zoella asked, jabbing Caesar's table with her finger.

'As I indicated before, personnel shuttles are certified for storm-laden flight paths,' Caesar replied. 'However, conditions are perilous. Caution is advised.'

'Do you think you can fly us there, through the storm?' Zoella asked Meru. 'And not crash this time?'

Meru pulled a face at her.

'I think so. We broke an engine last time because an arrow got stuck in it. Hopefully we won't run into that sort of problem.'

The comment made Zoella think for a moment. Meru was watching her as a frown crossed her face.

'What is it?'

'If I can hear the Obelisk calling me because of this … power … this gift,' she began. 'What if others have too? Maybe some of the priestesses have heard this as well? Maybe she has …'

'Kiri,' Meru whispered. 'But they're determined to attack Amar. They won't understand what the Obelisk is asking. They don't have Caesar to explain it.'

'But they might have the same vision, they might figure it out. Who's to say what other knowledge they have that could lead them there?'

Meru nodded. 'It's a risk, but they don't have flying machines. I doubt you could ride a dach through a thunderstorm. They can't get there like we can.'

'We should be on our guard all the same,' Zoella said. 'I'm going to see about food and water for the trip.'

She got up and left Meru with Caesar.

He sat still for a moment before turning around in his chair and leaning over Caesar's table.

'Can I ask you a question Caesar?'

'You may,' Caesar's voice intoned.

'When we were in Nireus,' Meru began. 'We saw this light in the sky. It was high up, beyond the clouds. I could see it in Coran's 'scope, it was an object. I did the maths on it and it doesn't make sense …'

'You are enquiring into the nature of this object?' Caesar asked.

'I guess so,' Meru said.

'That information is restricted based on a classification index. Only level two administrators and above can access restricted information. Emergency protective protocols are in operation. You do not have sufficient administrative privilege.'

'So you keep telling me,' Meru said. 'I think I've worked it out anyway. It's a ship isn't it? A ship in an orbit, just like this world Esurio orbits Lacaille.'

Caesar didn't respond for a moment.

'How did you come by this conclusion?'

Meru grinned. 'I landed at this place on my way to Drayden, found out a bunch of stuff. You will know it as waymarker thirty five, sixty four.'

There was another pause.

'That facility is listed as the Holroyd Radio Telescope,' Caesar replied.

'Yes, and the screens there told me that the last telemetry received before the telescope stopped working was a message from a vessel. It was called the *Du Maurier*. It was in a stable orbit. That's the light in the sky, isn't it?'

This time the pause was lengthy.

'Your determination is correct,' Caesar said. Meru fancied his voice was almost reluctant. 'Will you share your calculations with me?'

Meru took the scribbled notes from his pocket.

'Please place them face down on the table,' Caesar instructed.

Meru did so and saw a quick flash of light illuminate the paper.

'Your calculations are correct,' Caesar said. 'But your input data is in error.'

'How so?'

'You are correct in determining that the *Du Maurier* is in a stable orbit around Esurio. However your determination of altitude is in error. Fifty marks would be an insufficient height to clear the denser portion of Esurio's atmosphere.'

'So how high is it?' Meru asked.

'The vessel is orbiting at a mean height of seven hundred marks, to avoid interactions with the Esurio thermosphere.'

'Seven hundred! But that means ...'

'Your determination of angular diameter is crude, but is the correct method of determining size based on the angle subtended at the point of observation. The actual length of the *Du Maurier* is twenty six point eight marks.'

Meru blinked.

'Twenty six!' Meru leaned back on the chair for a moment before moving forwards. 'Caesar, what sort of ship is the *Du Maurier*?'

'That information is restricted based on a ...'

'Stop that,' Meru snapped. 'I worked it all out without your help. Before you said that the emergency protocols could be cancelled if an assessment of the current culture indicates that it has sufficient technological ...'

'And social and economic capability to assimilate the data,' Caesar finished.

'I worked this out on my own,' Meru said. 'I can understand it. Cancel the emergency protocols.'

Again there was a pause.

'Not all criteria have been satisfied,' Caesar replied. 'Technological understanding alone is insufficient.'

'Then give me level two administrative access,' Meru snapped.

'You are not entitled to level two administrative access,' Caesar replied. 'You are not an administrator.'

Meru glowered at the table top, but the machine was implacable.

A laugh came from behind him. He turned to see Zoella was watching him.

'Sounds like you need my help again.'

'How long have you been there?'

'Not long, just long enough to see you getting impatient.'

'No need to be smug just because …'

Her smile faded. 'And no need for you to be rude. I offered to help you before and you turned me down, seems to be a habit of yours. We're supposed to be working together on this.'

Meru sighed. 'I'm sorry, I just …'

'You want some answers,' Zoella interrupted. 'I get it. Provisions for the trip are ready by the way. Mel's already organised it.'

'I thought she might have,' Meru replied. 'Now, if I could just get …'

Zoella leant across him.

'Caesar, tell Meru what he wants to know, or he's going to be sulking for the rest of the stretch.'

'Administrator Zoella, are you granting a temporary override of emergency protocols on behalf of Meru?' Caesar asked.

Zoella rolled her eyes. 'Yes Caesar, I am granting a temporary override of emergency protocols on behalf of Meru.'

'Override exception noted,' Caesar replied. 'Please be aware that detailed interrogation of historical records is not recommended at your current cultural level. Please confirm you wish to proceed.'

Zoella and Meru exchanged a glance.

'Maybe we shouldn't ask,' Zoella said. 'The more we know …'

'The better we understand,' Meru countered.

'Or the more trouble we'll get ourselves into.'

'Please!'

Zoella shrugged. 'All right. Caesar, confirmed.'

'Meru, state your request.'

'Tell me what the *Du Maurier* is. Tell me all about it.'

'The *ICS Du Maurier* is a third generation self-contained hybrid embryo space colonisation and sleeper vessel. It was constructed in orbit about the Earth, in the Sol system, between Earth calendar dates 2245 and 2288. It was launched in 2289, the last such vessel to leave, under the command of Admiral Gregory Drayden …'

'Drayden was a person?' Zoella said.

'Shhhh!' Meru hissed.

'… embarking on a 632 year long voyage to the Lacaille 9352 system, arriving in orbit of planet Lacaille 9352B, later named Esurio, in Earth calendar date 2921. Initial colonisation of Esurio took place 22 years later and served as the basis for the start of the Esurio calendar. It is now 2307 rounds since the initial colonisation event. Continue?'

Meru swallowed, his throat dry. He looked at Zoella. She nodded.

'Continue.'

'The ICS *Du Maurier* remains in a stable orbit about Esurio with a mean altitude of 700 marks. Last communication from the vessel was received in round 232 indicating the ship had entered hibernation mode, on board life support had been terminated, but orbital elements remained within tolerance. Esurio-based observations appear to indicate that the station-keeping capabilities of the ICS *Du Maurier* are still operating effectively, however it is not currently possible to contact the vessel without operational ground based transmission capability. Summary report ends.'

'This Earth, is this another planet? We came from there?' Meru asked.

'That is correct. Earth is the third planet in the Sol system. The Sol system is 10.74 light years away from the Lacaille 9352 system. Humanity originated on the planet Earth.'

'Wait … a light year?' Meru asked. 'What is a light year? Come to think of it, what is a year?'

'A light year is the distance travelled by light in a single year,' Caesar replied. 'A year represents a single orbit of Earth around Sol. In Esurian measurements a year is approximately seven eighths of a round. Thus a light year is approximately nine million million marks.'

Meru blinked, trying to assimilate what Caesar was saying.

'Million million?' he said, his voice hushed.

'Then why did we come here from so far away?' This time it was Zoella's question.

'Due to a major environmental catastrophe Earth became uninhabitable. The ICS *Du Maurier* and her sister ships carried human embryos to nearby habitable systems within a 20 light year radius of the Sol system with the stated purpose to colonise worlds in those systems and preserve the existence of humanity.'

'Sister ships?' Meru asked. 'How many were there?'

'Records indicate that a total of 36 ships were dispatched from the Sol system.'

Meru looked across at Zoella. 'More ships, more systems …'

'So we didn't even come from here,' Zoella whispered. 'We travelled here from far away thousands of rounds ago. Our ancestors wanted to make this place a home. But what happened? What went wrong?'

'Colonisation was successful for the first 341 rounds,' Caesar replied. 'However the flare nature of the M2V class red dwarf Lacaille 9352 was not understood at the time. The first flare was unanticipated and caused widespread destruction and loss of life.'

'Sandra Morino,' Meru whispered.

'Who?'

'The remains of a woman we found here,' Meru said, his voice hushed. 'She'd recorded a message from that time, warning folks to avoid the flares. We found her body in this hangar, she was alone.'

'No detailed historical data is available post round 341,' Caesar continued. 'There was no access to this system between Sandra Morino's input and your access. In the interim time, communications with all facilities were impaired and continue to degrade. However, it should be noted that humanity was able to survive and prosper on Esurio despite the devastation, as your presence and the widespread human habitation of the planet indicates.'

'You were alone for two thousand rounds?' Zoella asked.

'No,' Caesar replied. 'One nine six four rounds.'

Meru smiled at the look on Zoella's face.

'What did you do in all that time?' Zoella asked.

'This unit entered a quiescent state and awaited further input,' Caesar replied.

'Didn't you get … lonely?'

'This unit is not programmed to experience emotional states.'

Zoella blinked.

'Caesar isn't a person,' Meru tried to explain. 'I'm not sure what he is ...'

'I am an automated diagnostic, forensic, reference simulation and decision making aid, providing terraforming support to the colonists of Esurio,' Caesar explained.

'Somehow,' Zoella said. 'That really doesn't help.'

CHAPTER ELEVEN

Airea, Capital of Taloon

Round 2307, Fifth pass

A gentle toll of bells summoned them. Kiri was reunited with Liana and the two junior priestesses. The others were dressed as she was, with variations in colour. Liana wore yellow, with the other two in a light green and a mauve. It seemed Taloon embraced colour wherever it could.

Kiri assembled her two younger priestesses and led Liana along beside her. Taloon did have many secrets. She was still marvelling at what she had seen beneath the streets of the city.

All their food, all their crops.

There was no time to think further on it now, she had to concentrate. The pleasantries could wait, negotiation between Drayden and Taloon was the order of business now. Her senses were attuned. She was ready.

A servant bowed and led them through the corridors of the palace. They arrived at a set of double doors which opened as they approached. Within was the palace courtroom, a riot of coloured tapestries and carpets adorned the place, with the interior space set here and there with great pillars of the same white stone she had seen from the air.

Along the sides servants stood, wafting cooling breezes with huge dark fronds.

Ahead of them, King Karquesh sat upon a wooden throne. It was emblazoned with intricate shining metal decorations. He was flanked by his guards, five on each side; tall stern looking men dressed in the leather armour of Taloon. In front of these, six women were arranged at his feet. They were scantily dressed, sitting upon cushions.

The servant walked forward and bowed.

'The priestesses of Drayden, your majesty.'

Karquesh got to his feet and strode forward, looking at Kiri with a smile upon his face.

'Welcome, welcome,' he called, his arms spread wide. 'We are most honoured to entertain you once again, priestess Kiri.'

Kiri bowed before him.

'The honour is ours,' she replied. 'You know my companions, Adrella and Tali.'

Karquesh looked at them, the smile not leaving his face. He turned his attention to Liana.

'And Liana, yes …'

'Liana of Scallia,' Kiri said in response. Liana bowed her head, but said nothing.

'My wives,' he said, turning to indicate the women behind him. 'Nia, Nala, Zahra, Ayah, Eshal and Kamile.'

'Six wives,' Kiri said.

'I know,' Karquesh said. 'A king should have more, I am always on the lookout for another.' Kiri caught his gaze and was unable to repress a shudder.

To be a mere token of his, how can these women have chosen that? Perhaps they have no choice.

She was conscious of Liana standing motionless next to her.

Is it much different to what we plan with her? If Karquesh can be swayed by physical appearances, so much the better.

Karquesh continued. 'You want for nothing, I hope?'

'Your hospitality continues to be without fault,' Kiri replied.

'The women of the palace know their duties well,' Karquesh replied. 'As we have already seen, things are quite different here than in your country.'

'Different … yes,' Kiri agreed. 'Yet, not so much that there can't be an understanding between us.'

Karquesh's smile broadened.

'To business then. Vandare tells me that your visit is not merely to appreciate the wonders of our city and our land, but that you have a request to make. Will you walk with me, Kiri of Drayden?'

Kiri nodded and stepped alongside him, her heels clicking on the floor. They walked to the side doors of the courtroom, which opened before them, leading out on to a wide veranda that overlooked the city. Kiri once again caught sight of the central thoroughfare, the bridges and the clear blue water of the river that flowed amidst the buildings.

She turned her thoughts back to her task.

'My request comes from Nerina, high priestess of Drayden,' Kiri said. 'She has decreed that we must complete a holy task, in defence of all peoples.'

'And what is this task?'

'You will have seen the flares,' Kiri said. 'The wrath of Lacaille herself.'

Karquesh paused. 'We have seen them, there was fire and damage here, some lives were lost, but we have fared well enough I think. You say this is the wrath ...'

'Of Lacaille, yes,' Kiri answered. 'The goddess looks down upon us and is displeased.'

'A goddess,' Karquesh said. 'This is the faith of the priestesses.'

'It is,' Kiri said. 'Her dictates apply to all peoples.'

'And why is the goddess Lacaille so displeased?' Karquesh asked.

'In times long gone the priestesses were instructed to rid the world of evil,' Kiri said. 'It was our great undertaking, we call it the "task appointed". It remains unfinished. This is why the flares come, it is our punishment for our failure.'

'Then what must be done to atone for that?'

Kiri looked at him. 'A foe of Drayden must be vanquished.'

'And this foe lies across the sea,' Karquesh said.

Kiri nodded. 'Then you already understand high priestess Nerina's request.'

Karquesh sighed. 'You wish to make war upon another land,' he said. 'With Taloon providing the means to do so.'

'It is called Amar,' Kiri said. 'It lies far to the shaderight.'

'I have heard the name,' Karquesh replied. 'Though I do not know much of it. An island to the sunright I understand. Perhaps our scholars will know more.'

'They are a force of evil that should have been vanquished long ago,' Kiri said. 'Long ago they built machines, machines which flew through the air, scorched the earth and poisoned the waters. Our first high priestess, Elena, she defeated them in battle, but the survivors fled overseas. Lacaille punishes us all with the flares, until such time as the evil is eradicated.'

'Flying machines?' Karquesh said, disbelief on his features.

'I have seen one,' Kiri said. 'Fought one on my very own dach and brought it down.'

'They sound fearsome indeed,' Karquesh said. 'And only a fool would attack an enemy without gauging their strength.'

'We know enough,' Kiri replied. 'Their strength is in their machines, not in their people. As we defeated Viresia, so we will defeat Amar. The priestesses will overwhelm them as before.'

'I have heard many tales of Viresia,' Karquesh replied. 'It seems your victory was decisive.'

Kiri straightened. 'The priestesses of Drayden have the means to cause pain in the bodies of others,' she said. 'Men cower and scream before us when we unleash it. We fly our dachs beyond the range of their weapons and then rain fire down upon them. Few survive such an assault, and those who do are swiftly despatched by overwhelming numbers.'

'Quite the formidable foe,' Karquesh acknowledged.

'Amar will fall, as all others have done,' Kiri said. 'We merely need to get there. Our dachs cannot fly all that way.'

Karquesh leaned on the balustrade that ran around the veranda.

'You ask much, priestess Kiri,' he said. 'Drayden asks much.'

'The rewards would be great too,' Kiri said. 'Which reminds me, I bring a gift for you.'

Karquesh turned to look at her. 'A gift?'

'Indeed,' Kiri said. 'Lady Liana.'

Karquesh paused and looked back through the doors at Liana with renewed interest, but he then turned his attention to Kiri.

'A generous gift,' he said. 'She is quite exquisite. How is she yours to give?'

Kiri smiled. 'The spoils of war,' she replied. 'I conquered Scallia, subdued their capital and … killed their King.'

She saw him swallow, but she continued before he could speak.

'I pursued her and captured her. A prize. She is royalty, of the house Tiamoi of Scallia.'

'Scallia tried to resist the might of Drayden,' Karquesh said, his voice soft.

'A mistake,' Kiri replied. 'They learnt a hard lesson.'

'And Drayden wishes to continue its conquests?' Karquesh asked. 'This land of Amar of which you speak …'

'Across the sea,' Kiri said. 'Yes. It is the will of Lacaille. None can resist her call. As I said, it is Drayden's great undertaking, our task appointed.'

'And yet Drayden has no fleet of ships,' Karquesh said. 'Taloon does.'

'Conquest,' Kiri replied and then shrugged. 'Or cooperation. A choice that lies before all who would contend with us.'

'Taloon is not without its strengths,' Karquesh said.

'Scallia thought so too,' Kiri returned.

Karquesh smiled and then looked back to Liana.

'A fine gift, a fine gift indeed,' he mused. 'But one with a metal-threaded cord attached.'

'You would also have the gratitude and favour of the high priestess of Drayden herself,' Kiri said. 'Such an honour is not easily bestowed, nor is it common, but it is to be highly valued.'

'And this land of Amar,' Karquesh continued. 'You wish to subdue it according to the will of Lacaille. For those of us not given over to such religious fervour, might there be spoils of war?'

Kiri smiled. 'Such women as we deign to take would be ours, all others are to be put to the sword as Lacaille dictates. Other treasures as might be found? They are yours. Coin, metals, anything else you may do with as you will.'

'And the land itself?'

'A province of Drayden with a tithe, but we would not be adverse to a ruler allied with us, who could exploit its riches for their own ends.'

Karquesh nodded.

'I will think upon this,' Karquesh said. 'You will have my answer by the end of the next stretch.'

Kiri bowed. 'I thank you, King Karquesh.'

'In the meantime, might I be permitted to give you a further tour of the city? There is still much to see. We have time before the banquet.'

'I should like that.'

* * *

Taryen watched the King and the priestess girl approach. Both were smiling, exchanging pleasantries as they walked together and the King pointed at various buildings visible along their route.

This girl is one of their greatest warriors?

Karquesh caught sight of him.

'Ah, Taryen,' he said, signalling for him to come over. Taryen did so, stretching up to his full height and looking down on the shorter woman.

'Priestess Kiri of Drayden,' Karquesh said. 'You remember my cousin, Prince Taryen, son of my late aunt.'

'I remember you from when I first arrived,' the girl replied.

She bowed her head, but Taryen could see she kept her gaze on him as she did so. She was unarmed and dressed in the flimsy garments beloved of the women of Taloon, yet her left hand was hidden within a black velvet glove that reached up to her wrist. None of the others wore such a thing; he wondered what it was for.

He could see firm muscle tone in her build and there were scars on her skin, showing through despite the colourings that had been applied.

'I'm honoured to meet you, Prince Taryen,' she said.

'You are the famous … warrior … from Drayden?'

She didn't miss the scorn in his voice. He saw her eyes narrow.

'I am a priestess of Drayden, of the warrior caste,' she said.

'Do you have no men that can fight in Drayden?' he asked. 'That you have to do all the fighting?'

'Do not cause offence, Taryen,' Karquesh rumbled.

'None is taken,' Kiri replied. She was glaring at him now. 'Men cannot fight the way we do. Too clumsy, too slow.'

'Then what use are we to you?' Taryen asked. 'Our women are civilised, they do not fight.'

'There are many things in Taloon that are of value,' Kiri replied. 'Drayden has many concerns.'

'Perhaps we don't want to share with you?'

'You would stand against Drayden?' Kiri asked.

'I would stand against all who seek to impose their will upon my people,' Taryen said. 'Taloon is not some minor power such as you have claimed victory over in the past.'

'Minor power?' Kiri asked.

'Oh, I credit you with a good story,' Taryen said. 'Defeating the Scallians with an army of women. But it will not happen here, not while real men defend Taloon.'

'That is enough, Taryen,' Karquesh said. 'You will honour our guest. She is a mighty warrior of renown. She has slain kings and princes in battle, your greatest deed is to have marched up and down the colonnade in fresh armour. You will show the proper respect to a true warrior.'

A true warrior? Your time will come cousin!

Taryen bowed, his words taut and grating as he spoke. 'All honour to you then, warrior Kiri of Drayden.'

The pair continued on. Taryen watched them go.

And upstart women will be taught their proper place.

* * *

'You must forgive my cousin,' Karquesh said. 'He is a disenchanted man. His mother sowed many seeds of entitlement into his mind as a child. He believes he should have been King. Though he is younger, he is old fashioned and does not perceive that the world changes around us, or that others have different points of view.'

'Can you not banish him to some remote province?' Kiri asked. 'That is what would happen to troublesome people in Drayden.'

'He is my cousin,' Karquesh said. 'Family is rarely as simple as that.'

Kiri nodded. 'I have seen that to be true. Does he fight?'

'Fight?' Karquesh said. 'In a manner I suppose. He has a fondness for weapons and fancies he has some skill. But Taloon is not and has not been at war for long rounds.'

'Born at the wrong time,' Kiri said.

'Consider him not,' Karquesh said. 'Come, the banquet will soon be ready. It is time for us to prepare.'

* * *

The banquet was as lavish as Kiri had expected. The heads of the noble families and the high rank or otherwise worthy folk of Taloon were out in force. Kiri and the other priestesses were the centre point of all conversations and much in demand throughout the event.

Wine and appetisers were served first. Kiri noticed that all the servants that swarmed about the guests had pale skin. Their eyes were odd too, not blue, brown or even green, they were a disconcerting pink. Their hair, cropped short, was white. None of them stopped or made eye contact with her. None of the guests acknowledged them either, so it seemed it was typical for Taloon.

The food was varied and excellent. Fresh sweetbuds, melps, corcuns and tupes, mixed with a choice of seafood and meats. All were choice cuts.

A bell tolled. Around her Kiri saw the guests taking their places at long tables. More food was imminent. Kiri, Liana, Adrella and Tali were placed near each other, interspersed with people from Karquesh's court. Their table was set in the centre of the hall with space either side. Perhaps there would be dancing later.

Karquesh was seated at the head of the table, but the chair opposite Kiri was empty. He clapped his hands and the muted buzz of conversation faded away.

'Honoured priestesses of Drayden, friends, nobles and guests,' Karquesh intoned. 'Welcome to my table. Eat, drink!'

Food was placed before them by the servants. They were fast and slick in their movements, almost balletic. Kiri picked up polished metal utensils, turning them over in her fingers.

Expensive. They try to impress us and they have succeeded. That a girl like me could come from the slums to eat at the table of a King ...

She had just finished her main course and the servants were beginning to tidy away the plates when she felt it. She stiffened, looking up and around to find the source of the strange sensation.

Metallic, that unmistakeable tang of ...

Someone nearby was familiar with the gift, someone had used the nexion, subtly for sure, but impossible to hide from one such as herself. She looked around herself at the table. Neither Adrella or Tali seemed to have noticed and none of the other guests had stopped their conversations.

Then, who?

Beyond the table the servants were in attendance, plates stacked high, moving in swift ordered rows to carry out their tasks.

One caught her eye, a servant girl.

Kiri stared into her eyes for a brief moment. She almost got to her feet, but another figure blocked her view and when she looked again, the servant was gone.

There is more to all this than meets the eye.

'So, we see fit to entertain these priestesses, do we?'

Kiri recognised the voice of Taryen. He was standing behind the empty place setting, glaring at her.

'Take your place, Taryen,' Karquesh rumbled.

'Have you given in to their demands?' Taryen asked. 'Cravenly fallen at their feet? Tempted perhaps …' He eyed Liana, who was sitting alongside Kiri. '… by Scallian flesh?'

'Sit down,' Karquesh said, as conversation dropped around them all. 'And act in a civilised manner.'

Taryen waited a long moment and then pulled out the chair and sat down. Food was placed before him but he did not eat it, rather he sat with arms folded and glared across the table at Kiri.

'Taryen believes that Taloon should forge its own destiny, without resorting to allegiances with others,' Karquesh said with a nod, addressing those around the table. 'What say you, priestess Kiri?'

Those around Karquesh nodded and muttered before looking at Kiri to see how she would respond.

Kiri looked at Taryen and then let her gaze slide away, focussing her attention on Karquesh.

'Taryen is wrong.'

Out of the corner of her eye Kiri saw Taryen unfold his arms and pull something from his waist. It was a dagger. She could just make out a jewel-encrusted handle. She poised, ready to jump to her feet and defend herself, but the man moved slowly, holding the dagger before him, before driving it point first into the table.

He then released it, leaving it quivering for a moment. All conversation ceased.

'Don't be a fool, Taryen,' Karquesh snapped. 'Take your weapon and leave before you embarrass yourself further.'

'I have made the challenge,' Taryen said. 'I will not retract it.'

'The priestesses of Drayden are not subject to our laws,' Karquesh said. 'Nor are they bound to our customs.'

'Nevertheless,' Taryen said, 'I challenge this priestess. What I say is truth. Those of Taloon should never bow the knee to others!'

'What is this challenge?' Kiri demanded.

'It is a duel,' Karquesh said, his gaze locked on her. 'A fight to the death according to custom. It is how differences of opinion between our warriors have long been decided. Naturally you can decline, we do not expect visitors to …'

And my chance of securing your allegiance if I decline? You are clever Karquesh. You could stop this, but you choose not to. Whether I win or lose … you win! You remove this troubling cousin of yours, or you make Drayden look weak and useless.

'You can afford to lose your cousin?' Kiri countered, still ignoring Taryen. 'For you will.'

'It is his choice to challenge you,' Karquesh replied. 'And yours to respond. We will understand if you do not …'

'I accept,' Kiri said, and dabbed at her lips with a cloth. She heard gasps of surprise from around the table. She deigned to give Taryen a glance. 'When do we fight?'

'First chime upon the next stretch,' Taryen grunted at her, raising his head, flexing his muscles and looking down at her.

Kiri raised an eyebrow.

'I have not the time for that,' she replied. 'Why not now?'

'Now?' Taryen echoed in surprise. Kiri saw his gaze rove over her silky dress and then look back at her face.

'Yes now,' Kiri replied. 'And before dessert, I will want something sweet afterwards.'

She held every gaze as she got to her feet and walked a short distance from the dining table. She pulled off her shoes and stood, arms folded, a few hands away, waiting.

'Well?'

Taryen got to his feet, his chair scraping back with a loud, rough grind. He stalked around the table, passing behind Karquesh. He leant across the table and pulled the dagger out, offering it to her, hilt first.

She took it, keeping her gaze locked on his. Then she turned it over in her fingers before handing it back to him. Behind her there were gasps of surprise.

'I do not wish to kill you.'

Taryen stepped back. He waved the dagger around in front of him. She spared a glance at his clothing, an embroidered shirt and baggy pantaloons. He was no better protected against a sharp blade than she was.

'You will fight me!'

There was space enough in the hall. Beyond that columns marked a corridor in which the servants were pulling back the food-laden trolleys out of range of the coming altercation.

'Are you resolved at this?' Karquesh asked. 'Once started, this cannot be stopped.'

'Yes,' Taryen snorted, a grin growing on his face.

Kiri nodded too. 'I am.'

'And will you bear no weapon?' Karquesh asked.

'None,' Kiri replied.

'Very well,' Karquesh said. He rose to his feet. 'Let this be witnessed by all, people of Taloon and Drayden alike, that this contest was willingly entered into by both parties. The rules are simple. Two enter, one leaves.'

Kiri and Taryen stood across from each other. Silence reigned in the hall.

Karquesh stretched out his arms.

'Begin.'

Taryen dropped into a deep crouch, the dagger poised before him. He swiped it through the air, the blade making a sharp whistling sound as he did so. Kiri sidestepped, her posture a little crouched, her gaze fixed on his, her hands ready before her. Taryen moved closer, jabbing with the dagger. Kiri ignored him, moving to keep a distance between them and continuing to step around.

Taryen yelled and came at her, his dagger raised high and striking down at her chest.

Fool! So obvious!

She stepped to one side, turning her body away from him. She grasped his wrist with her left hand on top and her right underneath as he came past.

She pulled her arms down and crouched, twisting his wrist around as she did so, all in a smooth fluid movement. Taryen surged past, stumbling forward before his legs went out from underneath him. He landed on his back with a heavy thud on the hard floor, a gasping moan of pain forced from his lungs, leaving him stunned and confused.

There was no time for him to recover. Kiri twisted his wrist further. Something cracked. Taryen yelled in pain and his dagger clattered from his grasp. She released her right hand and grabbed it, the other continuing to twist Taryen's wrist. Another crack. His screams filled the hall.

The blow was short and accurate.

Taryen gave a sharp yell as Kiri thrust his dagger into his heart. He flailed for a moment, gasping in shock before his body slumped and then lay still.

Kiri released the grip of her left hand and dropped Taryen's lifeless arm before smoothing away a lock of her hair that had come adrift.

She pulled the dagger out of Taryen's body, standing up from her crouched position. She walked back to the table before Karquesh and leant across him. There she jammed the point of the dagger into the table. A rivulet of blood rolled down the blade and pooled on the polished surface before the king.

There was silence all about her. Karquesh was staring at the dagger.

She sat back down at her place at the table. After a moment she looked around and beckoned for one of the servants.

'Where is my dessert?'

A plate, loaded with fruits and a syrupy topping was placed in front of her by a trembling servant.

She picked up her cutlery, scooping a measure of fruit from before her. She ate it slowly and then swallowed, nodding at the flavour.

'It's very good.'

There was no other sound. Everyone was staring at her.

After a pause she swivelled her head to look at Karquesh.

'As I said …' She stared at him and raised her voice. 'Taryen was wrong. I will have your answer now, King Karquesh. Will Taloon ally itself with the purposes of Drayden, as ordered by high priestess Nerina and blessed by Lacaille herself? Or will it not?'

Everyone in the room was looking to Karquesh now. Kiri placed her cutlery down, folded her arms and waited.

Karquesh cleared his throat and licked his lips.

'Priestess Kiri, emissary of high priestess Nerina of Drayden, herself the servant of Lacaille.' He paused for a moment. 'I place Taloon at your service in the pursuit of your goals. Faithful allies of Drayden we will be. Let us drink to the union of purpose to which we have set ourselves.'

Karquesh stood up, signalling for his goblet to be filled with wine. Kiri got to her feet too, finding her glass likewise filled.

'To Drayden and its conquests,' Karquesh pronounced.

'To Taloon, its honour and cooperation,' Kiri replied.

Both drank. Conversation rose from a whisper back to a hubbub. The servants, as quietly as they could, dragged Taryen's body out from the banquet hall.

* * *

Kiri returned to her room, her mind turning over the events of the stretch. She smiled and sent her thoughts out. The answer was swift. Nerina's presence filled her mind.

Kiri! How are you faring in Taloon?

Well. Liana was offered in tribute and King Karquesh has put his kingdom at our service. They are already preparing the ships.

You have done well, Kiri. Very well. Were there any problems?

Kiri would have laughed, but forced herself to suppress it.

I had to kill the King's cousin, but other than that, no.

There was a pause across the mental link.

It seems you have some tales to tell. Are you ready for the priestesses to arrive?

Yes. Send our warriors as soon as you can. We will be ready to depart within a few stretches.

And Amar, you are sure of its location?

I am sure, I have seen it. I know where it lies.

Then it seems we will soon complete the task appointed. Amar will fall and your renown will grow, young one.

I seek only to serve.

The words came easily to her now, she was adept at hiding her thoughts and feelings.

Have you considered the words of the Obelisk further?

There has been nothing. It seems you were right, the quest for Amar must be concluded first.

Lacaille would see things done in a certain order. Amar then, Kiri. I will assemble the flight and send them to you as soon as it can be arranged. Make things ready for our arrival.

Kiri allowed a sense of acquiescence and acknowledgement to filter across the link.

I will see it done.

Nerina's presence faded away. Kiri strode to the doors of the room and opened them, walking out on to the balcony. Before her she could see the harbour, many ships were already moored, with others sailing along the coast towards the city. Karquesh was honouring his word.

Standing at the balcony was Liana, still in the yellow dress she had worn for the banquet. She was staring out to sea.

She's my cousin, I'm condemning her to be Karquesh's plaything for the rest of her life.

Kiri reached out with her mind, but Liana's thoughts were nowhere to be found, there was just a void, no spark of life.

Her mind is gone, shattered when she tried to take my gift. There's nothing I can do. She'll probably be looked after better here than she would be in Drayden, at least her looks are an asset.

Kiri reached and took Liana's hands. The woman turned to her, looking at her. Kiri bound a cord around her wrists.

'You are to be married to King Karquesh,' she said. 'You will be his seventh wife. A position of honour in the court of Taloon.'

'Taloon,' Liana echoed, her voice bland.

'Do you understand?' Kiri asked.

'Understand?'

Kiri sighed and shook her head.

If someone tries to take my gift, I will fight to the death to avoid this fate! To be nothing more than a mindless shell ...

She thought she heard something from behind her and turned. A faint metallic crackle surged around her.

You!

But it was subtle, try as she might she couldn't intercept the thoughts of those who sent it, but the sense of identity was all too familiar. Kiri caught a mental glimpse of the inside of a machine. She spied clouds through windows and saw a brief glimpse of someone. She recognised him, a warmth spreading through her body in response. There was brief flicker and it was gone, but it had been close.

So, you spy on me, Zoella. You're coming this way and you bring Meru. Well then, I'll be ready for you both. Perhaps I will have what I want before we even leave for Amar.

As the link dissolved there was a faint flash in her mind, an image of a face. The face of the servant girl she had seen at the banquet. Kiri tried to focus on her face, but the image evaporated as she did so. She strained, seeking the source of the vision.

It was hard to detect, but she could tell it was coming from below her, down in the streets perhaps, or even lower.

Some other secret of Taloon?

* * *

Far away to the shaderight Nerina opened her eyes.

'News?' Merrin asked.

'Kiri has done remarkably well in a short time,' Nerina said. 'King Karquesh has agreed to our terms and the fleet of ships is being made ready.'

'So we will attack Amar?'

Nerina nodded. 'Yes. Let us subdue them and take the spoils. Kiri can have another moment of glory.'

'Is it not dangerous to elevate her so?'

Nerina thought for a moment. 'We have set her on this path, it is by my bidding that she went and under my instruction shall she prevail. We will unseat her later. Amar must fall first.'

'What of her being the chosen one of the Obelisk?'

'She will be revealed as a false prophet,' Nerina replied. 'She is not the only one who can manufacture a vision from upon high. Many now whisper that she has designs on being high priestess. We must show them all that Kiri's loyalty to me is wavering.'

'And how do we do that?'

Nerina smiled and gestured to the doors to the hall. They swung back and Rihanna walked in.

'High priestess, mother,' she acknowledged with a brief bow. 'You summoned me?'

'Indeed,' Nerina said. 'Come hither.'

Rihanna walked forward to join them.

'Good news,' Nerina said. 'I have just heard from Kiri, she has secured an alliance with King Karquesh of Taloon. His fleet of ships is at our disposal. The attack upon Amar may commence.'

Rihanna nodded. 'That was quicker than we hoped.'

'Assemble the flight,' Nerina said. 'I want you to lead the aerial attack.'

Rihanna blinked in surprise.

'Me? Not Kiri?'

Nerina looked away for a moment and then paced around.

'There is talk in the halls,' Merrin said. 'Talk that Kiri sees herself as high priestess elect.'

Rihanna looked uncomfortable. 'She is arrogant, proud and confident. She's been anointed by Lacaille and comes fresh from the victory over Scallia. But she should know her proper place, in service to you, Nerina.'

Nerina nodded.

'A test of her loyalty to Nerina,' Merrin said. 'Will she obey the high priestess' commands, or will she not?'

'If she will not agree?' Rihanna asked.

'Then you are to summon us immediately,' Nerina said, turning back to her. 'We will deal with her.'

'I shall see it done,' Rihanna said. 'When do you wish us to depart?'

'Kiri says they are already loading the ships with provisions,' Nerina said. 'As soon as you are ready.'

'I will begin now,' Rihanna said, bowing. 'High priestess, mother.'

Nerina nodded to her and Rihanna left the hall.

* * *

Rihanna left and found herself a quiet room away from the temple.

Kiri? Kiri! Can you hear me?

The answer was delayed for a moment, before Kiri's distinctive mental presence came back through the link.

Yes, Rihanna.

I have just spoken to Nerina, we are to prepare the flight …

She spoke to me just a spell ago. The ships are ready.

There is something else though.

Rihanna sensed Kiri's questioning thought from the other end of the link, she continued sending the mental thoughts to her.

Nerina has asked me to lead the flight … and the attack on Amar.

There was a blank response for a long moment. Rihanna waited.

So they don't trust me. This is a test of my loyalty then.

I played my part once more. I told them I thought you were becoming arrogant and proud. They are right when they say there are those here that think you plan to be high priestess.

They want us to fight, don't they? They really are trying to force us apart.

It seems that way.

But why?

I will try to find out from my mother. She hates you, perhaps she will reveal something to me.

Be careful!

I will. We will be in Taloon within three stretches. I will see you then.

The link dissolved.

Rihanna thought for a moment.

So, Kiri has her plan. Nerina has hers.

She smiled.

And I have mine.

CHAPTER TWELVE

The Deserts of Taloon

Round 2307, Fifth pass

'About five times as far as the flight we made to Nireus from Viresia,' Meru said looking at the map displayed on the screens of the flying machine. Zoella and Meru had been preparing for their flight sunwards, they were almost ready to leave.

'It took us nearly three stretches to cover that distance,' Zoella said. 'So this is going to take a pass or more.'

'Well you'll have enough food and water,' Mel said. 'You're stocked to the gunnels, or whatever they're called on flying machines. Enough to get you there and back to Amar.'

The flying machine was indistinguishable from the one Meru had flown before. It was a Class 6 Personnel shuttle, as Caesar insisted on calling it. Like the other machine, it had space for two people in front and two behind, further back was storage space for equipment, now crammed with provisions as provided by Mel.

'You still sure about this?' Coran asked.

Meru looked at Zoella. She nodded.

'It's got to be done.'

'Be advised,' Caesar's voice intoned. 'Flying vehicles have an important but limited energy reserve storage capacity aboard. In the event of power transmission failure due to Obelisk malfunction, on board avionics and propulsion will continue to function for a limited time to allow a safe landing.'

'Can I have that in Captain speak, please?' Coran asked.

'He means if the 'tricity fails we won't fall out of the sky,' Meru said. 'Though, by the sound of it we won't have much time to land.'

'Without external power, energy reserves will be depleted in approximately one spell,' Caesar replied.

'Could be worse,' Mel said. 'But that doesn't give you a lot of time to find a landing site.'

Meru nodded. 'Caesar, what happens if we're over water when the 'tricity stops?'

'In the event of landing on water, class 6 personnel shuttles are buoyant and will remain afloat unless damaged,' Caesar replied. 'Landing must be made at zero horizontal velocity.'

'Will we be able to take off again?'

'Class 6 personnel shuttles are able to lift off in that condition.'

Meru puffed out his cheeks.

'Then I think we're ready.'

'Go there, fix this damn thing and get straight back to Amar, agreed?' Coran asked.

Meru grinned. 'No detours this time.'

Coran pulled him into a hug. 'Safe travels, we'll see you in Amar.'

'We'll be there.'

Coran turned to Zoella. 'Please look after him.'

Zoella smiled and gave the Captain a hug too. 'Don't worry, I know what he's like.'

Coran pulled back, still holding on to Zoella's shoulders.

'Thank you,' he said, looking into her eyes. 'I had my doubts early on, as did many of us. But you've proved yourself a loyal friend to us all. Without you we wouldn't have convinced the senate to let us go, or saved as many people as we did. Proud to have you as a member of the crew. You're part of this family now.'

Meru saw Zoella swallow and blink back tears.

'And I want you back safe and sound, you hear?' Coran put a note of mock sternness into his voice. Zoella rubbed her eyes and nodded.

Mel was next. 'Look after each other, yes? I'd rather we were all together, but ...'

Ren pushed forward, clinging on to Zoella.

'I want go with you too!'

Zoella knelt down and hugged him. 'I know you do,' she said. 'But this is too dangerous. You must stay on the *Mobilis*, Mel will look after you.'

'I swear I will,' Mel said. 'Come on young Ren. If Meru's not going to be about I need you to do all his chores. I daresay you'll do them better than he did.'

Ren gave Zoella one more squeeze before he let go.

'Be safe,' he said and then went to stand by Mel.

'Anything from you, Fitch?' Meru asked, looking at the wizened old man, still sporting his wide-brimmed hat.

'Can't say I'll miss either of you,' Fitch said. 'But sounds like this needs to be done and it saves me doing it.'

Meru laughed. Even Fitch had a small grin on his face.

'I took the liberty of putting a rifle into your stores,' Fitch said. 'There's about twenty rounds in with it. Hope you don't need to use it, but just in case ...'

'I appreciate it,' Meru said.

He looked at Zoella.

'All set?'

She nodded. Meru gestured to the flying machine and she climbed up into the passenger seat. He jumped in behind her and pulled the door closed. Coran, Mel, Fitch and Ren stepped back out of the way.

Zoella had strapped herself in as Meru adjusted the controls.

'Promise you won't crash this time?' she asked.

He looked at her. 'I'll do my best.' He took a deep breath. 'I think we're ready. Sandra, can you hear me?'

'Affirmative Meru,' the disembodied woman's voice answered him.

'Activate flight systems.'

'Flight systems activated. You may depart when ready.'

Meru waved out of the window and then grasped hold of the controls.

The flying machine's engines whirred up, the vessel tilted forward and they were airborne. In moments the hangar swept past them and they were climbing into the sky, with the green landscape of Scallia falling away beneath them.

* * *

Coran, Mel, Fitch and Ren watched until the flying machine was lost in the glare of Lacaille. With a faint rumble the hangar doors of Caesar's facility rolled back and closed.

'That's it then,' Coran said. 'Our next step is to get all the other machines back to Amar.'

There was a soft mechanical clunk from a nearby wall and a hatch opened. Inside was a small black box with a tall metal pole jutting out of the top.

'Secure this device to your vessel,' Caesar said. 'It will enable the hangar assets to autonomously follow your position. Provided with this tracking device are handsets which will allow instructions to be passed to the hangar assets to aide transportation. I suggest you familiarise yourself with the operation of these devices prior to departure.'

'I never liked the way we get ordered about by a speaking table,' Fitch grumbled.

'Caesar is helping us,' Coran countered. 'Mel, think you can handle all that?'

'Sure thing,' Mel answered. 'And Ren here will help, won't you Ren?'

The boy nodded, his eyes bright with enthusiasm.

'We have our work cut out,' Coran said. 'I'd like to be heading home as soon as we can. Jump to it, folks.'

* * *

The flying machine droned on through the skies of Esurio, heading sunward. Spell by spell and chime by chime the Scallian landscape rolled away beneath them. Zoella watched the familiar shadeward forests, hills and valleys for a while. They reminded her of life before all of her recent adventures, stuck in the Lord Tarq's hall where she had grown up.

And Raga, dear Raga.

She recalled the times when she had fled through the forests, running from the King's men, the loyal old carn at her side, living on her wits and cunning before she had encountered Ioric.

I was good at that ... though it was full of fear. Those were almost happy times, without the weight of knowledge and sadness ...

The thoughts led her to Ioric, to Torin and Liana, the high spires of Viresia, the palace glinting in the bright light of Lacaille.

The confrontation before the gates of the city.

He was a good man ... and Ioric meant to lose the fight against Kiri. She was going to strike him but she herself was struck down. And then ...

Zoella remembered how Kiri was writhing on the ground in agony before her huge reptilian beast had killed Ioric.

It could only have been Liana but they blamed me, locked me up. Liana herself intended to defy and then control the priestesses, but Kiri was too strong for her ...

Zoella shivered as she remembered Kiri's ferocious attack on Torin, the brutality and the blood. She hadn't just killed him, she had tortured and mutilated him. She remembered feeling the fury emanating from the girl, white hot and blazing.

And Raga ...

She could see her loyal carn in her mind, bounding to her rescue, launching its heavy body at Kiri despite Zoella's protestation. Kiri had evaded the attack and brought Raga's life to an abrupt end with a blow from her staff.

Zoella moved in her seat, wriggling to get comfortable.

She didn't kill Ioric, the beast did – was it by her command or was it defending her, like Raga did for me? She had reason enough to fight with Liana and she hated Torin ...

A memory came back, something Kiri had shouted at Ioric before the battle, when they were all standing at the gates.

I was there! Your precious prince murdered our people, your cowardly brother burnt the treaty, killed our people and burnt Taranda to the ground. You're a filthy liar!

Zoella could remember the doubt that filled her mind at the time, but it was not the priestesses who were lying. Ioric had trusted Torin, yet if Kiri was speaking the truth then …

Torin forced the war with the priestesses? Kiri met him somewhere before and fought him. Liana tried to take Kiri and miscalculated her strength.

More memories surfaced. Guerren's last words to her through the mental link she had forged.

Do not hate Kiri! Myana, she was Ioric's sister, she was …

And then Kiri's own voice.

Stop, you're hurting him!

Zoella shivered.

Could it be that I was mistaken about her? That she was wronged and sought to undo those wrongs at Viresia? Perhaps the blame for Ioric's death lies with Liana. Raga attacked Kiri and she defended herself as anyone would. Even Guerren asked me not to hate her – and then Meru and her …

She looked across at Meru. He was still concentrating on flying, looking out of the windows of the machine as it flew onwards. Cloud billowed about them, the flying machine swaying in the air currents.

She could have killed him, she didn't. She spared his life … and mine. Was it just to track us to Amar, or was there something else?

She shook her head.

No. Kiri thinks only of herself. She schemes and plans. I've felt her mind; cold and calculating. Guerren was wrong, Meru is wrong. I must find out what she is planning next …

She closed her eyes, sending her thoughts outward the way she had done before, straining her senses to see if she could intercept Kiri's thoughts and visions. Forests, hills and vales sped through her mind's eye, before deserts replaced them. She saw a huge river delta and a white city before …

There was a sickening mental lurch.

About her she could see a palace, built of bright white stone and decorated with coloured flags and glass. Two women stood, facing away from her, both dressed in flowing gowns, one yellow and one cyan. The first was blonde haired, the other dark.

The second woman turned.

Blue eyes, dark black hair! Kiri!

Zoella gasped. She saw Kiri frown.

And Liana!

Liana's expression was blank, Zoella could see that her hands were bound with a cord, it seemed that Kiri was leading her away somewhere. The vision moved. Zoella caught sight of a big dark skinned man she didn't recognised, dressed in lavish garments of bright colours. Kiri handed the bound Liana over to him.

She saw Liana thrown to a bed as the vision went black.

Then her vision swept out and away, across the city, down through its streets and towards the bright sparkling sea.

There she saw something else.

Endless rows of seagoing vessels, ships of all shapes and sizes, some were enormous. She could see men loading crates, food stuffs … and weapons.

A fleet …

She had only a moment to assimilate the vision before it was wrenched aside once more. Amidst a wave of nausea her gaze was dragged back to the city and down. She panicked as it dropped straight into the white paved streets and then sank below. For a moment there was nothing but the strange sight of rock blurring past before she was in some other place.

Rows upon rows of green plants were set in order in great containers. Above her mirrors reflected the light of Lacaille in all directions. Tending the plants were people, dressed in plain and dirty smocks. Zoella could see guards here and there, whips in their hands.

One whip lashed out and there were screams.

Her vision was wrenched again and she saw a face, a girl's face. Pale, the flesh and hair white, the eyes a glaring reddish pink.

Like Ren!

Zoella reeled, trying to get her thoughts under her own control. The pale figure raised hands towards her, a cry of pain and despair ringing in her mind. There were no words, just images of pain, fear and terror.

'Zoella!'

She felt a nudge. She blinked, her vision clearing.

She was back in the flying machine. A great gasp surged into her lungs; she'd been holding her breath.

'Zoella? Are you all right?'

She turned to look at Meru.

'I …'

'What happened?'

She swallowed, trying to calm her beating heart and catch her breath. 'I tried to locate her …'

'Who?' Meru demanded, 'Kiri?'

Zoella nodded. 'She's near. Very near. She's already in Taloon. Meru, they're already loading the ships, they'll be able to sail in just a few stretches!'

'Shades,' Meru muttered. 'How can they be ready so quickly? It was supposed to take passes.'

'And she has Liana too …' Zoella cried. 'My queen, bad things are happening …'

'Hey,' Meru said, grabbing hold of her arm. 'Take it easy. Tell me what you saw. Woah …'

The flying machine lurched and Meru grasped the controls with both hands again.

Zoella took some deep breaths and explained what she had seen. Meru listened until she had finished.

'We can't ignore what you see,' he said. 'It's always a warning or something. So, Kiri's in Taloon, it sounds like she's succeeded in making an alliance with them. It's obvious that this city is by the sea and a fleet is making ready to attack Amar – and these other people below the city … slaves maybe?'

'Whoever she was she had the gift,' Zoella said. 'Strongly too, she was able to move my gaze around, I couldn't control it. There are gifted women there. We've got to help them.'

'Wait a spell,' Meru said in alarm. 'We're going to the Obelisk, we can't change course now …'

'Meru, if Kiri finds them she'll take their gifts, she'll be even more powerful. These people, whoever they are, might be able to help us defend Amar against the priestesses …'

'You mean go to the city? Just the two of us? And do what?'

'Rescue these people and escape.'

'Under the noses of everyone in the city and Kiri?' Meru asked. 'She'll find us, she'll know …'

'Not if we're careful,' Zoella replied. 'I can hide my thoughts from her.'

'What about the Obelisk? Caesar said we only had a few short passes to fix it before everything goes wrong.'

'Your father calculated it would take the fleet twenty stretches to reach Amar, maybe less,' Zoella answered back. 'They're almost ready to sail, the attack will happen much sooner … early in the next pass. The battle will be over before we even get back. We've got to save Amar first.'

Meru thought about it for a moment.

'I suppose,' he said. 'But the risk of going to this city, if we get caught …'

Zoella continued. 'We can't leave these people, and they could be useful to us, perhaps enough to stop the priestesses' attack. We need them on our side, not against us.'

'But the risk …' Meru argued back. 'If we're caught, Amar loses you – you're our best defence against the priestesses. That's what Coran will tell us when we call him on the radio, don't take the risk. And I just promised him, no detours!'

'Then we don't tell him,' Zoella answered after a moment. 'There's nothing they can do anyway. Their plan is to get back to Amar as soon as possible and make ready as best they can. Nothing we do will change that, let's not tell them.'

'We have to, we've got to warn them that the attack will be much sooner,' Meru protested. 'We need to check in. I can't lie to Coran …'

'You lied before,' Zoella said. 'You're good at it. Why is this different?'

She ignored the hurt look on his face.

'Meru, I can't defend Amar all on my own. There's a chance there are more gifted women here, if we can reach them, get them out before Kiri finds them, they might be able to help us …'

'Woah, slow down! What if it's a trap?'

'By who? Kiri?'

'Yes.'

Zoella gave him a tart smile.

'You're always telling me she's not evil. Maybe you'll get your chance to prove it. You can talk her out of attacking us.'

'She wants both of us,' Meru said. 'She might try to take your gift …'

'Then she'll suffer the consequences, won't she? We've got to try. '

Meru sighed.

'Coran's going to kill us when he finds out,' he said.

'I'll call him if you're that bothered,' Zoella said, gesturing to the radio. 'Switch it on for me.'

Meru swallowed and flipped the switches.

'Try it,' he said.

Zoella raised her voice and spoke.

'Coran, it's Zoella, can you hear me?'

The radio crackled and buzzed for a moment before they heard Coran's voice by return.

'Zoella?'

'Yes, it's me,' Zoella replied.

'Is everything all right?'

'Yes, everything is fine,' Zoella replied. 'Meru is still flying, so you've got me.'

'Good to hear, how goes the trip?'

'We're still heading sunright,' Zoella replied. 'I've sensed something though. The priestesses, they're massing, ready to sail soon. I think they'll be able to leave in just a few stretches.'

'So soon?' She could hear the dismay in Coran's voice. 'How do you know?'

'I saw it, sometimes I can spy on what they see …'

'We'll double our efforts,' Coran said, his voice heavy. 'You carry on with the Obelisk, but get back as soon as you can.'

'We will.'

'Is there anything else …?'

'No, we're fine,' Zoella said, keeping her voice light. 'We'll speak to you soon. Take care and love to everyone. Give Ren a hug from me.'

'Will do.'

Zoella nodded at Meru and he flipped the switches off. He was looking at her.

'I didn't lie.'

'You didn't tell the truth either,' he answered.

'Nothing I said was false,' Zoella replied. 'Are we going to do this, or keep arguing all stretch?'

Meru sighed.

'Which way do we need to go?'

'To the sunright,' Zoella said, pointing out of the window to her left. 'That way. The land will become a desert.'

Meru pulled on the controls and the flying machine banked to the left.

* * *

The spells ticked away. The flying machine cruised onwards. Meru looked at the map on the display, zooming it out by changing the settings. The monotonous display had changed.

'Look, I can see the desert and the coast line,' he said. 'You described a river, that looks like it there.'

He pointed at the map where a river delta could be seen.

Zoella looked across. 'That looks like it.'

'Sandra,' Meru asked, poking his finger at the map. 'Do you any information about this location?'

'Records indicate waymarker twenty two, forty three is located at that approximate position.' Sandra's disembodied voice replied.

'And what is the designation of that waymarker?'

'It is designated as the Talon Industries Hydroponics and Factory Farming Facility.'

'Talon,' Zoella said. 'Taloon?'

Zoella and Meru exchanged a look.

'Your turn,' Meru said, with a grin.

'All right, Sandra,' Zoella asked. 'What does all that mean?'

'Hydroponics is a mechanism by which to grow plant based food products in artificial environments primarily to improve productivity. Plants are grown in nutrient solutions as opposed to traditional soil. Factory farming is the process of rearing large numbers of animals for food in confined conditions for minimal production cost.'

'That's what I saw,' Zoella said. 'Rows upon rows of plants.'

'I guess we've got our destination then,' Meru said. 'Sandra, can you navigate us to that waymarker?'

'Course has been computed. Execute?'

'Yes.'

'Time to destination, two stretches.'

Zoella looked out of the windows of the flying machine. Already the thick forests beneath them were making way for grasslands. In the distance ahead she could see the ground was yellow and arid. They were leaving Scallia behind and entering the realms of Taloon.

'Let's hope we're in time.'

* * *

It was the early chime of the second stretch. Zoella and Meru had been taking turns at the controls of the flying machine. It had been Zoella's turn to sleep.

She felt a prod and woke up.

'We're getting close,' Meru said, gesturing out of the windows. 'We ought to start thinking about setting down; we don't want to be spotted.'

Zoella rubbed her eyes and sat up.

'How far away are we?'

Meru pointed at the map on the dashboard of the flying machine. 'Twenty marks now.'

'Long way to walk still.'

They both looked out through the windows. Below them was desert, they could see endless dunes of sand stretching as far as the eye could see.

'Are you sure we're close?' Zoella queried.

Meru rubbed his eyes. 'Yeah, pretty sure. Sandra, can you check how far we are from the waymarker?'

'Distance is nineteen point four marks, closing on target,' Sandra replied.

Zoella looked at the map. 'Meru look, the waymarker isn't on the coast, it's inland. The city I saw had a harbour with ships, wherever we're going … it's not the same place.'

Meru looked at the map.

'Looks like the waymarker is about ten marks inland of the coast. Close-ish, but not the same. They must be connected though. Ten marks is a safe distance through, we can't fly any closer than that, we'll be seen. When I flew into Viresia I had to land some way away to avoid being spotted.'

'Shall we land at the waymarker then?'

Meru nodded. 'Probably a good bet, but let's be cautious in case there is someone there.'

Half a spell ticked by as they approached the position on the map.

'There,' Meru said. 'Look, I can see the city!'

Tall white spires were just visible before them. They could see the coastline weaving along and disappearing over the horizon. Below them the dunes continued to roll past.

'Approaching waymarker coordinates,' Sandra said.

Meru slowed the flying machine down and it began to lose height. They flew over one dune and then crested the rise of another.

'There!' Zoella said, pointing to her left. Meru peered across out of the windows.

Below them was a large metal platform jutting up from the sand. One corner was submerged in a dune, but the rest of it seemed to be clear. A little further away was a thin tower that reached up perhaps two hundred hands into the air. Meru circled the flying machine around the platform, but there was no sign of life.

'I guess we found our spot to land,' he said, pulling the controls and bringing the flying machine to a stop above the platform. With a deft touch the machine descended. Meru triggered the landing gear as the machine lowered itself.

'Looks like it was made for this,' Zoella said, looking around.

With a gentle thud they came to rest in the centre of the platform. Sand billowed up around them for a few moments before Meru cut the engines. With a fading hum the flying machine grew silent.

'Now what?' Zoella asked.

'Let's take a look around,' Meru said. 'It's still ten marks to the city from here.'

Zoella pulled the door release and stepped out.

She gasped. The heat hit her like a blast, the air humid and close. She'd never felt anything like it before. The air in the machine must have been cooled somehow.

'It's so … hot!' she called.

Meru had walked around from his side.

'Yeah, really hot,' he agreed. 'I don't think I fancy walking ten marks in this heat even with water.'

'We've got to get to the city somehow, that's where …'

Meru had already wandered off. Zoella could see that he was looking at a panel that was connected to a railing that ran around the perimeter of the platform at waist height. It looked almost like a tilted desk. It reminded her of the material out of which Caesar was made.

'Zoella, look at this!' he called.

She hurried across.

'It's some kind of control,' Meru said. 'It's like the ones in Caesar's hangar. Look, this is definitely the place.'

He touched the surface and a number of symbols appeared, each accompanied by some text.

Talon Industries Hydroponics and Factory Farming Facility – Pad Delta
Pad occupied – Class 6 Personnel Shuttle detected.
Level G – Launch pad
Level 1 – Hydroponics Gallery
Level 2 – Maintenance Depot
Please select.

'Does it mean we can go down?' Zoella asked, when she finished reading.

'Only one way to find out,' Meru said. 'Gallery or depot?'

'I want to see the gallery,' Zoella said.

Meru pressed the symbol next to the gallery text.

A shudder ran through the platform. Sand vibrated and shifted about them, there was faint groan that shuddered through their feet.

The platform began to drop beneath them.

Zoella gasped. Both of them grabbed on to the handrail.

The platform descended, taking them and the flying machine down a huge metal tube of which the platform seemed to have only been the top section. Sand cascaded around the edges as the dunes moved up and out of their sight.

After they had dropped about twenty hands the metal tube ended and the platform emerged into a much wider space. It was dark, only the faintest grey outlines could be seen. Above them another platform like theirs slid across out of the darkness and took the place of theirs, rising up into the vacant slot above. As it did so, the bright light outside was cut off and they were plunged into darkness. The air was chill about them and it smelt old and stale.

'Meru!'

Zoella grabbed the handrail again.

Not the dark, I hate the dark ... ever since being locked in those catacombs in Viresia!

'It's all right,' Meru said from beside her. 'There are lights we can use in the flying machine ...'

There was a buzz from somewhere nearby, followed by a growing hum. Light blazed out of the darkness, blinding them for a moment with its intensity. Above them countless numbers of small lights similar to those in Caesar's hangar illuminated the ground.

They blinked and squinted before their vision cleared.

'Wow,' Meru said, open mouthed.

Zoella looked, releasing her grip on the handrail.

The platform was still descending, but they could see where they were headed now. Below them, still dozens of hands below, were endless rows of huge metal troughs. In them were what looked like dead branches; the twisted remains of long-dead plants. The troughs were in rows stretching left and right as far as they could see, parallel to each other, disappearing to the limits of vision before them. It was a vast underground vault.

The platform shuddered to a halt as it reached the floor level. The sound echoed around them for long moments before fading. Nothing moved.

Zoella and Meru looked at each other before stepping off and walking to the nearest trough.

It was about six hands wide and two deep. There was a stained residue coating the insides. Within was a mess of dried twigs and branches, long since dead. Above that was a complex collection of metal contraptions and tubes. Everything was coated in a thick layer of dust. Meru reached out and wiped some of the dust away, the tubes were transparent, but there was nothing inside.

Zoella pulled at one of the branches. It cracked and snapped in her hand.

Their footsteps echoed as they walked around, otherwise it was silent.

'I saw all this, but the plants were alive,' Zoella said. 'Green, healthy …'

'This can't have been used for rounds and rounds,' Meru said. 'Look, it's as dry as an old bone. No one has been here for a long time.'

'I know what I saw.'

'Perhaps there's another area,' Meru said. 'There must be a map, or something which shows us the layout of the place.'

They walked back to the platform, but the panel there was blank. When Meru prodded it, it only provided the same options as before.

'I think this just goes up and down,' he said. 'We need another …'

Zoella had seen something.

'Over there,' she said, pointing to the far end of one of the troughs. There was another panel. It was covered in dust too, but they wiped it clean, blowing the excess away. After a moment they were rewarded with it lighting up and more text appearing.

Talon Industries Hydroponics and Factory Farming Facility – Delta Sector
Gallery Offline, Maintenance Overdue
– Administration Functions
– Status Monitoring
– Internal Transport
– Schematics
Please select.

'Which one?' Zoella demanded.

'I don't know what this stuff means,' Meru said. He pressed the symbol marked 'Administration Functions'.

Authentication Credentials Required.

Nothing else happened. After a few moments the screen returned to the original set of text.

'Not that one,' Meru said. 'What do you think "schematics" means?'

'Try it.'

Meru pressed the symbol.

The text faded, being replaced with diagram made of a series of rectangles placed on a set of radiating lines. Each line was like a spoke in a wheel. There were six spokes, with three rectangles on each. The outermost rectangle on the lowest spoke was flashing.

'This is where we must be,' Zoella said. 'I guess this hall is one of …' she counted. '… eighteen.'

She touched the flashing rectangle. More text appeared.

Carousel 3, Hall 4. Status: Offline.

'Not being used, I guess,' Meru said. 'Try some of the others.'

Zoella touched some of the other rectangles. It was apparent that the outermost ring of six rectangles was called 'Carousel three'. Each hall was numbered sequentially from one to six around the circumference. All were shown to be offline. Carousel two was the same. It wasn't until she touched the fourth hall on the innermost Carousel one that they saw a change.

Carousel 1, Hall 4. Status: Online.

'It's on the same spoke as this one, but further in towards the centre,' Zoella said. 'Closer to where the city is?'

Meru nodded. 'My guess is that the city is above the centre of this map. Looks like that hall is the only one left working.' He prodded the remaining halls to check. 'Yes, the only one.'

'That must be what I saw,' Zoella said. 'And the people too … so, how do we get there?'

Meru stepped back and looked down the length of the trough next to them.

'Goes on as far as we can see,' Meru said, squinting into the distance. 'Best guess is that's a ten mark hike, at least we're out of the heat though. These halls are just enormous.'

'Then we'd better start walking …'

'Wait.'

Meru prodded the panel again, returning them to the original set of text.

'There's something about transport here.' He pressed the symbol.

- *Transport Request*
- *Cancel Transport Request*

He pressed the symbol for 'Transport Request'. The display changed.

Transport arriving in 00:02:00.

As they watched the timer started counting down.

'I hope you know what you're doing,' Zoella said.

Meru went back to the flying machine and grabbed the rifle, two lightglasses and a rucksack with food and water. Then he locked up the flying machine and gave Sandra instructions to stay put until they returned.

A faint whirring sound came to his ears. Signalling to Zoella he moved to the next trough along to see a wheeled machine moving up between the rows. Together they watched it drive up close to them, execute a neat turn and stop moving. It lacked a roof, but contained four chairs in two rows and a small panel at the front like the one they had been using. The whole machine sat on four black wheels.

'Fancy a ride?' Meru asked with a grin.

* * *

The wheeled machine bore them down the corridors at a speed far higher than they could have run.

Its controls were simple, similar to those of the flying machine. It was clear they shared a designer. The flat panel showed them a simple map and they were able to mark their progress on it. Meru checked the panel while Zoella controlled the progress of the vehicle.

After a short interval of driving, they reached the other end of the hall they were in. A set of double doors swung back as they approached and they entered a tunnel with metal lined walls. The air remained stale and dry about them. After perhaps five hundred hands the tunnel ended at another set of doors, which also opened before them. They drove into another hall. Lights flicked on as they entered.

'I'm guessing we're in Carousel 2 now,' Zoella said. 'Looks the same as the other one.'

'Offline,' Meru agreed. 'Which I guess means not used or broken. Shall we keep going?'

'Nothing else to do.'

Zoella pushed the controls and the machine moved off.

Progress was the same as before, but they became conscious of the air changing around them. The staleness was being replaced, but with something worse. Zoella wrinkled her nose.

'Something rotten,' she said, sniffing.

Ahead of them the corridor between the troughs was becoming littered with unidentifiable debris. Piles of refuse covered the troughs here and there.

'Rotten vegetables,' Zoella said. 'You can't ever forget that smell!'

'Slow down,' Meru said. 'Let's have a look.'

'Really?'

'Rotten food means it must be relatively recent,' Meru said. 'Someone, or something put it there.'

Zoella brought the machine to a halt and they got out, looking about them. The stench was increasing, the floor damp with fetid water.

'Tupes and corcans,' Meru said, prodding one pile with his foot. 'Some melps too.'

'All dumped within the pass,' Zoella said. 'Judging by the smell …'

She jolted, a vision flashing across her mind. The face of the girl with the white face and pink eyes.

'Zoella?'

'Whoever, they are, they're close,' Zoella whispered. 'I can feel them …'

Meru grabbed the rifle and loaded it.

'I don't think they mean us any harm.'

'Best to be safe,' Meru replied. 'Let's keep moving.'

Zoella nodded and they climbed back aboard, now driving around the piles of rotting vegetables. Before long they reached yet another pair of double doors. The area was in semi-regular use as a dumping ground. The marks of footsteps and other wheeled vehicles were visible in a thick layer of mud that now coated the floor.

The door opened and they drove into the next tunnel.

It was clear that something was different up ahead. There was a distinct glow coming from the doors before them, a bright green colouration that reflected off the walls of the tunnel. They approached a final set of doors and they opened.

Zoella brought the machine to halt as they emerged.

'Wow.'

Unlike the previous two halls, here the troughs were full of bright green foliage. Plants of all different types were suspended in the troughs, the machinery above humming with purpose. They could see fluids bubbling and moving around in the tubes, which were clean and untarnished. Flits and nargs buzzed about them alongside other small flying insects neither of them recognised. Also visible were massive mirrors that were shaped to cast the light of Lacaille down across the plants. They could make out a complex arrangement that stretched away into the distance, the beams of light glowing amber in the air.

'This is what I saw,' Zoella said, looking about her in wonder.

'Growing plants underground,' Meru said. 'I guess it's too hot to do it on the surface, but down here it can all be controlled. But this is the ancients' work, there's no way that …'

They were interrupted by movement, but when they turned there was nothing to see. They heard a scurrying of feet from somewhere nearby. Meru hoisted the rifle.

'No wait.' Zoella held out her hand.

Small figures emerged from between the rows of troughs, they were dressed in dirty white smocks, their bare arms and legs dirty, their hair unkempt. All had pale skin under the dirt, with cropped white hair. All had pink eyes.

Like in my vision, but these are so young …

There were about fifteen of them, all children, all young girls. They stood and stared without saying anything.

Zoella took a step forward. The children backed away, clutching at each other, fear and alarm on their faces. Zoella reached out her hand.

'Don't be scared. We won't hurt you.'

They were shaking their heads and still backing away.

'Meru, lower the rifle,' Zoella whispered, turning to him. He did as she instructed.

They were still wary. Zoella beckoned for the closest to come nearer, but the only answer was a tiny shake of the head.

'Who are they?' Meru whispered.

As he moved the children backed away. Zoella turned.

'I think they're scared of you,' she said.

'Me?' Meru said.

'Be quiet,' Zoella told him. 'Back away, put the rifle back in the machine and get in.'

Meru looked at her and then back at the children before nodding and retracing his steps. The children watched his every move.

'Put your hands where they can be seen,' Zoella said.

When Meru was sitting down with his arms raised, Zoella could feel the children relax.

'Who are you?' Zoella said. 'Do you understand me?'

One of the children, who had been standing near the back, stepped forward, pushing through the others. Zoella recognised the face of the girl she had seen. She was taller than the others, not long from adulthood.

'It's her!' she said, looking back at Meru.

The girl stopped a few hand lengths away from Zoella. She raised her hands and made some kind of strange gesture before standing still again.

'What is your name?' Zoella asked.

The girl did not respond. Zoella frowned, none of them had made as much as a whisper, much less spoken a word.

'I don't think they can speak,' Meru whispered.

At his words there came another gesture from the girl, a complex interweaving of her hands, ending with her palms open towards them.

'I don't understand,' Zoella said. She closed her eyes, holding her hand forward, the faint metallic sense rising up around her. She gently probed.

Can you hear me this way?

The girl gasped. She nodded.

An image came back to Zoella, a view of herself, reaching forward, Meru in the vehicle, the others clustered around looking at her. Feelings subsumed the link too; caution, wariness and … hope.

'Can you talk to her?' Meru asked.

Zoella opened her eyes.

'Not in words, no,' she said. 'She has the gift for certain though. She's sent me images of what she can see …'

The girl pointed at Zoella and then moved her hands in what was she took to be a 'follow me' gesture. Zoella nodded and moved towards the girl. She held out her hand and the girl took it.

Zoella felt feelings from her again; tenseness, anxiety and a growing relief. An image of a ramshackle camp, secluded and hidden amongst the machinery of the hall came into her mind.

Zoella turned back to Meru.

'Come on,' she said. 'Looks like they want to take us to their home.'

Meru climbed down from the vehicle once more.

Fear! Anger! Hatred!

Zoella gasped. The feelings from the girl were raw and directed at Meru. The girl held up her hand in a clear 'Stop' gesture. She pointed at Meru and shook her head.

You can trust him. He's a friend of mine.

The girl continued to shake her head. Images of whips, punches, beatings and worse came into her mind.

No … Meru isn't like that.

'What's wrong?' Meru asked.

'They're scared of you,' Zoella said. 'I think it's because you're a man. I get pictures of whips, beatings … men of the city above I think.'

'But I'm …'

'I've tried to explain.'

Zoella's mind was swamped with sudden images. Men, running, carrying sticks and whips. The children about her scattered like startled marsips and were gone in seconds. A moment later, Zoella could hear the sound of running and voices calling to each other.

'This way!' a gruff male voice called. Zoella watched in horror as Meru turned around to see a group of heavy set guards appear from behind one of the troughs.

'Who is that? Grab him!'

Zoella was yanked backwards by the girl. She tried to resist but the girl was strong. Lurid images of punishment flooded her mind, followed by the urgent need to conceal herself. She watched as Meru jumped off the vehicle, scrambling to grab the rifle.

No, just run!

Another yank. Zoella found that she was pulled under the nearest trough and out the other side.

But my friend! Meru!

She caught a last glimpse of him being caught by four big dark-skinned men. In horror she watched as he was turned around and forced across the vehicle, his hands wrenched behind his back. They tied his hands together and pulled him away.

Zoella went to get up, but the girl pulled her back, shaking her head.

I've got to help him! Let me go!

Zoella managed to get to her feet. One of the men spotted her between the rows of plants.

'Another one! There!'

She could sense their thoughts, rough and aggressive. It was clear what they intended.

Another image, the meaning clear; flee!

Zoella scrambled to her feet and was pulled away by the girl. She was fleet of foot and knew her way around. They darted between the troughs, finding gaps that Zoella would have missed, making a diagonal cross away from the men. They outdistanced them. The girl turned a corner and came to a halt. She pointed down.

There was a shaft, set in the floor. The girl pointed.

'Down there? But …'

The girl rolled her eyes and shoved. Zoella lost her footing and fell, plummeting into darkness, rolling and turning. She yelled out, panicking. She caught a brief glimpse of the girl jumping in behind her before something struck her head.

Stars rolled in her vision and then everything went black.

CHAPTER THIRTEEN

Airea, Capital of Taloon

Round 2307, Fifth pass

Kiri was called to the throne room within the palace of Airea. She brought Liana with her, leading her by the cord at her wrists. Upon entry she curtseyed, Liana copied her movements.

'Come,' Karquesh said. 'You are my honoured guest, there is no need for further ceremony. Taloon and Drayden are as one, are they not?'

'Your service is most gratifying,' Kiri answered. 'Your cousin …'

Karquesh smiled at her. 'As you no doubt surmised, you rid me of a troubling family member. Think no more of him. I do not.'

Kiri smiled.

'Then how go the preparations?'

'The fleet is being readied as we speak,' Karquesh said. 'It will be ready to depart in two stretches.'

'The priestesses will arrive soon too. Then we can depart.'

Kiri watched as Karquesh nodded.

'You bring the Lady Liana with you,' he said, stepping up from his throne and walking across to them.

'Your gift, as I promised,' Kiri said, holding out the cord to him. He took it, looking Liana up and down.

'Quite delightful,' he said. 'She says little, does she not?'

'Her thoughts are … elsewhere,' Kiri answered.

'A beautiful woman who does not speak,' Karquesh mused, a smile growing on his face. 'Perfection indeed.'

Kiri did not deign to reply.

'Now,' Karquesh said, stepping back. 'I also have a gift for you.'

Kiri's eyebrows twitched in surprise.

'Gifts are not necessary, King Karquesh,' she replied. 'Your hospitality and generosity has been more than enough already. With your allegiance to Drayden, I have all I could want from you.'

'Perhaps that is true,' Karquesh replied. 'But let it never be said that Taloon did not give abundantly when it could. And it is fair to say that a visit from the priestesses of Drayden should not go unmarked. I have something I think you will appreciate. Something to whet your appetite for the conquest ahead.'

Kiri tried to keep a bewildered expression from crossing her face. She wasn't sure if she had succeeded or not.

What is he talking about? The man is wily ...

Karquesh clapped his hands. Kiri looked over to the side of the hall where the ornate gilded doors opened. Two guards came in, holding someone between them. As she watched the figure was flung to the floor with a grunt.

'Caught in our midst, associating with criminals and vagabonds in the catacombs below the city,' Karquesh said. 'It seems we have spies among us.'

The figure got up on its hands and feet. Kiri watched in growing alarm. She gasped.

Meru!

Her heart lurched in her chest. She could feel it like a hammer blow against her ribs. A hot flush rushed across her body from head to toe causing her to gasp.

You let yourself be captured?

She almost ran to him, but had to quash her instinctive reaction. She schooled herself not to respond. She saw the recognition on his face too. His face and clothing were dirt-stained, his face marked by a bruise. She saw him stare at her in astonishment, taking in the sight of her in her glamour and dress. In that moment she formed a thought and aimed it at him.

If you want to live, do not speak or give any sign that you know me!

Meru blinked and then dropped his head.

'A spy?' Kiri said, looking back at Karquesh. 'From where?'

'He's not of our people,' Karquesh answered. 'And I assume he's not of yours.'

Kiri shook her head. 'No …'

'How he arrived is a mystery, perhaps one of those machines you talked about.'

'You think he's an Amaran?' Kiri said, licking her lips.

'Who else would be spying on us, seeking out our strength?' Karquesh replied. 'He claims to have come alone.'

'I find that unlikely,' Kiri said.

'My thoughts too,' Karquesh replied. 'We are searching for any companions he might have brought with him.'

Karquesh signalled to the guard and they brought some objects over.

'He was found with these,' Karquesh said. 'We have not seen their like before. Do you recognise them?'

Kiri looked at the objects. One was a transparent box with a black grip, the other a long metal tube with a wooden wedge at the far end. Neither were familiar to her. She aimed a thought at Meru.

What are these? Think to me, I will hear.

She could sense his worry.

The first is a light, the second a weapon, be careful, it is very dangerous!

'Do not touch them further,' Kiri said. 'They are Amaran weapons of some kind, for sure. I warned you of their devices.'

The guard put down both objects and stepped away from them.

'What else does he know?' Kiri asked.

Karquesh smiled. 'We haven't interrogated him … not yet, I thought you might have your own ways of … extracting information from him. Those powers of the mind you talked about …'

Torture Meru …? I can't. But if Karquesh doubts my abilities …

Kiri thought and then nodded at Karquesh, licking her lips again as she looked at him. 'Oh yes, there are ways.'

She got up and walked over to where Meru was crouched on the floor.

She walked around him once, aware she was echoing Nerina's habit, looking down upon him. Her shoes clicked on the marble floor.

'So Amaran,' she said, her voice sharp and aggressive. 'Come to spread your lies and deceits here? You're too late, Taloon and Drayden are already of an accord.'

Meru didn't answer. Kiri knelt down and grabbed his chin, jerking his head up, pulling him into a seated position. She looked at him, her face close to his.

'You will tell me everything you know, what are you doing here?'

I won't hurt you … but cry out, as if I am! Causing you horrible pain, like I did before. Do it!

Meru yelled, flinching in her grasp. Kiri renewed her grip as Meru flailed before her, she pushed him back and down.

And again! Scream! Scream as loud as you can!

Meru screamed, thrashing and writhing under her. Out of the corner of her eye she saw Karquesh and the guards flinch back.

Kiri released her grip and Meru fell back to the floor, gasping. Kiri got up and then placed her foot on his chest, pressing down, digging in the pointed heel of her shoe.

'That was just a warning, Amaran,' she said. 'Tell me what I want to hear and death will be quick and merciful. If not, your torment will be all the longer.'

She turned to Karquesh.

'A valuable gift,' she said. 'It will not take me long to find what I need to know. But he is filthy and disgusting. If I am to sully myself with close association with the likes of him I do not want his grime and muck as well. Put him in a secure room, have him cleaned and prepared for me. Then lock him away and …' She smiled at Karquesh, her tongue touching her teeth for a moment, '… give me the key. I will find answers soon enough.'

Karquesh nodded to the guards. They grabbed Meru and hoisted him up. He slumped between them.

'It shall be done as you request,' Karquesh said.

Kiri watched Meru being dragged out.

Saved him, thank Lacaille!

She felt the lust grow in her again. This time there was no subduing it. Having him so close and within her power was intoxicating.

And mine now, mine!

'Your powers are fearsome to behold,' Karquesh said.

Kiri looked at him. 'Drayden is mighty indeed.'

* * *

They had done as Kiri had requested. None too gently he'd been stripped, dunked in a bath and then scrubbed clean. A simple smock had been pulled over him and then he'd been lugged back through the hallways of the palace and thrown into a room.

It was dark within, heavy curtains were pulled across the windows.

He heard the sound of the key turn in the lock behind him. He tried the door, but it was firm and secure. The room was opulent, not a prison cell. He went to the windows, pushing the curtains aside, but was dismayed to find he was in a parapet hundreds of hands above the ground. Worse, he could see the ships in the harbour. Zoella had been right, they were close to being ready to depart.

The windows were locked and barred; there was no obvious way out.

Caught!

He sat on the edge of the bed and placed his head in his hands.

Zoella escaped at least. Where is she now? I can't contact her, but she can contact me using her powers, so why hasn't she?

That worried him. Zoella should have been able to send him a message via her gift, but there was nothing in his mind. What had happened to her? Who were the strange children in the hall?

We shouldn't have come here …

He looked around again, but there was nothing he could do. There was no way out, no escape.

And she's here. Kiri!

She had caught him now. She had saved him from interrogation by the Taloon guards. She wasn't far away. The thought was exciting and terrifying all at once.

He lay back on the bed, feeling exhaustion seeping through his body. It was a late chime in the stretch, almost into the sleeping. His body ached. In the darkness of the room sleep crept over him.

* * *

Zoella moaned and tried to sit up. She heard shuffling and movement around her. Next moment pain throbbed through her head and she felt a gentle push on her chest.

An image of a head bandage and blood came into her mind followed by a request to relax and rest.

She felt sick and dizzy, and lay back, feeling that she was lying on some soft material. She raised a hand and felt a bandage over her forehead. She pushed it up and opened her eyes.

Wherever she was it was dim. She could see little but some overhead metal beams, stained dark with age. Around the edges of her vision concerned faces were peering down at her. The children she had seen before.

The older girl appeared between them, pushing the others aside.

Zoella tried to sit up again.

'What happened?' she said. Nausea surged up through her. 'I need to find Meru ...'

The girl shook her head. An image of sleep flickered through her consciousness. Tiredness washed over her, she couldn't think. Zoella lay back and her thoughts drifted away.

* * *

Meru dozed, unable to shake the image of Kiri's blue eyes staring at him. The shock of seeing her, the abrupt recognition on her face, swiftly concealed. He tried to think of other things; home, the voyages on the *Mobilis*, the frozen wastes, even Zoella's friendly yet concerned smile; anything to keep that haunting face from his mind.

But whenever he lost concentration, there she was.

His dreams were tormented. He woke, drawing a shuddering breath.

There was a faint creak, a floorboard. He sat up, his heart pounding. The room was dark, but he could still see.

She stood there in front of the door, her blue eyes lit by the pale illumination that filtered through cracks in the curtains. She was still dressed in the same elegant cyan gown, draped from shoulders to feet, tied at her waist with a band.

Blue eyes, dark black hair.

I'm dreaming again …

She said nothing, but watched him for a moment. He felt his mouth go dry, heard blood rushing in his ears. She turned, locking the door behind her, before spinning around to look at him.

This is no dream.

Her mental voice echoed in his head.

Still keeping her gaze on him she stepped forward, teasing apart the band around her waist until it came undone, the folds of her dress falling aside. With an alluring shrug of her shoulders she let the dress slide from her and it fell to the floor with a faint rustle. She stepped over it.

Meru caught his breath.

She was naked, even the glove was gone. She walked forward, her gaze fixed on him.

I told you there would be a time for us … it's now …

He was transfixed, unable to take his eyes from the predatory gaze upon her face, yet beguiled by the contours of her body on the edges of his vision.

She knelt down as she reached the bed, moving on to all fours, crawling across the covers. He fell back before her, pulling up the bedcovers around him. In a moment, she was poised above him.

They stared at each other for what might have been an age, before she reached down and pulled the bed covers to one side. He tried to resist for a moment, but she grabbed his hand, forcing it above his head and back against the pillows, leaning across him.

The sight of her breasts, small but firm, drew a gasp from him. Her hair, deep black and perfumed, brushed across his chest and face. She pulled back, the faintest of coy smiles upon her face.

Desire growing in him, he reached towards her with his other hand, but she caught that too, forcing his arms above his head. He struggled for a moment, half out of fear, half out of dislike of being trapped, but she shoved him down, the strength in her lithe body startling.

You are mine, Meru of Amar, mine!

Now straddling him, she ground her hips against him, drawing another gasp and a half-snatched breath from him. Her head came down next to his, her breath hot across his ear and neck. He felt her teeth scrape down from his cheekbone to his jaw as if she intended to bite him. She pressed against his chest, the warmth and scent from her body a heady cocktail of lust.

He turned his head, her lips brushing across his as he did so. He tried to kiss her, but each time he tried she pulled back just out of reach.

If you want me, tell me so.

He stared into her eyes. She was waiting, still poised above him.

He couldn't articulate words.

Then her whole weight was upon him, her lips crushing into his to a point of violence. Both of them struggled, rolling and thrashing at each other in a lustful frenzy, the bedding flying unwanted around them, his clothing ripped away.

They twisted and turned, one atop and then the other, fighting for dominance, each trying to restrain the other long enough to gain control.

Breathless, Meru managed to pin Kiri down, but knew that she had let him do it. He likewise held her by the wrists, pinned against the bed. She was breathing heavily too, her chest rising and falling beneath him, accentuating her slight curves, but it was still her blue eyes that held him. She strained against him as if testing his strength. He pushed down harder.

So you do want me?

She relaxed under him, undulating her body.

Take me then, if you dare …

All thoughts of resistance evaporated. She knew he belonged to her, and he didn't care.

Her legs wrapped around him, pulling him towards her, ever inwards. As he slipped into the intoxicating warmth of her body, he felt her slip into the yearning of his mind.

* * *

Zoella woke a second time. Her body ached and her head was a solid lump of pain, but the dizziness was gone. She stirred; something was brushing her face, a damp cloth. She opened her eyes.

She sat up, taking her time to do so, moaning as her muscles complained.

The girl was holding a cloth and a small earthenware bowl.

'Thank you,' Zoella said.

The girl nodded. Zoella sensed a question about how she felt. She smiled by return. That seemed to satisfy the girl. She made a hand gesture and pointed at Zoella.

'Me? My name is Zoella.'

Zoella?

The word came back through her mind from the girl.

So she can hear me …

Zoella copied the gesture and pointed back at the girl.

There were brief flickers of images, snatches of childhood, views of the sands, the spires of the city and then …

Ira.

Zoella spoke it out loud.

'Ira. You're called Ira?'

The girl nodded.

'Where are we?' Zoella asked, looking around. 'How long have I been asleep?'

With a flurry of images Zoella saw that they were at a lower level in the hall complex. They had slid down a tube between the levels. Somewhere along the line she had banged her head in the rush of escaping the guards.

'You hide down here.'

Another nod.

Zoella sent an image of Meru.

'My friend, I must find him …'

Ira recoiled, shaking her head, images of the guards appearing. Zoella shook her head, sending back images of Meru rescuing her from Viresia.

Ira frowned.

'He's not like them,' Zoella said. 'He's my friend. I need to find him, he can help us escape from here. We have …'

She sent an image of the flying machine.

Ira gasped. The returned images were of the same vision Zoella had of the Obelisk.

She saw it too and the flying machine …

It took them some time, but Zoella managed to learn some of the gestures that Ira used, and Zoella taught her more words. Haltingly, they managed to communicate. Images and words were learnt, thoughts exchanged. Zoella's eyes widened as she began to understand.

* * *

Meru woke, the unexpected warmth of Kiri's body rousing him from his sleep. She was lying half across him, one arm draped across his chest, one leg curled across his. She was turned towards him, still asleep, her eyes closed, her dark hair half across her face. Her hand was clasped around his upper arm. The scent of her body was all about him.

He ran his own hand along her arm, feeling the softness but noting the thin white scars that peppered her skin. The left hand that clasped his arm bore an ugly mark, with roughen skin pulled tight about a wound now long healed. It was the hand she wore gloved. It was all evidence of the life she led. He ran his fingers over the scar, wondering how she had come by it.

His mind spun with the thought of her; she was wild, strong and lustful, yet somehow fragile and vulnerable at the same time.

What am I doing?

His mind was churning with thoughts. Kiri the priestess, the murderer of King and Prince, devoted to the destruction of his homeland, the ending of his people. She was here in Taloon to raise an army ready to sail across the sea and strike his homeland. She was his enemy …

But his heart rose up in defiance. Kiri the lover, Kiri the beautiful and irresistible, precious and unique. He alone held a special place in her heart. Beyond the fearsome fighter he alone had reached her softer side, seen her for who she truly was. He'd never felt this way about anyone.

She stirred against him, wriggling closer. He turned to look at her face. Asleep, it was relaxed, bereft of the scowl that was her habitual expression. He traced the line of one of her eyebrows with the tip of his finger, pushing her hair back.

He lay back, looking at the ceiling.

But what would my parents say, Coran, Mel … Zoella?

They wouldn't understand. He didn't understand himself. He was consorting with the enemy. This was madness. When she woke Kiri would laugh and scorn him, having found out what she wanted by probing his mind. Just a seduction. Maybe Kiri was doing this just to find out what he knew.

Maybe I am. But wasn't it a little more pleasant than being tortured by the guards?

He jolted and turned in surprise. Kiri was gazing at him, a smile on her face. He looked into her blue eyes, lost within them once more. Her expression was soft and alluring.

She moved across him, her body pressing down on his, the warmth and scent of her overwhelming.

Forget them, you have me.

A languid kiss followed and they were lost together once more, their love-making softer and slower now, not the frenzy it had been. Beyond the captivation of his physical senses she placed images in his mind, some lurid, some subtle. Not only could he admire and caress her curves and feel the softness of her skin, but he could sense her wants as she guided him to fulfil her desires. She was still dominant, still aggressive and impatient at times, her mind and body long denied and insatiable.

Once their passion was complete, she lay across him once more, her breathing fast and hot on his neck, pulling him into a tight embrace. It was a spell or more before she moved aside, rolling back to look at him.

He reached out to stroke her arm.

'Like silk,' he whispered, 'yet strong.'

She bent her neck to kiss his hand, wriggling into his embrace.

'I told you you'd be mine.'

Her body heat was still intoxicating; he could not help but run his hand over her lithe form. She sighed as he did so, moving closer once more.

So gentle, so demure … so unlike the warrior woman of before …

'I never said thank you,' Meru whispered to her. She looked at him. 'For saving me from the priestesses back in Drem … and the guards here.'

'Perhaps I haven't saved you,' she answered. 'I know you're here with her, with Zoella. You can't keep secrets from me. Perhaps I'll hand you over to them.'

'At least I'd die happy,' he said. She laughed. 'But why did you …?'

'I told you,' she said. 'You're mine. What happened between us … there's a bond, a link. You must have felt it.'

'Yes,' Meru whispered. 'I've been dreaming of you ever since. Every errant thought, every moment when I lost concentration … it was maddening.'

'And me of you,' she replied. 'I did not intend it, even tried to stop it … but now, I'm glad of it.'

Meru caught his breath, having this beguiling girl in his arms was the most glorious thing he'd ever experienced.

But what now? What would Zoella say? She'd be disgusted. She'd tell me Kiri was evil, irredeemable ...

But he couldn't bring himself to believe it, there was no lie in Kiri's deep eyes. He was sure of it.

'Kiri ...'

She placed a finger to his lips, rolling to look at him.

I know you care for your friends, and I know what they think of me. But they don't know the truth of who I am ...

Meru frowned.

'Truth? What truth?'

Kiri spoke now, her voice just a whisper. She ran a finger around his cheeks.

'When we met in Nireus, when I first caught up with you. There was an old man, remember?'

'We came to find him. Zoella's guardian ... Guerrun Sandatch. You killed ...'

'No, it wasn't me. I didn't hurt him. Zoella struck at me, but I was too deep within his mind to safely release him. I tried to stop her but she tore his mind with her attack. I know she didn't mean to hurt him. Yet, he was telling me about ... about both of us.'

'Both of you? Zoella and you? What do you mean?'

'We both share these powers,' Kiri said, a faint smile teasing her features. 'Don't you see?'

'See what?'

'We're sisters.'

Meru couldn't find words to answer. He looked at her in shock.

'Sisters?' he whispered. 'How can that be?'

'We're both daughters of woman called Myana Tiamoi, she was the sister of King Ioric of Scallia,' Kiri said.

Meru cast his mind back to the walled city of Viresia. He remembered the King, remembered his wisdom. But most of all he remembered the fierce battle outside the gates, against ...

'Ioric ...'

'I didn't know,' Kiri whispered, her face forlorn. 'He was my uncle. If I'd known …'

'I don't understand,' Meru said, propping himself up on one elbow. 'Zoella was just a maid in the household there, and you're from Drayden, not from …'

'Guerrun hid us on Myana's instruction, they knew we would both have these gifts,' Kiri said. 'As babes we were hidden in different places. He tried to keep us out of the reach of the priestesses by sending us to faraway lands. We're both Scallian, both royalty. Now that they are all dead, we are next in line.'

'Who knows this?' Meru asked.

'Just me,' she said, her finger now tracing his neck. 'And now you.'

Zoella and Kiri are sisters? Their powers, so alike. It makes sense …

'Then …?'

In a flurry of thoughts Meru perceived Kiri's dilemma. Raised as a priestess only to discover that she had brought destruction upon her own country. The death of the King, the subjugation of Viresia.

There is more I must show you.

Images lit up in his mind. He could see a vast metal edifice, rising into the sky, vast beyond imagining. Clouds swirled around it.

It calls itself the Obelisk …

He gasped.

Yes, it called to me. Chose me, instructed me. It is Lacaille's emissary on our world. Beyond the priestesses, beyond everything else, this is the truth.

Words echoed in his head, no longer in Kiri's voice, but with harsh male timbre, demanding attention and commanding in no uncertain terms.

The Obelisk Commands! The Obelisk Requires! Obedience and urgency!

Changes must be made! Lacaille must be sated, all must be set right or death and destruction will blossom, fires will come more devastating than any you have known.

Come to me, faithful one, servant of Lacaille. You are chosen! Come to me! This you must do! Carry out the task appointed! Changes must be made!

The mental connection faded, Meru gasped from the intensity of it.

'This is what Zoella saw too,' Meru said. 'We found out where it is, it lies in the uttermost sunward. We were going there to try to fix it when …'

'Fix it?' Kiri asked. Now it was her turn to frown.

'Zoella heard the same thing,' Meru explained. 'That the Obelisk was in trouble …'

Kiri shook her head.

'No, the task appointed is what the Obelisk requires. You don't understand. I have to subdue Amar,' Kiri said, her voice soft. 'I'm commanded to do it. Only though doing this can we stop the flares.'

Meru shook his head. 'Kiri, attacking Amar will do nothing but cause death and destruction to all. The flares happen anyway, they're just something that Lacaille does. It's the Obelisk that stops them and the Obelisk is breaking down.'

Kiri was shaking her head.

'You're wrong,' she answered. 'I know it, I saw it. It has chosen me, spoken to me!'

'Look into my thoughts,' Meru said, 'I won't stop you, go on. Look!'

He saw her swallow. Meru lay back as Kiri rolled across him again, but there was no thought of love now. She pressed her fingers against his forehead.

See, the cavern where we encountered Caesar … the true nature of the Obelisk!

Images flashed between the pair of them. Meru could feel Kiri's rising astonishment as she saw the hangar, listened to Caesar's words about the flares and the Obelisk.

* * *

It seemed that Ira's people had once lived in the city above long ago. Zoella couldn't quite work out why, but something had split the population, with many forced to work below ground. It seemed that generations had passed and the two became separate peoples. Those above had kept those below in slavery, forcing them to work on the plants and animals below whilst they lived in luxury above. With no exposure to the light of Lacaille they had become white-skinned and pale, with those above darker.

Then those with gifts had appeared; the girls. There were fights and unrest. The slaves had attempted to break free but had been brutally suppressed. Any malcontent was punished. The slaves had capitulated, going back to their labour amongst the plants and animals.

Ira seemed to be the exception. Zoella could sense her gift. It allowed Ira to confound the guards, lead them astray whilst the group of girls she looked after sabotaged the machinery. They seemed to have been running an insurrection against those above. The guards tried to find them and eradicate them, but they were too cunning, they knew their way around far better and were able to hide.

Those above were running short of food as a result.

Zoella had tried to explain her own story in pictures. Her own childhood, the priestesses, the city of Amar they were trying to protect.

They came at last to the Obelisk. Ira had received the same instruction as Zoella. The Obelisk needed them, the compelling call to go there was shared by both.

But Ira had seen something else. One image she portrayed showed a map, far more detailed than anything Zoella had seen, even aboard the *Mobilis.* It showed all the continents across Esurio, there were all sorts of markers and lines in addition. Ira tried to explain them, but Zoella couldn't grasp what she meant.

Zoella turned the strange conversation back to Meru.

Ira looked saddened. Zoella could sense regret. Images of torture and death came to her.

Ira shook her head and stretched out her hands, her eyes filling with tears.

'No ...'

Zoella shook her head. She sent her thoughts outwards once again, seeking, searching.

Meru! Meru, can you hear me? Meru!

* * *

Kiri pulled back, her gaze distant. Meru could feel her shuddering. Her outstretched arm was shaking, her fingertips trembling before his face.

'Kiri?'

She was staring past him, her eyes wide and unblinking.

'It's all lies,' she whispered. 'Everything I know, everything they taught me ... it's all lies.'

She rolled aside, sitting up on the bed. He reached out to her but she held up her hand and shook her head.

'Give me a moment.'

He watched as she swung her feet out over the bed, her back to him, her hands out to the side to steady herself. She bowed her head, her body shuddering. He could see her ribs rise and fall as she drew deep breaths. She shook her head from side to side.

She got to her feet and walked over to where her dress was pooled on the floor. She picked it up and deftly pulled it over her.

'I believe you,' she said, her voice shaking. 'You can't lie to me. And if what you have shown me is really true the priestesses are wrong, the religion is wrong and there is no goddess Lacaille. That machine... Caesar. What it says... there's just the Obelisk and whatever it needs from those of us with this gift.'

'What are you going to do?' Meru whispered.

'I'm going to defy her,' Kiri said.

'Who?'

'The high priestess. You saw her at Viresia. Her name is Nerina. It is she who has commanded the attack on Amar. She who controls the priestesses.'

'Stop her? Stop the attack?'

'Exactly,' Kiri finished fastening her dress. 'We can stop her, but she is powerful, very powerful. To do so I will need cooperation from others, from ...'

She turned to look at him. Meru gasped.

'You want Zoella to work with you to overcome this high priestess?'

Kiri stood tall. 'We are royalty, we are the true heirs of Scallia. It is us, not the priestesses of Drayden who have the right. I've seen this, Meru. With Zoella and you, we can end all this conflict, we can heal the Obelisk, we can set things right.'

'What about Taloon, the King?'

'Leave him to me. I must speak to Zoella first. The priestesses are coming, we have to be ready for them. Will you take me to her?'

Meru thoughts were wrenched aside by a heartfelt mental cry.

Meru! Meru, can you hear me? Meru!

He looked at Kiri.

'It's her, it's Zoella.'

Kiri nodded. 'I know, I can hear her. You'd better answer her.'

Meru closed his eyes and concentrated.

Zoella! Yes, I can.

Meru! You're alive, are you all right?

I'm fine ... I was a little roughed up by the guards, but not hurt.

It's so good to hear you, I thought you might have been ...

What about you? Are you safe? Those guards ...

They didn't catch me. The girl rescued me, her name is Ira, Meru, there's so much I need to tell you.

I need to tell you something too. Zoella ... She's here.

There was a pause in the mental connection between them.

Kiri?

Yes. She rescued me from the King's guards under the pretence of extracting information from me. We're safe for now, but we can't stay here for long.

Where are you?

We're in a room in one of the spires of the city palace.

In a … room?

Yes. We can escape, Kiri can get us past the guards … she … she wants to see you.

Me? Why?

I showed her the truth, Zoella. She knows the religion she's been following is wrong, she heard from the Obelisk too, the same vision as you! I showed her what Caesar said. She wants to stop the priestesses from attacking Amar, but she needs your help.

And she believes you?

She's still in shock, but her mind is made up. We can stop this battle, before it even starts. Kiri will help us!

Meru, we can't trust her, not after all the things she's done.

Zoella, I can prove she's honest. There's something else she needs to tell you, but it has to be in person …

Tell me now.

I can't … but it's so important, you must hear it from her.

I don't understand, what are you talking about?

We need to see you, will you meet with her?

There was another long pause.

She must come alone, no one else but you. She must not lead anyone else here.

Meru opened his eyes for a moment and looked at Kiri. She nodded. Listening to the mental voice was easier now.

She will do as you say.

Meru, you're asking me to trust you on this. There are lives at stake down here, if the guards find these children they will kill them …

I understand. We will be alone. I promise.

I will listen to what she has to say, nothing more. You remember what I said before?

I do. She won't hurt you, I promise.

We will see. We are beneath the city. I don't know how you get down here though. You'll have to find your way yourselves. Once you're in the hall with the plants wait there, we will come to you.

Kiri mouthed some words at him. 'I know how to get below the city.'

Kiri says she knows how to get down there. Stay safe.

I think you're the one who needs to be careful. Watch your back, Meru. I trust you, I don't trust her ...

The connection faded.

Meru took a deep breath.

'She will see you,' he whispered.

Kiri nodded.

'And what about you?' she asked. 'Do you trust me?'

Meru stood up and walked over to her, taking her in his arms. He kissed her and she responded as forcefully as ever.

'Does that answer you?'

She smiled, but said nothing.

CHAPTER FOURTEEN

Shadeward of Dynesia, Scallia and Amaris, Capital of Amar

Round 2307, Fifth pass

Mel had wasted no time in placing the tracking device on board the *Mobilis.* Caesar had given her instructions on connecting it into the ships 'tricity supply and was able to confirm it was working once she had finished.

'What does it do?' Coran asked.

'It sends out some kind of beacon,' Mel explained. 'Tells the other vehicles where we are.'

The other vessels were a mix of different machinery. There were two more small flying machines like the one Zoella and Meru had taken sunward. These were small and manoeuvrable, designed to carry small numbers of people or cargo.

There were six wheeled vehicles. Four of them seemed to be ground-based transports. They had four rugged wheels apiece, and a cockpit similar to the flying machines. A further two were different, with a series of smaller tracked wheels and a variety of fierce looking drills on the forward mounts. Caesar explained that they were mining machines, able to burrow into the earth or rock as required.

The other vessels were much larger. The two personnel transports were precisely that; large vessels with accommodation, seats and a series of beds within. The medical transport was the same on the outside, but its internal structure was different. It contained a series of what Caesar called 'autonomous operating and triage facilities'. These took the form of a series of alcoves within the vessel, each able to hold a person. There were six, three on each side. According to Caesar these could fix injuries from the minor all the way up to life threatening. There were a number of small cabins towards the rear which were named 'recovery and recuperation facilities'.

Coran decided that it would be best to understand the alcoves in more detail, so he summoned the crew and asked the onboard systems to give a demonstration. Sandra, as Meru had named the disembodied voice that responded inside the vessels, obliged. They saw a series of delicate mechanical manipulators fold out of the alcoves; tiny knives, drills, tubes and all manner of wires and other devices. Above the alcove were more of the black panel screens that showed information about the occupant.

Ren volunteered to lie down in one and they saw the alcove scan his body, showing a representation of his bones and muscles, along with his heart rate and many other statistics that meant little to them.

'Subject Ren is in excellent physiological condition,' Sandra concluded. 'No intervention is required.'

'They really knew their stuff,' Mel said, with a whistle. 'Every time we discover more about our ancestors, the more impressive they seem.'

'Yet they still were beaten by the flares it seems,' Coran mused.

Ren got back up.

'I won't have some machine fiddling with my innards,' Fitch grumbled as they watched the mechanism fold back into place.

'I'll remind you of that when your guts are hanging out over the gunwales,' Coran jibed back. 'Let's hope we don't need to use it.'

The final vessel was the biggest, dwarfing the others. It was empty within, it's purpose to haul cargo and equipment. It featured a massive set of rear doors and a loading ramp, along with sliding doors at either side. All six of the ground vehicles could fit inside easily with room to spare.

When it first emerged, rolling forward on a wheeled undercarriage, the crew stared at it in awe; it was twice as wide as the *Mobilis* and longer too.

'No way can that fly,' Coran murmured. 'That's impossible.'

'All vessels other than ground transports are capable of self-sustained flight,' Caesar answered. 'Observe.'

With a rising hum that soon became a thunderous roar of power, the big vessels stirred. Air blasted across the crew, forcing them to stagger back, their clothing whipped tight by the force. Coran shielded his eyes and stared in astonishment as the behemoths majestically rose up hand by hand into the sky.

Fitch was shouting something, but he couldn't hear it. Mel was gesturing at the vessels and Ren was jumping up and down in excitement.

Under Caesar's control the ships descended back to the hangar floor, their mighty engines spun down and the sound faded away.

'Wow,' Coran said, his mouth hanging open.

Fitch came up alongside.

'I don't know about those scorchin' witches,' he said. 'But seeing those things hanging in the air? Scared the living shades out of me!'

* * *

A stretch of testing had proved that the vessels were more than capable of following the *Mobilis* around. Coran, Daf and Creg had taken the ship down to the wide bay just shadeward of Dynesia, whilst Mel, Fitch and Ren had observed from the mainland.

When activated, the vessels rose from the hangar and flew sunwards, taking up a position to the stern of the *Mobilis* in a neat aerial formation. As the *Mobilis* moved, the ships followed half a mark behind, spread out in a phalanx.

'Look at that,' Mel said, watching the vessels turn in the air. 'It's ... amazing.'

The ability of the ships to follow the *Mobilis* was only half the story though. Manoeuvring them to land upon their return was another. Caesar had volunteered to do it for them, but Mel had declined.

'We won't have your assistance over in Amar,' she said. 'We have to solve the problem ourselves.'

'You may utilise the remote handsets,' Caesar instructed.

The handsets were also as described. They were designed to be gripped by both hands, and featured controls which were ideally placed for fingers and thumbs. In between those controls was another black panel display which showed a view from the front of the selected vessel.

Fitch tried and was hopeless. Mel was better, able to laboriously coax the vessels towards the hangar. After badgering them for an entire spell, Mel allowed Ren to have a go at the controls on one of the small flying machines and he took to it, able to move the flying machine with great precision.

'Looks like you were born to this,' Mel said, after supervising him for a while and finding he was able to control the machines far better than her. 'Can you bring them all in?'

Ren nodded and cheered. Mel continued to watch, but Ren brought each machine in via the handsets one after another and parked them in the hangar.

They were all parked and shut down by the time Coran, Daf and Creg returned.

'We're almost ready then,' Coran said as Mel brought him up to date. 'Nice work, Ren. Looks like you've been promoted to chief flying officer aboard the *Mobilis!*'

Ren beamed and then went on to demonstrate how the surface vehicles could also be remotely controlled by driving them up into the big transport one by one and then closing the hatch behind them.

'Next stretch we depart,' Coran said. 'Get some rest now, it's time to be getting home.'

The crew made for the quarters they had found scattered around the hangar.

'We'll look after them as best we can,' Coran said, his fingers tapping on Caesar's table. 'Not sure when we might be able to return them.'

'Hangar assets are at your disposal, Captain Coran,' Caesar replied. 'Approval has been authorised by Administrator Zoella.'

'Yeah I know, but I still appreciate what you have done for us,' Coran said. 'Is there anything we can do for you?'

There was a pause before the machine answered.

'This unit was created to act as an automated diagnostic, forensic, reference simulation and decision making aid, providing terraforming support to the colonists of Esurio,' Caesar intoned. 'Without the colonists this unit had no purpose for several hundred rounds. You now represent the colonists of Esurio and your presence has provided a renewed purpose. Their original aim was the peaceful settlement of this planet and to create a simple agrarian civilisation upon it. The original colonists eschewed religion and feudal hierarchical organisational structures. Judgement indicates that your culture, the people of Amar, is closest to their ideals based on available evidence. Your survival will be satisfactory reward for this unit.'

Coran blinked. He'd never heard Caesar give such a long speech before.

'We'll do our best. Once … once things are finished, we'll bring the machines back here.'

'That will be acceptable.'

Coran got to his feet.

'Thanks again, Caesar, and goodbye … for now.'

'Goodbye, Captain Coran.'

* * *

They were up early to load the *Mobilis* with supplies. The ship was ready to depart within a couple of spells. There was no further word from Meru and Zoella on the *Mobilis*' radio. Mel scanned up and down the frequency band without luck at the time they had arranged to try to make contact.

'Nothing new on the radio,' she shouted down from the deck. Coran was below her in the hold.

'They're travelling directly away from us into the sunward,' Coran said, looking up at her. 'Perhaps it's already too far. That thing was never reliable anyway.'

'I have fixed it you know,' Mel replied.

Coran chuckled. 'Not blaming you, but I wouldn't worry too much. They got their warning about the priestess through and they both know what they've got to do.'

'Let's hope they stick to it.'

She started hoisting the last set of crates down to him.

'Zoella is the sensible one of the pair,' Coran replied. 'I'm happy she's gone along with Meru. It'll keep him grounded.'

'She's an interesting young woman,' Mel said.

'The same power as the priestesses,' Coran mused. 'Yeah. At least she's using it in a good cause. Sounds like she's had a rough ride thus far.'

'She actually is an orphan. Has no idea who her parents are, and it seems the one man who did know something was killed just before he managed to tell her.'

'When was this?' Coran gestured for another crate.

'Back in Drem, before we picked Meru, her and Ren up.' Mel answered. 'She faced off with that priestess girl.'

'The one Meru has a thing for?'

'Yeah, Kiri.' Mel nodded. 'She sounds like a proper bitch to me.'

'Guess we'll find out soon enough,' Coran said. 'Doubtless she'll be amidst the priestesses who come for Amar, just like when they attacked Zoella's city.'

'We'll have to keep an eye on Meru then.'

'Yeah,' Coran said, stopping for a moment, a crate in his hands. 'You think his loyalty might still be split?'

Mel frowned and thought for a moment. 'I don't know. Zoella is closest to him. They were nearly scratching each other's eyes out at one point, but they seemed to make it up before they left. But whatever is going on there isn't resolved.'

The last crate was stowed.

'Then Meru's going to have to pick a side,' Coran said. 'Let's hope he picks the right one.'

They climbed back to the wheelhouse.

'All aboard who's going aboard!' Coran called.

'As if there's any of us who want to stay in this snuttin' place,' Fitch said. He'd been waiting for them.

'We all set to go?' Coran asked.

'We've grabbed pretty much everything that wasn't nailed down that we can bash a witch with,' Fitch answered. 'I'd say we're as ready as we can be.'

'Let's get going then,' Coran said and leant out of the window. 'Daf, Creg! Cast off.'

The two burly men were standing fore and aft. They untied the ships ropes and coiled them up on the decking.

'Take us out,' Coran said.

Mel adjusted the coil and accumulator controls and then pushed the throttles forward a notch. The *Mobilis* throbbed as its engines wound up to speed and began to move away from the quayside.

Within moments, they had left Caesar's hangar and were swinging out in the river once more. Coran turned the *Mobilis* sunwards to follow the flow of the river back down towards the bay of Dynesia where they could turn sunright and head out into the open sea.

It took them only a spell to reach the bay. Coran executed the turn and the *Mobilis* was facing towards home once more. He pushed the throttles up to half power, the ship leaving a churning wake behind it.

'Ren!' he called. 'Time to bring on the escort. Do your thing.'

Ren climbed on to a chair at the back of the deckhouse and began fiddling with the handset. His fingers were a blur over the controls.

'Ships coming!' he said, looking up for a brief moment, before turning back to his task.

'There!' Fitch called, looking back at the receding coastline of Scallia. The crew turned to look.

Above the horizon the six huge flying machines had come into view above the hills where Caesar's hangar lay. They were growing larger.

'Damn, that's intimidating,' Coran said, as he watched the ships turn and head towards them. 'It's going to give those priestesses pause when they see that!'

'Only when we get some weapons aboard,' Fitch grumbled. 'Otherwise all they can do is fly around ...'

It took less than half a spell for the six flying vessels to catch up to the *Mobilis*. Ren looked up from his controls as the machines adopted their phalanx posture above and behind the seagoing vessel.

Mel was grinning. Coran looked at her.

'What?'

'Looks like we should be calling you Admiral Coran of the Amaran defence fleet now.'

Coran grinned. Mel grabbed his arm and Fitch rolled his eyes.

'You've done good,' Mel said, giving his arm a squeeze before releasing it.

Coran pushed the throttles forwards to their stops and the *Mobilis* surged ahead out into the sea. The flying machines followed, tracking across the sky and casting huge shadows on the ocean.

'Best speed home,' Coran whispered to himself. 'And let's hope we're in good time.'

* * *

The crossing of the Straithian Sea was uneventful. There was a little rough weather to navigate, but it was nothing that the *Mobilis* couldn't shrug off with ease. The flying machines behind seemed likewise unaffected, they held their position and their formation regardless of sun or rain.

On the first chime of the fifth stretch all of the crew were on deck, looking for the island of Amar. It wasn't long before it came in sight.

'We're getting good at this navigation lark,' Coran said as the *Mobilis* closed the distance to the coastline. The weather was fair, but there was a stiff breeze blowing, the sea around them choppy, causing the ship to pitch and roll. They were all used to it now.

'You can thank Meru for that,' Mel said. 'He reset the timers and made the measurements before we left.'

'Good lad.'

'Looks like they've been busy,' Fitch said, pointing at the coast line. 'Look at the walls. They'd better not take exception to us again.'

Fitch's eyesight was good, but before long all of the crew could see the changes to the coastal defences of Amar. Along the walls were many more of the catapults they had seen on the recent return, now lined up at hundred hand intervals.

'That should give any approaching fleet pause,' Coran said.

'Assuming they try a head on attack,' Fitch said. 'If I were the priestesses I'd conduct an aerial attack first to weaken the city before bringing the boats in.'

Coran nodded. 'From what Meru told us about Viresia, that seems to be their tactics. The question is, how do we frustrate that approach?'

Fitch grinned. 'I left 'em with a few jobs to do for me. I have a few sneaky ideas based on what I saw in Nireus.'

As the *Mobilis* approached, they could see crowds of people lining the walls and the quays, the awesome sight of the enormous flying machines had drawn everyone out.

'Any suggestions as to where to land the beasts?' Coran said.

'No space in the bay or the city,' Mel said. 'But there's a flat plain above the cliffs overlooking the city a couple of marks inland. Easy enough to reach and more than enough space there.'

Coran nodded. 'Show Ren where it is, he'll be able to manage it I'm sure.'

Mel jumped down from the wheelhouse and ran aft.

The *Mobilis* slowed and turned into the harbour. The quayside they were approaching was thronged with people waving flags and banners.

'Looks like we'll get a slightly warmer welcome this time,' Fitch muttered.

They moored to shouts and cries of welcome. Senators Janaid and Henoch were waiting for them amidst a crowd of well-wishers. Coran raised his hands high and was rewarded with a loud cheer from the crowd. He shook as many hands as he could until he reached the senators.

'It is such a pleasure to welcome you back, Captain Coran!' Janaid shouted above the din. 'It seems your mission was fruitful.'

'We have brought what we can ...' Coran said.

He was interrupted by the thumping vibrations of the flying machines. Ren had brought them all in low across the bay and they cast the quayside into shadow as they passed overhead. A collective moan of awe and appreciation shattered through the crowd as the machines glided by above. Both senators were watching, mouths agape.

'My word,' Henoch managed to utter. 'I never imagined ...'

'Our lost legacy,' Coran said, unable to resist driving his point home. 'These are the machines of our ancestors, here to help us against our ancient foe.'

'They're truly coming?' Janaid said. 'The priestesses?'

'Aye,' Coran said, with a terse nod. 'They're coming all right.'

They were drowned out as the down-thrust from the flying machines echoed above them. The water in the bay vibrated and splashed in strange patterns.

'That little scamp,' Coran muttered, looking back at the ship. Ren was standing on the aft deck, having decided to bring the flying machines in at that angle before ordering them to rise up over the cliffs. The crowds watched as the machines receded, pointing and talking amongst themselves.

Henoch looked around him, casting his eyes over the *Mobilis*.

'Where is Meru and that young woman who was with him?' Henoch demanded.

'They're on a mission,' Coran said. 'I'll give you the full details once we're ashore.'

'But they're coming back?' Henoch demanded.

'That's the plan,' Coran said.

* * *

The flying machines were landed on the high plain beyond the city and seemed to be none the worse for wear for their trip. Once the crew were rested, the senate was called together to discuss progress.

As Fitch had seen, the residents of Amaris had not been idle whilst the *Mobilis* had been away. Along with the catapults, the city armoury had been working throughout, producing swords, bows and crossbows. Amaris had no standing army, there had not been need for one in living memory, but the guards of the city were trained and there had been no shortage of volunteers signing up to defend the city. Production continued, but it seemed that by the end of the pass anybody who wanted a weapon would have one. Training in their use lagged behind, and there had already been a few injuries from those over enthusiastic with their new-found tools.

'We'll have several thousand at the wall,' Janaid said. 'We're organising into manageable groups now, each under a guard who has some discipline and training. We have scarce two hundred of them though. Plenty of volunteers, but this is no seasoned army we have here.'

'They will fight to defend their homes,' Coran said. 'Or they will perish.'

The five original catapults that had been positioned along the walls had been joined by fifteen more. The city carpenters had been hard at work building them and they were almost finished. More weapon designs had been found in the city archives; giant crossbow devices that had been tried and found to work well.

Fitch's mysterious instructions had also been followed. Two odd contraptions stood on either side of the harbour entrance. They looked like a pair of enormous funnels or siphons, aimed outwards towards the sea. Connected to them were a furnace and bellow, along with a large metal reservoir of some kind.

'The smiths followed the instructions as best they could,' Henoch noted. 'But they are quite bemused by the function. We had to raid the entire island to find enough metal for them. What do they do?'

'I'll set them up soon enough,' Fitch answered. 'Should give those priestesses a nasty shock.'

'What happens if they don't attack the city directly?' Mel asked. 'They might try to land elsewhere and invade across the land.'

Coran shook his head. 'One advantage to these islands having rocks and cliffs. There's nowhere else to land a fleet, and no army would be able to set anchor off shore and wade in under fire from the cliff-tops. No, Amaris is the only way into Amar. They'll know that soon enough.'

'The priestesses might attack the outlying settlements from the air though,' Mel argued.

Coran nodded. 'That's true enough. We'll have to evacuate them as best we can. We can't defend everything.'

Much of the discussion had focussed on the use of the flying machines. When the call went out across the city for volunteers to help fly them, Coran had been met by many of the younger men and women. They had all been surprised when it was left with Ren, with some help from Mel, to train them in how the machines worked. Some could not grasp the concepts, but before a couple of stretches had passed Ren had selected those with the best aptitude for the task and assigned them each to a vessel.

'He's chosen five,' Mel said, when Coran inquired. 'So we now have a flying corps.'

'Five? Coran asked. 'He needs six.'

'He's flying one of the small ones himself,' Mel answered.

'No he's not,' Coran snapped. 'Mel, he's just a kid ...'

'Other than Meru he's the best flyer we've got,' Mel replied. 'And you'll not keep him out. He's determined to do his bit.'

'This is a war, a battle. Folks are going to get killed.'

'And if everyone is dead, who's going to be left to care for the youngsters?' Mel countered. 'He's got just as much reason to fight as any of us.'

'I'm not going to win this one, am I?' Coran muttered.

Mel grinned and shook her head. 'No, you're not. I've already told him he can.'

'I don't like it.'

'You don't have to like it, just let him fly.'

'All right,' Coran grumbled. 'Does he know what we need to use the machines for?'

Mel nodded. 'He sure does. We've already organised it.'

Coran narrowed his eyes. 'Already?'

The refitting of the flying machines had already been put into place under Mel's supervision. All the flying machines apart from the medical transport had large sliding doors along their flanks designed to make loading and unloading more straightforward. A series of rope harnesses had been rigged up within.

'Aerial shooting platforms,' Mel said. 'Crammed full of archers.'

Coran grinned. 'We can take the fight to the priestesses in the air.'

'Better still,' Mel said. 'The machines can hover over the city. The priestesses need to keep moving. We may even have the advantage.'

'We'll still be outnumbered.'

'But it will give them pause,' Mel said. 'An aerial defence is not something they will have encountered before. With their ships under fire and their dachs occupied, their strategy may collapse. They'll be expecting a quick victory from the air and then an invasion. All we have to do is repel them. We're the ones with the island. They'll be all at sea.'

'I'll crack the jokes around here.'

Mel smiled.

Later that stretch, under Coran's instruction, Ren had flown the medical transport down into the city. It did not have the sliding loading bays like the other vessels, and its primary role was far too valuable. Ren landed it as close to the main infirmary as could be managed. The ground vehicles had also been pressed into use, ferrying supplies around the city.

'Our strategy then,' Coran said, as the senate assembled. 'A spirited defence of the island. We must not seek to push the attack, only to prevent the island being overrun. Based on the description of the attack on Viresia, the priestesses will attack from the air first. They carry thrown weapons which turn to fire on impact, thus every section of the wall and as many parts of the city as we can manage must be well provisioned with water, particularly around our own weapons.

'Our own aerial defences will counter the priestesses in the air. This should frustrate their attack and force them to resort to the boats. Save for the *Mobilis,* we have no fleet ourselves, so we must rely on the defensive weapons we have constructed. Thus it's vital to protect the catapults and the crossbows from the priestesses.

'Once the ships reach the walls it will become a pitched battle of numbers. Our best hope is to make them reconsider their attack as too costly to continue.'

'And what of their mental abilities,' Henoch asked. 'Will they not strike us down before we can bring our weapons to bear?'

'We do not know the extent of their powers,' Coran said. 'And we do not know how to defend against them. We can only count to courage and fortitude, of that Amar has plenty.'

'What of the girl,' Henoch demanded. 'And what of my son?'

Coran sighed. 'Whilst on the mainland we discovered another threat, a threat not just to Amar, but to all peoples, all Esurio. There is a device that protects us all from the flares. It is ancient, another product of our ancestors' technology that you see represented here in these remarkable flying machines. It is called the Obelisk. Due to age or infirmity it is failing. Zoella and Meru have taken a flying machine to see if it can be repaired.'

'But the girl had powers alike to the priestesses,' Henoch said. 'Surely we need her here? When will they be back?'

'I would have preferred that too,' Coran admitted. 'But this threat is real enough. They will return as soon as they are able. With luck they will be back before the priestesses arrive, but we must see to the defence of Amaris now. We need every advantage we can get. Anything that gives us an edge. That is our priority.'

* * *

The preparations continued for stretch after stretch. Provisions were stockpiled, water carriers improvised and placed wherever they could be sited. The training with weapons continued for those who could wield them.

Above, cankers had once again begun to grow on Lacaille. It seemed another flare was brewing.

'It would be a fine thing if we get hit by a flare when we're being attacked,' Mel said, peering up at the sky.

'Might go in our favour,' Coran mused. 'I wouldn't fancy being at sea in a wooden ship during a flare. At least we can seek refuge in the city.'

Mel nodded.

'I don't suppose they might treat with us?'

Coran looked out to sea.

'If they want to talk we'll meet with them,' he said. 'If there's a way to avert this, let's see if we can find it. But from what Zoella said, they believe Lacaille has sanctioned our extermination. Unless we can convince them that their goddess isn't real, I don't see much hope in that direction.'

Mel sighed.

'Do you think we can win?'

Coran ran a hand through his hair and then stroked his beard.

'We'll give it everything we have,' he said. 'We have the advantage of the flying machines, we have the only land in the midst of the ocean hereabouts.'

'The ancient people of Nireus had all these things,' Mel said. 'They still lost.'

'I don't know, Mel,' Coran snapped. 'There's no surety to be found here.' He took a deep breath. 'I'm sorry, not enough sleep these last few stretches.'

'My fault,' she said. 'Daft question.'

Coran leant forward on the city wall, still gazing out to sea.

'I'd say we have a chance,' he said. 'Whether it's a good one or not is hard to tell.' He thought for a moment. 'Caesar told me something before we left.'

'Caesar?'

'Yeah,' Coran answered. 'He didn't quite wish us luck, but he wanted us to prevail against the priestesses.'

'I always figured that machine was impartial, never taking sides. He didn't seem all that keen for us to have the flying machines.'

'I remember,' Coran said with a chuckle and mimicked Caesar's metallic sounding voice. 'Conflict between Esurio colonists is strictly prohibited by original statute and is not permissible.'

'But he did let us have them,' Mel said. 'After Zoella asked him to.'

'And he identified she had the authority to do that,' Coran said. 'I reckon he found a way around the restrictions for us. He couldn't do it himself, but he guided us to a way that it could be done.'

'So what did he … it … tell you?'

Coran turned to look at her.

'He said something about the original colonists of this planet and what they wanted. Peace, quiet and comfort was the general impression I got. Caesar said they'd left religion and the idea of people in power behind them.'

'Sounds idyllic.'

'Doesn't it just,' Coran said. 'But he also said that we, us Amarans, were the closest culture to what those original colonists were aiming for. Our survival was important to him. If ever a machine had sentiment … well, there was something there.'

'Pretty touching stuff from a machine,' Mel said.

'Almost brought a tear to my eye, I'll admit,' Coran said. 'Made me think though.'

'Yes?'

'Two thousands rounds and more have passed since our ancestors found this place. Sounds like they had far greater challenges to overcome than we do. Meru told me some bunk about them travelling from another world umpteen million marks away in order to get here. Don't know if that can be true, but … imagine that, sailing between worlds, what must that have been like?'

‘They did achieve some amazing things,’ Mel said. ‘Everything we’ve seen points to abilities so great we’d struggle to even measure them. We all saw that sky-ship.’

‘And yet, despite all that,’ Coran said. ‘Despite all they could do, all the heights they scaled, what they wanted was the simple life; no politics, no war, no religion. Just people living and minding their business. Like they were trying to start over again.’

‘Sounds good to me.’

Mel moved closer to him. Coran put his arm around her and she rested her head against him.

‘Maybe we have right on our side,’ Coran said. ‘Perhaps we’re fighting for what was meant to be, what should have been. Not much comfort I know …’

‘It might just be enough,’ Mel whispered.

CHAPTER FIFTEEN

Airea, Capital of Taloon

Round 2307, Fifth pass

Kiri had left Meru locked in the room until the end of the stretch. The chimes of the sleeping had rung out through the city by the time she returned. She was carrying a pack of clothes tied up with string.

'I have told Karquesh that you were indeed a spy,' she said as she locked the door behind her. 'It's close enough to the truth. Since he gave you to me as a gift he is happy that I … dispose of you as I choose. I told him I would take you back to Drayden as my prisoner.' She smiled at the look on his face. 'I could hardly tell him the truth now, could I? He's released you into my care, that's the important bit. We are free to do whatever we choose.'

She came across to him and gave him a kiss. The lust flared up between them once more, but she pulled back.

'Not that, not now,' she breathed. 'We must …'

Meru nodded. 'Zoella.'

'I know the way into the great halls below the city,' Kiri explained. 'But there are guards we need to work around. I doubt they would let me in unescorted by someone from Taloon. We must also be finished before the sleeping is over.'

'Why?'

Kiri looked at him. 'Because the priestesses are on their way. They will arrive, ready to board the ships, on the next stretch.'

Meru swallowed.

'Quick now,' she directed. 'I brought spare clothes for you, change.'

Meru grabbed the pack and pulled out the clothing. It was a dull and simple smock, but at least it was clean. His original grey travelling tunics were in the hands of the guards somewhere. He'd likely never see them again.

Kiri was still wearing her gown, waiting for him.

'Don't be shy,' she said, with a wink. 'You have few secrets left from me.'

Meru pulled on the clothes.

'You still look like a prisoner,' Kiri said, appraising his appearance with a grin. 'Suits you.'

'Thanks,' Meru answered.

Kiri walked to the door, unlocking it, opening it and peering into the corridor beyond. She beckoned to him.

'All clear,' Kiri said, and turned to look at him. 'If we are stopped, you act submissive. I may have to mistreat you ...'

'I understand,' Meru said. 'Let's do this.'

Kiri led the way downwards through the palace. Most people had retired to bed and the halls and rooms were empty. Guards stood at the entrance, but Kiri was well known now and her presence went unchallenged as they left the palace.

'Come, Amaran scum,' Kiri said, pushing Meru before her. 'I want to show you your doom. The ships in the harbour spell your demise. Move!'

She pushed him hard. Meru staggered and stumbled forward. He heard the guards chuckle.

'So far so good,' Kiri whispered.

'You're enjoying this,' Meru whispered back.

Kiri grinned. 'Yes, I am.' She raised her voice and pushed him hard again. 'Faster, prisoner!'

They walked for perhaps half a mark before Kiri gestured for them to come to a stop across from an impressive looking tower in the centre of the city.

'This is the entrance to the halls below,' she said. 'Now we must be cautious. Stay behind me, we will keep to the shadows away from Lacaille.'

Meru could see there was a pair of guards outside the building, standing on either side of the entrance.

'What about them?'

Kiri already had her hand outstretched towards them. Meru watched as one clutched at his forehead, staggering to one side. The other caught him before he fell and pulled him off to one side Meru could just hear their conversation.

'My head … pain.'

'I'll get you some water, been a hot stretch standing here …'

The second guard moved away, marching to an adjacent building.

'Now,' Kiri hissed.

They ran across the courtyard, approaching from the side, and got inside the entrance before the second guard emerged from the other building.

'What did you do to him?' Meru asked.

'Gave him a headache,' Kiri answered. 'He'll be fine in a spell. Follow me.'

She led him down a stone-cut passage way. It was narrow for some time, veering left and right, but always descending. After a hundred paces or so the passage widened into a large vaulted space packed high with vegetables and fruits, boxed and ready to be shipped out.

Kiri moved toward to the centre of the space.

'Here,' she said, gesturing to a large circular metal shape on the floor.

'It goes up and down,' Meru said. 'I've seen this before.'

Kiri grabbed the lever that was set in the centre.

'Here we go.'

She pulled it back and was rewarded with the circular platform descending through the rocky walls. She stood back as it lowered itself. After a few moments she and Meru caught sight of the vast open space of the subterranean hall beneath the city. Uncounted rows of plants stretched out before them.

'The technology of the ancients,' Meru whispered, in awe once more.

The lift came to a halt. Kiri pushed the lever back and they both jumped off before it rose back up.

Kiri looked around her.

'So, we're here,' she said, looking at Meru. 'Where is Zoella?'

'She'll be hidden somewhere out there,' Meru said, gesturing to the rows of plants. 'Not near this entrance anyway. Let's walk.'

Zoella, we're in the hall. Can you hear me? We're in the hall!

* * *

In the towers of Airea, watchers were pointing upwards at the golden disk of Lacaille. For the last few stretches they had been watching the ominous dark cankers grow once again on the surface of the great disk. Crackles of fire had been seen on the surface, precursors of the burning rivers of light that had erupted during the flares.

Only now, the blotches were slowing, breaking and receding. Even as they watched they grew less, sinking back into the surface of Lacaille, its face becoming smoother and more placid by the spell.

'It's a sign,' one of the watchers muttered, staring up into the bright sky.

'Perhaps these priestesses truly are sent by Lacaille,' another muttered. 'Lacaille is pleased with what transpires. Our King is wise indeed to ally with them.'

* * *

Zoella sat cross-legged in the maintenance room Ira and her companions regarded as their home. She focussed on her breathing, trying to calm her racing heart, but her thoughts were awhirl.

Facing her. Facing Kiri.

She could feel an instinctive urge to strike out at the girl the moment she saw her. The fury within her at the death of Ioric and Raga still burnt hot.

But was she really responsible?

Zoella knew that if they were able to converse mentally she'd be able to judge the truth of Kiri's words, whatever it was she had to say.

And if Meru is wrong and she attacks me on sight? I'll be ready for that.

She clenched her fists.

Ira was watching her. Zoella sent an image of Kiri to her. Images of a fight came back to her.

Only if she strikes first. For Meru's sake I will give her the benefit of the doubt. Stay close, but do not show yourself to her, she's dangerous ...

As she thought of Meru she sensed him, much stronger now, closer.

Meru?

Zoella, we're in the hall. Can you hear me? We're in the hall!

Yes, I can hear you. You're not far. I will find you, keep walking this way.

Zoella got to her feet, took a deep breath and then walked to the ladder that led up out of the maintenance area. Above her was a hatch, she pushed it aside and climbed out underneath one of the plant troughs. Ira came up behind her and together they closed and locked the hatch.

Wait here.

Ira nodded.

Zoella crawled out of the narrow space and then stood up alongside the trough. Ira's little lair was about halfway down the length of the hall and off to one side. She could see two figures moving up an adjacent row.

Her heart was hammering in her chest.

She stepped into the same walkway, facing them.

'That's far enough,' she said.

It was them. Meru was dressed in a dull smock. Kiri stood beside him, dressed in a cyan gown unlike the tight leather armour Zoella had last seen her in. Her hair looked unkempt, as if she'd just got out of bed. Her blue eyes were as fierce and bright as ever.

'Zoella!' Meru said. 'You're all right?'

'I'm fine,' Zoella replied, keeping her eyes on Kiri. Kiri's expression was unreadable, but she was staring back at Zoella with narrowed eyes, as if scrutinising every detail of her face. 'You?'

'All good,' Meru said. 'Zoella ...'

'What have you got to say for yourself?' Zoella said, her voice harsh and directed at Kiri. 'Say your piece and go.'

I know you …

'Out loud,' Zoella snapped, as Kiri's voice echoed in her head. 'Meru needs to hear both of us.'

Kiri looked at Meru, who nodded.

'I know you hate me …' Kiri began.

'You have no idea what I feel,' Zoella returned. 'I don't care about your feelings. I know what you are. I'm only here because he wants me to listen. Say what you're going to say!'

Kiri raised her head, her voice direct. 'The other priestesses are coming, they will be here on the next stretch. The people of Taloon have readied the fleet. They will set sail for Amar as soon as they can.'

'We already know that,' Zoella replied. 'So?'

Kiri paused, looking at Meru. He nodded.

She's looking to him for support! Why is she worried?

'I want to stop them.'

Zoella shook her head. 'Why? Why would you want to stop them? You're one of them.'

Kiri dropped her head for a moment

'I was, I am,' she replied, looking back up. 'But I've learnt something, something about where I came from, where … we both came from.'

Zoella waited.

'The man in Drem,' Kiri said. 'Guerrun, Guerrun Sandatch.'

'Who you killed,' Zoella said.

Kiri shook her head. 'We both killed him. It was our fight that killed him. We were both in his mind. We broke it.'

Zoella remembered the altercation once again. Kiri's plaintive cry,

Stop, you're hurting him!

Followed by Guerren's last thought,

Do not hate Kiri! Myana, she was Ioric's sister, she was …

'You heard his thoughts,' Zoella whispered. 'What did he say to you?'

Kiri took a step closer.

'Myana,' Kiri said, her voice low. 'Myana, she was Ioric's sister, she was …' Zoella saw her swallow. 'She was our mother.'

The words didn't register for a moment. Then the full impact hit her.

Zoella reeled back.

'No.'

'You're my sister.' Kiri whispered.

'No, that can't be!' Zoella screeched.

'Zoella, it's true,' Meru said. 'It explains everything, your powers, your strengths …'

Zoella turned and threw her arms forward. She sensed Kiri's presence before her and sought it out, wrestling it close.

Liar!

To her surprise, Kiri didn't resist. She opened her mind to Zoella's aggressive search.

Memories flashed about her, Kiri's memories of Guerren.

A battered carriage, racing up a pathway, rain cascading down in sheets. Arrows whistling out of the dark. A woman, facing off against a cohort of priestesses … struck down by an arrow. The woman fell.

Myana!

Children. Two baby children. Two girls. One with black hair and bright blue eyes, another with wavy brown hair … an old couple, a farmstead, a friendly old woman and a grumpy looking man.

Then these are the last?

Scallia's most gifted, so I hope. Myana's daughters could be little else …

Long ago … it was long ago … to keep you all from the priestesses, they are not what they seem. I hid you in different places deep in Scallia, hoping you'd not be found.

I meant to come back once it was safer, but then the King sanctioned the searches and exiled me …

I tried everything I could to protect you from them. Kiri and Zoella, daughters of princess Myana, daughter of Marek Tiamoi of Scallia …

The link broke. Both Kiri and Zoella lurched backwards in shock.

'It can't be,' Zoella said. 'That means …'

Her mind flashed forward. Ioric … Ioric had been her uncle! Torin too. Liana … her cousin!

The kinship I felt with Ioric, he was like a father to me … he was family! And this means we're, both of us, of the royal line of Scallia …

Zoella stared at Kiri.

It can't be a lie. She tells the truth in this at least. The memory is pure and untainted. And Liana … she's here somewhere …

'What did you do with Liana?' Zoella demanded.

'Liana?' Kiri answered. 'She has been given to the King of Taloon. Her mind … she has no thoughts.'

Zoella remembered. Liana had tried to overpower Kiri, something had gone wrong. Liana had lost her gift, and with Turgan's death, her mind.

She is our cousin …

'There's nothing we can do for her,' Kiri said. 'I tried to protect her, but …'

Zoella looked at her anew. Kiri the indefatigable warrior of Drayden; the vicious killer who had struck down those in her way, who had chased her through the frozen wastes of Drem, who had tortured Meru for the location of his home, Kiri who had … let them go when she could have handed them over to the priestesses.

Is that why? We must have been together as babes … what happened?

'What do you know of our mother?' Zoella demanded.

'I don't remember much about being a child at all,' Kiri said, her voice soft as she answered Zoella's thoughts. 'And nothing of her. Just vague dreams. Shapes, a plague. I grew up in the forests around the city of Daine, an urchin. I was nearly killed when I … these powers we have … I killed this boy, the priestesses found me, they trained me … I didn't know anything else. They taught me everything. But I'm from Scallia, same as you.'

'Zoella,' Meru said. 'It's true, what she's saying …'

'You've known this …' Zoella began. 'Since Nireus?'

Kiri nodded.

'And still you've sought to kill us,' Zoella said. 'Seeking out Amar and making plans to vanquish us?'

'I believed,' Kiri said, her voice low. 'I believed in the will of Lacaille, the religion of the priestesses. The books and traditions tell us that Amar must be destroyed for the good of all. It's all I've ever known. But … it's not true, Meru showed me it wasn't true.'

Zoella was shaking her head, she pointed at Kiri.

'No. This is all a ruse to gain my trust. I don't believe you. I won't believe you!'

'I am a priestess of the goddess Lacaille,' Kiri shouted. 'But there is no goddess! It was all false, all lies! These gifts we share …'

'It's our ancestors again,' Meru said. 'Zoella don't you see? Caesar called you an administrator, something about nano … something! These powers were created by our ancestors. They're being used by the priestesses for the wrong purposes …'

Zoella swallowed. A memory from Viresia surged through her mind; when she had been down within the dark catacombs beneath the city. An ancient book, the tome of the Voren Empire long ago.

This power, the nexion and hereafter known as 'the gift', is essential to the running of the Voren Empire … the gift will then be put to its proper use, the ordering of the affairs of the empire in times of peace and the co-ordination of response in the times that Lacaille darkens. Administrators …

'The priestesses can be stopped before they set out,' Kiri said. 'They are led by the high priestess, a woman called Nerina. She is powerful in the gift, more powerful than either of us, but together, we could stop her. I have other allies within the priestesshood. I can call upon them. We can stop this war before it even starts.'

'No,' Zoella countered. 'We should flee before they get here. Amar needs us. If you're speaking the truth, then join us. Leave them here and come with us.'

'You can't fight the military might of Taloon and Drayden,' Kiri said. 'You know how the battle will go, you've seen it, you were there … both of you. Do you want to see that happen to Amar? We must stop it here, before it starts.'

'Amar has other ways of defending itself,' Zoella countered. 'You want me to stand with you to face down this high priestess of yours? How do I know this isn't a trap? You'll turn on me ...'

'I know you don't trust me ...'

'You're right, I don't.' Zoella replied.

'You can trust her,' Meru said. 'She's changed.'

'You've seen my thoughts,' Kiri said. 'What else can I do?'

'Come with us to Amar,' Zoella said. 'Fight for us, work with us in the defence of our home. Earn that trust.'

'It won't work!' Kiri answered. 'There's no time. Nerina must be stopped here. If the priestesses and the army of Taloon reach Amar in force then it will all be over. Come with me. Stop her here.'

Zoella turned away,

'I will not come with you,' Zoella returned, shaking her head.

'Zoella ...' Meru pleaded.

You must be lying! I will find out what you really intend!

Zoella snapped her hand outwards, pushing at Kiri's mind.

Kiri was taken unawares, she screeched as Zoella tore into her memories.

Zoella saw the images of Nireus and Kiri's memories of childhood. She pushed past them, searching for more recent memories. Images of Taloon, the hall, the King, the armada in the harbour, priestesses astride dachs high in the sky ...

More images. Kiri standing in front of a mirror, admiring her reflection, thoughts awhirl. Zoella could hear what she had thought.

And I'm truly as much a Queen as Karquesh is a King. It's my birthright! Elena strove to be high priestess. Nerina likewise with Drayden. But me ... I could take it all. Drayden, Scallia, Taloon, Amar too! I could reunite the lands. Not just Queen ... I could be the most powerful ruler these lands have ever seen. Empress of Voren ... Empress Kiri!

Zoella felt Kiri struggle against her and the thoughts were shut down.

Both women flinched back as the mental link between them cracked and failed.

'She's lying!' Zoella yelled. 'She sees herself as Empress! Empress of everything! She wants to conquer all. She has no intention of helping us …'

'No,' Meru said. 'That's not true, she's …' He turned to look at Kiri. Her expression was impossible to read. 'Kiri?'

Kiri didn't answer. Zoella saw Meru's face crumple in dismay.

'You see?' Zoella crowed. 'She won't deny it … she can't deny it! She's lied to you, Meru. Lying like she always does! You don't want to help us, this is just about you …. What were you planning, Kiri?' Zoella spat out her name. 'Use me to weaken the high priestess so you can attack her and take her place?'

Kiri didn't answer. She looked at Meru, but no words came.

'Answer her,' Meru whispered. 'Kiri, please …'

Kiri straightened.

'You leave me no choice,' she said. 'It must be done. I will do this with you or without you!'

'Kiri, no!' Meru cried.

Kiri's face was set, she struck out at Zoella. Zoella felt the grip of Kiri's attack tighten around her mind, a sense of grasping and clawing.

She's trying to take my gift!

Zoella fought back, but Kiri's ferocious assault was fearsome, strong, pummelling at her with a fury borne of determination and ruthless expertise.

She's done this before!

Zoella felt her defences weaken. She screamed out in fear and frustration, sensing Kiri's gleeful exhilaration as her grasp closed in on the burning warmth within her.

We could have worked together, sister! Daughters of Scallia united once again. We are royalty … but you are weak and cowardly! The priestesses will fall, you'll see! But it will be by my hand alone!

Zoella screamed as Kiri's mind pressed on through her defences, she could almost feel herself being ripped away …

There was another presence.

Anger, determination, flaring rage!

The link broke. Zoella reeled backwards, struggling to see through a whirling dizzying swirl of pain and confusion. She blinked, trying to see what was happening.

It was Ira. She stood between them, her hands outstretched toward Kiri. Kiri had likewise been thrown back, her face set in pure astonishment.

'Who?'

Ira struck out with her hand. Kiri screamed, rolling back end over end, yelling in pain and clutching at her head. Ira's assault continued, her fingers twisted and curling as she directed her powers.

Kiri was trying to crawl away, trying to shield herself from the attack. Meru ran to her, jumping between them.

'Stop it, you're hurting her!'

Ira relented. Kiri collapsed, rolling on to her back, gasping and wheezing in pain.

Zoella stepped forward, her fists clenched, pushing her foot down on Kiri's throat. Meru tried to stop her but she glared at him to stay away. Kiri struggled.

'I should kill you now,' Zoella said, her lips curled in distaste. She raised her fists to strike.

Meru pushed her back. Kiri gasped for breath as the weight was lifted from her throat.

'I won't let you kill her,' Meru said. 'She's hurt, leave her alone!'

Ira was at Zoella's side now, hands poised as Kiri got to her knees, cradled by Meru. Kiri was panting hard. She staggered, leaning heavily on Meru. It seemed she couldn't get to her feet.

Zoella's eyes narrowed as she directed her words at Meru. 'Then it's a choice you have to make. Stay with her or come with us. We're leaving, we're going home. And she's not coming with us.'

Zoella watched as Meru's expression fell. He turned to look at Kiri. She was looking up at him, her eyes pleading.

'Please …' Kiri moaned.

She has her claws so deep in him …

'She lied, Meru,' Zoella whispered. 'Lied to you, lied to all of us … she doesn't care about anyone other than herself.'

'No …' Kiri's voice was a croak. 'Remember what we shared, I didn't lie. I do care … Meru you know this … don't … please! I need you …'

Zoella saw Meru swallow, saw him gasp as he looked from her to Kiri and back again. He clenched his eyes tight shut for a moment …

And then stood up and stepped away. Kiri collapsed back to her knees, looking up in despair.

'Let's go,' he gasped. Zoella breathed a sigh of relief.

'Meru,' Kiri screamed, her voice shrill. 'Meru! Don't leave me, please.'

Meru turned and started back towards her. Zoella grabbed him and wrestled him to a stop.

'We need you to get us out of here!' she yelled. 'You need to fly the machine. Home, your friends, Amar! Remember?'

'But …'

'Leave her,' Zoella said, grabbing his shirt in her fists and pulling him to her. 'She lied to you. We need you, not her. Make your choice Meru, save your friends and your people, or betray us and go with her!'

Meru looked at Zoella and then over at Kiri. Kiri was crawling towards them.

He shook his head, tears dripping down his cheeks.

'Kiri …'

Kiri screeched, reaching a trembling arm out to him. 'No, please … Meru!'

'You lied,' he whispered. 'After everything we shared … you lied … why?'

Kiri turned her gaze on Zoella, rage suffusing her features. 'He's mine, not yours! You've turned him against me!'

'You did that yourself,' Zoella returned.

Meru staggered away, Zoella pulling him after her.

'Run!' Zoella yelled. Ira whistled and ran with her.

Kiri's howl of woe echoed around them. It was feral, a cry of pure animal rage. It resonated in the vast hall over and over again. Zoella could hear her thumping her fists into the dirt in her temper.

'I will find you, sister, I will come for you.' Kiri's voice was a shrieking rasp, twisted by fury and wrath. 'Amar will still fall. There will be no mercy. I will take everything!'

Zoella heard her scream again and again, but she ran on, Meru sobbing and stumbling beside her. More than once he fell, but she hauled him up and forced him onwards. Ira's companions appeared beside them, also running.

Kiri's screams continued to ring out, before fading into a keening wail then falling into silence behind them.

* * *

'What happened?' Nerina demanded, glaring at King Karquesh.

'That's how she was found,' Karquesh replied. 'Unconscious, in the lower levels. She shouldn't have been down there at all. She did not have permission.'

'Priestesses will go where there is need to,' Nerina said. 'Kiri doubtless had some task.'

'She was with the prisoner from Amar,' Karquesh added. 'We had no use for him, so we'd released him into her care. There's no sign of him.'

Rihanna was standing nearby.

'Perhaps he overpowered her?' she asked.

'Kiri?' Nerina scoffed. 'Impossible.'

Kiri was lying in a bed within the palace of Airea. She'd been noted as absent when she did not appear for the meal at the evening chime. A search of the palace had revealed she was nowhere to be found. Palace guards noted she had been seen earlier, taking the prisoner out into the city. A search was conducted, but she wasn't found until the first chimes of the following stretch, deep in the hall beneath the city. By that time, the priestesses had arrived, their dachs swooping into the city courtyards.

Kiri had been found unconscious, lying in the dirt. Around her were footsteps, the marks of a scuffle. There was no obvious sign of injury, but Kiri had not regained consciousness.

'We have tended her as well we can,' Karquesh said. 'If there is anything else we can do …'

'I thank you, King Karquesh,' Nerina said, with a short bow. 'My apologies for my short words. Kiri is most precious to us, to see her like this …'

'Distressing,' Karquesh said, with a nod. 'What could have rendered her thus? She is a formidable warrior. I have seen that much myself.'

'We will endeavour to find out,' Nerina said. 'How go the preparations?'

'Everything is ready for your inspection, high priestess.'

'Excellent,' Nerina replied. 'Lacaille blesses us too, the darkness upon its face has receded. This is a sign of her favour. We will depart as soon as we are able.'

'We will ensure it is so.'

'Might we be left alone with our injured sister?'

Karquesh nodded. 'If you require anything, please do not hesitate to ask.'

Nerina smiled as Karquesh left. The guards followed him out and the door clicked closed. Nerina's smiled vanished.

'Prisoner from Amar?' she asked, looking at Rihanna. 'Kiri omitted that detail when I spoke to her.'

Rihanna shrugged. 'It must be the boy she talked of.'

'It seems likely,' Nerina said, looking at Kiri. 'She has the answers. We will wake her, but be cautious of what you say before her. Remember what we discussed.'

Rihanna nodded.

Nerina stretched out her hand and placed her palm on Kiri's forehead. The girl shuddered at her touch, moaning.

Nerina pushed further, extending her thoughts into Kiri's mind.

Kiri? Kiri! Come to us, what happened to you?

Kiri stirred under her touch. Images, disjointed and confusing flashed through Nerina's mind.

Dachs in the air, ships in the harbour. A bloody blade stabbing the prince through the heart ... King Karquesh and the Scallian Queen Liana ... The boy ... Kiri standing close by, her foot on his chest ... A woman, with long wavy brown hair, arms outstretched ... and then nothing.

'No, no, no!' Kiri sat bolt upright. Nerina backed away in surprise.

'Kiri?' she asked.

Kiri looked at her with wide shocked eyes, her stare penetrating. She looked around her, breathing heavily, taking in her surroundings for long seconds before she looked back.

'Nerina! Rihanna!'

'What happened to you?' Nerina demanded. 'You were found ...'

'Beneath the city ...' Kiri whispered, her gaze darting around. 'Yes ... He ... the boy, he tricked me ...'

'The prisoner? The boy you formed a link with?'

Kiri nodded.

'Slow down, tell us what happened.'

'He was spying on us,' Kiri said. 'Karquesh caught him, I interrogated him. He had come from Amar in a flying machine to find out about the fleet. I thought it would be good to understand these machines better, so I forced him to take me to it. But, there were others with him, waiting for me. Women from Scallia who had not been found by our searches ...'

'With the gift?' Nerina demanded, staring hard at her.

Kiri nodded.

'I was caught unawares,' Kiri answered. 'They overpowered me. But they didn't know how to tear me.'

'Then you were lucky, 'Nerina said. 'And foolish. You might have been killed, or worse ...'

Nerina stepped back, pondering what Kiri had said.

'So,' she said, 'Amar has allies. We must alter our approach. Time is now of the essence. Word of our preparations will reach them if they have these flying machines. We must press our attack. Rihanna, assemble the flight and have them ready to board the ships this stretch, we will sail as soon as the sailors deemed we can.'

'Rihanna?' Kiri echoed.

'Yes Kiri,' Nerina said. 'Rihanna. Your judgement has been poor in this ...'

'I secured the alliance here,' Kiri snapped. 'I found the location of Amar!'

'Indeed you did,' Nerina replied, her tone hard. 'But then you may have given away our plans. They know we are coming and roughly what strength we have because you have an infatuation with this boy. You told me you hated men, and now look at you. Rihanna commands the flight, you will aide her. Is that understood?'

Nerina watched as a variety of expressions crossed Kiri's face. Defiance, anger, guilt ... and then acceptance.

'I will do as you say,' Kiri said. 'High priestess.'

'Regain your strength,' Nerina said. 'I will see to Karquesh. I expect to see you ready at the beginning of the next stretch. Time is of the essence.'

Nerina walked to the doorway before turning.

'Do not let me down again, Kiri.'

Then she was gone.

Rihanna walked around Kiri's bed.

'You're playing a dangerous game,' she said.

Kiri narrowed her eyes. 'It's my game to play,' she answered.

Rihanna chuckled.

'Was any of what you said true?'

'Truth is what it needs to be,' Kiri answered, her gaze going distant again. Rihanna watched her for a moment. Now that Nerina was gone, there was a strange sense of angst and sadness about Kiri.

'Did you find him?' Rihanna said, lowering her voice.

Kiri nodded.

'And?' Rihanna prompted, with a wry smile. 'Did you ...?'

Kiri looked across at Rihanna. A faint smile touched her lips, before she looked away.

'Kiri, coy?' Rihanna said. 'Such a thing has never been seen before. This boy has truly wormed his way into your affections then.'

'He is mine,' Kiri said and then her expression changed to one of sadness. 'He was mine ...'

'He escaped?'

Kiri nodded, her gaze going distant.

'I let him ...'

'Careless of you,' Rihanna said, with a laugh. 'I would have kept him under lock, key and perhaps a rope too had he given me a smile such as I saw on you.'

Kiri snorted. 'You never change.'

'Men are much like garments,' Rihanna said. 'They are to be used and then discarded once a change is desired.'

Kiri changed the subject.

'Did you ...?' she began. 'Your mother, Merrin?'

Rihanna sat down on the end of Kiri's bed.

'My mother is as she ever was,' Rihanna replied. 'She does Nerina's bidding. I found little amiss, but I listened closely. Certainly there was no love lost between your old mentor, Charis, and her, yet ...'

'Yes?' Kiri asked, her eyes narrowing.

Rihanna looked down. 'My mother did tell me one thing.'

'Which was?'

'You must not repeat this, Kiri. Both our lives ...'

'Tell me!'

Rihanna took a deep breath. 'She said something in passing.'

Kiri was sitting bolt upright now.

Rihanna swallowed. 'She said Nerina wanted a war with the Scallians, to train the priestesses for future conquests. She sent Charis to Varda knowing ...'

Kiri gasped. 'Knowing they had already taken up arms against us, that they would burn the treaty,' she said. 'There was no peace to be had, Charis and I walked into a trap!'

'Somehow she had already incensed the Scallians,' Rihanna whispered.

Kiri's eyes were cold now. 'I know how. It was Nerina that received the Scallian tithe that time. She insulted Prince Torin, she would not negotiate with Ioric. She wanted a war. And those who counselled peace … she had them killed, just not by her own hand. Charis … she had Charis killed.'

There was a long moment of silence between the pair.

'What are you going to do?' Rihanna asked.

'Other than avenge Charis?' Kiri said, her voice cold.

'Kiri, you can't fight Nerina. None of us can.'

'And what if many of us do?' Kiri said, looking at her hard. 'You and I?'

'Kiri … it's high treason!'

'She's been tearing women and girls from all the lands in secret,' Kiri said. 'She showed me how to do it. It's all in the sixth element. Rihanna … if she takes Amar she'll be even more powerful … she'll be able to …'

Kiri gasped, a sudden realisation coming to her.

'That's why …' she said.

'What?'

'That's why she hasn't torn us yet,' Kiri said. 'She's fattening us up, making our gifts stronger, but not so strong she can't overwhelm us. Rihanna, she's going to tear us the moment she's taken the women of Amar. We've got to stop her!'

'We cannot talk like this …'

'You'll see,' Kiri said. 'All this angst that they have tried to push between us, make us fight each other. It's a threat to her, don't you see? Together we are too strong; apart she can take us one by one. With our gifts Nerina would be unstoppable. She would take everything; Amar, Scallia, Drayden … all Esurio!'

'And you would stop her, would you?' Rihanna asked. 'Be high priestess yourself? So is it a choice between you and Nerina?'

Kiri stopped.

'Someone has to be,' she whispered.

Rihanna smiled. 'I know you want it. Maybe it's what you were born for, coming up from the slums like you did … rising from the bottom, who's to say you can't go all the way?'

'Would you?'

'My mother wanted me to be high priestess,' Rihanna said. 'And I was Nerina's favourite until you came along. Truth be told, I care little for the idea. But I prefer to be mistress of my own destiny whatever happens.'

'Then …'

'I do not want to be torn to favour someone else's rise,' Rihanna said. 'I don't doubt what you say. I'll support you when you make your move.'

Kiri leant forward and grabbed her hand. She felt a bright sense of admiration and excitement from Rihanna.

'But you must choose your moment with care,' Rihanna said. 'Nerina is no fool. She suspects you of much already, she watches you like a dach.'

'Loyal we shall appear,' Kiri said. 'We will follow our orders, attack Amar, be dutiful.'

'Until the time comes.

Kiri nodded. 'Until then.'

* * *

It took them a couple of spells to reach the far end of the assembly hall. Zoella had looked, but there was no sign of the wheeled vehicle or any of the panels with which to summon it in this area. They had been forced to walk all the way.

Ira had summoned her children to her. Including her there were fourteen of them.

'Can we get them all aboard the flying machine?' Zoella asked.

Meru was staring away into the distance, he'd not said a word since leaving Kiri behind.

'Meru!'

He jolted and looked around at her. 'What?'

'Can we get them all aboard the flying machine? There's sixteen of us.'

Meru looked around. 'I don't know.'

Zoella rolled her eyes and grabbed his hand, pulling him around.

'Focus!' she snapped. 'I don't care what happened with you and her, I need you here now. Understand? We've got to get out of here and we need you.'

Meru swallowed and nodded.

'With us?' Zoella demanded.

'Yes, sorry …'

They reached the connecting tunnel that led to the next hall. All seemed quiet. Ira was running ahead now, but she turned away from the entrance.

'Ira, where are you going? It's this way …' Zoella called after her. 'We can't afford to waste time …'

Ira had run alongside the tunnel, tracing the edge of the hall. The roof was higher here, leading into an alcove. Ira gestured, waving her hand for them to join her.

They moved across to Ira, who was pointing up. Zoella frowned and heard Meru gasp beside her.

Up on the wall was a map. Zoella remembered it. It was one of the images Ira had shown her when they'd been struggling to communicate, as Zoella recovered in the hidden maintenance room.

Meru walked up to it. It was filthy, covered in untold rounds of grime, but when he rubbed at the surface the dirt came away.

'Wow …'

The map was incredibly detailed, with a wealth of information that didn't immediately make sense. It wasn't printed on paper, but some hardwearing material that felt like the smooth surface of a glazed pot.

The outline of the continents was clear, they could make out Drem at the top, Scallia in the middle, Drayden off to the left and Taloon lower down to the right. There was also the island of Amar to the right hand side, surrounded by the Straithian Sea. Most of the names were marked, with the exception of Amar.

'It's so detailed,' Zoella said in wonder.

'And look here,' Meru said. He had rubbed away the dirt on the lower portion of the map. Below Taloon was another continent, marked as 'Kerun' and below that a further one called 'Nadir'. There was a small piece of writing in the very centre of that section. All the letters were in the strange austere block shapes that their ancestors seemed to prefer.

Substellar Pole Facility.
Atmospheric Processors and Magnetic Field Booster.
Obelisk Inc.

'Obelisk,' Zoella whispered. 'That must be where it is, but the rest of that ...'

'Sounds like something Caesar would say,' Meru said, his interest growing. 'He talked about magnetics and atmospheres and things. If only we could take this map with us, it would help us get there.'

'Ira has memorised it,' Zoella said. 'I think she might be able to draw it for us.'

Ira nodded. Meru traced his fingers across it, seeing contours and all manner of symbols marked.

'The maps in the machines are better,' he said. 'But this shows everything ...'

'We still need to go,' Zoella said. 'Come on.'

They found their way back to the tunnel, the children in tow. It was dark within, but it didn't take them long to emerge from the other side. The next hall was dead and dusty, with no living plants within the troughs.

'Long walk,' Meru said, looking around for one of the panels. There was one adjacent to the entrance, but prodding at it failed to give a response.

'Let's keep moving.'

It was a long slog through the hall, with nothing but the endless rows of troughs with long dead, dried plants within. A chime or more had passed before they reached the other side. Everyone was tired and footsore. The thought of the same distance again was weighing heavily on them.

'There must be a working panel here somewhere,' Zoella said. She thought an image of the panel to Ira and the group split up to look for one. It wasn't long before one of the children located one. Better still, after it had been wiped clean, it came to life.

'I'll ask for a transport,' Meru said, jabbing at it.

They waited, gasping in the dry air. They were parched, but there was no water to be found. Everything was bone dry and dusty.

'There's some in the flying machine,' Zoella replied to Ira's thought. 'We'll have to wait until we get there.'

With a rumble, one of the vehicles approached. Meru had been able to summon a larger one with an additional trailer being towed behind it.

'Well done,' Zoella said, relieved. 'That should make things easier!'

Ira directed the children to climb into the trailer, whilst she, Zoella and Meru climbed into the seats at the front. Meru began to program the destination.

Ira grabbed her shoulder. Zoella turned around. The children were banging on the sides of the trailer in alarm.

'What? What is it?'

Ira sent images to her. Zoella gasped.

Men and women, running! Bows, sticks, swords!

* * *

It was only when Rihanna had left that Kiri was able to let her guard down. The emotions were already close to overwhelming, but once she was no longer required to keep up the pretence …

Sobs wracked her, hot tears scalded down her cheeks. She muffled the noise in the blankets, rocking back and forth. The rage and the grief crashed about her.

He left me!

Her hands were so clenched that her fingernails cut into her palm, drawing blood.

And I know why he had to make that choice.

She didn't want to admit it, but it burned around in the back of her mind, swirling and angry. Meru's face swam in her mind. Fresh tears dripped down her face.

I didn't tell him the truth. Why didn't I tell him everything? I lied! I pushed him away. It's my fault!

Her mind buzzed back and forth, regret boiling into anger, twisting through rage and then back to regret at her choices once more.

We're supposed to be together, I know it. It has to be!

She clenched her jaw, biting her teeth together with a snap. Her determination came back to her, the ruthless side of her that had been honed by long rounds of fighting every stretch for life.

I do want to be Empress, Zoella saw it. She was right. I should have told Meru!

Regret was still burning within her, but a renewed flame of determination and desire was growing too.

It's my right, my destiny. With everything that he told me, this world needs someone to put it to rights. I need not care about Lacaille or the Element, nothing matters other than what we make matter! Nerina will fall. It should be me, I'm ready for this! And with him at my side …

The dream was a pleasant one.

And it will be, I will make it happen! I will get him back, I will get everything! Scorch Zoella, scorch Nerina, scorch Amar and Scallia and Taloon, Drem and Drayden. I will take what I can from the women of Amar, I will have Zoella's gift and I will depose Nerina. I will have Meru by my side. I will have what is rightfully mine whatsoever the cost!

* * *

'Meru, priestesses!' Zoella called. 'They're coming with the guards here – they must be looking for us.'

'I'm almost done,' Meru said, pushing at the controls before him.

The children were pointing now. Zoella leant out of the side of the vehicle to see better.

There were people, running towards them.

'They're here!' she shouted. 'Meru, we've got to go now!'

As she spoke an arrow pinged off the flanks of the vehicle. Meru pressed the last few controls and the vehicle jolted forward and began to move towards the nearby tunnel.

'Can't we go any faster?' Zoella asked, shouting above the drone of the vehicle's engine.

'I don't think so,' Meru said. 'There's no speed control.'

More arrows bounced around them with a sharp twanging sound.

Zoella motioned for the children to crouch down in the trailer. The vehicle turned into the tunnel and the door closed behind them.

'Made it …'

Their reprieve was short lived. Even as they were driving away from it the tunnel door opened again and they could see people silhouetted in the doorway.

'Stay down!' Zoella cried as more arrows flashed past them.

Moments later they arrived at the end of the tunnel and the doorways ahead of them opened into the final hall. They could hear yells behind them, and more arrows flew.

The vehicle was still crawling forward.

'They're going to catch us,' Zoella said, 'It's not fast enough!'

Meru continued to jab at the controls and then found something.

'Override!' he yelled. 'I think that means …'

The vehicle lurched to a halt. Meru grabbed the controls and pulled on them. The vehicle began to reverse.

'Not that way!' Zoella shouted. 'Forwards!'

Meru pushed the controls in the opposite direction as far as they would go. The wheels churned in the dirt and the vehicle shot forward, jolting and banging over the terrain.

It was fast enough now. A couple of arrows flew past and then they stopped. After a few moments Zoella pulled on Meru's arm.

'We've lost them …'

'They might be able to use these machines too, we need to keep moving.'

Meru slackened the speed a little, but he continued to look over his shoulder at intervals. There was no sign of pursuit.

'That was a little close,' Zoella breathed and then looked back at Ira, signing a question to her. Ira responded with a smile and a nod. Everyone was safe.

'Let's just hope they haven't found the flying machine,' Meru said.

His fears were unfounded. Everything was quiet at the far end of the hall. The flying machine was where they had left it, untouched. Both Meru and Zoella sighed with relief.

'Let's get aboard,' Zoella said. 'They will still be looking for us.'

Meru nodded and unlocked the doors.

'Going to be cramped inside with all these passengers,' he said. 'Will slow us down too.'

'We can dump some of the food,' Zoella said. 'We're going back to Amar, we don't need it.'

Both of them began unloading the machine, tossing the packaged supplies on the floor. The others joined in.

'Quick as we can!' Zoella called, herding them aboard.

Meru was right, it was cramped. Some of the children were crouched on the floor behind the main seats and all the remaining room inside was used by the others.

'Just manage it,' Zoella said. 'Let's get out of here.'

Meru jumped down and pressed the lift control buttons. The platform began rising, taking him and the flying machine with it. He ran back and jumped in, closing the door behind him.

'Sandra, start launch procedure.'

'Acknowledged, Meru.'

The platform continued to rise, overhead another platform slid out of the way, revealing clear blue sky. It jolted into place, the sand dunes rising above them.

'Launch ready.'

Meru pulled on the controls and the flying machine ponderously lifted off the ground.

'She's heavy,' Meru said, wrestling with the controls.

'Maximum recommended carrying capacity has been exceeded,' Sandra said.

The flying machine continued to rise, the dunes dropping down below them, allowing them a clear view of the horizon once more.

Zoella's expression dropped in dismay.

'Oh no.'

Meru was busy with controlling the machine, but he risked a glance out of the forward cockpit windows.

Above the distant city, flying shapes could be seen banking in the air and circling around.

The dachs of the priestesses.

Below them, the Taloon Armada was arrayed. Ships were set with full sail, already beginning to move up the coastline, heading shadeward in the stiff breeze.

'It's starting,' Zoella whispered. 'The invasion of Amar is starting!'

CHAPTER SIXTEEN

Amaris, Capital of Amar

Round 2307, Sixth pass

On the island of Amar, preparations were still underway. Provisions and stockpiles of water and other supplies were coming into the city of Amaris from the outlying districts. Scouts had been posted around the high-cliffed edges of the island with instructions to report any sightings of ships or flying creatures. The scouts were supported by runners and riders, the fastest available, aiming to send messages of any sightings.

Janaid, Henoch and the other senators had devolved the strategy and tactics of the battle to Coran and Fitch and they had been working non-stop for stretches in their preparation. Mel and Ren continued to work on the flying machines and the archers as often as they could. The initial results were not promising, but everyone gained confidence with practice.

The threat of the incoming invasion had galvanised the entire population into action. Scores of messengers had been sent across the island with news, educating the people with the long repressed knowledge of the past.

The history stored in the vaults of the senate was piecemeal, but it corroborated Coran's message. The records confirmed that the people of Amar had indeed come from the mainland, ejected from their home by an overwhelming hostile force. There had been an initial attempt to refer to their adversaries as the priestesses of Drayden, but the term 'witch' was taken up. It was simpler and far more pejorative, falling easily to the tongue and conjuring up images of ruthless evil, hell bent on their destruction. It was also how the records described them.

Many were scornful of the tales as they were told across the island, but Coran got Ren and his team to organise a fly past of the ancient flying machines and the few remaining dissenters were silenced when they encountered the awesome spectacle of their ancestors' remarkable accomplishments.

Mel had also been working on the *Mobilis*. Amar had no military vessels at all, just a fleet of fishing boats that were neither fast nor armed. As the *Mobilis* was the only vessel capable of mounting an assault, she had been working with Fitch on how to make it more potent. Fitch had issued instructions to the blacksmiths to copy some of the contraptions he had put upon the ship. The end result was that the *Mobilis* now had three sets of the rocket launchers rather than one. Two were positioned on the forward hull, with the other aft. A long metal beam had been attached to the bow, ready to act as a ram.

Mel had come up with a plan.

'No, absolutely not,' Coran said, once she explained it.

'We have to take the fight to them, you need this,' Mel protested.

'One ship against an armada?' Coran replied. 'That's insane.'

'I'm not planning on a suicide mission,' Mel answered. 'Just to slow them down and make them think twice.'

'Taking the *Mobilis* into battle?' Coran protested. 'She's no warship. She's supposed to be a small freighter, that's all.'

'She fought off those pirates,' Mel said. 'Remember that?'

'That was my idea,' Coran said. 'And you didn't like it as I recall. This is different, a pitched battle …'

'She's by far the most able vessel on all the seas,' Mel said. 'You know it, I know it. Maybe there have been better ships, our ancestors must have had warships, but right here and right now, she's the best there is. She'll do you … she'll do us all proud. You'll see. She's a good ship.'

'But you're talking about one ship against …'

'I'll assail the lead vessels with Fitch's rockets,' Mel said. 'Yes, we'll be first in the firing line, but we won't engage with them at close range, just see if we can set some of them ablaze. We'll retreat if they get too close and we won't get into bow range.'

'What about the dachs?' Coran protested. 'Remember how Meru described them, they'll drop fire on you. You'll be the only target! We won't be able to help.'

'I'll keep her close to full throttle at all times and keep coming about – we'll outrun any flames,' Mel said. 'The *Mobilis* is fast, hard to hit, even for a witch on a dach.'

'But if fire hits the ship ...'

'Daf and Creg have been practising drills for extinguishing fires,' Mel said. 'I've more than enough volunteers from the fishing fleet. Fitch has taught them how to use the rifles too, so that should discourage those witches if they take a fancy to us. If any do get too close, we'll shoot them down. Coran, it will make them think twice, throw their fleet into disarray, give you more time ...'

'Has Fitch agreed to this?'

'Yes,' Mel answered. 'He's keen to give the witches a bloody nose after all this.'

'And the witches' powers?' Coran said, saving his best argument to last. 'What about them?'

Mel shrugged. 'You know as well as I do we don't have an answer for that. But the more targets we give them, the more spread out they are. I'm guessing they won't be able to deal with everything.'

'That's a big guess.'

'No risk, no reward.' Mel smiled at him.

'You've thought of everything,' Coran said, sighing.

'Yes, I have.'

'Wish you hadn't,' he said. 'Then I could find a way to stop you.'

Mel smiled. 'We need every advantage we can get remember? Your words, not mine.'

'Yeah, you chose a great time to start listening to me!' Coran said. 'All right. She's your ship. Always has been really. But you're the captain now.'

Mel shook her head. 'I'll be the captain for the duration of this fight, but I'm giving her back to you afterwards.'

'I'll hold you to that,' he said. 'Not even a dent, agreed?'

'Not even a dent.'

* * *

Coran had walked up out of the city to see how the aerial defence preparations were going. Ren had organised the flying machines in a fallow field a couple of marks away in a natural sloping valley behind the cliffs.

Men, women and children were swarming around the various flying machines. Ren saw him coming and waved.

'How are you doing?' Coran asked.

'Good, good,' Ren said. 'Folk, bows, arrows.'

'And flying?' Coran asked.

Ren showed him. The big equipment transport was open on both sides and now strung with ropes to allow the people within to brace themselves and shoot their weapons.

'Twenty,' Ren said. 'Ship slow, no turn quick. Hover. Protect.'

Coran nodded. 'Makes sense. These others?'

There were two of the smaller personnel transports, also open both sides and strung with ropes in a similar fashion.

'Can move,' Ren said, with a shrug. 'Still slow, attack above.'

'But what about the dachs?'

Ren pointed at the two smallest flying machines. Caesar had called them personnel shuttles, they were of the same configuration that Meru had first flown, sisters of the one he and Zoella had taken.

'Very quick,' Ren said, with a grin. 'Archers back. Shoot dachs. Want to see?'

Coran thought about it. 'Yeah, I want to see.'

Ren scampered off and jumped into the nearest flying machine. Coran climbed in beside him. In the rear of the vessel the side doors had been opened. Two more youngsters, teenagers a little older than Ren, waved from that section.

Kids flying war machines. How did it come to this?

'Fun!' Ren said, flipping switches and adjusting the controls with an easy familiarity.

'This isn't a game, Ren,' Coran admonished. 'Those witches are coming to kill us.'

'Kill first,' Ren answered. He gestured to the pair in the rear of the machine. 'Ready?'

Both gave him a thumbs up sign.

'Scarecrow?' Ren said, pointing through the glass windows at the front of the machine.

'Aye,' Coran said, squinting. There were a number of them set up in the next field.

'Watch.'

Ren pulled on the controls. The machine's strange engines barked and whined, rising in volume. A moment later they were airborne, with the nose of the ship tilted downwards, about to crash into the stubble below. Coran yelled and braced himself as the ship tilted around him.

The ship didn't crash, but seemed to be gaining height. It levelled out and Coran could see they were already hundreds of hands above the ground.

'Shades!' he muttered, staring out of the windows at the unfamiliar sight of Amar from the air. As they rose he could see almost the entire island, though the far sunright end was lost in the mist.

They climbed even higher. Coran could see the city of Amaris come into view as they rose above the hills that guarded it and then far out to the sea, sparkling under the light of Lacaille.

He was holding his breath, gasping at the spectacle.

Ren was shouting something.

'Attack!'

The flying machine lurched, tilting over to one side. Coran yelled as the horizon spun about him, the flying machine now in a precipitous dive, its engines growling louder and louder with a scream of increasing pitch. Coran could see the other flying machines below, people looking up and them and pointing …

We're going to crash!

'Ren what in snuttin' shades are you …!'

The machine levelled out just in time, crushing Coran into his seat as it did so. Through the windows bushes and trees snapped past, only hands below the hull. Coran yelled again as Ren dodged one large tree, the flying machine canting to one side.

Then Ren swung the ship into another stomach twisting lurch. Coran clenched his eyes shut as the world outside became a blur of green, yellow and blue.

'Shoot!'

Coran heard the sound of taut bow strings being released, but he was only just able to keep the contents of his stomach in check. He opened his eyes as the gyrations eased. The flying machine was settling back down on the ground, the engine whine fading away.

'See?' Ren asked as the machine settled with a final jolt.

It was too much. His stomach heaved. Coran wrestled with the door, pushed it open and staggered out, collapsing to his knees and throwing up on the grass outside.

He spat the foul taste out of his mouth and staggered up against the side of the flying machine, turning to see Ren and his two companions looking at him.

'Better?' Ren asked. 'Look, see!'

Ren was pointing to his left. Coran wiped his mouth with the back of his hand and looked to where the boy was pointing. It was one of the scarecrows.

Four arrows were embedded in it.

'Good, yes?'

Coran blinked. 'You did that from the air?' he managed to ask.

All three were nodding.

I didn't even see the scarecrow …

Coran declined Ren's offer of a lift back to the city, deciding that a walk would give his churning stomach a chance to settle. He still wasn't right when he got back.

'What happened to you?' Mel demanded, looking at him. 'You look terrible. Actually … you look … green.'

'Ren happened to me,' Coran replied.

'You went in the flying machine when he was flinging it around the sky?' Mel asked, with a laugh. 'More fool you! I watched from the ground, that was bad enough.'

'I don't know what the witches are going to make of him and his flying machines,' Coran muttered. 'But he certainly scared the life out of me.'

'And most of your lunch too,' Mel said, still trying to stifle her laughter.

* * *

Fitch had also been busy. He'd been supervising the two contraptions that he'd arranged to have installed guarding each side of the harbour gate. With the help of some volunteers, large barrels had been carried up to the devices. From the sloshing sounds within it was clear that they contained some kind of liquid.

Once there, Fitch had supervised the barrels being emptied into the huge tanks that formed the aft part of the strange devices. Fitch had been very careful to ensure that no one bearing a flame or water was nearby as the liquid was poured.

It was some strange, thin yellow liquid with sparkles of metal within it. Fitch was careful to wipe away any traces of spillage as each barrel was emptied. Then he secured the tanks and locked them with a screw mechanism before checking the operation of the other end of the contraption. Those watching him could see that the siphon and its nozzle could be steered to points out to sea in any direction.

Fitch swung the device back and forth, making adjustments to the mechanism until he was satisfied it was working as he desired. Then he proceeded to walk around the harbour and repeat the entire process with the second contraption. Fitch had selected one of the blacksmiths who had made most of the componentry to man the second device.

Fitch ran through the instructions in a low voice, so as not to be overheard by the crowd of people who were watching from a discreet distance.

'You understand what you're doing now?' Fitch asked.

The man nodded.

'Not sure on the exact range,' Fitch said. 'We'll see how much pressure they can hold. Best to be cautious to start with, before we build the pressure.'

'What does it do?' one youngster asked, pushing forward, bolder than the rest.

'Never you mind,' Fitch said, glowering at him. 'Stay back. Not safe for the likes of you.'

'But it looks so cool!'

Fitch snorted.

'Nothing cool about this,' he muttered to himself. 'Nothing at all.'

* * *

Along the walls of the city the work was no less fervent. The stonework was strong, but it had been designed to protect the harbour and resist the battering of the sea and the wind, not an invasion by armed forces or an aerial assault. The few original catapults along the walls had been supplemented by new ones, but sturdy enough trees had to be cut down far inland and transported to Amaris. Once more, Ren's flying machines expedited the efforts and the surface vehicles proved ideal for dragging the logs into place. Every available carpenter was employed working all the hours they could to build new weapons both big and small.

Metal was in short supply. There were nowhere near enough swords available to arm even a tenth of the population of the city. Every available piece of scrap metal, valuable or heirloom was seized and given to the only pair of forges in the city. They were working all stretch to produce weapons as fast as they could, but they could only produce so many. Most folks would be provided with wooden weapons where that was possible, others brought in their farming implements, consisting of axes, cleavers, hatchets, spades and sickles.

The fishermen had been out at sea, working throughout. Their catches were salted down when they returned before the ships were sent back out again. Anything and everything was being burnt to keep the 'smokes' alight, enabling the fishermen to sail out of sight of land to bring in the biggest hauls. There hadn't been time to teach them the finer arts of navigation with Meru's new method, nor an easy way to duplicate enough maps.

The weather was growing colder once again, the spots upon the surface of Lacaille growing larger. Their rate of change seemed hard to predict, but all could sense another flare was coming.

* * *

Far out to sea, many of the fishing vessels were still plying their trade as they had done for untold rounds. Four vessels were fishing in the seas to the sunward and shaderight, equidistant from the island of Amar and the remote barrenness of the Scattered Isles.

The four ships could just retain visual contact with each other, spread out as they were across the ocean. The first mate of one of the ships was peering across the flickering surface, squinting at the other ships.

'Something up?' the Captain asked.

'Not sure,' the first mate said. 'That ship furthest out, looks like they've pulled up their nets and are making ready to sail.'

'Can't have filled their nets yet,' the Captain replied. 'Only dropped them a chime ago.'

'Don't make much sense, but yeah … look. Full sails! They've come about, looks like they're in a mighty hurry.'

The Captain looked for himself and nodded.

'Reckon you're right, but why?'

'Must have a reason.'

'Don't like this,' the Captain muttered. 'Ship our nets, let's head for home too.'

'Aye sir.'

The first mate barked orders and the men aboard began hauling in the big nets hand over hand. It was heavy work. By the time the nets were in and the sails were being hoisted the other boat was closing in on them.

'Skipper?' the first mate called.

'Aye?'

'Look!'

There was something in the sky, moving against the distant clouds, but drawing upwards. Small dark shapes, four or five of them, it was difficult to tell.

'What in shades are they?' the Captain asked.

'Reckon it's the witches,' the first mate said. 'Flying beasts, remember?'

'Aye,' the Captain said with a nod. 'Full sail men, get us underway right now!'

The sails flapped and then billowed out full in the wind as the men set the rigging. The wind was blowing towards Amar at a stiff clip, which allowed them to run before it. They could see the other ship keeping pace on their port side. The remaining two were still to starboard, sails down. The captain could see the men hauling in the nets in readiness.

'Scorched!' the first mate cried, pointing upwards.

The two ships were falling behind now. In the sky, the dark dots were taking form, winged beasts flying high in the sky. The captain could see the wings flap every few moments.

Fast, faster than we are ...

At some signal the creatures began to dive out of the sky, following each other in a descending pattern. They were heading towards the nearest vessel. Horrified, the crew watched as the great beasts closed on the beleaguered ship.

They turned aside at the last moment, climbing back up into the sky.

As they did so, flames erupted around the ship. More of the beasts followed the first, more fire blazed. Flames erupted within the ship, and the sails, rigging and masts caught within moments. The captain and first mate watched in horror as men jumped, their own bodies aflame, into the sea.

'Witches! With magic fire!'

There was nothing they could do but watch as the witches and their beasts bore down on the second ship. It was likewise hit by the mysterious weapons and burst into flame, its crew lost to the sea like the first.

The two remaining ships were fleeing under full sail, their hulls leaping over the undulating sea. The masts were creaking with the strain, the sails pulling the rigging taught. The ship was heeling over as they tried to maintain their course. The captain yelled at the men to clamber to one side to offset the tilt of the vessel.

Their companion ship was a hundred hands away, struggling with the wind and the waves in the same manner.

Above, the beasts were lining up once more.

'Get ready to turn hard starboard,' the captain said. 'On my mark!'

The first mate signalled for two men to join him and they grabbed hold of the tiller. The captain kept his gaze fixed on the skies as the aerial attack closed.

He could see them now, huge reptilian beasts with mouths full of sharp teeth. On their backs they bore the priestesses, dressed in dark leather. They were holding something up in their right hands. The Captain squinted, trying to make out what it was. As he watched the lead rider threw the object towards them, the following riders doing the same thing in sequence. They were round, spiralling through the air and falling straight towards the ship. The riders' aim had been good.

'Now! A-starboard!'

The first mate and his men pushed the tiller hard to the left side of the boat. The ship groaned and heeled further over.

The sea nearby erupted in flames. Some sort of oil had burst upon the water. It was behind them in moments as spray splashed up from the bow.

'Back a-port!'

The ship lurched in the opposite direction, its sails flapping for a moment before drawing true. The masts creaked with the strain. Another burst of flame from the other side of the ship, the heat intense.

Shadows passed overhead as the great beasts swept by.

The captain turned, just in time to see one more beast swooping down upon them.

'Hard a ...'

The order was never finished. Flame exploded across the deck, blasting the captain, the first mate and his men into the sea. The tiller shunted hard over, driving the ship into an abrupt turn. Without correction the ship kept turning, it heeled over in the wind and capsized, spilling those still aboard into the sea. Flames ran up its length as it went down by the head, a flaming mass of burning timbers.

The beasts circled in the air. One ship remained, still fleeing back towards its home. The beasts turned and flew away.

* * *

Coran was looking over the maps of Amaris when senator Janaid burst into the meeting hall.

'Fishermen have just reported in,' he gasped out. It was clear he'd sprinted from the harbour with his news. 'Those that had sailed to the sunward and shaderight. They said there are ships, warships, clustered around the Scattered Isles, too many to count.'

Coran nodded. 'As expected, the witches will use the islands as staging points and refresh their water supplies before moving on.'

'They say they came under attack from the air,' Janaid added. 'The dachs of these witches, dropping fire on their ships. Most of them ...'

'How many?' Coran asked.

'Three ships lost, over forty sailors. Good men ...'

Coran bowed his head for a moment.

'Another tactical move,' he said. 'They're going to blockade us, stop us going out for food.'

'What do we do?' Janaid asked.

'Little we can do,' Coran replied. 'Too dangerous to fish now, issue orders for all ships to remain in port. Close the gates to the harbour once all that are still out are back. We keep building up our defences as best we can.'

'And when that is done?'

'Then we wait.'

* * *

Another stretch passed, with the weather turning stormy, hampering efforts to complete the work. No more fishing vessels had been lost. Heavy leaden skies swirled overhead and grey waves crashed against the city walls. Rain cascaded down in thick sheets, soaking everything and obstructing the work of the carpenters.

In the early chimes of the following stretch the wind shifted, turning to come from the sunward, the weather warmer and brighter. The clouds lifted and the rain faded first to drizzle and then stopped. Lacaille blazed out once more, still scarred by the dark blotches on its face. The sea calmed.

Coran nodded as the gusts began to dry the rain-soaked streets.

'Fair weather for us is fair weather for them too,' he muttered, seeing the city folks returning to their tasks. He went back to his notes.

Mel on the Mobilis, Ren on the flying machines, Fitch on his harbour weapons. If Meru is able to bring Zoella back we might have some defence against their mental abilities. If not, all we've got is everyone armed in some fashion and wanting a piece of these wretched witches … is there anything else we can do?

Messages came in from the runners. Flying creatures had been seen high in the sky around the coastline. They had stayed out of range of the few archers that were stationed there, flying as far as the fire rocks on the far sunright of the island.

'Scouts all along the coast have reported them overflying the island in the last few chimes,' Fitch said. 'I guess they were looking for a way to avoid a frontal attack.'

'They won't have found one,' Coran said, with a grim smile. 'Amar's rocky coastline is one of the few advantages we have.'

'Guess we'll see them here soon enough then.'

They didn't have to wait long. Coran and Fitch were still discussing strategies when they heard yells from outside. They ran from the hall.

Cries of dismay were going up across the city. Coran and Fitch watched as three huge flying reptiles banked and swooped overhead. They stayed at altitude, circling high in the sky.

'We could send the boy up with his flying machines,' Fitch muttered. 'That would give them a nasty surprise.'

'Let them look,' Coran said. 'They can see we're readying for an assault and that this will be no pushover for them. Might give 'em pause.'

The dachs circled the city a number of times before flying back out to sea once more. They were swift and dwindled to points in the sky before being lost to the distance.

'Not long now,' Coran said, watching them depart.

'Next stretch,' Fitch replied. He was looking out to sea, with Coran's 'scope to his eye. 'Here, take a look for yourself.'

Coran took the 'scope and trained it on the horizon.

To the sunward and shaderight, sails could now be seen along the line that separated sea from sky. The sails were a bright orange in the light of Lacaille, more than he could count.

'A big fleet,' Coran said. 'I've never seen so many vessels.'

'Might be worth us doing some reconnaissance ourselves,' Fitch said.

Coran shook his head. 'Not putting Ren and his team at risk when we have little to learn,' he replied. 'Besides, I want the fact that we have an aerial defence to be a secret for as long as possible.'

'They may already know that,' Fitch countered. 'Those dachs had a pretty good view of the island from up there, they will have seen the machines.'

'But they won't necessarily know what they are or what they can do,' Coran said. 'With luck they may overextend themselves. We don't need to go looking anyway. We'll know how big a force they've mustered long before they reach the harbour walls. We're outnumbered for sure, the real numbers won't make much of a difference.'

Fitch nodded. 'They are going to breach the walls you know. Those ships will manage ten knots in this wind. We've got a spell before they get here, no more. We simply won't be able to stop all of them.'

'I don't think we can win this fight,' Coran answered. 'We can only make this island too hard and too costly to take.'

'Depends on how determined they are,' Fitch said. 'They sound scorchin' resolute to me.'

Fitch paused and adjusted his wide-brimmed hat.

'Think they'll treat before they attack?' he asked.

Coran rubbed his beard. 'Meru said that they did talk before they attacked Viresia.'

'Had much to say, did they?'

'Apparently not, some trial of champions, but that went to the shades soon enough. Given their religion teaches them we have to be exterminated I'm not expecting much talk.'

Fitch grunted in acknowledgement.

'Suits me,' he said. 'I'd rather cut to it and see if we can take down a few of these arrogant women.'

Mel came running into the senate hall.

'Ships have been spotted,' she said. 'On the horizon.'

'We saw them,' Coran said. 'You ready?'

Mel nodded. 'Aye.'

'You don't have to go through with this plan,' he said. 'We can still keep the *Mobilis* back.'

Mel shook her head. 'We can do this.'

Coran nodded. 'Time is now then,' he said. 'Good luck.'

'No sign of the others, I'm guessing?' Mel asked. 'We've heard nothing on the radio.'

'Meru and Zoella?' Coran said, with a sigh. 'No, nothing at all.'

'We could do with that girl here,' Fitch muttered, 'to stave off the witches' magic powers.'

'Hopefully they are far from here, dealing with the other problems,' Coran answered. 'Probably best they are spared this battle …'

'Going to get quite messy,' Fitch observed.

'I guess this fight has been coming for many rounds,' Coran said. 'A fight our ancestors lost last time.'

'Let's hope our descendants have something to be proud of,' Fitch replied.

'I'll settle for having some descendants,' Coran said, clapping him on the shoulder.

'That would be good,' Mel said, her voice hushed. She was looking at him. She hesitated for a moment. 'I … er … I'll be going.'

She reached to Coran and he pulled her into an embrace.

'Be careful out there,' he whispered.

'I will be.'

The moment passed. She pulled back and stepped away, turning on her heel and walking off.

'You'd better be getting ready too,' Coran said. 'Those weapons of yours …'

'You're a snuttin' fool, you are,' Fitch said.

'What?'

'That was your second chance to tell her,' Fitch said from alongside him. 'You're tempting fate letting her walk away, mark my words.'

'There's no time for that now,' Coran snapped. 'The witches will be here in this stretch …'

'There never is,' Fitch said, shaking his head. 'Don't blame me if you don't get to say all the things you want to say. Those witches are dead set intent on wiping us all out. They're coming …'

Above them, the dark stains on Lacaille continued to grow and fester.

The wind was picking up, blowing in cool from the shaderight. Coran stared into it, his lips tight and his expression set.

'Muster everyone we have,' Coran said before turning his gaze back out to sea. 'Let them come.'

CHAPTER SEVENTEEN

The Seas and Skies of Esurio

Round 2307, Sixth pass

The flying machine was struggling to gain height, its engines labouring as it struggled to pull itself above the rolling sand dunes. Zoella could see that many of the indicators around the controls Meru was holding were showing red.

'Too much weight,' Meru said. 'I can't get it any higher.'

'We can't leave anyone behind,' Zoella replied. 'Is there anything else we can throw out?'

'All the food, we've got to keep the water … maybe the rifles … but those things are precious, we'll need them if Amar is attacked …'

'Rifles?' Zoella asked.

'Metal weapons, they shoot … kill things. Really deadly.'

'Won't do us any good if we don't get there,' Zoella said, flinching as the flying machine only just skimmed over a dune.

'We've got other problems,' Meru said, jabbing at one of the screens.

'What?'

'Look!'

Zoella could see that one of the screens was somehow showing an image of what was happening behind them. Their take off had been noticed. Three of the dachs were heading in their direction.

'Oh no …'

'They're going to catch us,' Meru said. 'We don't have the speed to outrun them.'

'Just like last time,' Zoella said. 'These rifles, how do they work …?'

Meru spared a glance at her. 'There's no way I can teach you now …'

Zoella rolled her eyes. 'Just think it, I can learn from that. Quickly!'

She concentrated, pushing her thoughts towards Meru.

Rifles, in the side lockers. Fitch laughing, the planks, loading the weapon, pulling back the metal stock, holding it at the shoulder, astonishment at the noise and violence, the plank exploding into fragments ...

Then there was something else. Meru's mind was wavering, images of Kiri, her shoulders bare, moving toward him.

Zoella pulled away before she saw any more.

Her again!

Something hurt within her, something was twisted and angry.

'What are you going to do?' Meru demanded.

'Use the weapons,' Zoella said. 'Be ready to turn us so that the side door faces them.'

'But they're outside ... in the side lockers!' Meru said.

'Yeah, I saw that.'

Zoella undid the safety harness in her seat and jumped into the rear compartment of the flying machine, around her the children and Ira were huddled together, holding on as best they could as the flying machine rolled from side to side. Some were crying, already looking sick with the motion.

'Stay back!' she called, wrestling with the doorway.

She pulled the handle as the door slid back into its open position. Air blustered around her, whipping her clothing back and forth, her hair flapping in her face. She dropped down to the floor and crawled to the opening, leaning out to get at the side lockers. Ira saw what she was doing and braced herself against the interior, holding on as best she could around Zoella's waist.

Zoella could see the dunes rolling past below her, the movement dizzyingly fast, the flying machine was still only a few dozen hands above the ground. She reached out into the buffeting airstream, holding on to the door with one hand and fumbling with the catches to the side lockers with the other.

Her hand slipped, she almost lost balance as the flying machine tipped and gyrated.

'Hold it steady!' she snapped.

'I'm going my best,' Meru fired back.

Zoella reached again, managing to unclip the latch on the lockers. They were hinged towards her, which wasn't at all helpful, but she managed to grab both the rifle and the belt that came with it, yanking them back inside.

Ira was looking at her. Zoella tried to sign to her, but then sent an image of the packs of food still remaining in the midst of the children.

Throw them out!

Ira didn't understand for a moment, her face showing astonishment and confusion. Zoella nodded and gestured at the opening.

Ira nodded and the children helped her lug the heavy containers along the walkway before pushing them out one by one through the doorway. Zoella could just see them fall, tumbling away before smashing into the ground and splattering their contents over the dunes.

We're going to go hungry ...

'It's working!' Meru called, looking back from the front. 'Getting some lift!'

As the children and Ira continued with their task, Zoella busied herself pushing the strange metal capsules into the rifle. She struggled for a moment with which way around they went, but then pushed them home one after the other.

'Here they come!' Meru yelled.

A shadow flashed outside, gone in moments. Zoella looked up to see a dach arcing away from them. The flying machine jolted, but Meru corrected it.

A second dach came into view, Zoella could see the rider, clad from head to foot in leather armour and a face mask of some kind. They had a bow, tensed and ready to fire. Zoella thrust out with her mind, sensing the grip of the rider. She forced a jolt. She saw the bow release, but the arrow went wild.

Then she brought the rifle around, putting it to her shoulder as she'd seen from Meru's mind, and squeezed the flange.

The noise was terrifying in the confined space. The recoil threw her hard back into the interior. Smoke billowed about her, whipped around by the furious gale blowing about them. Zoella heard screams from the children, the flying machine bucked beneath her. Then all she could hear was a strange ringing in her ears and every other sound was muted.

The dach outside was gone.

She shook her head, trying to clear it. The flying machine was bucking around her, tossing her one way and then the other. She looked up, Meru was clutching his head with both hands.

The priestesses …

Out of the corner of her eye she saw Ira stagger forward, placing one hand on Meru and gesturing out of the windows with the other. Meru recovered, grabbing hold of the controls and steadying the machine. It levelled out once more, skimming over the sand dunes with a few hands to spare.

Ira stumbled back and crouched down next to her. She pointed out of the side exit. Zoella could see the dachs turning away, trying to get behind the flying machine.

'Turn us, Meru!'

The flying machine tilted to the right. The dachs came into view again.

Zoella reloaded and raised the rifle again. She saw the children shrink back, covering their ears.

She took her time to aim, waiting until the nearest dach was closer. She could see the priestess on its back readying a bow.

I hope it's Kiri!

She fired. The recoil flung her back, but she was braced for it this time. Through the smoke she saw the dach rear up in the air and then fall out of the sky, the priestess on its back thrown off. Both crashed to the ground, tumbled into the sand and lay still. In another moment they were left behind.

The two other dachs followed for a moment before giving up the chase. Zoella watched as they turned away, seeking the location of their fallen comrade.

Zoella lowered the rifle, conscious of the whimpering children and her own trembling hands. She put the weapon down and stood up, yanking at the side door and pulling it closed.

The noise from the rushing air outside was cut off, leaving just the ringing in her ears.

She looked up and saw Meru glance at her.

'They've given up the chase,' he said, before turning back to the controls. 'We made it.'

Zoella breathed a sigh of relief. Ira helped her up and she clambered into the second chair beside Meru.

'Well done,' he said, looking across at her.

She nodded, but said nothing, too tired to think, her ears still ringing from the loud noise.

'We're heading shadeward,' Meru said, 'The coastline bends towards Amar a little before turning away, that will make the trip across the seas as short as …'

He stopped. Zoella looked across. A series of red lights had appeared on the controls in front of them.

Meru touched some of the controls and was rewarded with several screens of text.

'What?' Zoella asked.

'Not sure,' Meru answered. 'Sandra, what does this mean?'

The flying machine's voice answered him. 'Magnetic induction systems aboard this vessel are no longer receiving a full power cycle. Power cycle amplitude is decreasing. Once levels fall below safety threshold this vessel will commence running on auxiliary power. It should be safely secured on the ground prior to battery depletion.'

'Auxiliary …?' Zoella echoed.

'We've got to land,' Meru said. 'And soon. You remember the *Mobilis*, that time we got stuck without power? That's going to happen to us.'

'Without power …'

'We can't fly,' Meru finished for her.

He looked out of the forward windows.

They had left the sand dunes behind. The flying machine was now travelling over a barren rocky wilderness filled with jagged spikes and arid looking promontories.

'And we can't land,' Zoella whispered.

* * *

Nerina and Kiri watched as the two dachs circled above Airea and then landed before them. Nerina stepped forward, seeing Rihanna pull her scarf off, allowing her red hair to blow in the wind. The second rider was carrying a slumped figure before her.

'What happened?'

'We tried to stop it escaping,' Rihanna said. 'Our powers were blocked.'

'Blocked?' Nerina asked. 'These women of Scallia you spoke of, Kiri?'

Kiri nodded, but said nothing.

'They had some weapon aboard that blew smoke,' Rihanna added. 'Then … killed the dach … Adrella fell …'

Nerina watched as Kiri walked over to help the other rider, and saw it was Tali. Adrella's body was lowered to the floor. Nerina could see Kiri crouched over her, but it was clear the other rider was beyond hope. Kiri stood up and walked back toward them.

'The fall broke her neck,' she said. 'You should have let me go. I could have stopped them.'

'You know of this weapon of theirs?' Nerina demanded.

Kiri shook her head. 'No …'

'Then you might have just as easily been killed,' Nerina said, looking across to Rihanna. 'They have escaped, we must let them go. Thanks to Kiri they know we're coming anyway. The ships are already underway. Kiri, see that Adrella's body is given to the flames and then take your place on the ships. We sail for Amar. Rihanna, come with me, we have much to discuss.'

Nerina and Rihanna walked away, leaving Kiri behind.

Kiri stared after them for a long moment before turning to Tali.

'Let us see to our sister,' she said.

Tali nodded.

* * *

'Power cycle threshold approaching,' Sandra announced. 'Landing is now imperative.'

'But there's nowhere to land!' Meru snapped back.

He had kept the machine on the course shadewards, hoping to come to an end of the rock field. Now it stretched out in all directions, unending, each rocky outcrop spikier and more dangerous looking than the last.

'What happens when the power is gone?' Zoella asked.

'We run on the batteries for a while,' Meru said. 'But they won't last long. We'll have to try setting down before that.'

'Can you do that?' she asked, looking at the passing landscape.

Meru didn't answer.

'We had to throw out all the food and most of the water,' Zoella said. 'If we land here and can't take off again …'

Meru looked towards the horizon.

'Then we've got a choice,' he said. 'We can continue shadewards and hope we come to an end, we can turn back and head for the sea, or …'

'Yes?'

'We can try heading shaderight and see if we can reach the forests we flew over on the way down from Scallia.'

Zoella looked out of the front windows and then to the side.

'If we go back to the sea the priestesses will find us and kill us or worse,' she said. 'No telling how far these rocks go shadewards. If we get to the forests there'll be water. I vote shaderight.'

Meru nodded.

The machine banked to the left, heading away over the rocks.

'Power cycle threshold breached,' Sandra announced. 'Auxiliary power enabled. Landing is now imperative.'

The landscape continued to roll beneath them as the flying machine droned on. Lacaille was to their left now, shining through the cockpit. Zoella could see their shadow on the ground, flickering up and down as the rocks flew past below.

'Look,' Meru said, pointing forward. 'Is that green, or are my eyes going funny ...'

Zoella squinted into the light.

'You might be right, it's our only shot, keep flying.'

'Tell everyone to hold on tight and strap themselves in if they can,' Meru said.

Zoella sent an image to Ira and turned to see both her and the children crouching down and hanging on to any available point on the interior walls.

'They're getting ready,' she said.

'You too,' Meru replied, pulling the straps tight around him. Zoella did the same.

'Auxiliary power at seventy percent,' Sandra said. 'Land immediately.'

Meru gripped the controls.

'This could get messy.'

Zoella looked ahead. The rocks were thinning out, the tall spiky constructs they had been flying over were less and less obvious, she could even make out small scrubs growing in between the rocks.

There was something else too ... when the power on the ship failed ... there was a message from the Obelisk ... and pain!

She could feel it, a pulsing burning pain growing in her head.

'Meru ...'

She managed to gasp out his name before the full force of it hit her. She screamed, lurching in her chair. A white hot pain flashed across her temple and burrowed into her brain. She was aware of screams from the back of the flying machine; Ira and the children were also affected.

'There!' She was barely aware of Meru's voice. 'I'm going to try there. Hang on!'

The agony was intense and unrelenting. Zoella clawed at her forehead to no avail, the world outside now streaked with pain, blurred and dizzying. More screams and cries of pain.

Ahead of them the ground was falling away. They reached a lip and it dropped away below into an arid valley filled with dry vegetation. It looked harsh and uninviting, but it was flat.

'Auxiliary power is now critical,' Sandra said. 'Land immediately.'

Meru brought the machine down as fast as he could, trying to find the least dangerous-looking spot to land in. There were twisted stunted shades everywhere, with no open space at all.

'Just got to …'

The flying machine was twenty hands above the ground when its power failed. The engines gave a final whine and then began to spin down. The machine dropped, tilting forward and crunching down into the shades.

A terrifying grating noise accompanied their headlong rush downwards. There was a hard thump, followed by a second. One of the front windows cracked, a spider web of lines arcing across it.

Then with a further jolt, the machine came to rest, lying canted to one side. The only sounds were the screams of those within.

* * *

Kiri and Tali stood watching as the pyre was consumed by fire. Kiri stared into the flames, wrestling with her thoughts.

Another fallen priestess, another death, and now we go to seek more conflict, more war. Elena commanded us to destroy Amar, but her religion is false. Amar is not the enemy, I'm not sure who is any more! Can I stop this now? If I defy Nerina now I will be torn, cast aside and likely killed; I am not strong enough yet. If I do nothing, Amar will be attacked and defeated.

Flames crackled, she could feel the heat on her face. Tears streaked her cheeks, but she stood immobile.

But Amar will not receive me, neither would Scallia. I am their sworn enemy! They will kill me as surely as Nerina would. Drayden has been my home all my life. Can I throw away my past? What of the command of the Obelisk? Meru said Zoella had received the same warning, we must go to it ...

She trembled, her grip on her kai tightening until her knuckles showed white through her skin. A vision consumed her mind once more. She gasped with the realisation of it.

Zoella was right. I do want it all. It was no dream. I hid it even from myself! But I would be a better high priestess, a better Empress than those who have gone before. I know what it is to be poor and hungry, I came from the slums ...

It should be her. It was she who was queen, royalty of Scallia. Nerina had no claim to be high priestess other than the power she had acquired. But to stop her ...

Nerina is too powerful. I can't stop her without help. Without Zoella ... would Rihanna stand with me? Can I trust her to betray Nerina? Would we be strong enough together? Which way will the priestesses turn, to us or against us? And how many more might die in such a power struggle?

More tears trickled down her face.

I was so sure before. The enemy was ahead, the priestesses righteous, our task clear! All I had to do was vanquish them and all would be right ... but now? Every choice I make leads to conflict. Who is right and who is wrong? All are set against me, Drayden, Scallia, Amar ... and the only one who did care for me ... I lied to ... I pushed away ...

A sob escaped her. Tali grabbed her shoulder.

'Kiri ... there was nothing you could have done.'

She nodded, blinking back her tears. She wiped at her eyes, her resolve coming back to her.

Amar is lost whatever I do. Let them all be weakened by the fight. Nothing matters anyway. If there's no goddess, there's no after, no reward for service, nothing! Just this life and what I can do with it. I will pick up the spoils, tear those I can in the midst of the carnage. Strengthen myself to challenge Nerina! I will show mercy to those who pledge themselves to me wherever they might come from. I will be Empress. There will be no Amar, no Scallia, no Drayden! I will be fair to everyone from the lowest to the highest. They will worship me, fall at my feet! They will love me! And Meru will sit at my right hand, my consort. This I will make happen!

The tears were gone now; her eyes were bright once more with purpose.

'It is done,' she said to Tali. 'Time for us to depart.'

Kiri stepped away, walking towards the harbour.

* * *

The flying machine was settled in a grove of twisted and thin looking shades. There was enough vegetation to hide them from the casual observer, but it wasn't thick enough to present a problem with landing or take off. One figure stood outside, walking around, surveying the damage.

Meru completed his inspection of the flying machine. It was scratched and dented, but as far as he could tell, it was still operational.

But without power, we're not going anywhere.

Inside, Zoella was slumped in the passenger seat, with Ira and the children curled up on the floor. All had fainted, overcome by the strange pain that seemed to accompany the loss of the 'tricity.

How can that be connected? Perhaps the 'tricity is what gives them their gifts somehow?

It didn't make much sense to Meru. The strange powers that Zoella and the others seemed to possess were of the mind, whereas 'tricity was a motive force, making engines turn and lights glow.

But it seems they share a common source. The Obelisk I guess.

A thought occurred to him.

If the 'tricity is failing ... does that mean these powers fail with it?

Zoella was stirring. He climbed back into the cockpit of the machine.

'Zoella?'

She looked across at him before looking around herself.

'We're alive?' she whispered.

'For now,' Meru answered. 'How are you?'

Zoella winced, propping herself up. 'It was like before, the pain … it's gone now. The others …'

Meru held up a hand. 'Still resting for now, they seem to be all right.'

Zoella undid the clasps on her seat and Meru helped her down from the machine. The temperature was soaring, so they both stood in the shadow of the machine's wings. Zoella checked on Ira and the children. She looked around the interior.

'We had to throw out all the food?' Zoella asked.

'The water too,' Meru said, 'With all of us aboard it's just too heavy. Unless we're planning to leave someone behind.'

Zoella shook her head. 'Out here? They'll die for sure.'

She walked away from the machine and grabbed one of the shades, it was brittle and dry, there was no nourishment or water to be found here.

'We're going to have to find some water then,' Meru said. 'We can go hungry easily enough, but three stretches without water and we'll all be dead. Look …'

Meru gestured inside the machine again. There was no power for the engines, but the screens still worked. He showed Zoella the map.

'See,' he said, pointing. 'The coastline runs shadewards before turning shaderight towards Dynesia. That's the closest point to Amar.' He moved his finger to the left. 'We're here, maybe a hundred marks inland now. We're going the wrong way.'

'We're not going anywhere at the moment,' Zoella said. 'Is the machine broken?'

'I don't think so, just no power,' Meru answered. 'It was only a spell last time before the 'tricity came back, but it's been longer than that already.'

'But if we can't go anywhere …' Zoella said. 'We've got to get back to Amar, the fleet … the priestesses!'

Meru shrugged. He tried the radio switches. As he did so the screens flickered and faded out.

'Without 'tricity, we aren't going anywhere.'

Lacaille burned hot above them. Both of them looked up at the shining disc, it was high in the sky.

'Last time,' Meru said. 'When this happened before, you heard a call, a message from the Obelisk. Did you hear anything this time?'

Zoella shook her head.

'No nothing, just the pain in my head.'

'I have this idea,' Meru said. 'I think your powers, these gifts and the 'tricity are all connected. Can you try … can you use them?'

'Now?'

'Yes, try it.'

Zoella concentrated for a moment.

Can you still hear me?

Meru looked surprised and then deflated.

'So much for that idea then,' he said. 'Thought I might be on to something.'

'They've got to be connected,' Zoella said. 'Too much of a coincidence to be anything else. Wait … what if I try to talk to the Obelisk?'

'Talk to it?'

'Caesar asked me if I could contact it,' Zoella said. 'Don't you remember? Perhaps there's a way. If it can talk to me, perhaps I can talk to it, make the 'tricity come back …'

'Worth a try.' Meru shrugged and looked at the arid landscape around him. 'Without it we're going to die out here.'

Zoella sat down in the passenger seat and closed her eyes, concentrating on the voice she remembered when she'd been aboard the *Mobilis*.

Obelisk, can you hear me?

There was no answer. She tried again, pushing her thoughts out as far as she could. She picked up on confusion and distress as she sensed the vague impressions of others. They were far away, perhaps it was the priestesses themselves. She pushed further, straining to the limits of her perceptions.

Obelisk, can you …

A voice, deafening, echoed around her head.

Administrator. Contact has been established. Access is granted.

Zoella gasped, struggling with the mental effort required.

'Can you …?' Meru began. She waved him to silence.

The 'tricity has failed, we need it back.

Failure of magnetic induction energy facility is confirmed. Diagnostics indicate axial alignment is now out of tolerance resulting in excess thermal load. Temporary shutdown is in place until cooling systems return this facility to safe levels.

Zoella frowned, trying to understand the words.

Will the 'tricity come back then?

Power distribution will be restored in approximately one stretch.

Zoella breathed a sigh of relief and was about to drop the link, but the Obelisk spoke again.

Administrator, on site repairs are mandated for a permanent solution. Energy distribution failure frequency will increase and become permanent within two passes. Without realignment, power distribution will halt and atmospheric erosion will reach critical values. Flare generated ultraviolet, x-ray and microwave radiation exposure will rapidly increase to fatal levels as ozone layer depletion rises exponentially. Please arrange a repair maintenance team and proceed to substellar pole, co-ordinates zero zero, immediately.

The connection ended itself. Zoella gasped and opened her eyes.

'What happened?' Meru demanded.

'Good news,' Zoella breathed. 'And bad. The 'tricity will come back on in a stretch or so, but whatever has gone wrong is getting worse. It told me that whatever it does … it's going to completely stop in two passes.'

'Two passes!'

* * *

Rihanna had seen to the organisation of the dachs. Whilst the fleet of ships made its way shadewards up the coast, the dachs flew with them stopping to rest on the land. However, when the fleet had to turn away from the land and sail into the sunright, the land was left behind. Now the dachs were settled on the big barges that had been brought along with them. Four dachs could be housed on each one, with every available ship pressed into service to carry them. A hundred of the great beasts were able to be transported in this manner, along with their food, water and handlers.

Another searing flash of pain had assailed the priestesses, some more so than others. Kiri had been lying down in her sleeping bunk aboard ship at the time and had been able to muffle her cries. It was short lived and she got no message as she had done before.

The Obelisk, it reminds us it needs attention. What does it need? Why does it need us?

The sense of urgency remained though. Whatever it needed, she had to make her way there and soon.

Kiri had watched Nerina and Karquesh board the flagship of the fleet. Dachs were in the sky, squawking. The soldiers of Taloon had also brought some of their phaunts with them too, in order to press the attack once the city had been breached.

Each priestess had been assigned a ship. Aboard her own, Kiri had little to do but ponder the upcoming attack on Amar. She stood near the prow of one of the military ships, loaded with armed soldiers from Taloon. They knew of her from King Karquesh, none came near her and they retreated whenever she walked about, bowing and scraping to get out of her way.

She looked out to sea as the bow rose and fell beneath her feet. She had never set foot on a ship before. The sensation was strange, but not unpleasant, but she would have preferred to have been aboard a dach.

The sea dashed away beneath, surging and splashing before the ship's bow. Amar was not far away.

* * *

They had spent the stretch making what few repairs to the flying machine they could and stripping out any other weight and non-essential items they could find. After deliberation they decided to leave the rifles and everything else associated with them. Everyone was hot and thirsty in the broiling heat, Zoella divided up the little water they had left between them all to ensure everyone got a fair share.

A stretch had passed and they'd spent a hot sleeping lying in the shade of the flying machine, with the unrelenting glare of Lacaille all about. Then, two chimes later, Sandra spoke.

'Power cycle restored,' she said. 'Auxiliary batteries recharging.'

'We can go!' Meru called.

Everyone climbed aboard, Meru ran some checks and was pleased to see that the crash landing hadn't broken anything critical. The machine lifted off and continued on its course.

'We should find the forest first,' Zoella said. 'Get some water. Before we all pass out.'

Meru nodded.

Another stretch saw them to the edge of the Scallian forests with the dry aridness of Taloon left behind. Zoella located a stream and Meru set the machine down nearby. All of them ran to it, dousing themselves in water and drinking their fill.

'We'll carry as much as we can,' Zoella said, 'But we can't store much, we'll have to keep stopping to find more.'

'Best we can do,' Meru said. 'If we follow the coast back sunright, there should be streams and rivers we can use. Once we cross the sea though, we're just going to have to keep going.'

The delay had cost them precious time, both Zoella and Meru knew that the priestesses' fleet was now far ahead of them. More stretches passed, but they reached the far sunright of the continent.

'This is it,' Meru said, at their final stop. 'Across the sea now. Either we make it to Amar ... or we don't.'

'Let's go then,' Zoella said, signalling to Ira and the children to climb aboard once more. 'No time to waste.'

The flying machine was still weighed down, but it was able to fly high enough to avoid the worst of the terrain. They left the continent behind them, turning across the sea.

'Let's hope we don't run into any more trouble,' Meru said, looking out at the distant horizon as the coastline receded past them. 'There's a lot of sea out here. If the power fails when we're out there …'

Zoella nodded. She looked behind her, Ira and the others were already asleep, with little to do they had huddled up and were resting as best they could in the cramped space to the rear.

She turned back and slumped in her seat, letting out a deep sigh.

'You did well with the Obelisk,' Meru said.

'Thank you,' Zoella said. Their conversation lapsed.

'Are we going to talk about what happened?' Meru asked, his voice low. 'About …'

'I don't want to talk about her,' Zoella answered, looking out of the window away from Meru.

'I need to tell you what happened … why … because Kiri …'

'I don't want to know what you did with her,' Zoella spat. 'I don't want to even think about it. You clearly don't care what anyone else thinks.' She turned and glared at him. 'It's nothing to do with me.'

'Zoella …'

'What?' She rounded on him. 'You made your choice, you live with the consequences. I need you to get us back to Amar. What you do after that I really don't care. Go join her if you wish. You'd better make your mind up which side you're on at some point.'

'She wasn't lying …'

Zoella shook her head and snorted in exasperation. 'I can't believe that you can even think that! She really has bewitched you, hasn't she? You can't see any fault in her.' He recoiled, but she continued to lay into him. 'She's a liar, Meru. She's manipulating you and everyone else. She wants it all for herself. The moment she didn't get her way she turned on us, can't you see that? She tried to take my powers. If Ira hadn't been there she would have succeeded.'

'She wants to stop the priestesses ...'

'No. She. Doesn't!' Zoella snarled out the words one at a time, her voice rising to a high pitch. 'That was just a story for you, don't you get it? She was after my powers, nothing else. She's a backstabbing, lying, manipulative, evil bitch. I should have killed her when I had the chance.'

'She's your sister.'

'So?' Zoella argued back. 'That grants her nothing, doesn't excuse what she's done or who she is. What am I supposed to do, embrace her as a long lost relative? I don't care that she's my sister. She's a liar and a murderer. That's all she is.'

'You don't understand ...'

Zoella sneered. 'Oh, I think I do. She's pleasant enough to look on, isn't she? I bet she taught you a few things in that bedroom she had you locked in.'

Zoella could tell from the flush on Meru's face that she wasn't far from the mark.

'Don't even bother denying it,' Zoella added. 'Seems you can't think with your head, only your ...'

'Shut up!' Meru yelled. 'Just ... shut up!'

'Thought you were better than that,' Zoella fired back. 'I was wrong. Don't be thinking I won't tell Coran and the rest of the crew about all this. They need to know. They're going to know.'

Meru looked at her, his face going pale.

'Yes, that's right. You're a liability,' Zoella said, looking back at him. 'I don't trust you, and neither will they. You've betrayed us, you betrayed me ...'

The tears she had fought back forced their way through. She could feel them dripping down her cheeks.

'... and you betrayed yourself.'

'Zoella ...'

'Don't,' she said, her voice cracking.

Zoella turned away. Time ticked away in the uncomfortable silence that followed. Zoella wiped at her eyes, listening to the interminable drone of the flying machine's engines.

'She doesn't really care you know,' she said, almost talking to herself. 'Women like her … You're just a trophy. Once she's …' Zoella shuddered. 'Once she's sated herself she'll throw you away too just like some old toy.' Her voice turned acid sweet. 'You'll see.'

* * *

The flying machine droned inexorably onwards, the sea rolling away beneath the windows. Zoella dozed. She felt the flying machine turn.

'You'd better wake up,' Meru's voice was toneless. 'We're here …'

Zoella stretched and sat up. She looked at him. He was staring out of the front windows of the flying machine, his mouth open. Zoella turned to see what he was looking at.

'Oh no,' Zoella said, her voice dropping in dismay. 'We're too late.'

Hundreds of ships, perhaps even a thousand, were stretched out below them. The island of Amar was beyond, the city of Amaris besieged. Even from here they could see fires, both on the walls and within the city, and smoke was rising far into the sky.

Ira and some of the children were just behind them, stretching forward to see.

Dachs circled over the city, their shapes flitting in and out of the smoke. Where they dived, new fires flashed.

'Hang on,' Meru said.

He pushed the flying machine into a dive, directing it straight towards the battle.

CHAPTER EIGHTEEN

Amaris, Capital of Amar

Round 2307, Sixth pass

Coran and Fitch watched from the harbour walls as a flight of the priestesses' dachs swooped overhead. There were five of them in a tidy delta formation. As they watched the formation broke up, the leader's dach descending to the breakwater at the far point of the harbour. The dach landed at the far end and they could see a figure step down from it. The four other dachs remained hovering nearby.

'Looks like they do want to talk after all,' Fitch muttered, shouldering his rifle.

Coran nodded to senators Janaid and Henoch. 'Let's go see what they have to say.'

The four men walked down the harbour wall. As they approached they could see the figure was a woman, standing before the great winged dach which opened its wings as they approached and roared at them. Henoch and Janaid staggered back, but Coran and Fitch were unfazed.

Looking up, Coran could see the other four riders were perched upon their dachs with arrows notched in the bows they held. The dachs hovered in the air, their great wings sweeping back and forth to maintain their position.

The woman was diminutive, her skin so pale as to be almost white. She was dressed all in black, her hair shining with a single silver streak. The left side of her head was shaved to the skin, with the hair grown long on the other side. It was topped by an elegant tiara that flashed and sparkled in the light of Lacaille.

'Who speaks for Amar?' she called.

Her voice was quiet, almost sepulchral, but it echoed around inside their heads in some strange fashion.

Henoch and Janaid both looked to Coran. He stepped forward, Fitch by his side.

'I do.'

'And who are you?' the woman said, looking him up and down.

'I'll have your name first,' Coran replied. 'You who come to our shores prepared for war.'

The woman raised her hand as if to strike. In a swift movement, too fast for Coran to see, Fitch had raised his rifle and taken aim just before the woman's feet. The abrupt noise, puff of dust and sharp impact made her jump back in alarm. The dach roared again, beating its wings.

Fitch reloaded and aimed the gun at her. She looked angry now, raising her arms out towards them.

'I wouldn't do that if I were you,' Fitch said, his aim sure. 'You'll be dead before you can utter one of your magic spells.'

Coran pushed down on the butt of the rifle.

'Peace,' he called. 'But I will have your name, woman.'

The woman looked at him for a long moment.

'I am high priestess Nerina Helios, of Darek, Daria, Kerchin, Farren, Goshe, Drem, and Daine in the realm of Drayden. Now, your name, man.'

'I am Coran,' Coran replied. 'Of Amar alone. Why have you brought a fleet of war to our shores? Depart these waters and we will not trouble you.'

'You are the exiles of Drem,' Nerina said. 'Cursed by Lacaille herself long ago and subject to her judgement. You were found wanting long ago, your death ordained. We come to finish that task.'

'We are not subject to your laws or your religion,' Coran replied.

'All are subject,' Nerina replied. 'Whether they believe or not. It is so written.'

'We do not want a war,' Coran said. 'Can there not be a peace between us?'

'We will spare your women and girls from that fate,' Nerina replied. 'Have them assemble in the harbour. We will take them away and they will be treated fairly. Your men and boys will be executed. We will be merciful. We will ensure it is done as swiftly and as painlessly as possible.'

'Quite the offer,' Fitch muttered, rolling his eyes.

'You think we will stand aside as you take our folk?' Coran asked.

'If you value their lives,' Nerina replied. 'Refuse and we will raze your city to take them.'

'Our people would rather die free than live as slaves,' Coran replied, his voice dark. 'Nor will we line up to be slaughtered by you.'

'So be it,' Nerina replied.

Her voice echoed in his head.

'You will soon be slain, Coran of Amar!' Nerina called. 'Your city in flames and your people massacred. History will count you as the greatest of all fools to defy the priestesses of Drayden.'

Coran turned away and then looked back.

'On the contrary,' he shouted back at her. 'History will record the people of Amar fighting against oppression and tyranny. We will not bow the knee to you or any other who seeks to impose their evil will upon us.'

'We have defeated stronger foes than you.'

'Then bring your battle!' Coran roared. 'You will not find us easy to overcome!'

Around them the dachs roared. Coran watched as Nerina mounted her own dach. It took to the air, back-flapping its wings as it gained height, rejoining the others in the sky above.

Then the entire flight turned, banking over the city with a rush of air and beating wings, before turning out to sea and retreating into the distance.

'Good,' Fitch said, shouldering his rifle once again. 'The pointless posturing was commendably short. Now we can get down to it.'

* * *

The *Mobilis* raced out of the harbour to the cheers of the people lining the walls. Coran and Fitch could see Mel leaning out of the wheelhouse with Daf and Creg aft and forward respectively, manning the rocket launchers. Lining the decks were six other men, volunteers from amongst the fishermen, armed with rifles provided by Fitch.

Clear of the harbour walls, the ship's wake churned thunderously and the ship surged forward towards the line of incoming vessels now approaching from the horizon.

'The flying machines are ready,' Fitch said.

'Don't want to play them too early,' Coran said, watching the receding *Mobilis*. 'Mel is under strict instructions not to get too close.'

'I'll keep an eye on the dachs,' Fitch said. 'That's where the fight is going to come from first.'

* * *

The *Mobilis* was running at a furious speed, leaping from wave crest to wave crest, spurring its way through the seas like a vast metal sword. It was closing fast on the front running vessels of the invading fleet. Mel could see them, row after row of moving wooden vessels, sails aloft, crammed with men.

'Ready on port side!' she yelled, turning the *Mobilis* to starboard. Daf and Creg swung their mounts around, aiming at the nearest vessels.

Five hundred hands I'd say, keeps us out of range of their bowmen ...

The *Mobilis* was now running adjacent to the line of ships, cutting across their direction of travel.

Crossing the T!

Mel squinted through the spray, judging her moment.

'Fire!' she yelled.

Daf and Creg yanked levers on their respective mechanisms. With a shrieking hiss, trails of smoke jetted from the *Mobilis*, arching out across the water towards the nearest pair of vessels. The first ship was struck a glancing blow, fire blossoming around its port side, blowing part of the hull and decking away.

The second vessel was not so lucky. The rockets hit it square on, the resulting explosion ripping out the centre of the ship, blasting its mast into the air and obliterating its crew. Timbers spiralled through the air as the mast crashed back down, the sea erupting with foam as the ship broke in two.

'Reload! All about!'

Mel pulled the throttles to half and swung the helm full to starboard. The *Mobilis* swung around, leaning hard with the speed and then headed back in the direction it had come from, splashing through its own wake.

'Ready on starboard side!'

More ships were approaching from the right, Mel adjusted course to bring the *Mobilis* across their bows. The captains had seen what she intended and the nearest ships were turning, but they were no match for the ferocious speed of the *Mobilis.*

They were in range once again.

'Fire!'

Rockets leapt from the *Mobilis* again, blasting across the water between the ships. Two more of the wooden vessels burst into flame. Mel could see men jumping away as the flames rose. A smattering of arrows splashed into the sea nearby, but the *Mobilis* roared out of range.

'Reload! All about!'

This time the *Mobilis* turned to port, turning back once again to commence a third run against the line of wooden shipping.

But this time there was something else. The men on the decks were gesturing to the sky. Mel leaned out of the wheelhouse to look.

Shades!

The sky was full of dachs, great wings of the beasts, travelling at different heights.

As she watched, the closest flight of the beasts folded their wings, diving down upon the *Mobilis.* Mel pushed the throttles to their stops and the ship leapt ahead, but even then, the dachs closed.

'Riflemen!' she yelled.

They were already prepared, braced in position with their rifles raised. Mel heard the shots fire, ringing out across the decks. With a roar one dach was felled, crashing down into the sea. Mel didn't see what happened to the rider.

Then, fire erupted around the ship in a plume of fury. Mel ducked as a flaming splash of some burning liquid exploded close by.

The *Mobilis*' prodigious speed saved it. The ship was through the flames in a moment, unharmed and unbowed. The dachs peeled away. Mel could see another group preparing to attack.

But now it was their turn again.

'Fire!'

A third series of rockets blasted from the *Mobilis*. Daf and Creg were practised now and the barrage was devastating. Two more ships were blown to pieces, with two more catching fire from the flaming debris that was flung around them. Mel could see men struggling in the water, sinking from the weight of the armour they wore.

Hundreds slain already ...

Her expression hardened as she watched.

They'll show us no mercy ...

More gunfire. The dachs were circling. Mel saw Daf duck as a shadow passed overhead. One of the fishermen was grabbed right off the decking by the claws of a low flying dach and cast, tumbling, into the sea.

'No!'

Then came more flames. The attackers were dropping small ceramic pots of some substance. It was catching fire the moment it came into contact with water. They were hitting the water about them, sending roaring flames up around the ship, but being left behind in her wake.

Then one struck the bow.

It did no immediate damage, but flaming liquid splattered across the forward part of the ship, forcing Daf and the two remaining forward riflemen to back away from it, struggling to douse the flames.

Before Mel had a chance to react another blast came from behind. She turned in horror to see the riflemen on the rear quarter aflame from head to foot, leaping into the sea in panic.

I can't save them ... we can't go back ...

Creg was further back, still clinging to the rocket launchers. She watched as he swung the mechanism around and pulled the levers again.

Rockets blasted up into the heavens, roaring into the formation of dachs that were dropping down to cast their fire at the *Mobilis*. With a devastating blast the rockets detonated, a plume of red flashed out in the sky, followed by huge trails of grey and black smoke.

Two dachs fell from the sky, their wings torn asunder and their riders dashed upon the surface of the sea. The others turned aside, abandoning their run against the ship.

That's all we can do. Time to retreat!

Mel turned the *Mobilis* towards Amaris and pushed the throttles to full.

* * *

Coran and Fitch watched the battle unfold. The *Mobilis* gave good account of itself and then the dachs swooped down upon it. Fire erupted across the ocean. There were dozens of dachs in the sky, taking turns in strafing the metal ship.

'That's enough, Mel,' Coran whispered. 'Get back now ...'

As if she had heard him, the *Mobilis* came about, driving headlong back towards Amar, the dachs forming up in the air and pursuing it.

'They're not just after the ship,' Fitch said. 'They're going to firebomb the city!'

Coran nodded.

'Archers to the walls! Fitch, raise the flag for the aerial defence!'

* * *

Kiri had been assigned to a tertiary wing of dachs by Rihanna. She and her group of priestesses were stationed on a ship on the far right of the fleet. Kiri watched as a single ship left the harbour. She recognised it as the one she had seen fleeing from Nireus. The strange metal ship seemed ridiculous sailing alone towards the fleet that outnumbered it. She gasped as it unleashed smoke and noise at the wooden vessels in the leading line, smashing them into flaming timbers.

Such weapons! Can we prevail against them?

Rihanna's voice echoed in her head.

Priestesses, to your dachs! Attack that vessel!

By the time they were aloft, the leading line of Taloon vessels had been decimated, nothing more than flaming wrecks. The metal ship was moving with unbelievable speed. From high up they could see its wake trailing far behind, the water at its stern churned white by its strange motive power.

Rihanna led the attack. Fire was dropped on the ship. Kiri watched as it turned in a vain effort to evade the attack. She could see men on the decks holding up weapons.

Not those ...

A dach was slain, crashing into the water behind the ship. Fire erupted around it as Rihanna's flight swept past. The second flight had even less luck, with two dachs killed as they swept around the ship, unable to damage it.

Kiri, now you!

Kiri signalled to the priestesses with her and her own flight turned and swept down upon the ship. Kiri could sense the trajectories of the defensive fire that was aimed at her and brought her dach in low. She saw an opportunity ...

Grab him!

Her dach swept across the decking, its talons outstretched, bodily grabbing one of the men from the ships and casting him, screaming, into the sea. Fire blazed out as her companions dropped their vials of oil upon the ship.

A third wave of dachs assailed the vessel. Kiri, now climbing back to altitude, watched as they dived down.

With a thumping detonation, red fire, smoke and flames erupted in the sky. Kiri watched in horror as two dachs were ripped apart in the air, their bodies and those of their riders tumbling into the sea. The ship was turning below, now running for the safety of the harbour.

Rihanna's call sounded in her head.

It is time! Attack the city!

* * *

The fleet of ships was closing on the harbour, but it was the aerial attack that had the defenders of Amar staring in dismay. Hundreds of the winged beasts filled the sky, their shapes silhouetted against the bright light of Lacaille.

Archers lined the walls of the harbour and the high towers of the city.

The flags were raised.

Coran turned and saw the acknowledgement from the cliff tops behind the city. The *Mobilis* was almost back to the harbour walls, thick black smoke trailing from the burning fluid that still coated its aft decks. Coran couldn't see who was left aboard.

The dachs began to dive.

'Wait,' he called, staring up in the sky. He could see the riders now, poised with their weapons in their hands, ready to drop fire upon the city. 'Wait!'

He could hear them now, both the roar from their throats and the rush of air over their wings. They were magnificent and terrifying all at once. He saw the leading riders dropping their weapons.

'Loose!'

* * *

Kiri was behind the leading wave of dachs as they swooped down upon the city. The priestesses could sense the trajectories of the arrows unleashed against them, but the response was more co-ordinated here than they had experienced at Viresia. Riders and dachs were slain in the fierce response, but then the fire dropped.

Flame burst out in the ranks of the defenders, throwing some of them off the walls to die in the streets, burning others alive or sending them over the walls to drown in the sea. As the dachs swept inwards fire erupted in the streets and around the high towers where more archers were located. Dachs fell and riders were lost, but the defence began to become more haphazard as the fires took hold.

Kiri could see people running in the streets trying to douse the flames, but it was to little avail; the oily compound the priestesses had learnt to use burned despite their efforts. Kiri threw her own vials at one of the towers, seeing it burst into flame and disappear behind as she pulled her dach into a climb over the city.

Then she stared in surprise, her mouth dropping open.

Over the cliff tops were flying machines, huge, far bigger than the one she had pursued Meru in. They were descending towards the city. Kiri could make out people within, armed with bows.

Rihanna!

The machines were enormous, careening straight into the fight. From their flanks arrows flew, dispatching riders and dachs alike. Kiri watched in horror as arrows whistled through her own flight, slaying two of her own. She turned her dach to avoid the assault.

They fight well, as Meru said they would! We have never lost so many …

The priestesses were well trained. Rihanna signalled for them to re-establish their wings and return to the attack.

Do not attack from the sides! Attack from above if you can!

The dachs tried to climb above the flying machines, but their moves were countered as the machines rose in place, able to hover over the ground with ease. More arrows flitted through the air and more dachs fell.

The priestesses were struggling to apply their mental powers too. The twisting and turning of the attack and the defence made inflicting mental pain impossible, they were having to put all their efforts into flying and avoiding the arrows of the defenders.

They fight well, the fiercest resistance we have ever encountered …

An arrow pierced the wing of her dach. Kiri could sense the pain and felt the dach convulse beneath her thighs. She looked behind, only to see one of the smaller flying machines was pursuing her. An archer was hanging out of the side, fitting another arrow.

As she yanked her dach aside she saw the tidy formation of the dachs was now in disarray. Any pretence of order had been abandoned. The battle was joined, it was a fight of attrition now.

Below, the Taloon ships were closing on the harbour walls.

Another arrow whistled past, forcing her to concentrate on her own survival. Whoever was at the controls of the flying machine knew what they were doing, it was right on her tail, twisting and turning in the air whilst arrows snapped past too close for comfort every time she made a turn. Her dach rose into a stalled turn and then closed its wings and fell from the sky, the flying machine in close pursuit.

* * *

The smoke cleared. Ren could see the other flying machines were still hovering over the city. The largest one had been hit by the flaming weapons of the dach riders, but it seemed to be coping with the attack without much difficulty, its metal hull resistant to the flames.

The dachs were swarming them, trying to rise higher than the machines and drop their flaming weapons on them from above. Ren watched in horror was one of the medium sized machines was struck. The first attack sent fire blazing into the open interior of the machine and the second hit the windows on the front. They smashed, and flames burst into the cockpit.

Trailing smoke the ship dropped from the sky, spiralling downwards out of control to crash into the city far before, exploding and shattering into fragments.

'No ...'

A shadow passed above. Ren saw a dach before him. He twisted the flying machine around to follow. The two smaller machines were almost as nimble as the dachs, and in his hands they were evenly matched in the skies. The dach rolled and pitched, unable to shake his pursuit. He angled the machine aside for a moment, to give his two companions a chance at a shot.

One loosed an arrow. Ren saw it hit the dach in the wing.

'Got it!' he yelled.

The dach was wounded, but they hadn't finished it. Ren saw the rider look behind them and catch sight of him.

'Going to get you!'

He swung the flying machine back the other way and his second companion unleashed an arrow. It missed and he watched the dach fold its wings and drop away. He nosed the flying machine into a dive and continued the chase.

* * *

Coran lost sight of Fitch in the smoke, but ran along the lines of archers defending the walls, encouraging them to keep shooting at the dachs. Fires were burning all across the city, many were dead or dying, but the priestesses' attack, whilst devastating, had not overwhelmed them.

Above, the flying machines were giving good account of themselves, the dachs unable to assail them. Coran couldn't see much of that battle through the smoke, but the machines were still there and were keeping the dachs occupied, allowing the defenders to regroup along the walls and deal with the fires.

But now the main attack was being unleashed.

The invading ships were closing on the harbour walls. Coran could see men standing on the gunwales, armed with swords and bows.

But now they're in range of our weapons!

Coran ran up one of the sighting towers and bellowed out instructions 'Catapults!'

Along the wall ropes were pulling from the catapult restraining harnesses. In a balletic ordered sequence the catapults' stored tension was released and huge chunks of rock were hurled into the air.

Many rocks splashed down into the sea, drenching the attackers with spray, but doing no harm. A couple hit, smashing the hapless vessels into kindling and dashing their occupants into oblivion.

'Reload and release at will!'

More rocks continued to fly, striking down more vessels, but there were still hundreds coming towards the walls. The smaller faster ones were striking for the harbour entrance. The *Mobilis* was blocking their path for now, but its supply of rockets was exhausted and there was little else it could do.

Archers were turning their aim back towards the sea as the aerial battle continued above.

The invading vessels were close now, driving in using their oars, heading for the harbour entrance. Coran ran back to set more flags, but he could see Fitch on the opposite wall, gesturing to his own counterparts.

Fitch had swung the strange siphon device around and was pointing it out to sea. As Coran watched he took a flaming torch and lit the end, as did his counterpart on Coran's side.

Coran saw Fitch raise his arm and then lower it with a snap. As he did so, a flaming river of liquid sprayed out from the siphon, arcing out over the sea and engulfing the nearest vessel. The siphon near Coran did likewise, splashing hot fire over the next vessel in line. Both vessels were ablaze from stem to stern in seconds, their crews and soldiers diving out into the water.

The heat was intense, forcing Coran to stagger back. The liquid continued burning on the surface of the sea, splashing around and spreading to the other vessels queued up behind the first. Coran could see the panic on the faces of the crews. Orders were shouted and those ships still free of the flames reversed course, their oars digging hard into the water as they tried to retreat.

* * *

Nerina watched the carnage from one of the ships further back in the fleet. The aerial assault continued. One of the Amaran flying machines had been brought down to cheers from the crews around her, but then the fire had burst from the walls as the Taloon ships approached.

Cheers turned into cries of fear and trepidation and the ships slowed their progress. Those nearest the conflagration were torched in the flames, sending men screaming and diving into the sea. The waters before the city were a mass of flames and sinking wrecks.

'We cannot fight against such weapons!' Karquesh called to her. 'We lose too many!'

'Hold fast!' Nerina said. 'Do not fear the weapon of the enemy. We will soon render it of no consequence. Make ready to attack the city.'

Karquesh issued the instructions. The men around her looked subdued, but turned back to the oars at her instructions. Nerina turned her attention outwards.

Rihanna!

* * *

Kiri turned her dach in the air and then swooped downwards. The flying machine was unable to make the turn and it vanished into the swirling smoke behind her.

Rihanna's voice sounded in her head.

They have a weapon on the harbour that spits fire! The ships cannot approach!

Kiri looked down and saw it, twin jets of burning flame that had set the lead ships ablaze as they approached the harbour entrance. She circled overhead to get a sense of the machine that was spewing the fire. She could see it being turned to one side and then the other, covering an arc that stretched along the harbour walls. Dozens of ships were ablaze.

I will destroy it!

She pushed her dach into a steep dive.

* * *

The dach was swooping lower and lower, it turned to avoid the spires jutting from the city. Ren tried to turn with it but realised he couldn't without endangering the machine. He pulled back on the controls and forced the flying machine back up, abandoning the pursuit.

The dach spun around below him. He could see it heading towards the harbour walls.

He realised what the rider was aiming for.

'No you don't!'

The flying machine came around again, he turned it towards the harbour.

A light glinted across the sea, he squinted, trying to make it out.

It was another flying machine.

'Zoella! Meru!'

His heart hammered in his chest as he saw a dach diving towards the distant machine, approaching from above and behind.

* * *

Fitch saw the huge dach descending through the smoke, its wings folded as it dropped down towards him.

'Scorchin'...' he managed to utter, trying to bring the siphon around to aim at the approaching beast. The rider must have seen what he intended as the dach extended its wings and rose above him before descending across the harbour entrance towards the second siphon and its crew. Their attention was elsewhere, on the ships in the harbour. In horror, Fitch watched as the dach's rider dropped two of the burning vials from on high.

The rider's aim was good, fire blazed out around the mechanism, forcing its operators to run or cast themselves into the sea below. Fitch saw some men running back towards it, carrying buckets of water.

'Get back!' he yelled. 'Get back!'

It was too late. With a blast of ignition the mechanism exploded. A huge fireball erupted upwards from the harbour wall, a cloud of burning flame mushrooming upwards, throwing burning bits of debris, metal and bodies high into the air, to fall, crashing down upon the city.

* * *

Coran was nearly thrown from the harbour walls when the mechanism was consumed by the explosion. He fell back along the stone paving, his hair singed, feeling his skin rip against the rough surface. He rolled over before he came to a halt and looked up, amazed to find himself alive.

The harbour wall before him was in flames, with debris and twisted metal wreckage everywhere. Around him were bodies, some still alive, others twisted and burnt. Smoke was all about him, wafting back and forth, stinging his eyes.

Beyond the flames he could see the ships swinging about, preparing to drive back towards the walls again. He got to his feet, yelling to the guards and people about him

'To the walls! Everyone to the walls! Now comes the fight!'

* * *

Kiri braced herself as the dach crashed into the ground. She was flung from her saddle, forward over the dach's head. She curled herself into a ball to limit the impact, but still smacked down hard, rolling over and over before she stopped.

A strangled roar sounded behind her and her dach breathed its last, with a shuddering snort.

She got to her feet, grabbing her kai in one hand and a vial in the other. She stepped forward through the smoke.

Before her was a man. He was thin and bent, wearing a bizarre looking wide-brimmed hat. She could see a pointed crooked nose that protruded almost to the rim of the hat. His long coat was smoking at the tails.

He turned to regard her as she stepped towards him, a snarl curling his lips.

'Been wanting a piece of you witches …'

He snatched around the metal weapon he was carrying, pulling back a lever with a thick click. He was hoisting it to his shoulder with a practised air. Kiri could sense the muscles in his arm, his fingers tightening, the intent and direction behind his aim. She ducked aside.

A bang, something sparked against her kai and wrested it from her hands. The man advanced, reloading the weapon.

'Very pretty, but not enough, witch …'

Kiri flung out her hands, straining at the man's mind and crushing at it. He yelled, the weapon firing again. She felt an impact and fierce stinging pain in her left arm. She was spun around and flung to the floor.

She looked up, gasping with the pain. Blood was coursing down her arm, but the weapon had come close to missing, though it had ripped the skin out just below her shoulder.

The man was standing over her, the weapon pointed down at her. Kiri found herself staring into a dark barrel. Flames and smoke roared behind him, casting his face into shadow. She struggled backwards, crying out as her arm stung. He stepped after her, reloading the weapon.

'Third time's the charm,' he said and pulled the trigger.

* * *

Meru had tried to fly down towards the city, but the air was thick with flames and smoke, he could hardly see anything. Dachs swirled around them, duelling with the flying machines that hovered over the city.

'They're everywhere,' Zoella said. 'Look, there's Fitch! Put us down there.'

'I'll try to …'

A dach flashed by the windows of the flying machine. There was a horrible thump from outside and then the machine was spiralling out of control. Zoella screamed as the motion flung her against the side door, the harnesses cutting into her skin. Outside was nothing but a dizzying whirl of motion.

'We're going to crash!' Meru yelled.

For a moment they saw the harbour, the walls aflame. Meru was wrestling with the controls, trying to pull the machine out of its death dive. Dachs, fire, smoke, people running, ships …

The flying machine hit hard, its engines screaming. Zoella saw sparks and flames before the machine rolled over on its side, a deafening metallic squeal assaulting her ears.

* * *

The gun spat fire, Kiri flinched, clenching her eyes shut, but a moment later realised she was still alive. Something had gone wrong with the weapon, it was smoking at both ends.

'Snuttin'…'

She thrust out at him, gripping at his mind again. He yelled and staggered backwards, trying to shield himself with his hands. Kiri rolled aside and grabbed her kai, swinging at him. He managed to block her thrusts twice with his weapon before she curled her attack, wrenched it from his hands and sent it spinning away.

A thudding impact sounded nearby, accompanied by a horrific screeching noise. Kiri turned to see one of the flying machines had crashed behind her, its metal shell crunching as it rolled on to its side, sliding towards her. It cannoned into the carcass of the dach and came to a halt.

Kiri took her chance, she uncorked the last vial she was carrying and hurled it at the mechanism beyond.

* * *

Zoella couldn't see through the spidered glass of the windscreen, but something was moving outside. She was pinned at an awkward angle in the seat, the harness still holding her in place, with the machine on its side. She battered at the harness and it came free. She caught herself by one hand and braced her foot against the dashboard of the flying machine. She looked around inside.

'Meru!'

He was lying below her slumped in the pilot's chair, blood running from his forehead. She could hear faint movement from behind, cries and moans.

'Ira?'

Flames flickered outside. She tried to open the doorway above her, but it wouldn't move. She pushed at it as hard as she could but only managed to cut and bruise her hands. Ira appeared beside her. She appeared unhurt and joined her in trying to open the door. Even together they couldn't manage it. It opened a hand's width and then jammed. Smoke was filling the interior. They coughed, still struggling together.

* * *

Ren watched in horror as the dach lost control and crashed into Zoella's flying machine. The dach, stunned, fell like a stone and dropped into the sea beyond the harbour wall. The flying machine, damaged by the impact, spun out of control and landed hard on the wall itself, rolling on to its side, sparks streaming in its wake.

It fetched up against the body of the dach he'd been pursuing, it had been shot down as it had attacked Fitch's own weapons.

Ren circled for a moment, seeing no one emerge from the downed machine.

'Zoella!' He turned to his companions in the rear. 'We go to help her!'

He dropped the machine down, landing it to the rear of the other machine. He ran out, clambering over the wreckage of the other.

'Zoella? Zoella!'

He could see her through the glass. She was with someone else he didn't recognise, but both were trapped inside, the door was buckled. He stood up, yanking at the twisted metal, trying to lever it up. With a groaning creak it bent back and Zoella was able to clamber out.

'Ren!' she said, pulling him into a hug. 'What are you doing here?'

'Flying!' he said, pointing back to the other machine. Dachs screeched overhead. Ren helped the other woman out, staring at her white hair and pink eyes.

'Like me …' he said.

'No time,' Zoella said. 'There are others inside. Meru too. He's hurt, I couldn't get to him …'

They were interrupted by a huge explosion. Flame burst up into air, debris showered about them and a hot wind almost blew them off the top of the wreckage. They all turned to see that Fitch's contraption had been blown to pieces. Bits of hot metal and flaming debris clattered down around them.

Ren looked up to see two figures silhouetted against the flames.

Before Zoella could stop him, Ren had launched himself from the broken door and was running towards the figures, a knife in his hand.

* * *

Fitch staggered to his feet, batting at his clothing, it was singed, aflame in places, even his hat was smoking. The wretched witch had succeeded in her aim, the siphon was destroyed; a burning inferno behind him.

He'd seen her throw the vial and thrown himself at the ground before it went off. The rifle wasn't far away. He grabbed it, wrestling with it, cursing the third cylinder for mis-firing. He pulled it out, snapping another in its place.

Not gonna save you this time, witch.

The woman had been thrown back by the blast, not anticipating how powerful it would be. She was crawling to her feet, grabbing the staff she carried.

She looked up as he raised the gun, stretching her arms out towards him.

A headache pulsed across his temple, burning and stinging. He grunted, pulling the trigger. The rifle fired.

She was running towards him. He just had presence of mind to raise the rifle to stop the swinging blow of her staff. Twice more he parried, backing away. Then a blow hit his wrist with a sharp crack. Pain lanced up his arm and the rifle fell from his grasp.

He yelled, but before he took another step another blow caught him in the shin, knocking him to his knees. A kick pushed him over on to his back.

The witch was before him, holding her staff ready.

'Well fought,' she said.

Fitch looked at her fierce expression and gave a brief nod.

* * *

Rihanna landed her dach at the rear of Nerina's ship.

The defences are down, the flying machines overwhelmed. We can attack the city now.

Nerina nodded, but then she frowned.

She could sense pain, a power and a struggle ahead of her. She squinted through the smoke.

Kiri is in danger. We must go to her. Fly me!

'Karquesh!' she called. 'Now is the time. Lead the attack on the city. We will deal with what little of the defence is left.'

Karquesh nodded, signalling to his men. The ship turned and began heading towards the walls.

Nerina ran back to the dach. Rihanna hoisted her aboard. The dach took off with a mighty down stroke of its huge wings, lunging towards the harbour walls.

Around it the ships of Taloon were now advancing on the stricken city, the soldiers climbing the walls.

Victory will be soon, in more ways than one.

* * *

Karquesh's flagship was rowed in between the flaming piers of the harbour, his men shooting arrows at the failing ranks of defenders. Behind, more ships were following, all surging into the breakwater. Victory was at hand.

'Sire!'

Karquesh turned to see the mysterious metal ship ahead of them. It was alone, its strange sails crackling with flickering blue discharges like lightning.

It was turning.

With shocking abruptness Karquesh saw the ship lurch, its stern digging down into the water, its prow riding high over the waves. A long metal beam jutted from the bow.

Karquesh stared in horror, unable to utter anything as the massive vessel bore down on his ship. He heard the yells of fright all about him, but he was rooted to the spot.

Wood splintered and smashed about him. He was thrown backwards.

Water, blackness.

* * *

The guards and people of Amar had put up a brave fight. Along the harbour walls the ships of Taloon had made themselves fast, soldiers were pouring over them, charging along them and into the city. Coran found himself forced back in the crush, battling forward and backwards with the push of those around him. It was a dirty fight, sword against sword in places, sword against spades and shovels in others.

Above him the dachs were swarming, it seemed the aerial defence had been broken down under overwhelming numbers. Coran had lost sight of them and of Fitch too, but he'd seen the second siphon destroyed. More ships were coming in.

We're losing, despite all we tried, we've failed …

He struck at one of the Taloon soldiers, his sword grating through bones and into flesh. Yells and shouts were all around him, yet still they were pushed back. The walls were lost, overwhelmed now by the soldiers. More ships remained at sea, closing in.

Coran caught sight of the harbour.

There lay the *Mobilis*. He could see it was coming about as the Taloon warships rowed their way into the harbour led by what seemed to be their flagship. He could see the wake churning at the back of the ship and, in a moment, knew what Mel had planned.

Against so many …

The *Mobilis* rushed forwards, smashing the flagship into kindling, riding over it and smashing through a second and a third vessel.

But her speed ebbed with each onslaught. The prow of the *Mobilis* stuck fast in the fourth ship and held there. Coran saw the *Mobilis* try to reverse, but it was too late. Soldiers from the ship jumped on to the deck plates of the *Mobilis*, surging towards the wheelhouse.

More bows and shouts. Coran was borne down to the ground as the press of the fight pushed onwards. He could see nothing but arms and legs, struggling, punching and kicking.

* * *

It should be merciful, quick and accurate. The man was gasping, lying before her, helpless.

He deserves as much.

She raised her kai to strike a killing blow.

There was smattering of footsteps from behind her.

'No!'

Kiri turned, only to find agony burning up her right thigh. She yelled and looked down in shock to see a knife stabbed into it. She fell to the ground as the knife was pulled out. She saw it flash above before it slashed down at her.

'Die witch!'

A boy!

'Ren, no!' someone screamed from behind her.

The boy jabbed the knife down at Kiri. Kiri managed to grab it and stop herself having her throat slit. The boy stabbed down at her again, she caught his wrist, her fingers crushing into his skin, trying to loosen his grasp, but he was stronger than he looked. The knife turned towards her, his weight pressing down. He jammed his knee into her wounded thigh causing her to scream in pain. The knife came down point towards her throat. She struggled to stop it.

She threw her weight to one side, rolling on top of the struggling boy. She lost sight of the knife, crushed somewhere between them as they rolled and struggled.

She managed to catch him beneath her, trying to free the knife so she could throw it away. She felt his wrist snap back in her grip.

He gasped, his hold going slack in her hands. He was staring at her, a thin rivulet of blood dripping from his mouth. He choked.

Voices and visions assaulted her. Words, screams, images.

Like Tia, so sudden, so shocking, blood, always blood, blood everywhere!

A vision of Tia's voice flooded her mind. Her childhood friend, impaled on a sword, slipping to the floor, her eyes staring at nothing …

The boy struggled for a moment and then lay still beneath her. A bloodcurdling shriek filled her ears. She staggered up, her hands slick with blood … but it wasn't hers. The boy was small, a child, not even a teenager …

She couldn't focus. Her vision was blurred, her tears blinded with tears.

A child ... like Tia ...

The scream came again and then a furious pain lashed through her head. Kiri reeled back, falling to the floor. She felt the impact with the ground, but it was nothing compared to the fire in her mind.

Anger, resentment, and immolating fury surged around her, white hot.

Killer! Murderer!

Kiri recognised Zoella's hate-filled familiarity in her mind. Fragmented images of the boy being cuddled, being hugged, a cheeky smile and an infectious laugh scattered through her mind, followed by another dizzying mental blow. Kiri screamed and twisted on the ground, trying desperately to crawl away.

You killed him! You killed him!

Kiri could not frame a thought. She tried to hold up a hand to defend herself against the barrage, but the onslaught remained ferocious, fuelled by grief and heartbreak.

She sensed Zoella's own murderous intent, to crush her mind, to destroy her consciousness. She felt her powers weaken as Zoella's own gift pummelled into her. Around them the nexion fizzed and crackled, both subsumed by the strange influence. Kiri could taste metal in her mouth mixed with the hot taste of blood.

You will not escape this time!

It was the last thing she heard. Zoella's relentless attack overwhelmed her. The pain and regret in her mind cascaded inwards. Blackness closed around the edges of her vision and she collapsed to the floor, senseless and prone.

* * *

Zoella screamed and raged, striking out again and again. Kiri fell before her, Zoella sensed her mind and body crumble under her onslaught. She clenched her fists, ready to administer the final blow, to strike down her hated sister, once and for all.

Rage and grief consumed her. Kiri had killed again. Ren.

No mercy!

She struck, using the same mental technique she'd learned in the high pass of the frozen wastes to crush a mind. She pummelled down on Kiri's unconscious mind, aiming to mash it out of existence.

But her mental blow was turned aside.

A dach dropped out of the swirling smoke. She heard Ira scream from alongside her. Two figures dropped down before her, arms outstretched.

Who are you, girl?

The first figure was dressed all in black, only her hair showed a narrow streak of silver. Zoella recognised her. Nerina, the high priestess herself, she who had launched the attack on Viresia. By her side was another priestess she had seen before, with distinctive blood-red hair.

Those that came with Kiri at Viresia!

In her wrath, Zoella struck out at both of them, but her blasts of mental fury were blocked by an imperious gesture from the high priestess.

So. You are the maid, the maid from Viresia!

She could sense what they wanted. They were here to steal what gifts they could; rich pickings from the devastation all about.

An image of the flying machine burst into her mind and she was grabbed from behind.

It was Fitch.

Zoella was yanked backwards.

'Ren …'

Another yank. She was running, Fitch was pulling her away, past the downed dach, past the wreckage of the flying machine and towards the other one. Zoella could see Ira and the children clustered around it, Meru's unconscious body hauled between them.

A single thought entered her head.

I can save them …

A mad scramble had them aboard the second machine. Zoella tried to remember what Meru had done to make the machine fly as she strapped herself into place.

'Sandra,' she yelled. 'Start launch procedure!'

A blast of mental pain shattered her thoughts. She reeled, feeling the priestesses' thoughts nearby. She looked up to see them before the flying machine, arms outstretched. Next to her, Ira had her own arm outstretched, wrestling with them. The engines of the flying machine whirled into life.

The pain in Zoella's head lessened. She yanked on the controls and the flying machine lurched into the air, rolled and bucked before making headway, turning inland and across the city.

* * *

Kiri was barely conscious. The pain in her head was gone, but she could feel her body trembling with the aftershock. Her body convulsed with the hurt of her other wounds.

She opened her eyes. She could see the stone paving of the harbour wall before her, flames still rising in the distance, smoke wafting across her. Of Zoella and the others there was no sign. She frowned in confusion.

Footsteps echoed somewhere close by, heels clicking on the stone.

'Just in time it would seem,' said a voice.

Kiri moaned, trying to crawl to her knees. The voice was Nerina's.

She managed to look up. Nerina was standing before her, with arms folded, looking down at her with an unreadable expression on her face.

'Nerina,' she croaked.

Nerina knelt down, extending her hand towards Kiri. Kiri moved to take it.

Nerina swept it out of the way and dealt Kiri a fierce blow across the face. Kiri yelped and fell back to the ground.

'You stole the queen's power,' Nerina snarled. 'You set the Scallian girl free against my wishes ...'

Kiri's eyes widened as she remembered Gemma. She'd left her in the mountains on the borders.

What happened to her?

'Yes,' Nerina said, seeing the look on her face. 'Her name was Gemma. You didn't succeed. She's dead.'

Kiri gasped. 'No ... but ...'

'Then you hid the maid's power from me,' Nerina continued. 'Lie upon lie, upon lie.'

Kiri gritted her teeth against the pain. Her leg was agony, her face stinging and her arm hung useless. Blood loss was sapping her strength.

'And then you plotted to overthrow me,' Nerina said, her voice twisting into a laugh. 'Thinking that you would be high priestess in my stead. But I had the measure of you long before you even began your rebellious thoughts, young one. All this while you have been doing my bidding, not your own.'

Kiri was shaking her head, trying to clear it.

'You grew arrogant and cocky,' Nerina said. 'Such traits have their use, but now it is time for you to fulfil the purpose I spared you for. I didn't save you because of Charis, I saved you for me.'

Kiri saw Rihanna step out from behind Nerina, her hands raised. Hope flared in Kiri's mind.

Together ...

Now Rihanna, now!

Kiri somehow staggered to her feet, thrusting outwards with the fading reserves of her mental strength. She looked over to Rihanna. The girl stepped forward, her own hands raised towards ...

... her.

She found her arms wrenched down to her sides. Her legs gave way and she fell to her knees, shock and betrayal burning in her heart. Fresh agony burnt up through her.

Nerina smiled down at her.

'Oh, such naivety is touching to behold,' Nerina said, her voice mocking. 'Rihanna was never your friend, Kiri. She's been my servant throughout it all.'

Kiri looked at Rihanna, hope dying as Rihanna's face twisted into a hate-filled sneer.

'Yes guttersnipe,' Rihanna spat the words. 'You were right, you have been fattened for the harvest. Yes, I told Nerina everything you told me … and the Scallian girl is dead because of me. You should have torn her yourself, she might still be alive now.'

'No …' Kiri said, despair and anger burning through the last of her strength, she slumped forward on to her hands and knees.

Nerina grabbed her by the chin, pulling her head around. Kiri looked up into her cold, dark eyes. Behind her she could see the soldiers of Taloon climbing the walls of the city, it seemed the battle was lost for the Amarans.

Nerina caught her look.

'Yes, our victory is at hand,' she said. 'My victory, not yours.'

Kiri struggled in vain. She grabbed at Nerina's arms, but she couldn't break her hold.

'And now, at last, I will take your gift,' Nerina said. 'Oh … but don't you worry, you will serve the priestesses well for the rest of your life. Merrin has need of a scullery maid, a wench … or a whipping girl.'

Nerina's fingers probed around Kiri's face, strengthening their hold. Kiri could already feel the numbing sensation that preceded the tearing. Nerina was too strong, there was no way she could resist.

Her mind screamed out as she felt her powers about to drain away.

* * *

But there was another power, indifferent and unconcerned with the petty squabbles taking place far below it. Far beyond the boundaries of what the priestesses, the Amarans or the soldiers of Taloon could comprehend, primal forces were stirring once again. Indefatigable, irresistible, it glowered down upon those assembled below. Some thought it a force of nature, others a vengeful goddess. Regardless of what it was, it made its influence felt, awesome in its unleashed fury.

Above the battle, Lacaille blazed in the sky. Not even the ancient settlers of Esurio had fully mapped its moods and behaviours. It had unseated them long ago with its mercurial temperament, bringing their age of machines and technology crashing down about them.

No darkness warned of the wrath to come this time. Lacaille had her own store of woes and sorrows to inflict upon Esurio.

With shocking abruptness Lacaille's fury was unleashed.

* * *

Coran saw it coming. The blue tinge in the sky; the sudden whiteness of the light.

He'd forced his way back to his feet in the press of people.

'Flares!' he yelled. 'Flares!'

Others about him, those of Taloon and Amar alike had noticed the abrupt change in the sky. A blast of heat rippled across them. In horror Coran saw a wave of fire rippling across the horizon out to sea beyond the harbour. As he watched, it raced towards them, the wooden ships consumed like the paper boats that the children of the city made to sail in the ponds. They flashed into fire and smoke.

'Take cover!' he yelled.

There was a wild scramble all about him. Folks pushing and shoving to get indoors. Struggling he was borne by the crowd inside, animosities forgotten in the desperate panic to escape the wrath from above.

* * *

A burning wall of heat swept across the harbour walls. Kiri saw the sky go white, tinged with a fierce blue, actinic light. She remembered it from the mountains of Drem.

She heard screams and yells.

Nerina and Rihanna turned to see the cause of the commotion.

In that moment, Kiri pushed out all her remaining strength,

grasping at their minds in fury. The blow overpowered them, breaking their grip.

No! You won't have me.

Kiri staggered up, tottered backwards to the edge of the harbour wall. Nerina and Rihanna scrambled to reach her.

Kiri!

Kiri shook her head, then raised her arms and stepped back.

She let herself fall into the churning waters of the harbour. She saw white fire, blue streams of writhing colour, then a shocking cold and darkness.

Nerina and Rihanna ran to the edge, looking over it. There was a splash of white churned water bubbling back to the surface, but nothing else.

Kiri was gone.

Epilogue

Round 2307, Seventh pass

Smoke rose from the city of Amaris. Buildings were blackened and burnt, some smashed down by fire, others by the impact of dachs or the flying machines as they fell from the aerial battle that had taken place overhead. Around the harbour lay smouldering wrecks in the shallow water, and further out to sea was drifting flotsam from the vessels. Of the dachs that had been airborne as the flare struck there was no sign, none had seen what fate had overtaken them.

Hundreds were dead, their bodies immolated in the streets as the fire had blasted down from above. Few Taloon soldiers had survived, and many of those were killed in retribution before the guards could restore order. Those that survived were locked away.

The *Mobilis* lay beached in the harbour, its prow dented and the hull burnt and blackened.

Coran ran to the ship, jumping on to the tarnished decks. The burnt remains, scattered planks and rigging from the vessels it had rammed lay all across it, tangled in the forward mast, which was bent at a cockeyed angle. It was listing in the water, rolling to starboard.

Through the smoke he could make out a figure. He staggered forward, waving smoke out of his eyes. The figure straightened, having pulled back the hatch at the rear of the ship, just above the engine bays.

More figures. Shapes he recognised.

'Daf, Creg … Mel!'

The two men were hauling the battered engineer up between them. She was cursing at them.

'I'll be all right, had worse burns than this.'

Coran stepped through the smoke and then ran to them, clapping the burly men on the back and pulling Mel into a bear hug.

'You're alive,' he managed to say.

'Yeah, just,' Mel replied. He could see she was covered in grime, soot and grease. 'Thought we'd bought it at the end there.' She caught sight of the ship as the smoke blew aside. 'The *Mobilis* ... the ship ... my beautiful ship!'

'Damn the snuttin' ship,' he said. 'We're alive!'

'Did we win?' Mel asked, holding on to him for support.

'Hard to say.'

Reunited, they started searching the city for survivors as teams of workers began clearing rubble and dousing the remaining fires.

Two of the flying machines remained. The big equipment transport, though burnt and blackened, had proved indefatigable in the face of the dachs' attack. One of the mid-sized personnel transports had survived as well. The other two had crashed in ruins on the city. Of the smaller flying machines, one could be seen wrecked upon the harbour wall, the other two remained unfound.

The medical transport, unused in the fight, now came into its own, the remarkable technology aboard healing those with the worst injuries.

Coran and Mel were triaging the wounded when a whirring came from overhead. One of the small flying machines descended into the senate square alongside the medical transport. Dust whirled about them as the machine settled down. It was battered and dented, its exterior caked in dirt and streaked with scorch marks.

Coran looked at Mel.

'Ren?'

The doors opened.

Zoella stepped out. Behind her was Fitch, his hat burnt and frayed. From the opposite side of the machine another figure stepped forward. Coran squinted, seeing another woman, her hair bright white in the warm light of Lacaille.

Mel ran to Zoella, grabbing her and pulling her into a hug.

'Zoella!' she gasped. 'Are you all right? What happened? Where is Meru? Who is ...?'

Zoella didn't return her hug. Mel drew back, looking at her. Zoella looked shocked, her gaze distant and unseeing.

'Zoella?'

'Meru's alive,' she whispered. 'He's only a little hurt ... Ren ...'

Her expression was angry. Mel grasped her, her own eyes wet with tears.

'Oh no ...' she said.

'You said you would keep him safe,' Zoella said. Her gaze was locked on Mel, but she was pushing her away. 'I trusted you ...'

Mel swallowed. 'Zoella, we ...'

'On the harbour wall,' Zoella sobbed, her voice breaking. 'Why was he there? Why ...? You let her kill him!'

Coran came up behind them both, to put his arms around them. Zoella pushed past him, ignoring them both, striding away.

* * *

Ren's body was found on the harbour wall. With great reverence it was taken down, covered in fine linen and then laid to rest in the custom of the people of Amar. He was accorded a special place in the senate halls, lying amidst worthy figures in the history of the city.

Coran was called on to mark his passing with a eulogy.

He stepped forward, his head bowed. Mel was at his side, Zoella standing away from both of them. Meru was still unconscious, in the care of the mechanisms aboard the medical transport.

'Ren. I didn't know him well. Just a kid ...' Coran stopped for a moment, his voice catching on the words. 'But maybe the bravest soul I've encountered on my travels. He didn't let his age stop him from doing what needed to be done. He fought ...' Coran's own voice cracked, but he struggled on. 'He fought with the same determination shown by the mightiest of us. This wasn't his homeland, but he defended it as if it were.

He gave his life for this city, for Amar. I'm proud of him, and we'll never forget his sacrifice.'

There was a mumble of approval around the senate hall.

'To Ren,' Coran said.

His words were repeated by those present. All except Zoella. She stood stock still, staring at the linen draped over Ren's body. There were no tears.

Folk around them were leaving, giving the crew of the *Mobilis* time to themselves. They stood there for a long time, lost in their thoughts. Daf, Creg, Fitch, Coran, Mel and Zoella.

Fitch gave a nod and walked away, followed by Daf and Creg. Coran went to touch Zoella, to give her a reassuring clasp around the shoulders, but she shrugged him off, stepping away.

Coran watched her. He could see she was trembling, her lip curled and her teeth clenched.

'She's not in a good place,' Mel whispered. 'No grieving, just anger.'

Coran nodded. 'She won't talk to any of us. What do we do?'

Mel guided him outside and out of earshot, leaving Zoella within the hall.

'I don't think there is much we can do,' Mel said. 'She's blaming us … blaming me … for putting Ren in harm's way. If I hadn't persuaded you to let him fight …'

'The boy wanted to do his part,' Coran said. 'And he did, he may have saved us all.'

Mel's face was streaked with tears. Coran pulled her into an embrace.

'It's not your fault.'

'If I hadn't said what I said, he might still be alive …' Mel said, her voice choked.

Fitch wasn't far away. He looked over at them, peering out from under his hat.

'He made his choice,' Fitch said. 'We all did. And I almost had her too.'

'Who?' Mel asked, looking up.

'The witch girl,' Fitch said. 'Had her on the floor and almost blew her away. Snuttin' rifle jammed on me. She scorchin' near killed me; she'd beaten me down on the ground. It was Ren who saved me. He distracted her, stabbed her right in the leg.' He grinned. 'How she howled.'

Coran looked at him. 'The witch girl?'

Fitch nodded. 'Yeah, vicious little bitch. Knew how to fight though, wielded her staff with a fury, not going to forget that in a hurry. That and her black glove.'

Coran swallowed. 'Black glove ... on her left hand?'

Fitch frowned. 'Er ... yeah ... why? Is that important?'

'It was Kiri,' Coran said, looking at Mel. 'Kiri killed Ren.'

Mel nodded. 'That's what Zoella meant ... something in her eyes, the hate ...'

There were shouts from outside, from the road that led down to the harbour. As they emerged from the hall they could see a crowd of people down at one of the quays.

'What's going on?' Coran demanded.

'No, it can't be!'

Coran and Mel turned to see Zoella standing behind them. There was a fierce expression on her face. Her mouth was set firm, her lips a thin line.

Before they could stop her she pushed off through the crowd.

* * *

The sound was the first thing she sensed. Chants, jeers, cries of anger and frustration all about her. Then came a lurching sense of motion, her body not under her control, but being pulled and pushed back and forth. Pain in her arms and legs.

She was being dragged.

She opened her eyes, her vision was blurred, but she could make out a shoreline, ships, a harbour ... and a crowd of people. Her arms were above her head. She craned her neck to see both her hands were in the grasp of someone else and she was being pulled, her legs dragging along the rough ground. She twisted and yelled out.

Her cry brought an answering shout of surprise.

'She's alive! The scorchin' witch is alive!'

She was hoist upright and stood, swaying on her feet, her vision blurry, facing her captors. All around her the crowd was growing, pushing closer, every face full of anger and the intention of violence. She could feel water running from her body, the warmth of Lacaille upon her skin.

I must have washed up on the shore ... in Amar ... Nerina and Rihanna tried to tear me ...

'Witch!' someone shouted. The chant was taken up. She could feel their murderous fury. She steadied herself, holding her hands up and striking out at the owner of the voice, seeking their mind and applying pressure. With a screech someone behind her fell.

'Witch!'

She whirled around, her arms raised. She sensed another person grabbing at something, all about her hands were clenching. She felt fear and terror.

As it should be!

'Witch!'

She sought out another, crunching into their mind as they raised their hands.

But there were too many.

Something struck her in the temple. She was thrown to the ground, her vision reddening with blood from her forehead, her head ringing with the impact. Dazed, she tried to get up, but she staggered and fell back to the ground, too dizzy to stand.

Then came the blows. She fended off one, but another caught her in the chest, another in the side. She felt her body spin and sprawl across the ground, feeling the dirt grind into her skin. Someone stamped on her outstretched hand sending fresh paroxysms of agony crashing into her.

'Witch! Witch!'

A hand gripped her hair and yanked her up. Another blow struck her full in the face, another in the stomach. She collapsed, only to be yanked up again. She was winded, wheezing and gasping for breath, her vision a jumbled whirl of colours tunnelling into blackness at the edges.

Numbly now, she felt her hands stretched out before her, felt a rope bound around her wrists. She was jolted forward, staggering to keep upright as she was hauled along.

She could barely see. They had roped her to the back of a cart. Hergs were pulling it, hauling her along a road, leading away from the harbour and up into the city. More projectiles struck her. She caught a whiff of rotting vegetables. Faces loomed close, she felt their spit upon her face.

Something struck the back of her legs, she lost her footing and yelped in pain as she was dragged along the ground by her wrists, still secured to the cart. She felt her clothing rip and tear, and then more pain from her legs and side as her body was scoured over the rough paving.

The motion stopped. More commotion, more yells. They were dull in her hearing now. Somehow this seemed familiar. Visions flickered in her mind.

I am here, Kiri.

A girl, a young girl, with bright eyes and an innocent face.

Tia? You can't be here ... you're in the after ... so long ago ... it must be my time ... my time to join you ...

The rope around her wrists went slack. She fell to the ground and lay there, immobile, still gasping. Someone was arguing, she couldn't hear. Her vision was tunnelling in about her.

I will be with you soon, Tia. We'll be in the after together, there will be no more pain there ...

'Kill the witch! Kill the witch!'

Another blow was coming, she was sure of it. She could sense fingers tightening around a club. The blow would crush her skull. It would be the end of her.

More voices, more shouts. She blinked, trying to clear her vision. The crowd was backing away. She couldn't move, every breath sent shooting pains through her midriff, she could taste blood.

'Bind her eyes first, she's dangerous! Then kill her.'

A woman's voice. She recognised it. It was accompanied by a sense of white hot wrath and anger.

Zoella!

She felt her head lifted up and a swath of material was wrapped about it, cutting off her fading vision.

Murderer!

Kiri could not form words to retort.

Another voice. A scuffle.

'Back off! Put those down! We will deal with her. She will be brought to justice, but not like this.'

This time, it was another woman's voice, gruff and sharp. It was a voice used to being obeyed.

Kiri could still hear the rumblings of discontent, but she could sense the crowd was backing away. A man's voice reinforced the message.

'Go back to your duties townspeople. We have won a victory. This woman will stand trial for her crimes, do not fear!'

A moment later the woman's voice was close by her ear.

'Shards,' it said. 'She's been ripped to shreds.'

Kiri felt a finger on her neck.

'She's still alive,' the voice continued. 'Looks like we got to her just in time.'

Kiri felt herself hoisted up none too gently. She yelped as something grated in her chest, the renewed pain was too much for her body to bear. Consciousness slipped away and blackness claimed all her senses.

* * *

The Scattered Isles were many marks sunward and shaderight of the island of Amar. For the most part they were barren and inhospitable, but they were the only land between Amar and the continent.

Brief stretches before they had served as a staging point and waymarker for the mighty fleet of Taloon, now barely a dozen vessels remained and those were burnt and scorched. Above, festooning the cliffs and outcroppings, hung huge reptilian creatures; the dachs of the priestesses. They too were vastly reduced in numbers. Many were injured, either from the aerial battle above Amar, or from the ignominious retreat before the wrath of Lacaille blazing from above.

Higher still, on the exposed tops of the isles, the priestesses had gathered to tend their own wounded.

Rihanna had organised the efforts as best she could. She had made impossible choices, choosing between those who might live and those whose passing could only be eased. Less than half of the priestesses who had set out from Taloon remained and many of them would likely not survive the next stretch.

And then there was the decimation of the soldiers of Taloon. The lives of men might be of little concern, but Rihanna had never before seen such death and destruction as when the fleet of ships was consumed by the flare. Only the tiniest fraction had been spared.

Amar. We overreached ourselves. We underestimated them. Nerina's obsession with Kiri ... we even lost her, drowned! Nerina's folly has brought us to this.

The high priestess stood on the cliff top, facing away from the carnage, staring out to sea.

Nerina's eyes closed.

Merrin!

It was several moments before she received an answer.

High priestess? I did not expect to hear from you so soon ...

The battle did not go well.

Another significant pause.

But, the might of Taloon and our own people combined, surely ...

We were poised on the edge of victory, but Lacaille dashed our chances. A flare scorched our hopes, the fleet destroyed, our priestesses cut down. We have retreated. Many are hurt.

Nerina could feel the shock and dismay echoing back to her.

What can I do?

Send forces into Airea. Their King is dead, slain in the attack. There will be unrest, we will subdue it before it starts. Taloon is ours now.

I shall arrange it immediately. What of …?

Nerina allowed a little feeling to seep into the mental connection.

Rihanna survived, she acquitted herself well. She will lead our priestesses home.

That is good to hear. And …?

Now there was satisfaction.

Kiri was weakened, broken. I tore her … almost. I took much of her power.

She lives?

No. She fell from the harbour wall. She is dead, drowned. But she knew her place before the end.

Now a sense of gratification flowed in both directions.

So, the guttersnipe is no more and her power is yours. Amar is merely a setback, high priestess. Return home, we will regroup, subdue all the lands as we have planned. The exiles may be cunning, but we will find another way to deal with them.

Nerina nodded, smiling to herself.

We shall.

The mental link faded, leaving Nerina to stand alone once more at the clifftop.

I shall return, and there will be retribution for all our losses. I am Empress of Esurio, none will dare defy me!

* * *

'She's alive,' Zoella said. 'She'll live, she'll heal … more's the pity.'

Mel looked around at her. 'Zoella … they almost tore her to pieces. Her wounds. She's half dead.'

'She should be dead,' Zoella replied, her gaze firm and her eyes cold. 'You should have let them kill her.'

The remaining crew of the *Mobilis* stood in the council hall. Daf and

Creg stood at the entrance, as taciturn as ever. Mel and Zoella were facing off against each other. Coran had intervened. Fitch was watching the proceedings, interjecting as he saw fit.

'This is definitely her, the priestess woman Meru spoke of?' Coran asked. 'The one that …'

Zoella nodded. 'Kiri. She killed …' Her voice shook and she glared at Mel. 'She killed Ren.'

Mel's jaw tightened.

'So what are we going to do with her?' Fitch asked. 'She's our enemy after all. She tried to kill me. I almost blew her away with a rifle. If the snuttin' thing hadn't mis-fired …'

'She needs to die,' Zoella said.

'We can't just kill her now,' Mel protested.

'Then pretend she died in the fight,' Zoella countered.

Coran bit his lip. 'It might have been better if she had been killed outright; drowned, or shot.'

Zoella nodded. 'All the time she's alive, she's dangerous. If there are other priestesses nearby she will be able to talk to them. Spy on us, let them know …'

'Nothing stopping us from sticking an axe in her right now,' Fitch said. He was leaning against the wall, his arm in a sling.

'You can't just murder her in cold blood,' Mel said. 'It's wrong. She's our prisoner now.'

'She killed Ren,' Zoella snarled, not taking her eyes off Mel.

'Many are dead because of her …' Coran replied, swinging around. 'All the death and destruction. She attacked us, all that fanaticism! I'm half tempted to kill her myself …'

'You couldn't,' Zoella replied, her voice sharp. 'She'd sense what you intended the moment you got close. She'd crush your mind … just like that.'

'You could do it,' Fitch said, looking at Zoella. 'You could end her.'

'Fitch, no …' Mel said. Coran and Fitch exchanged a look.

Zoella nodded. 'I could,' she said, her fists clenching. 'Perhaps I should.'

'I tend to agree,' Coran said, his voice dropping to a whisper. 'She kills anyone who gets in her way. She's hurt, she may never be weaker. We could end this now. Now is the time, send a message back to those priestesses …'

'Yeah,' Fitch said. 'We've made mistakes before now. Let's not make another one. Best to be rid of her, I say.'

'Amar has no death penalty,' Mel countered. 'It would be murder by our laws! Is that what we're sinking to?'

'No one is going to care,' Fitch said. 'The crowd almost did away with her. She would have died of her wounds if we hadn't treated her, and that's more than she deserves! Look at our city. We've got to do what's right, laws be scorched. If she lives, then what? We can't let her go, can we?'

'If we abandon what we believe because it's convenient …'

'She's a killer,' Zoella shouted. 'What about vengeance for Ren?' She glared at Mel. 'Or have you forgotten him?'

'I haven't forgotten,' Mel said, her voice calm. 'But we can't just kill her. She must stand trial for her crimes. We can't sink to the level of the priestesses, we're Amarans. We have laws, civilisation. That's what makes us better than them. That's what we fought for, isn't it? Is it so easy to give that up?'

Coran made to protest, but then stopped. He shrugged and raised his hands before clenching them. Then he lowered his head into them and rubbed at his brow.

'And what about Meru?' Mel added. 'Doesn't he have a say?'

'Meru forfeited his say,' Zoella snapped. 'He betrayed us to her. He slept with her! He's entranced by her; she uses him like a puppet. If you want him back she needs to die.'

'Does he love her?' Mel asked.

'Just lust,' Zoella replied, her voice rising. 'She has him bewitched. I know how powerful she is and what she can do. She's a murderer and a liar. She's evil!'

Coran and Mel exchanged a glance as Zoella finished her tirade.

'How do you know all this?' Coran asked. 'What happened out there?'

'There's no time to tell you it all,' Zoella said. 'We met her in Taloon, Meru and I.'

'Taloon?' Coran asked. 'But you were heading to the Obelisk …'

'We never got to the Obelisk,' Zoella cried. 'She got her claws into him. He betrayed us to her, told her our secrets, led her to me. She tried to steal my powers, but Ira and the others stopped her. She tried to turn me to her side. She's …' Zoella's lip curled in distaste. 'We share the same mother.'

Mel's mouth fell open.

'She's your sister?' she asked. 'How can that be?'

'We were separated at birth,' Zoella replied. 'Some scheme of the man who hid us, the man we found in Nireus, Guerren. That's why our powers are so similar. They are the same.'

'Two sides of a coin,' Coran whispered. 'One light, one dark.'

'So I know exactly what she is,' Zoella said, her eyes pleading. 'And that's why she has to be killed, otherwise this will never stop and more people will die. Don't you understand? She's got to die!' She was crying now, the tears dripping down her cheeks.

'The girl's not wrong,' Fitch said.

Coran gave out a deep sigh, thinking it through.

'No,' he said with a heavy sigh, 'Mel's right as usual. There's too much here to think through and the grief is too recent, too raw. None of us are thinking straight right now. Meru deserves a say in her fate …'

'Don't be a fool …' Zoella cried.

'… but we lock her up and keep her bound for now. The Amaran senate should decide what's to be done. This crew,' he said, looking around at them, 'needs to deal with the Obelisk, or it's not going to make a difference either way.'

'I don't care about the Obelisk,' Zoella said, her voice flat. 'And I'm not bound by your laws. Scallian justice. She once inflicted it on my people, murdered those close to me. She's still murdering … she will keep on murdering!'

Coran straightened, his voice dropping. 'Decision made, Zoella. Mel is right. That's enough.'

'Captain's made the call,' Mel said.

Zoella was shaking her head.

'She has to die.' Zoella's voice rose into a twisted scream.

'Zoella, she's your sister!' Mel gasped.

'So?' Zoella grated out. 'She has killed or taken everything I have ever cared about. She intends to kill me. She killed Ren … dear little Ren …' Her voice cracked, but then it hardened once again. 'She killed all the others, she poisoned Meru against us. Isn't that enough? That we share a mother makes no difference. She's never going to stop. This must end now.'

Zoella stepped forward. Fitch moved away from the wall, bracing himself.

'No,' Mel said, stepping between her and the exit. 'This is wrong.'

'Take it easy, girl,' Fitch rumbled.

Zoella faced Mel. 'Out of my way.' Her voice was just above a whisper.

Mel shook her head.

'Zoella,' Coran interjected, standing alongside Mel. 'Maybe you're right, maybe Kiri deserves to die, but this isn't the way. She must be subject to our laws, otherwise … what are we fighting for? Maybe the senate will override the law, sentence her to death, but it's got to be fair, done the right way …'

'She's too dangerous,' Zoella replied. 'I'm going to kill her.'

'Not going to happen,' Mel said, her tone cool.

'Get out of my way,' Zoella's voice was colder.

'Back down, Zoella,' Coran rumbled. Fitch was also alongside Mel now, the three of them facing Zoella.

'Do as the captain says, girl,' Fitch said, his eyes narrowed. 'You might be right, but this isn't the time.'

Mel reached out for her. 'Zoella …'

Zoella screeched, gesturing with her hand, a snarl upon her face. Mel screamed in pain, clutching at her forehead, sinking to her knees. Coran tried to grab her, but Zoella struck out at him too and he yelled in pain, falling to one side. Zoella strode past them.

Fitch went to block her but she pushed him aside with another claw-handed gesture. He doubled up, sprawled against the wall with a screech.

'Daf, Creg,' Coran managed to utter. 'Stop her!'

Zoella turned around as the two burly men approached her from either side, they were both huge, dwarfing her, but she was not intimidated.

'You can't stop me,' Zoella cried. 'None of you can.'

Daf and Creg almost got close enough to grab Zoella, but she stretched out her arms towards both of them, her fingers talon-like. Both men grunted and staggered back clutching at their foreheads, felled by Zoella's power. They collapsed full length on the floor. None of them could move for the fire in their heads.

'I decide her fate,' Zoella said, turning around, her eyes flashing with anger. 'Her life is mine to take, it is owed to me. You're all cowards. I will do it!'

Then she was gone.

* * *

Meru blinked. His vision was blurred. For a moment he couldn't remember anything at all. Then visions swirled in his mind, memories, thoughts and feelings.

The flying machine. They'd been above Amar, circling down when they had collided with a dach. The machine had crashed. He could remember the impact, the cracking of glass, a jolt …

Then there was nothing.

What happened? Where am I?

He tried to sit up. His head spun with the effort, but something held him in place, some kind of restraint.

Lights flickered above him. He squinted, recognising them.

I'm on the medical ship. I must have been hurt. What happened to Amar? Did we win or lose? Where is everyone?

'Please remain still.' Meru recognised Sandra's voice. 'Restorative procedure has not yet completed.'

'I need to find out what's going on,' Meru protested. 'Sandra, cancel procedure.'

'Cancellation of restorative procedure is not recommended, please confirm.'

'Confirmed! Let me up!'

He felt the restraints unclick. A tube that had been embedded in his left wrist detached itself and snaked away.

He pulled himself upwards, still feeling dizzy and faint. He staggered to the windows of the medical transport and looked out. He could see smoke drifting upwards from the city, but there was no sign of the Taloon fleet or the priestesses.

Maybe we won ... if so, then what happened to ...

As her face came to mind, a mental thump of anguish cascaded all around him, causing him to yell out in surprise and pain. His knees give way beneath him and he collapsed to the floor, a plaintive cry of distress and despair echoing around his head.

Meru ... please ... help me!

Kiri?

She's going to ...

The mental connection stopped mid-word; there was nothing, not even an echo of the words.

Kiri? Kiri!

There was no answer. Meru staggered up and lurched outside.

* * *

Zoella made her way down to the cell where Kiri was being held. Two guards stood either side of the doorway. They stepped forward as she approached.

'Who goes ...?'

Zoella didn't even bother to acknowledge them. They were

inconsequential, a minor irritant. She clutched at their minds, their yells of pain and surprise going unnoticed. It was easy now, just a brief thought. She pulled the key from the belt of the first, turning it over in her hand.

The anger burned in her, a flame that had been long smouldering, ignited by Ren's death and now raging in her soul.

Across the room were Kiri's possessions, the tattered clothing she had been found in and the metal staff that had been found on the harbour wall.

The staff that killed Torin, Raga and Turgan! She called it a kai ...

She walked over and picked it up. She was surprised by how little it weighed. It glinted in the light that was filtering through the narrow windows high above. Zoella's grip on it was tight, her hand clenched, the knuckles showing white through her skin. It was a simple device, but Zoella had seen what could be done with it.

I know what I have to do.

She turned and moved to the cell door, unlocking it with the key, pushing the door open.

It swung inward with a creak.

The cell was empty save for a solid shadewood chair. Upon it, now dressed in a simple short gown and tied in place by ropes at her neck, wrists, waist and ankles, was Kiri. A tight blindfold was still in place around her head.

She seemed insensible; her head dropped forward, her long dark hair hanging down to her waist. Her wounds had been cleaned and bound. Zoella could see the bruising all over her body, the bloody stain on her thigh from the stab wound that Ren had inflicted. The crowd had almost finished her.

They should have been allowed to. Time enough for that now.

Zoella didn't bother to try and hide her footsteps.

Wake up!

Zoella prodded Kiri with the kai. Kiri jolted awake, gasping for breath. Her head came up, turning from one side to the other. Zoella could see the congealed blood and the ugly blue and yellow bruises across her face and neck.

Zoella reached forward and pulled the blindfold away. Kiri blinked in the brightness. Zoella saw her eyes focus and watched as her expression dropped in dismay.

'You …' Kiri whispered through parched lips. Her voice was a dry croak.

'Yes,' Zoella said, her voice a snarl, laced with hostility. 'Me. Sister. And we're alone this time.'

Zoella saw Kiri swallow.

They stared at each other for long moments. Zoella paced back and forth before her.

'We can talk,' Kiri said. 'Please. The Obelisk, only you and I can…'

With no warning Zoella swung the kai around and then brought it down as hard as she could across the fingers of Kiri's right hand, crushing them against the arms of the shadewood chair.

Kiri screamed in shock and surprise. Zoella waited, watching as the other girl writhed in pain. The blow must have broken at least one of her fingers.

Hope that hurts like fire!

Just as Kiri was recovering from it, Zoella swung the kai again, striking the same hand. Kiri's screams echoed around the cell a second time, collapsing into a stuttering helpless whimper of pain and anguish.

Zoella grabbed Kiri's chin and yanked her head up. Kiri was gasping, her eyes clenched shut against the agony.

'I am going to kill you,' Zoella whispered into her ear. 'But you're going to suffer first. You're going to understand the pain you have caused.'

Kiri's eyes opened, and Zoella felt the sting of a headache. A burning metallic taste welled up in her mouth. She could feel the bright burning orb of Kiri's gift, scalding hot before her.

No you don't!

Zoella drove her own thoughts against the flow, pushed past the resistance and turned the attack. She grasped at the power before her, luxuriating in its strength, pulling it towards her, barely conscious of Kiri's moan as she did so.

So that's how it's done. Stealing the gift of another!

Zoella felt a strange sense of elation, her powers stronger. She could feel it buzzing within her, energizing her, her body responding to the thrill. Zoella backed away, readying the kai once more.

For moments the only sound was Kiri gasping for breath. Zoella watched.

'Do you member King Ioric?' Zoella asked.

Kiri didn't answer. Her head lolled forward, her body shaking, slumped against the ropes that held her, her breathing coming in ragged gasps.

'I said do you remember?' Zoella screeched. She jabbed Kiri hard in the chest with the kai.

Kiri retched, choking, but managed to look up.

'And Torin? Remember how you tortured him? You're going to remember exactly how that felt!'

Anger washed out from Kiri, Zoella felt it bombard her.

'He deserved to die,' Kiri gasped, her teeth bared. 'He killed my mentor, he lied … about the treaty, he started … the war! We were defending what was …'

Zoella swung the kai and cracked it across Kiri's thigh where Ren had stabbed her. Kiri screamed again, jolting against the ropes, writhing against the pain.

'Lies!' Zoella shouted at her. 'Everything is a lie with you!'

'No …' Kiri was shaking her head, trying to form words.

'You killed them both, you killed Raga, my carn!'

'You set it on me …' Kiri's screeched back.

'Liar!' Zoella screeched. 'Liar, liar, liar!'

The madness cleared, a moment of lucidity.

Zoella stepped away and paced back and forth, watching Kiri, enjoying her torment. Kiri's body was shuddering from head to toe now. Zoella saw tears mixing with blood on Kiri's face, but she didn't relent.

The anger ruled her.

'And Guerrun, and Liana!'

Zoella lifted the kai.

'And you killed Ren,' she screamed, howling her pain and misery, hysteria in her voice.

The final blow went wild, catching Kiri across the face. Kiri's head was knocked back against the chair and she slumped in her restraints.

Zoella grabbed forward with her other hand, lifting Kiri's chin again. Zoella saw blood flowing from her lips. Kiri's eyes rolled in her head, unfocused for a moment before she managed to look at Zoella.

'I didn't …' Kiri whispered. 'I didn't want to hurt him …'

'No,' Zoella screeched, tears burning her eyes. 'Always lies. Always murder. Now it stops … stops forever!'

Zoella let go of Kiri and stepped back, raising the kai above her head, a screech of unbridled rage coming from her.

She saw Kiri look up at her, realising what was to come. Zoella saw the fear and hopelessness in her blue eyes, the dread …

Now die!

In a vicious swinging arc, Zoella brought the kai down.

The Shadeward Saga concludes in book four,
Shadeward: Expiation

Appendix

TIME-KEEPING

Measuring time on Esurio is problematic. There is no night/day cycle. The only readily available visual cue is the crossing of the planet Mayura (a 'hot Jupiter' gas giant in an inferior orbit) across the face of the star Lacaille, which is easily visible from the surface of Esurio. The duration of this transit is known as a 'Chime' and the time between 'Chimes' as a 'Pass'.

Spell
A short duration in the order of fifteen earth minutes. There are eight spells to a chime.

Chime
Many cultures on Esurio use sand timers to count 'chimes' and they are also used for sleeping, waking and marking time for meals. A chime is the time taken for the inferior planet Mayura to cross the face of Lacaille. A chime is considered the typical length of time it takes to do a job. A chime is around two hours long.

'The Sleeping'
This is the gap between the eighth chime and the first chime. The time set aside for being asleep. It is four chimes in length. Analogous to 'night'.

Stretch
A cycle of eight chimes and followed by 'the sleeping'. Analogous to a complete day.

Pass
Length of time for the planet Mayura to return to the same point on Lacaille. It lies in on the ecliptic plane as seen from Esurio, thus transits each orbit, visible from the surface. A pass is analogous to a month. All other timings are taken from this. There are twenty stretches in a pass.

Round
A round is twenty passes, which are counted manually by timekeepers (a specialist role on Esurio). Analogous to a year, although slightly longer in duration, being four hundred stretches.

MEASUREMENTS AND DIRECTIONS

Measurements are more easily understood and are based on hands and the typical length of a stride. These are not accurate terms and they will vary somewhat depending on the culture that is using them at the time.

Hand
The width of an adult's hand with fingers outstretched. Approximately a quarter of a metre.

Span
The length of an adult's span fingertip to fingertip with arms outstretched. A little under two metres.

Pace
The length of an adult's stride. Roughly a metre.

Mark
Used analogously to an earth 'kilometre' and of similar length.

Traipse
A long way. Many 'marks'. Typically the distance one can walk comfortably without stopping to sleep. Around 40 kilometres.

Shadeward
If you orient yourself so that Lacaille is directly behind you, you are facing shadeward.

Sunward
If you orient yourself so that Lacaille is directly in front of you, you are facing sunward.

Sunright
If you orient yourself so that Lacaille is on your right hand side, you are facing sunright.

Shaderight
If you orient yourself so that shadeward is to your right (or Lacaille is to your left), you are facing shaderight.

FLORA

The flora on Esurio are unique to the planet and have their own distinctive characteristics adapted to the conditions. The primary ones are listed below.

Furlers
Rather similar to earth Redwood trees, but significantly larger in the low gravity. These trees give Esurio a 'hardwood' from which much building material is taken. These trees also capture rainwater from above, rather than by roots as on earth. Their roots are for stability only. They are found in the cooler areas, where they are not swamped by faster growing vegetation. Some of these furlers can be thousands of years old. Their

leaves are dark green and edible like a sweet fruit, a good source of vitamins and nutrition, but they are high above ground, accessible only to the marsips, who typically live in them. The leaves are regarded as a delicacy in some areas, and a prized commodity in others depending on rarity. The leaves can be fermented into the fierce liquor known as 'Ochren'. Furlers escape destruction by the flares on account of their size and have evolved to utilise the extreme ultraviolet light by throwing out fast growing branches of leaves to trap the high energy light – hence the name 'Furler'. These can be quite dramatic.

Shades

These are curious entities, straddling the line between the planet and animal kingdoms. They look rather like mushrooms in general appearance, but with the 'cup' inverted so as to look rather like a dish. These capture rainwater and sunlight. The tops of the cup are black, but they have a light coloured underside which gives off a milky phosphorescent glow. They form large forests over much of Esurio. Their trunks are also a pale cream colour and grow straight and true, but are lightweight, rather like bamboo when dried out. These plants are able to move around slowly and have a sophisticated musculature, growing to angle their cups towards the sun, competing with each other. They quickly shrivel when detecting ultraviolet radiation to minimise exposure. It is possible to 'tap' their bark for water, though it is bitter, with a 'cinnamon' like taste. Many infusions and brews can be made from shadewater. In boiled and concentrated form it is a good painkiller. The bark can also be stewed to produce a cinnamon like drink which is mixed with milk from a herg to produce 'Chai'. Shades are found throughout Esurio, but thicker in warmer areas. They are a few dozen metres tall at best, with trunks up to 30 centimetres diameter. Shades survive the flares by sacrificing their top cups in to the ultraviolet and growing back afterwards. Shade forests are the best place (outside of a cave) for animals and humans to hide during flares due to the thick overlapping canopy, hence the name.

Snares

A parasitical and carnivorous plant. It can be found hanging from shades and furlers. Completely black in colour it is tendril and vine like. It hangs glistening tendrils down (in the manner of a spiderweb) towards the ground attempting to snare nargs and marsips primarily, though it is capable of immobilising a human. It is completely black and difficult to see in the gloom, though it gives off a smell like aniseed. Its tendrils are poisonous like a jellyfish. This poison is harvested by many hunters for use on arrows. When touched the tendrils whip around rapidly, catching the unfortunate creature and reeling it in. Snares have a hollow centre 'stomach' which contains strong acid which dissolves the prey whilst still alive. Snares are able to move slowly around from week to week. They gain their water from the plants they grow on. Generally snares are a nuisance, but there are reports of people being killed by larger infestations.

Mulches

Mulches are a composite microscopic lifeform that infests stagnant lakes, dykes or any other trapped water. They are quiescent most of the time, but are capable of overwhelming large creatures by swarming together and emerging from the water in a continuous stream having detected them. They immobilise their prey by anaesthetic stings, entering the body and then consuming them from the inside out. They can move at a surprising speed for their size (a slow amble to humans) but will not venture far from water otherwise they dry up and die.

Sweetbuds, Melps, Corcuns and Tupes

Varieties of vegetable commonly found in Esurio. Sweetbuds are particularly useful as they are rich in sugar, found mostly in the warmer climes of Taloon. Dried Sweetbuds are regarded as 'sweets'.

FAUNA

All Esurian creatures share some common traits. They have nictitating membranes or double eyelids. They have thick fur or skin, covering heavy bony structures on the upper part of the body (to protect against flare radiation). They are able to keen sense ultraviolet radiation, which precedes the flares, via a special third 'eye' on the back of the head, giving them a chance to reach safety, typically underground or deep within shade forests. None of them sweat or pant, but have various different wing-like or fan-like protrusions which they pump blood into for the purposes of cooling or territorial threat displays. Their eyes are adapted to the infrared, allowing them to see well in the gloom. None of them sleep, the mechanism having never evolved on this planet, but they go into temporary trances on occasion, resting one side of the brain at a time.

Narg

There is a wide variety of insect life on Esurio, but the primary one of note is the narg. It is regarded as a pest by the colonists, but it is essential to the food chain on the planet, being at the bottom for the most part. Nargs come in a number of forms but they are hive based, with a queen, workers, hunters and nest builders. They are large and black in colour, in order to absorb as much heat as possible, they are not found in the colder regions of the planet. The males are winged and the females are not. The society is strictly matriarchal, a pattern much admired by the people of Drayden and copied by them. Nargs create large structures similar to termites, but much more extensive due to the low gravity. Their primary food is vegetation, but they are known to make concentrated attacks on marsips, cainers and even dachs and hergs if they gather in sufficient numbers. They have a sting that is alcoholic in nature rather like a shot of Tequila, thus their venom is cultivated as a delicacy. It is possible to be killed by alcohol poisoning by multiple stings. This has led to the phrase 'Stung drunk'. Nargs can be up to six inches long, due to the high oxygen levels. Narg females consume the male after mating.

Flits

Flits are larger insects akin to dragon flies, although with six wings rather than four. Like dragonflies they are iridescent and have many colours including green, blue, red and purple. They primarily hunt nargs for food. In most lands they are quite rare and infrequently seen, thus are regarded as an omen of good luck – they are welcomed as they are known to keep down the population of nargs. By contrast in Drayden they are considered a delicacy and cultivated for that purpose. Flits are also eaten by dachs, but are so agile in the air that they are rarely caught. Flits have strong mandibles like the praying mantis and always hunt on the wing, hardly ever touching ground. They can grow up to 30 centimetres in length, filling the small 'bird' role on the planet.

Marsip

A small rodent like creature, varying in size from a rat to a large cat. They have much evolutionary potential as they have opposable thumbs, but they are close to the bottom of the food chain, subsisting on vegetation and insect life. They are lightly furred and make excellent pets due to their high intelligence. In the wild they live in burrows to escape from the flares. They are excellent climbers, which is their primary defence against cainars and dachs. They have exceptional eyesight and agility. They are found throughout Esurio. The fans of the marsip are folds of skin between their arms, legs and body, making their cooling displays rather amusing, and allowing them to glide between trees to some degree. They can grow up to a metre in length and can stand on their back legs like a meerkat.

Cainar

A large wolf-like creature. Rather bigger than earth creatures and longer in the leg due to low gravity, standing about a metre high. They have sabre teeth and are a dappled brown colour. They tend to inhabit the shadeward parts of the forests as they are acclimatised to cool weather. They hunt in packs and have a high intelligence. They have a mane like fan which they use for cooling and in territorial threat displays. They head sunwards on occasion depending on the availability of food. They hunt the marsips and hergs and have been known to take on a phaunt in desperation. There is also a domestic version of the cainar, called a 'carn' which is analogous to a dog and frequently used for similar purposes. Like most Esurian creatures they have bony plates across their backs to shield against flares. This makes them extremely tough, but less agile than might be expected.

Fellin

A cat like creature, subsisting on nargs and marsips, known for its agility and poise. They tend to be smaller in the sunward areas and larger in the shadeward. They mostly live in deep in the shade forests and are the only creature known that seems to make a living out of hunting and eating the snares. They appear to be immune to the poison of these plants. They are lone creatures and exceptionally shy, most inhabitants have never seen one. Due to this rarity and their ability to take on the snares they are regarded as mysterious and an omen of bad luck. They are smaller than the cainar but are notoriously bad tempered and will fight viciously if cornered or threatened. They do not possess the bony back plates of the other creatures and thus tend to stay confined in the forests in the protection of the shades and furlers.

Dach

A large flying lizard like creature preying on marsips and larger insects primarily, mostly in the sunwards parts of Esurio. They counterpoint the cainar in many ways, and their territories do not naturally overlap that much. They are usually to be found in the more mountainous areas where they have their eyries. The people of Drayden specialise in breeding tame collections of these beasts and then growing them to a great size. Thus these are ride-able by individual humans or a pair as long as they are not too heavy. The fans of the dach have evolved as wings, making them supreme aerial hunters. Dachs are able to attack marsips in their furler top homes, prefer flits and will eat nargs out of necessity. Dachs also utilise the shades and furlers to escape the flares.

Herg

A creature like a cross between a buffalo and a horse, but with a massive bony back. Naturally found in herds of up to one hundred, they are one of most useful creatures on Esurio. Easily tamed and used wildly through the lands they fulfil the role of the ox, mule and horse. They are the main mode of transport and food in Drayden, Scallia and Drem, less so in Taloon. In the wild they graze the temperate areas of the planet, moving around as the vegetation is eaten and then grows back. They are heavier in the front shoulders like an ox, but have the longer legs of a horse.

Phaunt

A large creature of comparable size to an extinct earth Triceratops, but having the neck of a giraffe. These tend to inhabit the tropical parts of the planet, where they browse on vegetation high up in the canopy, pushing down the Shades. They are a dark green in colour, with thick skin. They move slowly and stay within the highly vegetated areas in family troupes. Some phaunts have been domesticated by the Taloon people for the purposes of pulling equipment and battles, but they are generally too big to be used for agriculture. Much of Taloon culture is built around adulation of the phaunt. These creatures make a startling noise when alarmed by means of a trumpeted mouth piece. Phaunts are unique in having multiple fans on their necks, often with different colours. It is not clear how they survive the flares.

ALSO BY DREW WAGAR

In the Shadeward series published by Fantastic Books Publishing

Shadeward: Emanation

Shadeward: Exoneration

Authorised novels of Elite: Dangerous

Reclamation published by Fantastic Books Publishing

Premonition published by Frontier Developments plc

Authorised novels of The Lords of Midnight published by Fantastic Books Publishing

The Lords of Midnight

Doomdark's Revenge

ABOUT THE AUTHOR

Drew Wagar is a science fiction and fantasy author. He lives in Kent with his wife, two sons, one girlfriend (not his) a dog and a cat. His favourite colour is dark green. He drives a small convertible car which occasionally works. He doesn't require a conservatory or any double glazing.

You can reach Drew as follows:

Drew's Website: http://www.drewwagar.com
Facebook: http://www.facebook.com/drewwagarwriter
Twitter: http://www.twitter.com/drewwagar

If you have enjoyed this book, please consider leaving a review for Drew to let him know what you thought of his work. You can find out more about him on his author page on the Fantastic Books Store. While you're there, why not browse our delightful tales and wonderfully woven prose?

www.fantasticbooksstore.com

Printed in Great Britain
by Amazon

60725776R00251